an
imperfect
certainty

an imperfect certainty

a novel

Richard Samuel Sheres

Vendemmia
Press

An Imperfect Certainty

A Novel

Copyright © 2019 Richard Samuel Sheres

ISBN: 978-0-9890602-2-6

Also by Richard Samuel Sheres

Ingersoll

Keeping Gideon

For my children.

For the generations.

Part I

Thus the sum of things is ever being renewed, and mortals live dependent on one another. . . . In a short space the generations of living creatures are changed and like runners hand on the torch of life.

Lucretius

The Wroth Family, 1944–1950

Chapter 1

Spring 1944: The Graduates

THE ENLISTMENT LINES WERE longer than usual on the morning of May 30. It was the Tuesday after Memorial Day. The previous Friday was graduation day for many of the city's high schools. Now, the men-children graduates were waiting in various states of anticipation to be interrogated, stripped, and poked by the medics.

Criticized when it was built in 1889 as an ugly, imposing fortress of red sandstone and brick, the structure at 39 Whitehall Street in lower Manhattan now seemed appropriate to its purpose. The walls inside, recently repainted drab gloss green and smelling of oil and linseed, complemented the formidable exterior.

Some of those in line were reluctant and had waited to be called to duty. But many others were eager to get into the fight.

The recruiters sorted the would-be soldiers alphabetically, which kept Stephen Wroth and Henry Zimberg together, as they had been for many of their Taft High School days. Henry, small, wiry, and full of nervous energy, had been talking nonstop since he and Stephen met up at the 170th Street el that morning.

"What did the guy say? First letter of your last name?" Henry asked Stephen, who stood in front of him. "Isn't last name enough? How stupid does he think we are?"

The remark drew a glare from a prototypically no-nonsense sergeant who walked with a limp that caused him to grit his teeth. It also drew a low "Shut up, would you?" from Stephen, who craned his neck to look briefly at Henry. "If you don't mind, I'd like to get through the first day without getting into trouble."

All the men now had their shirts off, ready to have the medics listen to their hearts before moving on to the more embarrassing stage of shorts-down, heads-turned coughs.

"Messing up already, Henry?"

"Well, lookie here, another future army reject," Henry said to the source of the pseudo question, a Taft graduate in the RST line named Ronald Trott. "You're just lucky both your first and last names get you to the same place, so they won't see what a moron you are trying to figure it out."

Ronald took a beat to think of a suitable response. He settled on "Tell it to the Japs," and turned to stare at nothing that required his attention.

Henry poked Stephen in the back. "See? What sense does that make? He is a moron. And what makes him think we're being sent to fight Japs? I'm betting on Germans."

"We'll find out soon enough," Stephen said without turning around, arms folded to his chest.

"Well, I do speak German."

"You speak Yiddish."

"I can gussy it up if I have to."

Stephen half-turned to Henry. "I'll take either front."

"If you were a real Jew, you'd want to shoot Nazis."

"I am a real Jew," Stephen replied, irritably and more loudly than he intended.

"I thought you were an atheist."

"Agnostic."

"And Reform. Not real," Henry responded with another poke.

"Cut it out, goddammit!"

"See?" Henry laughed triumphantly. "You even take His name in vain."

Stephen shook his head. There was no point in responding. Experience putting up with Henry's nonsense—not to mention the frequent schoolyard rescues he'd performed, though not without resentment, standing up to Irish toughs when they'd decided they'd had enough kike for one day—had taught Stephen, when he had the presence

4

of mind to remember it, that silence was the only effective way to get back at him.

In any case no retort was necessary, as the sergeant pointed at Henry and barked, "You!" In response to Henry's stagy innocent, questioning look, he repeated, "Yes, you! You'll want to shut your face if you want to get off on the right foot. You do want to get off on the right foot, don't you?"

Stephen grimaced, hoping the smart-ass retort he was sure Henry had ready would be suppressed.

"Yes sir, I do," Henry said to Stephen's relief. He wondered whether the sergeant could hear the sarcasm his own finely attuned ear detected.

For Stephen, the pluses of being friends with Henry sometimes seemed to be matched almost point for point by the minuses. This balance, worked out over time, had required patience to appreciate, and there was no simple explanation for Stephen to have had that patience.

They had gotten to know each other as opposing candidates for president of the junior class. It was an uneven match, and, some said, ridiculous.

Stephen was the sure thing—confident, clean-cut-handsome, and poised. Solidly rooted in a middle-class family—his father a respected cardiologist—at a time, the fall of 1942, when these Rockwellian all-American traits were exactly what people, including the great majority of his fellow students, were looking for.

After a decade of national privation, Stephen, naturally and often unconscious of his attributes, offered something bright and optimistic. He was intelligent in a conventional way, making good grades without challenging norms or rocking boats. He lettered in basketball (at five feet eleven, he was tall for his time and age) and track. He was on the debating team, where he won points on charm and common sense more than creative argument. Not that he lacked substance or wit, but rather that style was what tended to tip the balance in his favor. He scored on smile alone, displaying newly straightened white teeth and the vague remains of dimpled cheeks. And he was genuinely nice, devoid of the hubris to which he might have succumbed.

In short, Stephen was the kind of kid people, his classmates included, liked to root for. If during his upbringing he had more in the way of ease while others had less, it was not held against him. He was the very image of a fresh start, and if this reflected a climate of wishful thinking or escapist yearning in the face of the current national challenges, so be it.

And then there was Stephen's opponent, Henry. If Stephen had the good fortune to be what his times desired, Henry was in the opposite position. He was scrappy and haphazard in appearance, with an outsized nose and light brown kinky hair that tended to remain close-cropped even when he was overdue for a haircut. He had a distinctively nasal voice that became more irritating as his fervor grew. Henry won his points on zeal, effort, humor, and genuineness. Without a doubt, Henry was Henry, a stand-in for nothing but himself, and likeable, quirks and all.

Henry wore his Jewishness as a badge. This won him a narrow, but enthusiastic, following in the student election, though it caused discomfort among some Jewish students who might have been considered part of Henry's natural constituency had they not been drifting toward the more fashionably liberal, secular persona typified by Stephen. For his part, Stephen was uncomfortable with what he saw as the shallowness of his support and the ardor of Henry's camp, imagining his own followers to be less loyal than Henry's.

Henry possessed an obvious intelligence that, unlike Stephen's, was not distributed across the range of subjects in the school curriculum. He cared little for math or science and very much for history, politics, literature, and philosophy—in short, for anything that could spawn a good argument and, preferably, one that would remain unresolved.

If Henry fretted over any of his deficits, he didn't show it. He possessed sharp powers of observation and a sardonic wit, which he expressed with little regard for self-image or the opinions of others. These qualities appealed to Stephen, who was sufficiently self-aware to appreciate what he considered to be his own excessive concern with what others thought. Later, in a moment of stark confessional honesty, he would reveal this shortcoming to Henry, whose response was that Stephen was paying the price of easy popularity. He said this was like having money you were afraid to lose.

The class election, then, was no contest. But Stephen was generous in the aftermath of his landslide victory, partly because he was a nice guy who wouldn't like to think of himself as a gloating winner and partly because he had come to appreciate Henry's contrarian thinking and whatever it was—bravery or lack of awareness—that caused him not to censor his thoughts. When Stephen closed an election debate by thanking all of the teachers who were supporting the war effort by preparing the future generation, Henry seconded these thanks but added the qualifier that as in other areas of society, teachers don't all pull their weight ("you know who you are"), and in these dangerous times those at Taft who fit this category might serve the country better by enlisting.

A FEW OF the Taft grads decided to meet up for the subway ride home. Stephen, Henry, and two guys Henry knew slightly from history class had found out straight off that they were bound for the infantry, though not to which front.

Two others, good friends Anthony Manucci and Chris Bruni, were likely to become pilots. Their jubilant voices bounced off the porcelain tile walls of the station and rattled the straphangers on the train. "I can't believe they gave me exactly what I wanted!" Chris repeated over and over.

"Just think. We'll be up in the nice blue sky giving you dogfaces cover," Anthony chimed in with a laugh.

"That's if you learn to fly before the war ends," Henry said, raising his voice to be heard over the metal-on-metal squeal of wheels rounding a bend in the track.

Hulking Jack Greenburg, who played left tackle on the varsity football team, sat stone-faced, hunched over and staring at the floor, ignoring the enthusiasm around him.

Henry elbowed Stephen. "What's with Greenburg?"

"They didn't take him. He's 4-F. Some kind of heart murmur."

"You should tell him to see your Dad."

"I've never flunked a physical in my *life!*" Jack declared, suddenly looking up. "I'm an athlete, for Christ's sake!"

7

"Maybe they made a mistake," Stephen said. "Happens all the time," he added, supposing it did.

Jack shook his head and resumed his silent downward stare.

"Hey, Russo!" Anthony, the prospective pilot, called over to the boy sitting across from Jack. "What's so funny?"

"Wasn't laughing."

"Pretty big smile then."

The boy, Russo, just shrugged.

"He's 4-F, too," Henry said out of the corner of his mouth. "But he never wanted to go."

"How do you know?" Stephen asked.

"He told me so. He said the war will probably be over by the time he gets there, and there's no point risking his life for a done deal."

"Really? He said that?"

"Exact words."

Anthony shook his head violently. "Chickenshit excuse! Hell, we haven't even invaded Europe yet."

"It'll be soon, I think," Henry said.

"Anyway," Anthony pressed, "does Russo really believe the Nazis will roll over and die as soon as we touch the coast of France? And I don't see much sign of the Nips surrendering, either. It's just a chickenshit bill of goods, that's all."

This was said loud enough to get Russo to look over and then look away without saying anything.

"Who's chickenshit?" Jack Greenburg, the 4-F athlete challenged.

"Easy!" Stephen said. "Not you. No one would say that about you."

"Darn right! I'd knock his block off!"

"We know, Jack. Settle down, would you?" Henry said. "Jeeze."

"He's just a little touchy right now," Stephen mumbled so that only Henry would hear him.

"Well he needs to cool it," Henry mumbled in return. "After Pearl Harbor there were guys who committed suicide because they were 4-F, you know."

"Yeah, I know, but that's not Jack."

Everyone got off at the same station, all but the two 4-Fs in high spirits. They parted with a round of "V for Victory" signs, and a few words of encouragement to Jack.

From Broadway Stephen and Henry headed east toward the Grand Concourse, the Bronx's jewel boulevard. There Stephen would split off to go a few blocks north where his family lived in a large and well-maintained apartment building, while Henry continued across the Concourse to his family's more modest, more crowded apartment.

They made a stop at their favorite candy store, its facade highlighted by a large metal sign that wrapped around the corner, each end sporting a raised Coca Cola sign.

"How will your parents react to today?" Stephen asked, picking up several of his favored chocolate-covered jellies. "To being taken by the army," he added.

"They're expecting it. They're afraid for me, of course. But they know if I don't enlist Uncle Sam will draft me anyway." With a nod toward the jellies, he said, "You know those things are disgusting, right?"

In silent response, Stephen pointed to the coils of red licorice in Henry's hand and rolled his eyes.

"At least mine won't leave brown and red sludge on my teeth," Henry continued. "The bright side for my mother would be if they put me on permanent K.P. duty or something. Before I left the house this morning, she said as far as she's concerned she'd be happy for me to spend the rest of the war peeling potatoes in New Jersey. How about your parents?" he asked as they exited the store.

"Same as yours. Mom says she understands that everyone has to do their bit. But every time she sees a casualty list or especially when someone receives a telegram, she gets really quiet, and you just know what she's thinking. It's all focused on me, too, since my brother's young enough that he'll probably miss the war, and there's my sister, of course, not much worry about her."

"Well, with three brothers coming up behind me plus my two sisters, Mom and Dad spend most of their time worrying about ration books and how they'll feed us. Maybe they'll be relieved to have one less mouth."

"I seriously doubt that. Speaking of food, you want to come for dinner tonight?"

"I can't," Henry said. "I've got a date with Judy. Her uncle's out of town," he added with a mischievous smile. "And she has the keys to his car."

"But neither of you drive," Stephen said, slightly bewildered.

"So, who needs to drive? All we need is a back seat and blackout curtains."

"Lucky man," Stephen said, catching on. Henry and Judy had gone all the way—a subject about which Henry was uncharacteristically stingy with details as far as Stephen was concerned.

THE DINNER HOUR in the Wroth home was treated as almost a ceremonial occasion. Stephen's father would come home in his suit and tie and not remove either one until after the meal. His mother wore a dress, sometimes pearls. The children were expected to show up in clean clothes and with any exposed skin bearing the marks of a good scrubbing.

Stephen sometimes teased his mother, saying she had watched too many movies about aristocrats and tycoons. She would laugh, but she never wavered. Nor, despite her insistence on a tablecloth and good, not the best, china, did she ever concede that the daily event was in any way formal. It was, she said, simply a daily *occasion* on which more than the food was to be savored.

None of this was to say that the occasion itself was somber. To the contrary, it was lively. The parents treated the children as budding citizens of the world. They quizzed them about current events—mostly the war, though as Stephen's participation in it drew nearer they tried to focus on other areas—as well as social issues, science, and whatever improving subject came to mind.

That evening Stephen's father, normally talkative at least about his day or the latest headlines, was subdued, taking and passing food with a murmured "Thanks." Stephen's mother was quiet, too. Occasionally, she would emit an absentminded sigh. Once or twice Stephen noticed her eyes go moist, which she tried to hide by excusing herself to retrieve something or other from the kitchen. Stephen wished Henry had been able to join them; he would have lightened the mood.

Stephen's brother, Robbie, nearly two years younger, was the only one who appeared to be energized by the day's signal event. He seemed not to notice that answers to his requests for details were rendered tersely, subdued by the parents' mood. Meanwhile, Barbara, thirteen and obviously adored by all despite her father's by now tired joke that her birth had ruined plans for a trifecta of boys, took unspoken cues from her mother and silently moved her food around the plate.

"You know I had to do this," Stephen said, finally, stroking his mother's freckled arm. "There's no point waiting to be called up."

She nodded. "Just because something has to be doesn't mean it's not difficult. But why the infantry? Why not the navy or the air corps? And you'd think the high school class president would be in demand for his brains, wouldn't you? Let someone else shoot. You be the one to tell them what to shoot at."

Stephen patted her arm again, and said with a smile, "It doesn't work that way, Mama," suppressing the response that in any case the casualty rate for officers, sailors, and pilots wasn't exactly low.

"It'll be okay, Mama," he added. "Besides, it looks like maybe Henry and I will go together."

"Wiseacre Henry?" his mother said with the first smile Stephen had seen since he came home. "That's not so reassuring."

~ ~ ~ ~ ~

Chapter 2

September 1944: Transitions

IT WAS A HOMECOMING of sorts—the kind usually reserved for the long gone—when Stephen and Henry returned on a three-day pass following twelve weeks of basic training. Neither of them had ever been away from home on his own for more than a week.

Their families learned by telegram with only a day's notice that they would arrive on Friday and ship out on Sunday. Mrs. Wroth went into overdrive to throw them a combination welcome home/bon voyage party, the former anticipated with infinitely more enthusiasm than the latter. But the going away could not be ignored, as it would appear like a smile missing a front tooth. "We can hardly welcome them home without saying a proper goodbye when they're leaving three days later," Stephen's father said. The welcome-and-farewell theme was artfully captured on a banner, drawn by Stephen's sister, proclaiming the boys heroes.

And so Mrs. Wroth scrounged as many ration coupons as she could and set to work. The guest list grew rapidly and forced her to do what she, as a proud hostess, hated: ask some of the guests to contribute coupons or dishes. "Who knows what we'll end up with?" she sighed.

Family and friends crowded the narrow entry hall. By the time Stephen knocked on the door—followed a short time later by Henry, who had arrived home to find a note telling him to go directly to the Wroth's apartment—well over thirty people were jostling to pat the boys on the back or kiss them. All were focused on the homecoming and trying to ignore the imminent leave-taking to an unknown destination. Because of the need for fresh troops in the aftermath of D-Day, it was generally assumed to be Europe. Nevertheless, both the purpose of their having been away and the possibility of their being sent to the Pacific were evident in hand-drawn posters depicting the boys putting outsized boots to the rear ends of a startled, toothbrush-mustachioed Hitler and a squinting, buck-toothed Tojo.

Stephen's mother locked him into something resembling a permanent embrace. "Look at you!" she exclaimed as she placed a hand on each of his shoulders. "You look just like a real soldier!"

"Well, I should hope so, Mama," he responded with a laugh.

"Wait until you see the feast I prepared for you and Henry," she said over the din. "Chopped liver, potato latkes, pastrami—the last piece of lean pastrami in New York, I might add—all of your favorites. And don't forget to compliment your sister on the cake. She made it herself, and let me tell you, getting enough flour and eggs took some doing."

Everyone remarked on how fit the boys looked. The difference was even more marked in Henry, who, unlike Stephen, had not started out as an athlete. He was happy to flex his arms and mug theatrically for anyone who commented on the contrast.

Henry found his family banded awkwardly together in the far corner of the living room. He embraced them one by one—mother, father, three younger brothers and two sisters—but didn't linger as he spied his girlfriend, Judy. He rushed over and whispered something in her ear that made them both break into conspiratorial smiles.

Stephen hugged his father, who appeared more careworn than Stephen remembered. Had he not noticed before? He had only been away for a few months, after all.

"You boys have matured a lot in a short time," his father said.

"I hope so. Basic was tougher than I thought it would be. I was in good shape, and there were times I didn't think I would make it. I still don't know how Henry survived. Sheer gumption, I guess."

"Something to keep in mind if you're in a jam. And we only have you until Sunday?" his father confirmed in what seemed an awkward attempt to change the subject. It occurred to Stephen that his father, usually a ready source of advice, whether solicited or not, had held back

13

in his letters over the past several weeks. Perhaps he wanted to avoid appearing gratuitous or condescending at a time when the world in the guise of the U.S. Army was yanking his son into manhood.

"Only until Sunday," Stephen confirmed.

"Well, I don't think your mother intends to let you out of her sight. You'd better go mingle before she nabs you again."

"I think I'll start over there," Stephen said with a resigned smile and a half wave in the direction of Henry's parents, now sitting alone. That they looked stiff and out of place was predictable. He had never warmed to them. They weren't unfriendly, merely dull, reserved, and fretful, in stark contrast to their garrulous, high-spirited son.

Stephen was surprised to be embraced by Henry's mother. "You look so tan and healthy," she exclaimed. "I was so worried about you two. I'll bet there was nothing to eat but *tref*. You must have been very hungry."

"It wasn't so bad," Stephen said, not bothering to remind her that his family didn't keep kosher or that Henry, who at first tried to observe the dietary laws, fell from grace early on by wolfing down the army's version of spaghetti and sausage meatballs with grated cheese.

"God will forgive a soldier, don't you think?" Henry had asked.

Seeing Henry across the room, Stephen excused himself.

"You'll look after each other, won't you?" Henry's mother said, clinging to Stephen's sleeve.

"Of course we will," he responded with an awkward pat on her arm.

Henry's father extended his hand. "You're good boys," he said as they shook.

"Some do, huh?" Henry said with a nod to the dining room table, which had been set up as a buffet in the center of the room.

"Yeah. Nice welcome home."

"And sendoff," Henry said with less enthusiasm. He had not tried to hide his nervousness about what was to come. He struggled to get through basic and was particularly worried that he was the worst shot in the company. "How do they expect us to be proficient at all this stuff in a few measly weeks?" he'd complained. Stephen tried to reassure him the training would kick in when they needed it.

"You've got more faith than I do, buddy," Henry responded.

"They're taking big casualties over there, I bet," he said now. "The newsreels play it down. Plus, we'll be replacing guys who have probably been together for a couple of years. What do you want to bet they give us the cold shoulder like we're just fresh meat for the grinder?"

"You worry too much," Stephen said, though he had many of the same fears. "What happened to Judy?" he asked, scanning the room.

"She couldn't stay. Something with her parents."

"I never got a chance to talk to her," Stephen said, sounding more regretful than he was. He never knew what to say to her. She was shy and lacked spontaneity. He thought her plain-looking, with mousy brown hair, glasses, and a stickish figure. And as far as he was concerned, she was entirely too deferential to Henry. He supposed Henry liked this about her and liked even more that she was willing to put out for him. Henry might have been cagey about sharing the details, but he was annoyingly eager to bring up the subject in general.

Stephen wouldn't admit it, but it was also embarrassing. The closest he'd ever gotten to full-on sex was when he fingered a girl and she rubbed him—over his pants—until he came. It had taken what seemed ages merely to be allowed to touch her breasts.

He found his lack of success difficult to understand. Henry wasn't the only friend in the not-particularly-handsome category who had succeeded. Stephen was not boastful, but when he reviewed the inventory of his assets, he concluded that he should have fared better. This conclusion was buttressed by the fact that the girls he went out with were almost always sexy and popular. Was he not insistent enough when making out? Maybe he was drawn to the good girls. That they were both attractive and good presented an acute dilemma and intensified the pain. It was particularly hurtful when a girl he dated, a persistent virgin, turned up pregnant after she started dating other boys.

Anticipating the answer, Stephen asked anyway, "Is your plan with Judy still on for tomorrow night?"

"You bet it is. It'll be the last time before we shove off."

Stephen nodded, trying not to show disappointment. Henry had reserved a room at the nicest hotel around, the Concourse Plaza. Stephen was doubtful when Henry told him about it. His impulse then was to raise all the obstacles he could think of. "Have you ever stayed at a swanky hotel?" he'd asked.

"I have," Henry said, a little indignantly. "In the Catskills."

"That's a bungalow colony, Henry. For Christ's sake." Stephen, who had stayed in a hotel once, during a family vacation in Florida, added, "One thing I know is hotels don't like renting rooms to unmarried people."

"So what? You think no one's ever pretended to be married?"

"Hotels have private detectives, you know."

"Oh, come on! I don't believe you! Why do you always have to be the good boy?"

Later, gazing into the bathroom mirror, Stephen acknowledged it was a good question. He allowed a smile at the thought that he could be inadvertently emitting signals that he was, indeed, the good boy. Girls could trust him. The girls' parents always liked him, another telling sign. They said he was a *gentleman*. Maybe the girls didn't want his reputation sullied.

~ ~ ~ ~ ~

Chapter 3

September 1944: Vers les Vosges

A T EVERY POTHOLE AND rill, the truck bounced and lurched. Stephen and Henry were among fifteen soldiers being tossed this way and that on the road from Marseille to Dijon, a terrestrial reminder of what they had experienced over sickening weeks at sea. And Dijon wouldn't be the end of the line but merely a transfer point to who knew where.

The long voyage over had been made even longer by the zigzag course they followed to avoid U-boats. Rough water all the way, particularly when the captain took swells on the beam, causing the ship to roll. The condition of the men, jammed into bunks in a huge airless space, was made worse by the pervasive smell of diesel oil and vomit from the many who couldn't make it to the slop buckets, some of whom thereafter displayed constant reminders of the experience in the form of dribble stains down the front of the life vests everyone was required to wear at all times. Stephen was constantly seasick.

"I don't know how you can stand it," he exclaimed in envious frustration to Henry, who was somehow immune. "I think this whole cruise is an army plot to make us unafraid to be killed. Anything has to be better than this."

"Cast iron stomach and seasick pills," Henry replied.

"Those pills do absolutely nothing for me."

"I can tell."

Henry was sitting on an upper bunk with his legs tucked under him, playing gin rummy for cigarette points (a convenient currency for him, since he didn't smoke) with a New Jersey boy he had befriended in basic named Carl.

"Find a spot on the horizon and fix on it," Carl suggested to Stephen.

"What horizon?" Stephen replied, struggling to fight off the heaves. "The way we're jammed in here, you can't look farther than three feet without something blocking your view. I'd sleep on deck if they'd let us."

"Gotta take turns up there," Carl said unhelpfully. "Too many of us to all be there. Gin!" he declared, throwing down his hand with a whoop.

Henry tossed in his losing hand and looked over to Stephen. "Hey, Mister Obedient, Mister Perfect. Why don't you go up there anyway? Maybe they'll take pity. What's the worst they can do, send you back down here? At least you'll get some fresh air while you're pleading with them."

"They might throw you overboard," Carl said with a laugh.

"That's no threat," Stephen replied, the end of the declaration muffled by a lurch to the slop bucket.

Now here they were bouncing along on land, two groups sitting on benches in full gear, facing each other, their backs to the ribbed canvas of the truck bed. "Shit!" Henry exclaimed. "I'm sick to death of feeling like a billiard ball." He chopped his teeth for effect. "At this rate my fillings will be all over the floor."

At the end of the bench opposite, one of the soldiers shook his head at Henry in disgust. "Fucking replacements," he muttered.

Stephen looked at the soldier, a three-striper called Russell. Ordinarily Stephen might assume that this was the man's first name. But hardly anyone used first names in this man's army. Stephen was always Wroth, Henry was Zimberg. Monikers of various kinds, some imaginative, others merely stupid, were acceptable substitutes. As an instructor said during basic, it's easier to deal with a nickname when you watch the guy next to you with his guts hanging out. So far, no name had stuck to Stephen, Wroth probably not being a very interesting root. One guy in basic liked to call him Grapes ("of Wroth, get it?" he declared to an apparently obtuse Stephen), but it didn't stick. Henry, on

18

the other hand, had the misfortune to have a pimple attack at just the wrong time, whereupon long after it subsided he was Zitberg.

Since they had left Marseille, Russell had taken pains to separate himself from the others. They might have belonged to the same division, but he wanted no confusion over the point that he wasn't one of them. As Stephen understood it, Russell had been wounded, but not badly enough to punch his ticket home. He'd been released from the hospital and was on his way to rejoin his company.

"Someone has to be a replacement," Henry said, reasonably. "We can't all have been there from the beginning."

"Well, the least you can do then is shut the fuck up," Russell said. "You new guys have some fucking nerve complaining about bumps in the road. You haven't earned the right to complain about anything."

"What do you expect from a bunch of sheenies," one of the men said in a Southwest drawl, a transparent attempt to curry favor with Russell. "Especially ones from New York. If it wasn't for the kikes, we wouldn't be fighting this damn war." His name was Murch. He was from Tulsa, and he took pride in having shaved his head before the army could do it for him. The bald head accentuated his weathered skin, lately turned doughy white during the time at sea. He was missing an incisor, which caused his teeth to do a wide-spaced shift. At about six feet tall and sinewy from years of manual labor, he was someone Stephen thought worth avoiding in a brawl.

"What do you know, you stupid Okie son of a bitch," Henry shot back.

Murch started to get up, but the truck went into a curve and he fell back like a sack of slag. His friend, a fellow Oklahoman named Coins, put a restraining hand on his arm when he tried to get to his feet again.

"Right, there'll come a time to deal with these two," Murch said, looking through narrowed eyes at Henry. "Funny thing about war," he said with the sleazy theatricality of a Hollywood mobster, "you never know where the shot that kills you came from."

Stephen almost retorted, "You should keep that in mind yourself," but decided it was the kind of thing best left unsaid. This wasn't his first run-in with Murch, and it had occurred to him that the threats might be more than just talk. Someone might actually need to shoot the bastard, maybe Coins too.

Russell shook his head in wonder and crossed his arms in front of his chest. "You assholes don't know a goddamn thing—none of you. Just wait until it's real Krauts you're up against. You think this is a fucking game, Oklahoma boy? You really think you'll be going after each other when an enemy machine gun is mincing your dumb asses?"

Coins made the mistake of saying, "And what the hell would you know about it?" Before he could so much as blink, Russell was on him. Whatever wounds Russell was recovering from were not evident as he pinned Coins by the throat. Stephen thought Russell might crush his windpipe, as he was strong enough to hold the stunned Coins with one hand while with the other he pulled a pistol and pointed it at the forehead of Murch, who had moved as if he might want to aid his friend.

"Let me tell you what I know about it, you retard motherfucker."

"All right," Coins croaked, "I didn't mean anything by it."

Russell pulled back, managing to keep his balance as the truck bounced along. He held his gun on Murch and Coins until he was convinced they were staying put. "You guys were all just transferred into the division, right?" he asked no one in particular as he holstered his gun and returned to his seat.

Seeming still surprised by the suddenness of Russell's movements, a few of the others just nodded.

"Well, let me tell you a few things before you get your tiny dicks shot off, which you probably will anyway," Russell continued. "While you fat-assed jerkoffs were home worrying about stupid shit like ration coupons, the 45th was fighting, and I mean *fighting*, as in killing and being killed. I was with this division in June of '43 when we landed in Morocco to get ready for the invasion of Sicily. That July, we led the amphibious landing there. On orders from Patton himself, we crawled—and I mean belly-scraped—over the island to Messina, taking big casualties the whole way.

"Then it was the mainland. The names Salerno, Monte Cassino, or Anzio mean anything to you?"

Everyone nodded. The fighting—and, even though the censors tried to minimize it, the dying—at those places had shocked people back home.

"The 45th was on point there, too. Then it was on up the boot to Rome. I've been wounded three times, the last time when we landed in the South of France as part of Operation Dragoon, which let me tell you was a breeze compared to Italy. And now we're all here, listening to shithead over there"—he nodded toward Henry—"piss and moan about how uncomfortable he is riding in this vehicle. You don't even know you're lucky to be riding instead of walking, do you?" he said to Henry. "You know why you guys are replacements? Because we need to fill in behind all the real soldiers who've been KIA or wounded." Russell sat back, his point met with newfound silence.

"What's it been like here?" Henry asked.

"Here?"

"In this part of France."

"So far, not near as bad as Italy. But you can bet your bottom dollar it's going to get worse when we cross into Germany. If I were you—all of you—I'd get on the stick real fast."

Stephen glared at Murch, who returned the look. In Stephen's opinion, Murch and Coins were more than your run-of-the-mill anti-Semites. The word "psychopath" wasn't too strong. It applied especially to Murch, but Coins behaved like a low-IQ acolyte, a beguiled simpleton, and in some respects that made him even more dangerous. He looked the part, too, with army-short, tomato-red hair; pale green eyes; Silver Cup–white, freckled skin; and elephantine ears. Stephen wondered about the luck of the draw (if it was luck) that had him and Henry in the same platoon as Murch and Coins. Considering the large number of recruits from their neighborhood back home, it was hard to figure out how he and Henry had ended up so isolated.

The problems with Murch and Coins had actually begun during basic when Coins saw a yarmulke on Henry's head and asked what the hat was hiding. Henry and Stephen had heard stories about guys, especially from rural areas, who wanted to catch a glimpse of Jews' horns. They never took the stories seriously, but the way Coins asked came close. At first it was difficult to tell whether he was pulling Henry's leg. This was before they knew Coins well enough to realize he didn't have the intelligence to ask a question in jest.

But not for the first time, an irritated Stephen told Henry he wished he wouldn't wear "the damn thing." He didn't add that he was tired of being dragged into situations where he had to defend Henry. What he did say was that it was tough enough to get through basic "without having to deal with this crap, too."

Murch and Coins were the most virulent of the anti-Semites Stephen and Henry had encountered. However, more jarring was the simple fact of finding themselves for the first time in a world in which they were a distinct minority. In self-ghettoized New York, with its neighborhoods of Italians, Jews, and Irish, among others, one could count on being in the majority at least some of the time, which created a loose balance of power that mostly kept the peace. There might be fights, but their nature was tribal, not based on the fundamental ignorance of a large population that had never so much as seen a Jew, or often, a Catholic, for that matter.

At home, Stephen and Henry confronted their share of taunts alleging Christ-killing and various forms of blood libel. But, as Henry observed about their New York antagonists during basic, "They might be ignoramuses spouting bigoted nonsense, but at least they sort of know their Bible. They know enough to be angry over something specific, even if it is ridiculous. These guys," he'd added with a thumb over his shoulder to indicate the general basic training population, "these guys are still in some kind of magic newt-and-toad phase."

To which Stephen responded, in somber tones with an obvious glance at the skullcap, "Well, just make sure you keep your horns and cloven hooves hidden."

"My spike tail, too."

Most of the time, the others in the company, including the yokels, as Henry preferred to refer to them, seemed to view Stephen and Henry with benign curiosity or indifference. Only a few followed Murch's lead. Most were preoccupied with survival. One or two befriended the boys and seemed willing to come to their aid should it get to that point.

However, Murch and Coins displayed a constant animus, the depth of which Stephen found difficult to understand. Whatever its roots, the pair grew angrier as their taunts were ignored.

Ignored except in one instance, which probably derailed any possibility, however slight, that Murch might let up and find some more gratifying target for his ire. That was the day Henry tripped Murch in the mess hall. Perfectly timed, it resulted in a cinematic fall and a plate loaded with spaghetti and meatballs splattered over Murch's shoes, his uniform, and a nearby instructor, who placed blame for the incident entirely on Murch's clumsiness.

As Murch bent over next to Stephen, who had watched the episode with undisguised glee, to clean up the dinner detritus, he hissed through gritted teeth, "You motherfuckers just made sure you'll never get out of this war alive."

Stephen returned a determined smirk, but he knew the homicidal cretin wasn't kidding.

~ ~ ~ ~ ~

Chapter 4

Late September 1944: Épinal

NOT UNTIL THEY REACHED the northeastern city of Épinal, capital of the Vosges region, were Stephen and Henry shot at. They had talked about missing the action and how the Germans were in retreat everywhere. They could even begin to believe that German military prowess had been exaggerated, though occasionally their musings allowed for reminders that Germany had been competent enough to conquer most of Europe. A related hopeful thought, mostly on Stephen's part, though Henry had to admit he hadn't personally witnessed much evidence to the contrary, was that the stories of Nazi atrocities might have been overstated.

Almost certainly overstated, as far as Stephen was concerned. He had growing doubts about the reliability of, and the motives behind, the drumbeat of reports circulated in the Jewish community back home. No question the Jews of Germany had been targets of extreme discrimination. They had been robbed of their possessions, brutalized, sometimes murdered—but these things had been known since the Nazis came to power in the thirties. There was little doubt that in the conquered territories Jews were often treated savagely, and it was probable that many had been killed. So what was new? Pogroms were a way of life and death for Jews. What's more, Jews might have been the main targets, but they were hardly the only ones. Homosexuals, Gypsies, mental or physical so-called defectives, communists, political opponents—in short, anyone who fit the voluminous and infinitely amorphous category labeled "Undesirable."

Stephen allowed to Henry that it might be worse this time, with everyone killing everyone in Europe. "And Asia, for that matter," he added. "Let's not forget about the Japs."

The Warsaw uprising had been excellent fodder for what Stephen referred to as their debates. This in itself rankled Henry. As much as he had always enjoyed intellectual give-and-take, he accused Stephen of callousness and "flippancy" for treating this, as well as the unprecedented catastrophe being perpetrated by the Nazis, as a mere game. When the desperate Jewish revolt that shocked the Nazis ended in defeat, Henry took aim at Stephen for blithely describing the outcome as "predictable." ("That's what Jews *do*, Henry. They fight lost causes. Think Romans and Masada.") Anyway, Stephen maintained, tales of heroism in Warsaw were probably exaggerated ("Whose reporting can you trust?"). And even if they weren't, how was it different from the fighting that had leveled cities all across Europe? "How about Stalingrad, for just one example. Practically nothing left of the place. The story there wasn't about dead Jews, was it? It was about dead Germans and Russians."

And the reports of camps dedicated to the killing of Jews? Also exaggerated. "What sense would it make?" Stephen asked Henry. "I mean, here you have the Germans fighting on all fronts and becoming desperate. Why would they divert things from the war effort just to kill Jewish children?"

"And yet," Henry replied, "we have it on good authority . . ."

"Which would be what?"

"Reliable reports . . ."

"No such thing in the chaos of Europe."

"You've got to be kidding!" Henry sputtered. "We've known about the Nazi extermination plan for almost two years. It was in all the papers."

"That doesn't make it true."

"But it *is* true, and you know it! Don't make it sound like we haven't been over this before, either. If you still don't believe it, it can only be because you don't want to."

"And why would that be?"

"That's between you and your shrink. Maybe because you'd feel like you might actually have to do something about it."

"You mean something like join the army? Put my life on the line? Even if the stories are true, what could we do about it that we're not already doing?"

"We could bomb."

"Bomb what? The camps?"

"Yes."

"So instead of Germans killing Jews, we'll have Americans killing Jews, maybe even Jews killing Jews! Wouldn't Murch and Coins like *that*!" Stephen replied, his voice rising in a tone of arrogant incredulity. "I'll bet the dead Jews will feel much better, too."

"No, idiot!" came Henry's spittle-laced retort. "Bomb the parts of camps where they kill people. And yeah, let's say some of the prisoners die. They were going to die anyway. At least we'll make it hard to kill the next ones."

"Oh, come on, Henry. It's not like bombing a factory."

"It's exactly like bombing a factory."

"Well, anyway," Stephen continued with a dismissive wave, "I'm not so sure we can bomb anything that precisely. You've seen the newsreels. When the bombers hit a place, the bombs go all over. They get the job done by leveling everything, not a building here or there."

"How about railway lines? We want to destroy them anyway. If the Nazis are using trains to haul Jews . . ." Henry stopped, shook his head in disgust, told Stephen to get off his high horse, and wondered aloud at how Stephen could be so "insufferably deluded" as to sound like an apologist for the Nazis.

"So they'll switch to trucks," Stephen said, and added, "The single best thing we can do is what we are doing: win the war."

And so on.

They knew enough to keep thoughts about exaggerated German capabilities or less than absolute evil to themselves. After all, Henry reminded, they were, as Sergeant Russell had put it that day with so much derision, replacements for the many killed or wounded. That their journey thus far had been more uncomfortable than catastrophic was primarily the result of good timing. Their arrival in the south of France at the end of September meant they missed bearing the brunt of that landing earlier in the month, but even more so missed the bloody D-Day invasion and subsequent push inland. Their experiences—not to mention their chances of survival—might have been vastly different had they joined up just a little earlier.

In Épinal they saw firsthand the widespread destruction of a once-lovely city. It had been captured from the Germans on September 24, two days before Stephen and Henry arrived, and their initial reaction was to view things at a remove—the fighting that must have been intense, the hollowed-out edifices of what must have been a charming medieval town.

But it didn't take long for the immediacy of what they were witnessing to set in. Wounded men were still being evacuated, fresh graves still being dug; a large cemetery was becoming larger still at the edge of town. The Germans had chosen to make a stand. Combat was house to house. Allied casualties were high; it hardly mattered that enemy casualties were higher.

They were assigned to a platoon that had been badly depleted. The surviving veterans no doubt would be even less patient than Russell had been with any hint of complaint from the new men. To the extent they were welcomed, it was only because they offered the possibility of relief for the veterans. It was a utilitarian proposition: fill the ranks, help out where you can; we're beyond caring if you get killed or wounded; we're more likely to call you by your status (*Hey you! Replacement!*) than by your name. They were, one veteran said, GFF: Good for Fodder.

The result was the existence of strata in which each layer represented a bonding of contemporaries, as often occurs in a new school class. Each layer was simultaneously unique and part of a larger, shared community, recognizable but not necessarily recognized by that community until, occasionally, the demands of combat forced compression of the layers.

Stephen, Henry, and the other new arrivals clung to each other in a way that all the vets recognized. A vet called Bilbo, passing a group of them, remarked on the phenomenon, calling over his shoulder, "Good to see you hanging together, boys. First rule of combat: Your buddies are all you've got." But clearly, he meant your buddies, not we, not us.

"That's reassuring," Henry said. "We've got pricks like Murch and Coins to look after us."

"The good news is I haven't seen either of them," Stephen said.

"Oh, they're around. Filling in on some other squad. We haven't seen the last of them. I'm still gonna watch my back, believe you me."

* * *

THE ORDER OF the day on September 27 called for the squad to patrol the eastern edge of the city, where small pockets of Germans, including snipers, had been reported. The squad leader, a sergeant named Pugliese, gave an offhand briefing. The vets were only half listening—it was strictly routine to them—while Stephen, Henry, and three other replacements paid nervous attention. "Just do what we do and keep your heads down where snipers can't see them," he said for their benefit but in a voice that suggested he understood, belatedly, that he'd better be a little reassuring before one of them panicked and did something that would get them all killed.

The patrol started out walking slowly northeast in spread formation, through an area that had been secured earlier. They passed the remains of houses and shops that had stood for hundreds of years. Shards of brick and plaster crunching underfoot were often all that was left.

Stephen tried to envision what piece had gone where, a particularly challenging jigsaw puzzle. Here, there must have been some sort of living room or parlor. A wall must have been over there, separating what was probably a bedroom. Wrecked furniture on the ground floor must have started out on the floor above. In one place Stephen was brought up short when he came upon the detritus of a child's life: a tiny woolen dress, torn and plaster-encrusted. He saw now that the dress lay next to a wooden model automobile and concluded that there must have been a brother and sister here. He had not yet seen death close up. He realized

28

this could not last and dreaded the day, probably soon, he would have to confront human remains. He hoped he could cope with whatever it was, *only please don't let it be a child.*

As they went on, what had started out as a cool but sunny day became gray and drizzly, turning plaster dust into a slurry that made cobblestones particularly slick. The temperature was falling. Occasionally the rain would stop; the damp remained.

They came upon an arched stone entrance to an enclosed plaza. Pugliese held up a hand. He looked over to the new men. "Watch yourselves here," he said. He motioned to two of the veterans to proceed through the archway and scout the area. They went through, pressing their bodies close to the wall, covering each other. They scanned the plaza. A few moments later they gave the all-clear and the remainder of the patrol eased through the archway.

There was less destruction here, in this cobblestone space. A large statue stood in the center of the plaza. Shops of all kinds, most with residences above, surrounded the space. However, there was no sign of life. The area had either been abandoned during the fighting or whoever was left was well hidden. The men scanned the windows, looking for signs of snipers. Seeing none, they relaxed a little, but only a little. Stephen walked carefully toward the center of the plaza, saying over his shoulder to Henry that he wanted to check out the statue; wanted to see who Épinal saw fit to honor in this way. "Some guy named Durkheim," he called back with a shrug.

"New guys!" Pugliese called, "Spread out! You're too close together! You!" he pointed to Stephen. "What the fuck are you doing over there!" He ordered the men to pair off and begin working around the plaza, checking out the houses and shops. They had hardly begun when a high-powered rifle cracked the silence, and a replacement named Warrenton, who was paired with Henry, was shot through the forehead, pieces of his skull exploding like visceral shrapnel.

"Sniper!" someone called needlessly, as everyone had already leaped to what little cover they could find, including a few abandoned carts and wagons, and began looking for the source of the shot. Henry, who for a perilous moment stood motionless, slack-jawed, with pieces of Warrenton stuck to his face, gathered his wits and dropped to the ground, using Warrenton's body as a shield. It was inadequate but the best he could come up with.

"There!" Pugliese yelled, pointing. "On the right, second floor, second window from the end."

Caught out in the center of the plaza, Stephen pressed himself against the granite base of the statue, trying to get out of the sniper's line of sight. Another shot, this one coming close enough to his head that he could feel the air separate. Then a bullet smashed into the statue base, sending fragments of dust and stone into the air.

The men opened fire at the sniper's position. Henry, on the ground and using Warrenton to brace his rifle, tried to calm his shaking hands. His shots went wide.

Stephen's movements had been driven by adrenalin-fueled instinct. Now, caught out in the open plaza with only the statue of a son of Épinal to protect him, it felt like his whole body was trembling uncontrollably.

"Hold fire!" Pugliese called after a minute. "You think he's still up there?" he asked the veteran he trusted most, Brad Parsons, who had been with him since the division arrived in North Africa.

"Maybe not," Parsons said.

"I'd be surprised if we got him."

"Might have taken his shots and scrammed. He might want to set up somewhere else."

"I wouldn't mind lobbing a couple of grenades his way to make sure, if we can get close to his window. You think there's a way for him to get out? A back door? Something that doesn't face the plaza?"

"Don't know. Probably windows in the back, I'd guess."

Pugliese ordered two of the men to retreat through the archway and circle around back. "If there's no door, cover the windows. If the shooter tries to get out that way, put him down."

"Stay where you are behind the statue," Pugliese yelled to Stephen. "We'll get you out of there. Don't expose yourself until you get the all-clear." He called for suppressing fire to cover a couple of men while they made for the sniper's windows.

At that moment a barely perceptible movement occurred—the appearance of a shadow or silhouette on the opposite side of the plaza, on the second floor. "Trap!" Pugliese screamed, pointing. "Crossfire trap! Everyone back out of here the way we came!"

Before anyone had a chance to move, there was a sound, like ripping canvas, recognizable to the veterans after a beat as a machine gun they sometimes called Hitler's zipper. The gun raked the plaza. "I need suppressing fire! You, behind the carts—get that gunner!" Pugliese yelled, trying to be heard over the gunfire and spattering cobblestones. "The rest of you, back through the archway as soon as you're clear!"

Two men scrambled toward the exit. One was hit in the back of the thigh and screamed for help. The other had almost made it to the archway but turned around and raced back as the machine gun kept firing despite the efforts of the men behind the carts to shut it down. Somehow, he was able to drag the wounded man through the archway.

When the machine gun fell silent as the shooters reloaded, Henry and most of the others dashed to the archway. Just then the sniper reappeared and took another shot at where Stephen lay, trying to cover up. "Stephen!" Henry screamed desperately, too late to warn but instinctively needing to do something.

"Stay put!" Pugliese called to Stephen again. "He doesn't have a good angle on you!"

On the safe side of the wall, two men were trying to put pressure on the wounded man's leg, which was bleeding profusely. "We'll have to use a tourniquet," one of them yelled.

Pugliese ordered his radioman to call in the encounter, but the man only shrugged and pointed. In the panic to get off the plaza, the radio had been dropped and now sat useless, the German shooters no doubt hoping someone would try to retrieve it.

"Hell, we're not that far away. Someone's got to have heard the gunfire," Parsons said.

Pugliese flinched as another shot scattered stone near Stephen. "What a fucking mess! The sniper must be just a hair off. We have to keep him from moving to the next window, where his angle will be better. And we need to get close enough to those zippers to lob in grenades."

"The zippers have to be taken out first," Parsons said. "If we can get under their window, staying close to the wall, they won't be able to get at us without exposing themselves."

Pugliese ordered his men to give him and Parsons covering fire. Pointing at Henry, he said, "You, Zitberger . . . whatever the hell your name is. I want you to keep firing at the sniper's windows—both of them, the one he's been shooting from and the one to his right to keep him from getting a better shot at your dumbass buddy. Is there any sign of the sniper?" Pugliese asked, looking around and receiving negatives and head shakes.

"Well, we thought he was gone before," Parsons reminded.

"All right, Zitberger, until we're sure he's dead or gone, you keep shooting at those windows. Use the archway to give yourself whatever cover you can, but you'll probably be exposed while you line up your shots, so watch yourself. You others train fire on the zipper."

Pugliese nodded at Parsons. They had become so close—sometimes called the Two Ps, one wag dubbing them "Two Ps in a Squad"—little more was necessary. Parsons could be relied upon to make the right decisions. Just as important, he had an accurate throwing arm to get the grenade through the open window.

And a final instruction to the others: "Make sure you keep firing or we'll be sitting ducks out there."

Pugliese gave the go signal, and the men commenced firing. The men behind the overturned carts had some cover, but the ones sheltering in the archway had to move back into the plaza where they were more exposed.

Out of the blocks, Parsons slipped on the slick cobblestones but quickly regained his footing. The plan was to stay close to the building walls. From there they could work their way under the machine-gun nest and lob a grenade through the window. They made the dash across to the first stage, where they were most vulnerable to both the machine gun and the sniper, if he was still there. The machine gun opened up, returning fire toward the men near the archway. Stone, plaster, lath, and bits of glass flew. The sniper's position remained quiet, but Henry kept up a steady fire. Accuracy wasn't as important as making sure anyone in either window was forced to stay low.

When the zipper stopped to reload, the Two Ps moved again to get under the window.

"Shit!" Henry called out suddenly. "My gun's jammed."

32

The pause was all it took for the sniper to reappear and get off a shot. Parsons' helmet flew off. Pugliese looked over for the split second it would take anyone to comprehend that it was hopeless—Parsons had been struck in the temple—and finished his sprint, diving against the wall under the machine gunners' window.

Pugliese landed hard and clutched at the shoulder of his right, throwing, arm. But everything depended on getting off a grenade before the zipper took out more of the men. He moved crab-wise, kicking his boots along the cobbles to push his body along and get an angle from which he could make the throw left-handed. He reached for a grenade and ripped it away from his jacket. Even this small movement made him cry out. Somehow, he managed to hold the grenade in his left hand and pull the pin.

With a scream of effort, Pugliese heaved up a hook shot. The throw was true, but not true enough; there was not enough arc in it. The grenade glanced off the window ledge with a clunk of metal on stone, and bounced back onto the plaza, landing only a few yards from where Pugliese lay. "Shit!" he exclaimed as, eyes wide, he rolled as far from it as he could. When it went off, the explosion sent ancient cobblestones everywhere and left Pugliese looking dazed and buzz-deafened.

The machine gunners opened fire again at Pugliese's men near the arch. They returned fire, hitting the second German gunner, the spotter, who fell hard from the window. He was a small man. His helmeted head disproportionately heavy, it banged like a steel pot against the cobblestones. As the gunner fell back and stopped firing, Stephen took advantage of the lull to move. But he didn't try to make it back to the archway. Instead, he raced toward Pugliese, firing at the machine gunners' window as he ran. When he came to the dead German, he dove next to him and rolled his body over to use it as a shield.

Stephen watched as Pugliese shook his head hard as if to clear it and then pulled the pin on another grenade. Again, it clanked against the building wall and landed, this time near Stephen. Only later did the horrified look on Pugliese's face register with Stephen, as without thinking he scrambled to the grenade, picked it up, and threw a line drive into the open window. Half a second later it exploded, sending bits of machine gun and gunner to the plaza below.

The men in the archway who had been covering the zipper now made a dash for the building where the sniper was hiding, leaving a trembling Henry to continue firing at the open windows now that he had cleared the jam in his rifle. The men breached the front door without opposition and raced upstairs. Muzzle flashes and a grenade bang were followed by one of the men signaling an all-clear. "No one here," he called out. "Shooter's gone."

Suddenly, shots again could be heard, but this time in the near distance. "Doesn't sound like Germans," one of the veterans said. "Sounds like our shit."

A short time later, the shots were explained with the return of the two men Pugliese had sent around to the rear of the plaza. "Sarge nailed it," one of them, Collins, said. "We caught one of the Germans trying to get out through a window. And blam! No more German. We checked his rifle. It was the sniper."

"We figured as much," said one of the men who had stormed the building where the sniper had been.

In a daze, Stephen approached Henry, who was staggering in an obviously confused state of his own. Two of the other men slapped Stephen on the back and congratulated him on making a great throw. Stephen nodded vaguely.

"Where's Pugliese?" asked one of the veterans, named Royce, who had gone behind the plaza.

Another vet pointed. Pugliese was kneeling over Parsons's body, his helmet off, palm to his forehead, his other arm drooping off the injured shoulder.

"Holy shit! Parsons?" Royce exclaimed. "Are you shitting me? Goddammit!"

The men began tentatively to converge on Pugliese, silent now. Pugliese stood. When he saw Henry, the grief on his face turned to rage. "You, you fuck!" he bellowed, and charged at Henry. The others grabbed him and held him back. "Where the fuck was the covering fire on that window!" Pugliese demanded.

Henry, bereft and close to tears, said simply in a near whisper, "My rifle jammed."

"The fuck if it did!" Pugliese yanked free of the men who were restraining him. It seemed for a moment that he would go after Henry again. He pulled up short, but he wasn't finished. "You dumb prick! Didn't they teach you how to keep your weapon from jamming?"

Stephen, becoming alert now and emboldened by his successful kill, was about to speak out of turn and venture what he believed was the simple truth—that guns jammed all the time, and it had been just the worst luck at that moment. He didn't have the chance to say it, though, as Pugliese tromped off, grasping at his useless shoulder.

* * *

IT BECAME COLDER on the patrol's march back to its temporary quarters, a collection of homes, barns, and shops—some no more than bombed-out shells—that the division had occupied. The men's spirits, already low after their losses at the plaza, became lower still under a drenching, freezing rain that chilled them to the marrow and gave a foretaste of winter.

At least today they could look forward to a roof over their heads—good news, particularly for the veterans who had seen much worse weather in foxholes, tents or lean-tos. Many of the structures had no heat or hot water. Still, it was an improvement.

The majority of the French citizens of Épinal had welcomed the Americans and demonstrated this by sharing the little they had. The troops could count on an abundance of fruit and vegetables picked and put up not long before. They were appreciative, though all of that sudden fruit gave them the shits. They shared their C-rations, which they were sick of but which the locals liked—at least at first—because they were different. Some of the men shared the bounty of parcels from home.

Fueled by a successful performance in his first combat experience, Stephen was as exultant as the elements and the circumstances of the squad's losses permitted. He was under no illusion that his fears had vanished. Nevertheless, he allowed himself to savor the moment.

At the same time, he felt bad for Henry, who was morose and continued to berate himself even as he resented the veterans who, taking Pugliese's lead, were giving him the cold shoulder. Had their guns never jammed? He'd bet they were lying if they said no.

Over the next two days, Stephen and Henry went out on more patrols. There had been a shuffling of men to rebalance specialties. Medics were in short supply, which made Pugliese particularly angry because none had been with them on the plaza, even as he must have known that there would have been no saving Parsons.

Henry was assigned to a new platoon. Stephen asked for, and was granted, permission to stay paired with him. Henry was given no reason for the transfer, and he made clear to Stephen that it bothered him not to have one. Had Pugliese requested it? There was no indication this was the case, but Henry said he couldn't stop replaying the events in his head. It troubled him greatly that now he wouldn't get a chance to demonstrate to Pugliese that he was a good soldier. Yet he also feared that the incident put him on some unspoken form of probation—that his fellow soldiers had no faith in him, and that in fact he might fail again.

"Let it go," Stephen said. He pointed out that, considering how close Parsons was to Pugliese, it was probably unrealistic for Henry to think he could remedy the situation. How would Henry feel if it had been Stephen who had been killed because of what he thought, even wrongly, was someone else's incompetence?

"I can't. It's a stone in my shoe."

"Look, Henry, all of the vets have told us time and again that losing buddies is something they had to get over or they'd have gone crazy. You remember that guy who held up a hand to silence us when we tried to introduce ourselves? You remember him saying, 'No offense, but I'd really rather not learn your names unless I need to?'"

Henry nodded. "I understand all that. The difference is I keep wondering whether I'm responsible for the loss of someone's buddy. And I just don't want to be known as the company screw-up—the guy no one will partner with."

"You're not. You're imagining things. I *asked* to stay with you, didn't I? I mean, look at it as objectively as you can. Your gun jammed. Did you do anything on purpose to make it jam?"

"Don't be ridiculous."

"Okay, did you do anything accidentally that made it jam?"

"No. But I keep playing it over and over in my mind. Did I do something I didn't realize I did? Could I have cleared it faster?"

36

"You've got to stop it, Henry, before you get so distracted it really does get you or someone else killed."

"I tell myself that. And then the scene comes into my brain again."

"Well, don't let it."

"I'll keep that in mind."

* * *

MAIL CALL GOT Stephen five backed-up letters. Three were from his mother and father (his mother did most of the writing, with his father appending miscellany). One was from his sister. And one, a surprise, was from a girl he knew slightly from school. But this letter had a canned quality to it, and Stephen concluded that she was just doing her bit for the troops at the local USO.

Meanwhile, six of the letters Henry received were from Judy. She had written him almost every day, sometimes more than once in a day, sometimes just a line or two to cheer him up, and sometimes long, loving missives, including occasional mawkish poems. The letters came with regularity despite far less frequent, usually much shorter, responses from Henry, all of which included the disclaimer that he was constantly busy and she should not interpret gaps or delays in his correspondence as meaning in any way that he cared less for her.

That day they were enjoying a reprieve from the raw weather. Henry found Stephen sitting on a low stone wall, staring off at some unfixed point, a letter in hand. "Nu?" Henry said. "What's on your mind?"

"Nada."

"Doesn't look that way, pal. Everything okay back home?"

"Seems like it. Unless they're playing the same game we are of not mentioning worrisome news. My sister is dating a guy from school. She says it's serious—whatever that means at her age—but that she's trying not to let Mom and Dad know it. She's apparently not doing a very good job, since Mom wrote that she's head over heels in puppy love, as she called it, and her grades are suffering. That's about it. What's your news?"

"The usual slew of letters from Judy. Tell you the truth, I'd like to hear a little less from her—a lot less, actually."

"You know, if you feel that way—and especially if you want to break it off—you owe it to her to tell her."

"I would, if I knew. It's not that I'm sure we're not right for each other. It's that I'm not sure we are. Meanwhile, she's way out on a limb, and I feel pressured with every letter. *When we're married and have a home of our own*, and so on and so on."

Stephen tamped down the end of a Lucky (a habit he'd picked up somewhere around Dijon) and lit it. "Look who's headed our way," he said through a cloud of smoke.

"Great. My day is complete," Henry responded as he caught sight of Murch. "Ready for a rumble?" he asked Stephen.

"With that scumbag? Always. He won't want to, though. He doesn't have his me-too Jew-baiting ignoramus friend with him."

They eyed Murch conspicuously as he approached. Stephen hoped his glare was sufficiently truculent to let him know that if he wanted a fight, he could have one. He crushed the just-lit cigarette under his boot just in case.

But Murch didn't pause. As he passed he merely smiled and pointed as if his hand were a gun. He cocked his thumb, took a pretend shot in their direction, and blew imaginary smoke from the phantom muzzle. He issued a laugh as he walked on, leaving Stephen and Henry to stare at his back.

~ ~ ~ ~ ~

Chapter 5

March 1945: A Bronx Thunderbird in Germany

HELLO LITTLE BROTHER,

Long time no hear from. I have a little time off and I'm thinking about you, wondering how you've been. I suppose I haven't been so great about writing either, so we're even. We'll call it my turn.

Henry and I are veterans now. That's how we think of ourselves at any rate, and even some of the guys who have been here from the beginning are treating us less like dumb replacements. Funny thing is, when new guys arrive now, we treat them like dumb replacements!

I was wounded in the Vosges campaign. Did I write about that? This was back in October. Come to think of it, maybe I didn't write. I was a little out of it for a while. Anyway, I wouldn't have wanted to cause concern on the home front. Mom and Dad don't know about it, and I'd just as soon keep it that way.

The wound wasn't too serious. I caught some grenade fragments in my back. One of them went in pretty deep, but I was only out of action for a week or so. The guys here don't have much patience if they think you're malingering. Especially the "old timers"—with the things they've seen, you've got to be pretty much dead to get any sympathy. I got a Purple Heart out of it.

You probably haven't heard much about the Vosges, where I was wounded. It's a really rough, mountainous area of eastern France. It was tough going there. The Germans put up quite a fight—more than people expected, I think. But, then, it's not the only time we've underestimated their willingness to keep fighting. There may not have been much in the news about the Vosges, but I'll bet there was plenty about the Bulge and Bastogne. Some of the guys here were transferred quick-time to help out there. Not me, though. I was one of the lucky ones who stayed put. Things are tough enough here.

They say a soldier's life is equal parts boredom and terror. I don't know about the equal parts. But I can tell you for sure about the terror. It's being shot at, yes, but also the uncertainty—the never knowing what's around the next corner, and not to be melodramatic, but never knowing if this day will be your last.

In my old life at home (that's another thing, there's a clear line in my head between then and now), when I got out of bed in the morning there wasn't much thought given to whether I'd be alive at dinnertime. You go to class, you practice with the team, you stuff your sweaty gym clothes into a bag, and you come home. Needless to say, that's not the way it is here.

Mind you, I have no regrets about joining up beyond the obvious one that I wish it hadn't been necessary. But it is necessary. You don't have to be here long to realize that, and I bet the guys in the Pacific feel the same way.

I've learned a lot about myself. For instance, I've learned I can overcome fear. All of us wonder about that—how will I behave when the bullets come at me? I'm proud to say I have been through it. I have contained my fears and done my job—done it well, I think. Trouble is, I can't just pocket what I've learned about myself and go home! There's always next time, a next fight, and I wonder whether I'll be up to it.

But you know, everything is relative. After you've been here awhile you start thinking about getting shot like, "Well, at least it will be quick." That's not necessarily true, of course, but you start brooding over all the other ways you can die, and getting shot doesn't seem so bad!

For instance, coming over on the ship, sealed up below decks with a zillion other men, I couldn't stop thinking about being torpedoed. They make you wear Mae Wests twenty-four hours a day. But, seriously, do you know how fast a ship can sink? I'd have nightmares about being trapped down below, trying to claw past all the other guys panicking to get out. I'd dream I couldn't breathe as we went under and imagined what it would be like to die this way. I'd wake up wondering if it wouldn't be better to kill myself—cut my throat, maybe—to make it quicker. Then I'd think, hell, even if I managed to get off the ship before it went down I might die of thirst or be eaten by sharks—well, you get the idea. All of a sudden getting shot looks like a pretty good deal! (Again, this stuff is for you—NOT Mom, Dad, or Barb.)

Have I ever told you that my division, the 45th, is called Thunderbird? There's a swell patch on my shoulder. But there's a funny story. The division was created in Oklahoma after the last war (how did a kid from the Bronx end up in a division from Oklahoma, you might ask, and I'm not sure I could tell you). Well, the division's first shoulder patch insignia was a swastika! Really! You may not know this, but the swastika is a common American Indian symbol. Needless to say, it was changed (sometime in the thirties, I think). It's pretty funny to picture how the Nazis would react to us if we still had swastikas on our uniforms!

Most of the men in my platoon are good Joes. But you don't know for sure with the replacements. I sound like one of the vets who needed me to prove myself, and really, I understand it now: The whole question every day is, "Can I trust the man next to me?"

I don't know if I've told you how grateful I am to have been together with Henry all this time. It's more than having a piece of home with me. The thing about fighting a war is you get close to some people in ways you can't imagine. Simply put, we've gone through the kinds of things together that you only experience in wartime (thank God), and only people who actually go through them can truly understand. I worry that when I return home the only people who'll really get me will be other vets.

Henry may have his annoying quirks, but these things don't mean much when someone is shooting at you. Of course, it's exactly for these reasons many of the guys are afraid to get too close to someone. The guys who have been over here from the beginning, especially the ones who have been through the Italian campaign, have lost enough friends to make anyone wary of forming attachments.

41

In some ways you wouldn't recognize Henry. He's become much more serious and moody than you probably remember. I guess that's true of me, too.

Henry blames his moods on the reports we're getting—more of them all the time, maybe you're seeing them too—about German atrocities, especially against the Jews. The worst reports are coming from the eastern front, particularly Poland, where the Russians say they've overrun camps that are too horrible to describe.

Personally, I'm not so quick to completely believe these reports, especially since they're coming from the Russians, who would be happy enough to portray the Nazis as even worse than they are. And it still doesn't make sense that as much as the Germans are struggling they would bother to spend so much time and effort murdering Jews, even if they'd like to.

Henry gets angry with me when I express these doubts. He says our own side has witnessed enough that even if the Russian reports are untrue, it would be bad enough. Maybe so, but I keep telling him he shouldn't jump to conclusions. He tells me I'm an ostrich—that I wouldn't believe my own eyes—and stomps off.

One day it got really nasty. He was crazy-angry. I'm not sure what set him off. He called me a self-hating Jew who would rather not be a Jew at all. Then he said if I were German I'd be more at home among Nazis than Jews. He realized he'd gone too far and apologized right away. After being mad as hell for a minute, I decided to chalk it up to Henry being Henry. What can I say? It's the one subject we've tried to stay away from since.

That's it for now. I need to get a move on. One more thing, though, and the censors will almost certainly cut it out, so you'll have to take my word for it that it's a good thing: The division is about to cross the Rhine—the Rhine!! Into the heart of Germany! It's hard to believe.

Love to you all. Let me hear from you.

Your Big Fight'n Man Brother

~ ~ ~ ~ ~

Chapter 6

March–April 1945: Aschaffenburg

T HE PLATOON PULLED UP on a ridge overlooking the Main River valley in mid-afternoon. The men had hopes of resting for some time. Stephen scanned the horizon, breathed deeply, and said to the man next to him, "If you didn't know better, you'd be amazed to hear there's a war on."

Visible below were the twin cities of Schweinheim and Aschaffenburg, the latter dominated by the huge red sandstone Schloss Johannisburg. Henry stood next to Stephen, pointing to a railway bridge over the river. "I guess we cross there," he said. The tracks had been covered with wooden planks.

"What's next, Sarge?" Stephen called to Frank Baker, who only recently had taken over as senior non-com for the platoon.

Baker replied with a shrug and a nod toward the valley and the cities below. "Looks like we're headed down."

"Brilliant deduction, Sarge," one of the men said. "Can't miss a chance to shoot up a peaceful place."

"Third Army secured the bridge a day or two ago but then moved on. I don't see anyone, either our guys or Krauts," said Baker. "What the hell, just hang tight. All will be revealed." He left to walk along the line.

"That's what we're afraid of." The comment came from Murch, several yards over, and was quickly seconded by Coins.

Henry nodded in Murch's direction. "Great," he said to Stephen. "Now we have to watch out for them, too."

"When did those assholes join up with us?" Stephen asked.

"Don' rahtly know," Henry responded in a bad imitation of an Oklahoma drawl, which he quickly abandoned. "First time I've seen those crackers in awhile."

A replacement named Riggs edged over to Stephen and Henry. While the two of them had adopted the veterans' wariness of newcomers, Riggs had managed to break through the barrier. He had a disarming awareness of his surroundings—an eighteen-year-old who comprehended the generational difference between himself and vets who might be only a year or two older. He dealt with it by approaching them in a way that was irreverently deferential. "What's the best way to handle this or that?" he would ask the vet in serious tones, and then attenuate the question by addressing the vet as "wise old fart." He was the kind who tended to be adopted as an earnest mascot. "I'll bet there are some nice, comfy beds in those pretty little towns," he said now.

"I'll bet there are," Henry said. "I'll also bet that the chances of us getting to sleep in them tonight are somewhere south of zero."

"Ah, well," Riggs said with a shrug. "We've had it pretty easy for a while. It got me to hoping maybe the towns have been abandoned."

"No law against hoping," Stephen said. "Looks like some of the guys are shoving off."

"Seriously," Riggs said. "What happens now? Do we go through one or both of the towns? Or maybe around them?"

Henry barked a laugh. "Like anyone would tell us."

"It'd be nice to see some activity down there," Stephen said. "Have the Krauts left, or are they just laying low to kick the shit out of us?"

"What do you think, Sarge?" Riggs asked Baker, who had come up next to them.

"Rule One: Never bet on unoccupied until you're sure of the bet. Rule Two: There is no Rule Two," Baker said. "The one thing I can tell you for sure is we've got no fording equipment, so if we're going there, the only way is over that bridge, and that's giving me the willies. I understand a platoon is being sent to check it out. I don't know which one, but I assume it's not ours or we'd probably have gotten word by now."

"Well, there they go," said Stephen, pointing toward the bridge.

The men took turns looking through Baker's field glasses. They could see troops moving cautiously across the bridge. When the last man reached the other side, Stephen and the others breathed easier. Until they looked at Baker.

"This doesn't make sense," Baker said. "You mean to tell me the only bridge over the river is not being defended? I ain't buying it."

"Didn't you say Patton's boys secured the bridge?" Henry asked.

"Yeah, but that was at least a couple of days ago. You don't take an important bridge and then leave it unguarded."

"Either way, the main thing is the platoon made it over without getting shot at," Henry said. "Looks like they're headed for Schweinhundt or whatever the hell it's called."

"Schweinheim," Stephen said.

"So now what?" Riggs asked.

Baker said, "We stay put 'til we get orders."

The wait was not long. A few minutes later they heard the crash of mortars and small arms fire in the distance.

"And there we go," Baker said, appearing relieved to have an answer. He caught the eye of the platoon lieutenant, who was passing nearby.

The lieutenant, a recent West Point grad named Morrison, had not yet led the men in combat. He was tall and lanky. When he bent low, he took giraffe-like steps, swinging his legs from the hips. "We're going in," he said as he approached.

"Just us?" Henry asked.

"All of us. Whole battalion."

"Sir, if there are Krauts over in Schweinheim, why didn't they defend the bridge?" Baker asked. "It would have been easier to stop us there, don't you think?"

"Third Army took the bridge."

"That's what we heard, but where the hell are they?"

"There's a cavalry recon group positioned upstream. You can't see them from here. We've got two companies going across, plus artillery support staying on this ridge."

"Lucky bastards," Henry said.

An hour later Stephen's platoon made the crossing and headed for Schweinheim. The gunfire had stopped as they pulled up at the edge of town. Stephen caught sight of a man he recognized from the group that made the initial crossing. "What's the deal?" he asked.

"Hell if I know," the man, a corporal, said. "We went in, met resistance, and pulled back here. To regroup, I guess."

"So much for an easy day," Stephen said.

"Not happening," the corporal responded. "I mean, when we crossed the river without opposition, we figured maybe the enemy had pulled out. Then we entered the town, and let me tell you, my friend, the dream died. There must have been a Kraut in every window. We started going house to house, and it was slow. Ten of our guys would go in. You'd hear shooting and explosions, and we'd clear the house all right—killed most of the Krauts and led a few out with their hands in the air. But we'd lose four or five of our guys along the way. Can't deal with those kinds of numbers for too long. There is a shitload of houses in this town, and that doesn't even count Aschaffenburg, the town with the big castle up there."

"Asshole Germans. You'd think they'd know when to call it a day," Stephen said.

"What for? The only thing the sons of bitches are good at is fighting. And I'll tell you something else. Forget all that crap about the collapsing Nazis relying on geezers and kids. The ones we ran into were almost all SS. If that's the way it's gonna be the rest of the way, taking this place is gonna be hell."

Just then, the corporal and Stephen flinched as explosions ripped across the town, hitting also the Schloss Johannisburg. "That's us," Stephen said. "We left our artillery back on the ridge."

"Yeah? Well, if you ask me, just let them level the place and starve out anyone who isn't turned into itty bits. I gotta go." He turned toward men from his squad who were gathering. "Anyhow, why the hell do we have to occupy every piece of real estate on the way to Berlin? Just bust up the town with the big guns and watch everyone who's left scatter like roaches."

There was a reprieve overnight as the battalion continued to mass forces and prepare for an assault the next morning. By this time no one was suffering under an illusion that the coming fight would be easy.

46

Stephen and Henry did their best to find a place to catch some sleep; the former they found under a copse of elms, the latter eluded them. Both of them smoked now, and they lit up one after another. Henry justified taking up the habit by saying it was one of the few pleasures that could be had reliably. Food rations might lag, but the smokes always seemed to get through.

"It pisses me off," Henry said.

"What does?" Stephen lit a cigarette off the remains of another.

"Risking our lives this late in the game. It was one thing when the outcome of the war was in doubt. But especially after the Bulge, it's clear now. What's that expression—something about being killed by the last bullet of the last battle of the war. What a waste."

"Keep that in mind when we go in, and don't do anything stupid."

"Believe me, I won't. But there is one good thing about this battle. If the Krauts defending the town really are mostly SS, killing as many of them as possible will be an act of justice. They're the ones responsible for killing the most Jews, so they'll be getting what they deserve."

"Not that again, Henry . . ."

Henry gave his cigarette an angry flick. "Yeah, that again. Why the hell not? If we're going to risk our lives, it might as well be to kill the baddest of the bad."

Stephen gave Henry an impatient look. "Because even if you're right about what they've done . . ."

"Even *if?*" Henry interjected. "Are you blind, intentionally blind, or just plain stupid!"

Stephen glared and stood to go. "I'm not starting this again, Henry. When the war's over, it will be over. There's no changing anything," he said as he walked away.

"Not for you, maybe," Henry called to his back.

* * *

"I HEARD WE'VE taken over a thousand prisoners so far," an exhausted Stephen said to Henry during a brief rest period. It was early morning on the third day of fighting. They had finally taken Schweinheim and moved into Aschaffenburg.

Henry was playing absently with a Luger he had taken on the first day. It had come from the first man Henry had ever shot at close range. He had been ordered to cover a hallway in a large house they were clearing while Stephen and the rest of the squad split up and began going room to room on the floors above. Suddenly, a German soldier flung open the door to one of the rooms at the end of the hallway. Henry, standing near a stairway landing, got out of the line of fire just in time.

Amped with fear and adrenalin and acting on automatic, he stepped from the landing into the corridor and began shooting. The German slumped where he stood; a jerking finger let off a final, wild round before he collapsed. Henry ran to him and pulled the body to the side to create a clear run to the floor above. The shot had hit the man high in the chest, just below the throat. Blood soaked his uniform, spreading to the lightning SS patches at the collar.

Acting on impulse, Henry reached into the German's holster and pulled out the prized souvenir Luger. But it wasn't the souvenir value of the gun that mattered so much to Henry, as he took a furtive look around to make sure he was not being observed, pointed it at the dead man's heart, and pulled the trigger. "Just because," he muttered in the moment before he was joined by others in the squad as they started up the stairs to begin clearing the rest of the house.

"You can shoot them all as far as I'm concerned," Henry now said bitterly. To Stephen's skeptical look, he added, "Like I said, call it justice. Call it revenge for all I care."

Stephen began to respond, then thought better of it. "Nice souvenir," he said with a nod to the Luger. Henry had not told him about the extra shot. "You okay?" Stephen asked.

"Yeah," Henry said after a distracted pause.

They looked up as Murch walked by. He ignored them, as he had since he rejoined their platoon. There was still no sign of Coins.

"Too bad no one's taken him out," Stephen said after Murch had passed.

Henry only nodded, Stephen's remark not spurring the agreement it usually did.

After a moment, Stephen said, "Word is that the reason we've been in it up to our necks here is that Aschaffenburg is a major SS training base, and they've been ordered to resist to the end. For every one we kill or push back, it seems like there are two more ready to counterattack or reinfiltrate. Come to think of it, maybe that's why Murch hasn't been hit. They wouldn't want to shoot one of their own. You sure you're okay, Henry?"

"Just tired." Henry shrugged.

"Because, maybe it's killing that German that's got you? I mean, I know they're evil scum of the earth and all, but still. . . . You remember? I had that delayed reaction to the ones I got with the grenade back in Épinal? Henry?"

"Maybe. I can't think of any people who deserve killing more than these . . . " He waved his hand at the surroundings to indicate what he couldn't find a potent enough word for. He released an audible sigh. "But . . . it's true that every so often I'll have a blink of a memory of myself, what, ten months ago? Seems like ten years. And I think, *little Henry*." He gave a small, wistful laugh. "Whatever happened to little Henry, the smart-ass kid? He must be in there somewhere, but damned if I can find him."

* * *

"ANOTHER HOUSE TO clear? You'd think we'd have run out of them by now," Stephen said to Baker, who was walking with a limp. He'd had a shrapnel fragment removed the previous day but insisted on returning to the fight.

"Apparently there's one more," Baker said in a resigned, dismissive tone. He gathered the men in front of a low stone wall and winced as he set one ass cheek on it in a contorted effort to favor his better leg. "We're here," he said, pointing to a map of Aschaffenburg. He counted and read out the names of three streets. "We need to get up here, behind the castle . . . or schloss or whatever. If we can get over to this big street, Pfaffengasse (he pronounced the Pf combination with an aspirated 'P'), we'll have a pretty clear shot at our objective. Bravo Company cleared the street a little while ago, but watch for reinfiltrated snipers anyway.

"Just up from there, closer to the castle, we'll come to a large house. Or what's left of a large house—I've been told it'll be obvious. Apparently, there's a group of Alamo-minded Krauts who are moving around the rubble, using large chunks of it for cover. We've been ordered to dislodge them."

"Why can't we just waste the place?" Murch asked. "Isn't that what artillery's for?"

For once, Stephen agreed with him.

"The fighting's been at close quarters—sometimes hand to hand—all over that area. There's too much risk of hitting our own," Baker answered.

"Yeah? Well, like I said, just pull ours back and tell the big boomers to fire at will."

"Write the general a letter, Murch," Baker said. He gave the order to move, and the men spread out, scanning intently for snipers as they picked their way through the rubble-strewn streets.

"There." Murch, staying low, pointed at their objective. The difficulty encountered in the earlier assault was immediately evident. The front of the house had been demolished, appearing almost sheared off, leaving a field of debris that included man-sized chunks of concrete, which the Germans were using to cover themselves as they moved about shooting at the comparatively exposed attackers. Meanwhile, the part of the house that was left standing was almost a perfect half, like an architect's cross-section elevation or an elaborate dollhouse. Approaching it from the opposite side, one would never know the house was incomplete.

"There's the problem," Henry said. "If we push them back, they'll just retreat into what's left of the house, and we'll end up going room to room to root them out."

Baker split the squad into three four-man teams. By bad luck or unspecified design, Murch was assigned to be with Stephen and Henry. These three, plus a replacement, Jarman, were designated Team Alpha. Henry's frowns and eye-rolling over Murch's assignment made no impact on Baker, who had made it plain as first order of business when he took charge that he'd have no truck with individual spats or squabbles among the men. If he was aware of the animosity within the sub-team he'd just created, he didn't let on. They were given the task of

50

approaching the house from the left flank. The eponymous Team Baker, which included Riggs, was to come at it from the right. Team Charlie would take the central position.

On Baker's signal the teams began to move forward, staying low and zigzagging through the rubble toward the house. They met no opposition, but they had learned from hard experience not to place much stock in such moments.

Stephen signaled to Henry, Murch, and Jarman to pay attention to a cluster of masonry forms that were large enough to conceal enemy gunners. It took only another few crawl-steps forward for the Germans hidden there to begin shooting.

All three teams of the divided squad immediately returned fire and looked for positions where they would be less exposed. Clouds of disturbed stucco and plaster filled the air. Jarman screamed as he was hit in the chest close to the shoulder. The reaction on his face, more than pain, was surprise, as if he couldn't believe that his first exposure to battle could end so quickly. The cry went up for a medic. Henry ran to Jarman. It was difficult to tell how serious the wound was. Jarman remained conscious despite the presence of a large amount of blood.

When a few well-placed grenades finally succeeded in taking out the most threatening of the German positions, the remaining troops began to retreat into the house. Murch pointed up to the exposed rooms—the ones that were wide open to the elements—where new enemy troops had emerged to cover the ones retreating from the rubble. What they lacked in cover from these open rooms they made up for in height and angle. Their clear field of view enabled them to shoot down on the attackers.

The remaining three in Stephen's team opened fire, trying to protect the medic who had arrived to treat Jarman. The fusillade, joined by firing from other parts of the squad, pushed the Germans back. When one of them, shooting as he went, stood too tall, Stephen took a bead on him and fired. The German disappeared from view. From the squad's position, it was impossible to see whether Stephen had hit his mark or the man had retreated into the house.

"Now!" Baker yelled, and the three teams moved forward.

There were two staircases, one on either side of the building shell, both opened to the air. Stephen's team gathered at the bottom of the staircase on the left, while the other was covered by the team containing Baker and Riggs.

The two staircase teams got ready to rush to the floor above. They prepared grenades to toss into the rooms. Henry said, "I sure as shit hope these do the job; otherwise, we'll just keep forcing the SS fuckers back and up to other floors and rooms."

"Either way," Stephen said, "there are only so many floors and rooms they can retreat to."

"I'll go first," Henry said in an emphatic tone that cut off any objection. Stephen noticed a more fierce concentration on his face than he'd ever seen. His eyes looked almost wild. If Henry had a bloodlust, this is what it would look like, and Stephen was afraid that it signaled a determination devoid of caution.

"No, I want the lead on this one," Stephen said, pushing past Henry and leaving Murch in the rear.

"What the fuck, someone just go!" Murch spat out as Stephen began to do just that.

There was no resistance on the staircase. They reached the first landing and gathered around a closed door. Standing off to the side, Stephen readied a grenade and reached for the doorknob. The knob turned, but the door opened only a crack before it met resistance. "Shit, we've got to force the door wide enough to lob a grenade in there. I can't pull the damn pin until we do that."

"Well," Murch said, "I'm sure as hell not hurling my shoulder into it only so's they can shoot my head off the minute I break through. Why don't you try it, Jew boy," he added, looking at Henry. "You're all fired up to go."

Stephen, still afraid of what he saw in Henry's eyes, began to say he would do the battering, but before he could move Henry shoved Murch aside. "Chickenshit Okie cocksucker," he said as he put his shoulder into the door, staying low and driving his legs. He managed to get the door and whatever was blocking it pushed back about six inches.

Immediately, a hail of bullets splintered the wood just over Henry's head. He dove to the side.

"Try it again, limp dick," Murch said, and it occurred to Stephen that Murch was trying to take advantage of the same reckless determination

52

from which Stephen was trying to protect Henry. Before he could say or do anything, Henry, getting as low as he could while still being able to drive his legs, crashed into the door.

This time, the door opened another foot. Stephen grabbed Henry by the collar and pulled him back just as the next fusillade hit. "That's enough!" Stephen yelled at him. "Just stand back!"

Stephen pulled the pin on a grenade, waited the necessary beats to make sure it would not be returned, and pitched it as well as he could through the narrow opening. He had another ready just as the first went off with a reverberating bang, and he heaved that one in, too. Behind them, they could hear the gunfire of other fights.

"Go! Go!" Murch yelled.

The room was large, used as an office of some kind and filled with a jumble of desks and filing cabinets. Two Germans, apparently hit by grenade fragments, lay on the floor. One was motionless, the other writhing as if trying to expel the hot metal from his body.

Stephen and Henry kept firing until it was clear there was no opposition. Henry looked back and saw Murch. It was plain that only now was he entering the room, and that he had let the two of them move in alone.

It took that mere instant of distraction for a third SS man, mortally wounded and until then unseen behind an overturned desk, to get off a final shot.

The bullet hit Henry in the leg. "Damn!" he screamed in both surprise and pain as he reached for the wound and collapsed onto the floor.

Stephen yelled for a medic, but he couldn't tell whether he could be heard over the echoing din of gunfire from elsewhere in the house.

"Okay, okay," Henry said, as if gathering his wits and taking stock. "Only a leg wound."

But Stephen saw in an instant that it was more than that. Blood had already soaked through Henry's pants. Clearly, the femoral artery had been hit—something they all feared. He grabbed Henry's pants leg, ripped the fabric, and put pressure on the wound, blood seeping through his interlaced fingers. He again bellowed for a medic. As he did, he looked up and saw Murch, just standing there, casually scanning the room.

Henry was beginning to babble and lose consciousness.

"Murch, you motherfucker, get help!"

But Murch didn't move. "Medic," he called in a mocking whisper. "Jew hit."

"Medic! Help!" Stephen screamed again, trying to stanch the flow of blood that was everywhere, soaking Henry and covering Stephen's hands. He ripped off Henry's belt and fashioned it into a tourniquet. "Hold on, Henry, just hold on. Doc will be here in a minute. It's only a leg wound. All we need to do is stop the bleed and pack it. Easy-peasy." He kept up the reassuring patter. "I'll be damned if you punch your ticket home before me. You don't want to have to deal with Judy." Again, he called for help. And then again.

And then Henry's seeping blood stopped flowing.

"No, goddammit!" Stephen cried. He flailed. He slapped Henry's face hard, and then slapped it again and again. Finally, every bit of him depleted, he buried his head in Henry's lifeless chest.

When he looked up a moment later, Murch was going through the pockets of one of the dead Germans.

In an instant Stephen would always think of as one of the most fateful and defining of his life, he realized his hand was resting on the souvenir Luger in Henry's waistband. He pulled it and looked at Murch, whose back was to him as he rifled through the dead man's pockets.

Stephen aimed. "Murch, you motherfucker."

Murch looked up. "Yeah, right," he said with an expression of disdain. He added something unintelligible to Stephen as he began turning to continue stripping souvenirs off the German.

He never completed the turn.

Stephen fired, hitting him just below the armpit.

Murch cried out, collapsed like an unstrung marionette, and began to writhe on the floor, not knowing what part of himself to grasp.

Stephen could feel his movements take on a slow, ethereal quality as he walked toward Murch and stood over him. His thought—his fear now—was that Murch might not die. He couldn't leave him alive to tell what happened.

"Medic," Stephen whispered with a sneer. He wanted Murch to plead for his life. But there was no time for that satisfaction, as he heard voices coming closer. "I just can't let you win," he said in a low voice, spitting out each word. "For Henry's sake, I just can't let you win." He looked into Murch's confused, frightened eyes, and put a round from the Luger through his forehead.

Moving quickly now, he wiped down the gun as well as possible with his shirttail and dropped it near the outstretched hand of one of the dead Germans.

A moment later, he heard a noise behind him and whirled to find Riggs standing there.

~ ~ ~ ~ ~

Chapter 7

April 1945: Bavaria

A N HOUR LATER, THE house at last secured, Stephen watched a pair of stretcher-bearers prepare to remove the bodies. He dropped his helmet and placed his hands like a vise to both sides of his skull as they shifted Henry's body onto the stretcher and started to pull a blanket over him. When they began to cover Henry's face, he squeezed the vise until he felt as though his head might shatter like a glass.

"Wait!" he called out suddenly, startling the bearers. "I need a minute with him."

"We can't," the one holding up the blanket said. "There are still Krauts sneaking around."

"Just one goddamn minute, that's all! I need to talk to him!"

Stephen dropped to one knee beside the body. His eyes were wild and unfocused. Avenues of tears and sweat ran down his cheeks, creating ravines through a drying coat of plaster dust. He caught the suspended blanket and pushed it away from Henry's face.

"Make it fast," the bearer said. He turned to his companion and nodded toward Murch's corpse. "We can start with the other guy."

Stephen ignored the kindness. He looked into Henry's face, plaster-crusted like his own. Blood-drained and plaster-crusted. A true death mask, but falsely tranquil, as if the ire and querulousness—the sometimes-joyful querulousness—had drained through Henry's shot artery.

In the near distance, new firing and explosions. "Let's go!" the bearer said.

Stephen ignored him and drew his face close to Henry's. "Come on, Henry!" he shouted into the mask. "Argue with me! Tell me about the fucking Nazis! Tell me I was wrong to do what I just did to the scumbag! Or thank me. And then tell me it was wrong."

The bearer bent to cover Henry's face. "We have to get moving. He's not the only one."

Stephen reached out and stopped him. He grabbed Henry's collar, bunching it in his fist and slightly lifting the body. "Idiot!" he screamed. "How am I supposed to get home without you! What am I supposed to tell your parents!"

"Out of the way!" the second bearer said, interposing himself between Stephen and Henry.

Stephen nodded, resigned now, drained. He stretched to touch Henry's face for one last time—an index finger to the forehead, leaving his print in the plaster dust. A battlefield benediction.

And then the face was gone, covered, the rough army blanket pulled tight. It puckered slightly over Henry's nose and mouth. A death mask relief of the death mask beneath.

Stephen stood, dazed and at a loss as the bodies were removed. Like most of the men, he had grown an emotional exoskeleton to protect against the loss of comrades-in-arms and to see him through from one day into the next. This was different. This was Henry. For this death the armor was too thin. It had grown, layer upon layer with—yet always a season behind—the friendship itself.

Worse, in this instance grief was compounded by the galling reality of seeing the bodies of both Henry and Murch removed with the same degree of respect. It was a sick joke.

* * *

WHEN THE SQUAD reassembled, Baker approached Stephen and told him he was sorry about Henry. "When your head clears, tell me what happened. His family will have to be notified."

Stephen nodded vaguely. Tell him what happened. When his head cleared. He was grateful to have a moment to collect his thoughts. He would have to make it a straightforward account. A firefight. Two men down. Just the worst luck that the bullet struck Henry where it had. He would not pretend to mourn Murch. He had no doubt that the most incompetent of investigations would show that the German could not possibly have hit Murch from where he had fallen. He had to pin his hopes on the knowledge that in the slaughterhouse of Europe early in 1945 there would not likely be that cursory investigation.

But Riggs. How long had Riggs been standing there? What had he seen? The shot that killed Murch? Probably not. The look on his face was more one of surprise and sorrow over fallen comrades, even if in fact they had not had that status for very long. No, if Riggs had seen the act, something would have signaled it; some tell would have shown in his face.

Yet certainly Riggs was there when Stephen stood up after placing the Luger near the dead German's hand. Did he see that? Or if he did, perhaps he thought that, rather than putting it down, Stephen was planning to pick it up and take it as a trophy. If so, it would be a terrible misunderstanding to have to live with. Whatever exculpatory benefit there might be would have to be weighed against the hideous thought of Riggs concluding that Stephen was trophy hunting before Henry was cold. It would be a notion Stephen would be in no position to contest, but the thought of Riggs holding it made him sick at heart.

The reality was that Stephen had panicked. His response to seeing Riggs was to fly into a rage that was partly spontaneous and yet on some level a performance flash-calculated to distract Riggs's attention. He kicked the German soldier's body, then kicked the gun he had just placed near his hand. The gun flew over a desk and skittered across the floor to the wall. Only later did it occur to Stephen that kicking it out of sight and away from the dead German might have been fortunate. Considering the popularity of German pistols as souvenirs, someone coming behind him and Riggs otherwise might well have wondered at the excessively good luck of finding two pistols on one corpse—one recently fired, the other still holstered. In any event, it was all speculation, as Riggs had not said anything, and Stephen had no intention of being the one to broach the matter.

All of which was distinct from the fact of Stephen continually finding himself—startling himself sometimes—looking around for Henry as if he would reappear at any moment. All along he had imagined them returning home together. The goal felt so close. Stephen could only think of the Germans hanging on and not surrendering as an act of petulance. It made no sense. They themselves had even tried, and failed, to assassinate Hitler, yet Der Führer's sacrificial whims still held sway. The last bullet of the last war. . . . Goddammit, Henry, we came so close to making it.

Several times he began to write home. The army would tell Henry's family. That would be the worst of it, but it didn't spare him the need to write them himself. To write his own family, too.

And Judy. The situation with her was particularly awkward. Only a month ago Henry had gathered his courage and sent her what he referred to as a Dear Jane letter. Her unending stream of letters outlining their shared future had finally gotten the better of him. Henry said one day that her increasing ardor seemed to move in lockstep with his decreasing certainty that she was the one for him. Stephen remembered suggesting back in Épinal that if he felt that way, he owed it to her to cut her loose. Even more problematic, by the time Henry got around to doing so, she had become close to his family, assuming a de facto position of dutiful daughter-in-law awaiting her beloved's return.

Judy had responded quickly (it was one of the rare occasions when slow mail service would have been welcomed). Henry looked woeful as he read the letter, which was equal parts grief and vituperation. A paragraph pouring out the reasons she was heartbroken and couldn't imagine life without him would be followed by one that painted him as the most cruel man who ever lived and wishing him nothing but pain as great as he had caused her.

Stephen felt obligated to tell Judy something himself. But what? Would he stick to the basics—some bromide about how we all miss him—or create for her something like psychological widow's weeds (*pay no attention to the epistolary excesses of a man in combat; he adored you to the end*)? He concluded that the latter was more suitable, but in emphasizing the adoration, he would be careful not to encourage mourning so profound that she would consider entering a convent.

He resolved to focus on his mission. As the division pressed on into Bavaria, it became ever more challenging to concentrate on the work at hand. Henry's death made it clear that nothing should be taken for granted. He would not be home safe until he was home safe. Allowing himself to be distracted by personal tragedy would only lessen the odds of this coming to pass. Still, he missed Henry, pure and simple.

~ ~ ~ ~ ~

Chapter 8

April 29, 1945: Unspeakable

THE STENCH—A PECULIAR mix of rotting flesh and decaying filth—got to him before the sight. Stephen thought he was sufficiently accustomed to the smells of war—to the bloated corpses, human and animal, and to the particulates that went airborne from pulverized structures of all types and took up permanent residence in his lungs and sinuses. This was different, unlike anything he had ever encountered.

Riggs pulled up next to him. "What the hell is that stink?" Stephen asked. Riggs and others nearby answered with obvious gagging. One man vomited into a ditch. The men gave him a wide berth but not wide enough to be unaffected by the compound of the man's breakfast and the putrid air.

The roads were crowded as troops from three divisions converged on Munich. Up ahead was a railway siding and a long line of freight cars. Several men were milling about, distracted and aimless. Stephen could see as he got closer that most wore an expression he would forever think of as the definition of dumbstruck. The stench was growing stronger. Oddly, he was becoming less affected by it as his brain and body went about the well-practiced work of accommodation.

There was no need to ask what was going on when he reached the siding. To have posed the usual, casual "What's up?" would have been grotesque in itself.

Before him and several others who had stopped in the warm April sun stood railcars—forty or fifty of all types, for freight, for coal, for cattle. Every single one spilled the contents of the most wretched corpses he could imagine: ragged bone-sticks of the starved in various states of decomposition. Some must have survived long enough to claw themselves out and die on the ground. Many wore on their faces a final rictus of wonder at how their lives could have come to such a state— what anyone could have done to warrant such an end.

As he shuffled forward in a daze, all Stephen could think to ask the first soldier he encountered, a young lieutenant as stupefied as any of the rest, was, "Where did they come from?"

"More like, where were they going?" the officer replied after a pause that was long enough to make Stephen wonder whether he had been heard. The officer continued without looking at Stephen, softly in a Virginia Tidewater drawl that might have suggested he was talking to himself and rank was no longer a consideration. "I understand the Nazis have been shipping people all over from their camps, trying to stay one step ahead of us. We've been finding scenes like this everywhere, even worse than this, I've heard."

"How could anything be worse than this?"

The officer shrugged. "Well, that's what they say. Mostly Jews, apparently." He nodded toward the corpses. "Division says it's not only Jews here in this camp, though. Anyone the Nazis didn't like—political enemies, queers, gypsies. Someone said they used this place for some weird medical experiments, but I don't know what that's all about. All I know now is it's nothing but fucking disgusting confusion."

Something about the way he said *fucking*, a flicker of hesitation perhaps, suggested to Stephen that this was a man who had to be pushed beyond comprehension to utter such a profanity.

The officer continued, "Even while trainloads like this are arriving in one place, others are being sent someplace else. I heard one guy talking about a death march from here to God knows where. If you can believe people in this condition could walk at all. Supposedly, anyone who couldn't keep up was shot. That would have been most of them, probably. The lucky ones."

"You'll see for yourself when you go into the camp," the officer went on, now addressing Stephen directly. "Piles of dead people everywhere. There's a cremator—I'm not sure what the word is . . . a huge building where all they did was burn up dead bodies."

"Is everyone in the camp dead?" Stephen asked.

"Anyone who isn't looks like he is . . . might as well be. They look like they haven't eaten anything in months. A bunch of them wearing these . . . I don't know what to call them. Striped uniforms of some kind . . . filthy things. Whatever they are, they hang off the living, if you can call them that. If I wasn't a good Christian, I'd doubt there is a God."

"Not me," Stephen said. "I have no doubt there isn't one."

"That's a shame, then. I'll pray for you. Damnedest thing I ever saw," the officer continued, once again musing to himself as he looked toward a distant, indistinct vanishing point. Turning to Stephen he added, "When the first of our guys arrived, they began to hand out their rations, until the medics made them stop. Apparently, if you give a starving man too much rich food at once, you'll kill him. That's what the docs said, anyway. How's that for a bitch of a problem? Anyhow, we've taken as many of the living as possible to rescue stations. Still going on, I think. You'd better get moving and help."

Stephen stammered, finally asking, "Where are we, anyway? I thought we were headed for Munich."

"Yeah, well, good luck with this disaster in the way. I guess we'll get there eventually. We're close. Right now we're stuck in this place; it's called Dachau, I think." He pronounced the word with a soft "ch," as he would say "chum."

* * *

"WROTH!" STEPHEN TURNED to see Baker approaching in quick time.

"Where are the rest of the guys?" he asked. He looked around in disgust. "Hell of a thing, isn't it? We heard about hellholes like this, but who would think even fucking Nazis could do shit this bad? Where are the others?" he asked again.

Stephen pointed. "Riggs is over there. I don't know about the others. Probably wandered. Some of them were losing their lunch."

"Can't blame them for that. Round up as many as you can and meet back here in twenty minutes. Anyone we can't find will just have to catch up. We have to go through the camp, then go into town . . . something about making the fine local citizenry deal with all this."

A short time later, they had succeeded in gathering about half of the squad. Baker led the way into the camp. Ambulances and any truck or jeep that could be used for the purpose rumbled in and out, ferrying survivors and slowing only to avoid the dead and the walking dead.

Baker, standing next to Stephen, recognized one of the medics, who was directing traffic from the bed of a truck. "Pankow!" Baker called. "What are we supposed to be doing?"

"You believe this?" Pankow answered as he waved an ambulance through. "I don't know how many of these poor wretches are here. Thousands, I'm guessing, most of 'em dead or on the way to being dead.

"I don't know what to tell you," he continued while simultaneously trying to direct traffic. "I wish an MP would get his ass over here, so I could do my job. Some of the other squads have been combing these huts." He waved toward a cluster of low structures, while with his other hand he directed a truck loaded with empty stretchers. "They're looking for anyone still alive. All I can say is it's lucky we're not doing much fighting. We've got more than we can handle without having to deal with our own wounded."

As if on cue, the group was startled by the rattle of automatic weapons fire in the near distance. Pankow flinched. "What the hell! It figures!"

"Sounds like our guys shooting," Baker said.

"Spoke too soon about the fighting, I guess." But then the gunfire ceased.

Stephen felt a tug on his sleeve. He whirled, reflexively bringing his rifle up.

If being at the business end of a loaded weapon fazed the two people standing at his elbow, they didn't show it. A skeleton of a man—an old man, but how could you tell—with caves for eyes looked into Stephen's face. He was being propped up by another, seemingly younger skeleton, though one not quite so wasted.

"*Ww'as'r*," the old man whispered, then gathered himself to try again. "*Wasser*," he managed to get out.

"Someone get them some water, quick!" Baker commanded.

"Make sure they don't gulp it," Pankow, the medic, said. "Or it'll come right up."

More gossamer words from the old man: "*Hylp myr, byt. Myyn prwy.*"

"I don't understand. What's he saying?" Baker asked.

"It sounds like maybe Yiddish," Stephen said. "But I don't know."

"You don't?"

"No, goddammit, I don't. Not every Jew speaks Yiddish."

"*Www yz . . . myyn prwy . . .*" the old man tried again.

"His wife," the younger man managed to get out. He spoke haltingly, searching for each word. "He is tries to see . . . to find . . ."

"Maybe find his wife?" Stephen ventured.

The younger man nodded. "For long time." He shook his head with a look of futility. "I think not live."

Pankow held up his hand to stop an approaching ambulance. "You got room for two more?" he asked, pointing at the two.

The driver stuck his head out of the window. "No, but give them to us anyway."

Baker yelled for one of the men to help them aboard. "Can't believe it will be any more uncomfortable for them than what they've already gone through," he added under his breath.

"I'll do it," Stephen said. He approached the weaker man, then realized each of them was propping up the other. Yet they were so thin, his arms could have fully encircled both of them. His reflex as he got close was to pull back. All he had experienced during his time as a soldier, all of the filth and the stink and the gore, had not prepared him for the overpowering smell of decay of these walking corpses. The smell was different; it was less of dirt or uncleanliness—in a sense it had gone past these things, as rotting fruit might stop smelling after it becomes desiccated—and more that it had become one with the person who embodied it. These thoughts must have passed across Stephen's face as the younger of the two seemed embarrassed. Stephen, in turn, was mortified at the thought that with all these men had gone through they were still capable of feeling shame.

When the men had been crammed into the waiting ambulance, Baker sighed and said the squad had better help comb the camp. He spied two more of his men, both looking wan and confused. He ordered Riggs to collect them, then looked around and saw that Riggs was gone.

"Goddammit, where is everybody!"

Just then, the gunfire resumed in bursts. "What the . . ." Baker continued. "It still sounds like our guys, but I don't hear anyone shooting back."

"Cleaning out nests, maybe," one of the men suggested.

"Wroth!" Baker called. "See what you can find out. And while you're at it, see where the hell Riggs went."

Stephen made his way cautiously in the direction of the firing, which was sporadic; he had to stop occasionally to listen for new sounds. All the while he tried to avoid staring at the horrors he was forced to pass. "All dead, maybe fifty of 'em," he heard one soldier shout to another as he emerged from one of the camp huts.

A new burst of fire, prolonged this time, led him toward a pair of concrete watchtowers. "What's over there?" he asked a man coming from that direction. The man looked as dazed as Stephen felt.

"A yard of some kind. Somebody said maybe they stored coal there."

Another clattering burst of fire. Stephen inched toward the sound. As he rounded one of the towers, he collided with another soldier, who was rushing and didn't stop. It took him a second before he recognized that it was Riggs. "What's going on here?" he asked to his back. "Riggs!" he called again.

But Riggs kept going, slowing just long enough to yell, "Whatever it was, it's over! Fucking Germans!"

Stephen turned and almost ran into another man. This one slowed long enough to issue a warning. "Let me tell you," he said, "if you don't want to see these Kraut sons of bitches all dead, don't go in there."

But he did go in—peered in at first. In front of a concrete wall he caught sight of GIs wearing patches from his division. The smell of cordite was intense, and close to the wall bodies of Waffen SS were piled in a heap, blood still seeping.

He thought about moving closer, but quickly concluded there was nothing to be gained by doing so. He had already seen more than he wanted to report back to Baker. If it was what he thought had happened, he would have an obligation to report it formally, and he simply didn't want to know more. Two things registered with him: First, his hatred for the Nazis at that moment was so strong, he didn't care what might have been done to them. Second, even though Riggs had never broached the subject of Aschaffenburg, the possibility remained that he knew about Murch. Now Stephen had ammunition to use against him if it became necessary.

* * *

LATE IN THE day they stopped to rest. No one had eaten anything. No one would. You cannot eat in front of starving people.

Somehow, most of the living had been evacuated. That still left the piles of corpses, some half-burned in an effort by the fleeing camp masters to hide the evidence—an exercise in absurdity, like trying to hide a murder victim under a napkin.

Stephen stood off by himself while the men waited for a ride into town. He was blank, emptied out in every way; weary of body, vacant of spirit, at last devoid of tears as, without warning, the liquid had spilled from his eyes and fallen to the ground with no regard for others who might witness his unsoldierly demeanor.

Over and over he could say only one thing, speaking as if his listener were present: "My God, Henry, I am so sorry." He thought about the debates—no, call them by the right name, the arguments—they had over what the Nazis were or were not doing, and he cringed at the image of his haughty self-assurance, his arrogant conviction. He was grateful that Henry was not present to witness the scene, and, in the only moment that prompted a ghost of a smile, he reflected on the thought that Henry never missed a chance to crow when he was proved right. But this— even Henry could not have imagined this. "I am so, so sorry, Henry."

"Who is Henry?"

Startled, Stephen looked up. "What . . ."

"Who is Henry who you were saying you are sorry to? You must have done something very bad."

It was a woman asking the question, a camp inmate. Ragged, sunken-cheeked, but not so much as the others. She had the yellow *Juden* star on her breast. It was falling off. Either the stitches had come loose or, more likely, she had attempted to tear it off. But why was it still hanging there? Did she not have the strength to finish the task?

Stubble, white except for hints of russet near the temples, had begun to appear on her shaved head. But she seemed younger than he took her for at first.

"I could not decide whether to take it off or leave it," she said in answer to his unasked question. "I am this thing. It is all that I am, whether I want it or not. So now, like me, it is half off, half on."

Amazing to Stephen, she said this with a wan smile. "You speak English," he said, as if he had only now noticed.

The phantasmal smile again, this time with a small shrug, the "obviously" left unsaid.

"How?" Stephen asked.

"I am a teacher. Or I was."

Stephen was intrigued by this waif and wanted to know more about her but did not know what to say next. Finally, he asked, "Why are you here?" To her confused expression, he quickly added, "I mean still here. Why didn't you go with the medics . . . the doctors?"

"I know what means medics."

"Or run away? Many people ran away if they were able to."

The shrug again, one more little mystery among all of the day's vast unknowables. "There seemed no hurry now," she said.

Despite her sorry condition, Stephen found himself drawn to her—to some mix of intelligence and spirit that was not quite definable but which he believed he glimpsed. How else to explain the fleeting smiles, the inner strength, whatever it took to not only survive but also decide she would not go with the others? The more he looked at her, the more he was able to see remnants of physical beauty as well, something her captors were unable to extinguish.

He came back to the earlier question of why she was still there, deciding it had been worth asking, even if poorly worded. And he wanted to know how she came to be in this camp. Was it only because she was Jewish, or something else too? How long had she been here? Why was she alive, and why was she not as wasted as the other survivors? It seemed too personal, too intimate to ask such questions, but he was intrigued nonetheless. Why had she ended up in a place like this?

He tried to be more diplomatic. "How long have you been here?"

She considered this for a moment. "In this camp? Not so long. Months. This isn't my first. About a year and a half all together. I can't say for surely . . . for sure," she corrected. "I remember the day I was taken. It's easy to remember that. It was my birthday, 14th July 1943."

It seemed she would stop there; he expected her to stop there. But she continued. "Born on the French independence day. You know, a strange thing happens in places like this. Time doesn't go as it does in the usual world. There is no clock to look at. Here time feels smashed together; it just does. Maybe because you have no future. And yet . . ." She paused to collect her thoughts.

"And yet," she went on, "this is very strange—hard to explain. You are always knowing about minutes passing. My father used to tell me to take difficult times day by day, make it through one, and then the next, and so on. Here that is too much. Every hour, every minute you keep living is like an anniversary. Can you understand what I am meaning?"

"I think so. I don't think I could tell you in words though—it's more a feeling of understanding. In combat—when we are in battle—it's different. The future is a mystery, and it can hurt to think about it, so you just hope time passes and you're around when it's done."

She nodded, vaguely. "But anyway, I can't answer your question exactly. I know when they took me away, but I don't know what today is."

"April 29th," Stephen answered. He added, "1945," just in case she had really lost track.

"Ah, so I was close. A little more than a year and a half since they took me away."

"Did you live in Munich? Is that why you're in this particular camp?"

This question brought a bitter little laugh. "I did for some years. But I was born in Heidelberg. That's really what I think of as home, even though it's many years ago. This isn't my first camp. Did I tell you this? Yes, I think I did. My brain gets mixed up. Actually, it's my third. I'm very popular, you know." The strained laugh again—ironic, sad, wistful.

Stephen was waiting for her to go on. For a moment it seemed she would, but then she said, "I don't want to . . ."

"It's okay," Stephen interrupted. "You don't have to tell me anything."

She nodded. He wasn't sure whether she was relieved at not continuing to explain or sorry to have lost a sympathetic ear.

He felt awkward, a little embarrassed for asking his questions, afraid she might think him voyeuristic. "Well, anyway, come with me. You shouldn't spend another night here. What is your name?" It was the first time all day he had asked this question. Once or twice the information was volunteered. Mostly it was superfluous in a place where nothing was permitted to be superfluous: it either was, or was not, essential to live.

"Greta," she said after a pause, as if she had to decide whether to loan one of her only possessions. "I'm Greta."

"Well, come on, Greta. Let's see if we can find someplace for you to stay tonight. Not here," he added, just in case she needed reassurance.

* * *

STEPHEN WANTED ONLY escape, any kind, any way it could be found. Alcohol? Bring it to him, the more, the better. Sleep? He was exhausted enough. But if he were to collapse onto the soft bed in the house he imagined had been requisitioned in Dachau town, would he be able to fall asleep, or stay asleep if he did? Could he stop the thoughts and images, keep the dark at bay?

About sleep he needn't have worried. The soft bed was sometime in the future. First, he and the rest of his platoon were ordered to start knocking on doors or posting notices. They were to inform the good citizens of Dachau that they were to muster at 0600, ready to work, and work hard. After this day no one was in the mood to brook excuses. Prior commitments, rheumatism, bad feet, bad heart, old age—show up at 0600 or we will drag you to work. We won't be gentle about it.

70

Some young mothers asked what they were to do with their children. They were informed that infants could be slung on their backs. It was tempting to tell the ones with children who were older but not old enough to look after themselves that they should be brought along. But it was decided that children were the only ones who could legitimately claim innocence and seeing the sights of the camp would be too damaging to them.

"So what?" one of the men said. "The people here didn't give a damn about the children or anyone else they damaged to death." He had taken the words out of Stephen's mouth.

"We're not them," another answered. Besides, the kids would only slow the work.

The solution was to designate a few people who for legitimate reasons could not go to the camp to care for the children.

Given only the information that they would be on death detail in the camp, some protested. They knew nothing about what went on there. They should not have to go.

No excuses, the officers said again. Anyone who doesn't know didn't want to know. A captain said he had it on good authority that this was the oldest camp in Germany, the one the Nazis set up first to deal with their enemies—a list that got wider and wider. There might be worse places, unimaginable as that was, but none older. "These fucking people are going to see what happened right under their noses," he said.

One of the men teamed with Stephen said he particularly liked the idea of banging on doors late at night. "Scare the shit out of them, that's what I say. Let them think the motherfucking Gestapo is beating on their door."

Early the following morning, the labor details were in place. Most people did show up on their own, perhaps fearing the consequences of not doing so, perhaps because that's who they were—authority is authority. "What else would you expect?" said a man from Stephen's platoon, giving voice to the thought. "They're fucking Germans. They follow orders. *Jawoll und Sieg Heil* Motherfucker!"

The few no-shows were rousted from their homes or businesses, or grabbed off the streets. When a middle-aged woman who couldn't hide her elegant pedigree complained to Stephen, he simply looked at her coldly and said he hoped for her sake she hadn't eaten a big breakfast.

Throughout the day Stephen supervised the laborers and tried to guess their reactions by the expressions on their faces. He caught sight of the woman to whom he'd given the caustic warning about breakfast. Her mouth and nose covered by a fine silk scarf, she was pulling stinking corpses from a pit and passing them up the line. What could she possibly be thinking about this Dante-esque vision? Was any part of it remorse, or was it all resentment over how her beautiful life was turning out? Does it really do any good to put a dog's nose in his shit?

What would Henry have said? Surely not "I told you so"—or at least not only that. Would he be all anger, or would parts of him be reserved for something else? Certainly, Stephen concluded, he would feel an overwhelming compassion and sense of loss for the victims, as well as rage and simple wonder that anything like this could come to pass. Even he could not have conceived of something this demonic. And he probably also would conclude that people who could feel only anger at the scene were protecting themselves from feeling other things, worse things that might have immobilized him and them.

Stephen ran into Baker. They nodded to one another and stood in silence as corpses and pieces of corpses, some hardly recognizable as having human provenance, were dealt with. Most of the gagging had stopped. They must have become used to the sights and smells, a frightening idea.

Stephen broke the silence. "I hope someone pays for this."

Baker responded in a low voice, passing on a cryptic confidence. "I understand some already have."

Stephen gave Baker a questioning look.

"You know some of the guys went apeshit yesterday, right?" Baker continued.

"Yeah, well, I think we all did."

"No, I mean really. I heard they rounded up as many of the Nazis who were running the camp as they could find, SS especially. Rounded them up and executed them on the spot."

72

"What? Are you sure?" Stephen said, squelching an impulse to say exactly what he had seen and wondering how cagey he should be in light of his anodyne report to Baker the previous day.

"It's what I heard. Well, in any case, don't go spreading it around." He shrugged. "What the hell. It would be payback for what they did to our boys at Malmédy," he said, referring to the murder of American prisoners during the Battle of the Bulge.

Stephen nodded, torn between the automatic impetus of his old self to condemn such an act and the thought rooted in his present existence that the executed couldn't have suffered enough.

~ ~ ~ ~ ~

Chapter 9

Summer 1945: Feldafing

FOR STEPHEN, THE DAYS following VE Day were strange, a time of anxiety, uncertainty, and drift. Some of his buddies were going home. A point system rewarded time abroad, battles fought, wounds received, and honors won to determine who got to go home first. Stephen was somewhere in the middle of the list. For the moment this was irrelevant or, as the men had taken to saying in such situations, *macht nichts* (it doesn't matter, the verbal equivalent of a shrug, which he and his comrades pronounced and wrote as *mox nix*). Any way you sliced it, he wasn't going home soon. Adding to his anxiety was the likelihood that he and remaining Thunderbirds would be redeployed to the Pacific.

Stephen also found it strange adjusting to something resembling peacetime. The end of the almost daily terror of combat, or of its anticipation, was welcomed with predictable relief. But the sudden transition following the German surrender was hard to comprehend. The wartime Stephen had a purpose, however terrible. He likened the abrupt change to skiing downhill into a snowbank.

Faced with the tedious chores of occupation, Stephen gained understanding, if not equal desire, of some of the men who were eager to fight Japs. They had become combat junkies. Insane as it appeared, especially to those who had not become addicted to the rush of battle, Stephen thought he knew what they were about.

The mindlessness of many of the daily tasks gave him too much time to think. About home. About Henry. About his future. Oddly, about the girl, Greta.

He told himself that thoughts of Greta were rooted in simple curiosity about her experiences in the camps and about what had become of her. He had not seen her since the day he settled her in one of the houses in Dachau town that had been commandeered to assist camp survivors on the less urgent tier of the triage list. Stephen was confident that, unlike many of the survivors, Greta would rebound, physically at least, with some decent food and shelter.

One day, curiosity got the better of him. Finding himself near the house where he had left her, he stopped in to see how she was coming along. He approached a house matron, interrupting her to ask about the girl—the woman, he amended—he had brought in. He told the matron he was looking for a woman named Greta, but he had no last name. He described her—thin, malnourished, shorn, maybe pretty if you could see it. He got the kind of impatient stare he might have expected had he thought about it in advance, as if he had told someone in New York City to meet him by the tall building. "Speaks good English," he finally offered as possibly a useful clue.

It wasn't. The matron pointed out that since the house was used primarily as a triage center, the survivors, "including this Greta," would not have stayed long after determining what services were needed.

Stephen thanked the matron and left. He might have stopped his search then, but if anything, he became more curious and determined. He made further inquiries with various military and civilian organizations, but with nothing more to go on than he had provided to the matron, they, too, were unable to help.

In late May, Stephen, who had received his second stripe shortly after reaching Dachau and was thus now Corporal Wroth, was seconded to the army's Civil Affairs Command and assigned to the recently opened Feldafing Displaced Persons Camp nearby. To Stephen's "why me?" posed to the officer, a captain named Wilding, who informed him of the transfer, he was surprised to get an honest answer. Feldafing was probably going to be converted into a predominantly Jewish camp, and being Jewish, Stephen was a logical choice. As a matter of principle,

Stephen was unhappy at being so pigeonholed. But he was not being given a choice, merely the unnecessary courtesy of an explanation. And, as Captain Wilding concluded, "Besides, why not you? I have to send someone."

Despite his annoyance over the presumption of his Jewishness, Stephen gradually came to consider that, yes, take the presumption out, and he might actually prefer to work mostly with displaced Jews. After all, some sense of kinship might be helpful in dealing with them. Moreover, helping Jewish survivors was probably the least he could do to atone for the guilt that still plagued him over being so determinedly blind to the extent of Nazi atrocities, and to honor Henry's memory.

Further crowding Stephen's mind, as well as diluting the purity of his compensatory righteousness, were allegations of war crimes committed by his own division the day Dachau was liberated. He was questioned by an army investigator who was attempting to assign responsibility for the summary execution of anywhere from a handful to hundreds of SS. The allegations were lent credibility by similar crimes committed by the division in Sicily in 1943, before Stephen's time.

Stephen reluctantly told the investigator about hearing unexpected machine-gun fire, which "someone" said came from pissed-off men in the general area of the coal yard. The shooting was said to be in reprisal for what the Germans had done in the camp. He said he also thought he remembered someone mentioning retribution for the German atrocities at Malmédy during the Bulge.

When the investigator asked if he could identify that "someone," Stephen said he didn't know who it was and that it was only a remark he had overheard. In truth, he remembered clearly that it was Sergeant Baker who mentioned the Malmédy connection, but he had no intention of revealing this. Whatever happened that day, he was certain Baker played no direct part in it, and he had no desire to put him in the investigator's sights. He also decided it would be best not to mention rumors he heard subsequently that some of the camp survivors were given pistols and left to take whatever revenge they wanted.

Stephen knew it was wrong, and in fact illegal, to withhold this information. Nevertheless, he was able to rationalize it. He worked himself up thinking of the investigator resentfully as an after-the-fact interloper who wasn't present to see what he had seen when the camp was liberated. He put the matter out of his mind with the thought that the very fact that his army investigated such allegations made his side morally superior to the Nazis and Japs, who celebrated crimes that were many times worse. Besides, it was better not to think about it, because thoughts of murder inevitably drew him to the incident with Murch.

* * *

STEPHEN AND THE others assigned to Feldafing reported to a young chaplain, a first lieutenant named Prentice, who, Stephen soon discovered, took a chameleon-like approach to the fact that he was half Jewish. To the Jews in the camp he had let it be known that his mother—"the half that counts"—was a Jew. It was a hard, if not impossible, sell and won him no points considering that in practice he followed his father's faith as an Episcopalian and was, in fact, a Christian chaplain. To the religious Jews in the camp, he would have been better off presenting himself as a whole Christian, instead of trying to pass as both fish and fowl.

Still, Stephen credited the man's motives. Prentice's desire to demonstrate an ability to empathize with the survivors seemed sincere, however ineffective his methods might be. At their first meeting, Prentice explained that their orders were to help oversee proper administration and order in the camp, and to coordinate with the various relief agencies such as the International Red Cross and the United Nations Relief and Rehabilitation Administration, UNRRA, which had been created in 1943 in anticipation of postwar needs. This was mostly routine work, Prentice said, as to a surprising degree the survivors— recategorized as displaced persons, or DPs—were effective in managing their own affairs through a series of committees, many of which were religious in nature.

"I think we're headed for trouble, though," Prentice added. He went on to explain that the military wanted the DPs repatriated as soon as possible. The initial plan called for a target of six months after the war ended to accomplish this. "It's a nice round number, but completely unrealistic. Many say they won't go. The surviving remnant, as they call themselves—*Sh'erit haPletah*, in Hebrew," Prentice added with a self-conscious smile over the pedantic moment—"say they refuse to return to places that butchered their families. Many want to go to Palestine, which will create a huge headache for our British allies."

Almost immediately after beginning work in the camp, Stephen discovered that the chaplain was right on all counts. The committees were practically running the place, and far more efficiently than Stephen would have imagined possible in light of the DPs' all-too-recent ordeals. But mention of repatriation immediately created friction.

Stephen received a cautious welcome from the DPs and their committees. Some warmed up a little when they found out he was Jewish, though the devout among them made it plain that he was no Jew as far as they were concerned. "And Wroth?" one of them said. "What kind of a way is that to spell Roth, with the W? Who does he think he's fooling?"

The spelling of his name was not something Stephen had given much thought, and only now did he reflect on the fact that no one he knew with the name, including a few distant relatives, fronted it with the silent W. It was something to ask his father about.

On the surface, Stephen's relationship with the committees appeared to be relaxed. They worked together amiably. The rabbis liked to tease him, offering at every opportunity to "make a real Jew" of him.

Such lightheartedness didn't extend to the question of repatriation. The DPs were adamant on the subject, while Stephen was obligated to hew to the official line: The DP camps were by definition transitional; they existed only for the purpose of resettling the survivors in their homes. Given the realities Stephen found in the camp, it became increasingly difficult to state the official position with conviction.

One day, after he had been working at the camp for a few weeks, Stephen was accosted by one of the senior rabbis. As the rabbi had drawn a bead on him and strode in his direction, Stephen braced for what was obviously going to be a confrontation. The rabbi, dressed all in black, his sidelocks, or *payos*, trailing behind him like smoke from a locomotive, hailed him: "Hey, you! Mr. Army!"

Stephen was surprised to hear the man's colloquial English. He had expected to have a difficult time understanding him. "How can I help you, Rabbi?" he asked, warily.

"I hear you say you're a Jew, right?" He was several inches shorter than Stephen, and when he got close and looked up, there was an appearance of truculence in his expression, which Stephen nevertheless had the impression was neither mean-spirited nor without a sense of humor.

"Well, it's not something I run around yelling over a loudspeaker," Stephen said with a smile. "But yes, I am."

"No, you're really not," the rabbi retorted. "But that's beside the point."

Stephen maintained his bemused smile, wondering what the man was about. "You brought it up, Rabbi."

"Only to make a bigger point. That's how we rabbis work."

"And the point is?"

"That you don't have to be Jewish. You only need to have half a brain in your head to know why your new policy is stupid."

"Excuse me, Rabbi . . . sorry, I don't know your name."

"Rabinovitch. No W."

"Yes, Rabbi, very funny, but I think I've heard that one before. What policy are you talking about?" In fact, Stephen knew what was coming. The army major in charge of the DP camps in his area had threatened to cut rations if the DPs continued to resist resettlement. Stephen was only surprised at how quickly word must have spread considering the policy had not yet been announced. He himself had learned of it officially only that morning. In his opinion, it didn't take much to see that if the policy really was more than an empty threat, it was indeed stupid.

"You're going to cut our rations?" The rabbi's tone might have been termed belligerent incredulity, and it didn't change as he continued before Stephen could respond. "Half a brain," he repeated, poking a pencil-thin index finger into Stephen's chest on each beat. "You only need half a brain to understand our situation. Half of us are surprised to be still alive, and the rest are sorry they are. And your army wants us to return to the places—to the ashes—we left behind? Haven't you heard that our former neighbors—the same greedy bastards" (he pronounced the word with an Eastern European inflection, *bisterds*) "who couldn't wait to move into our homes after they betrayed us—are welcoming us back with open daggers? And you know what's really stupid? Thinking that, after all we've survived, we'll listen to you because you cut a tin of sardines from our rations. You'll have to do a lot worse than that, let me tell you."

"Rabbi, you're complaining to the wrong person. Even if I agree with you, I don't make these policies. You may have noticed that I'm just a dogface." Stephen tapped the stripes on his shoulder.

"A what?"

"A lowly soldier."

"You have a mouth, don't you? You're too afraid of your superiors to tell them what you think? Fine. Then tell them what you're hearing from people like me. Make it an intelligence report."

NOT LONG AFTER his encounter with the rabbi, Stephen was meeting with a group of committee representatives at one of the women's barracks. The mood among the women was sour, as it was also among the men, a reflection of widespread and growing resentment over the army's new policy. One of the women echoed the rabbi's incredulity that anyone in the army was so detached from reality as to believe they might be influenced by such threats in a matter as important as resettlement. The only thing the threats accomplished, she said, was to allow anger and bitterness to displace the gratitude the Allies had earned.

As the meeting was breaking up, Stephen ventured to ask some of the women about Greta, using much the same inadequate description he had provided at the triage house.

And he received much the same answer, but in tones tinged with the resentment that suffused the meeting. "Do you know how many Gretas we have around here?" one woman, a matron in the barracks, said.

"There can't be that many in these barracks," Stephen responded.

"There are enough."

Stephen had posed the question in an offhand manner. He had not been planning to pursue it, but the woman's unhelpful attitude irked him. "Let me see your ID roster," he said. He could have checked the records on his own. The officious command was the point.

After a moment or two of obvious dithering—long enough to show that, while she might have to listen to him if he pushed, she was not a slave to his wishes—she produced a cloth-covered binder listing camp residents.

Stephen hefted the book. There were hundreds of entries, including the names of people who had already been repatriated or had otherwise moved on. The good thing was that the entries included recent photographs, taken when the DPs were registered and used also for ID cards with which they could obtain camp services.

He took the binder over to a beat-up oak desk, its top covered in cigarette burns and cup rings, and began to leaf through it. He focused on the photos, thinking it would be the fastest way to identify "his" Greta.

He paused at the photo of a woman who looked familiar. Her name was not Greta, however, and he moved on.

When he was finished, he pushed the chair back and gave a resigned shrug.

"No one?" the matron stated more than asked with a note of triumphant condescension. "Well, Greta is a common name."

Indeed, it was. Stephen's eye had stopped at a number of Gretas only to find no resemblance to the young woman he was looking for. He was about to depart when he decided to take another look at the photo that had first caught his attention. He found it and was again struck by how much it looked like Greta. But the name . . .

"Do you know this woman?" he asked the matron.

She gave a dismissive shrug, as if to say, if I did, why would I care? "I may have seen her around."

"Where can I find her?"

STEPHEN WALKED OVER to Barracks 3 and asked for Annalise (née, he hoped, Greta) Gerber, the name attached to the photo. He had mixed feelings about continuing the search. If Annalise and Greta were the same person, why did she give him a false name? Did she not want to be found? Had he said something that caused her to mistrust him? What did he hope to accomplish by looking for her, anyway, and what would he say if he found her?

Obviously, there was some deep-seated attraction, but putting a label on it defied simple explanation. Her looks? Given her physical state when they met, it would be hard to figure, though he did remember seeing the makings of beauty. What else? She was obviously intelligent, and the fact that she spoke English well was appealing, particularly at that moment, after a day filled with straining to communicate with DPs in pidgin.

He was attracted, as well, to her self-possession, though he would have been at pains to describe it in these terms. He thought about the casual attitude she struck when she first approached to ask who Henry was, after she caught Stephen mumbling his name in apology. Then there was the matter-of-fact way she referred to her time in the camps, and also her seeming unconcern over not being evacuated with the others.

And he was lonely.

A woman in the barracks told him he could find the woman he was looking for with a group outside, behind the building, though after she said it he had the impression she regretted revealing anything to someone from the army. He resisted the impulse to inquire further of the woman. There was no point in worrying someone who was trying to be helpful.

More pressing as he followed the woman's directions was deciding what to say to Annalise/Greta. Should he pretend they just happened to meet? No, it would be too obviously contrived. Or perhaps he should own up to looking for her. In that case, what reason should he give? He could tell her he was following up since he helped her get settled. Whether or not she accepted the explanation, by now he acknowledged to himself that there was more to it.

It was a beautiful summer day, and outside, behind the barracks, a group of men and women were gathered in the shade of a large elm tree. They were having an animated discussion, which he could not yet hear clearly and in any case seemed to be in a babble of non-English languages; Yiddish, German, and Polish appeared to predominate.

Stephen scanned the group as he approached but saw no sign of the woman he hoped to find. The discussion halted when they caught sight of him, with some people shushing others.

The group leader was a young man in perhaps his early thirties. He had thinning, ginger hair and wore clothing—loose khaki pants and a powder blue button-down shirt with sleeves rolled up tight over his forearms—that set him apart from the DPs. Also setting him apart was the robust appearance of one who had not experienced recent starvation. Smiling in Stephen's direction, he made a weak stab at the kind of levity that fails to mask one's true concern, saying in heavily inflected English, "Quiet, please! An army spy is coming!"

Stephen returned a thin smile. In fact, the purpose of the group's meeting was already clear enough. Despite the army's attempts to discourage such gatherings, they were occurring all over the camp. The leader was undoubtedly a Zionist, sent from Palestine to encourage and organize resettlement there. It wasn't this so much as the group leader's lame remark that irritated him. He was tempted to say, "Yes, here is the spy for the people who gave their lives fighting the fucking Nazis; the people who are responsible for the fact that every one of you sitting here is safe and not mingling in a heap of ashes outside the Dachau crematorium." Instead, he said only, "I was looking for someone. I don't see her, though." He turned to go, still irritated by the group leader's remark.

"May I ask who you are looking for?" the leader called.

Stephen considered whether it was wise to announce a name. In a what-the-hell moment of pique, he said, "A young woman named Annalise Gerber. Or maybe she calls herself Greta."

He turned away and so didn't see the woman stand and say in German what Stephen thought meant, "I think I know who he is looking for." As she approached, Stephen could see what he couldn't when she was seated with the group. The face was fuller than he remembered. And she was losing her gaunt frame, regaining a defined figure. Hair more auburn than white had formed a mossy irregular covering on her head. "Continue the meeting," she called back to the group leader in English. "I can answer this man's questions."

She gave Stephen a wispy smile. "And what would those questions be?"

"There are many."

They walked out of earshot of the group and found a bench. It was missing odd slats, and most of its dark green paint was worn to the raw wood, now going soft.

"First question," he said after they had seated themselves. "Am I talking to Greta or Annalise?"

"Both." She was looking around, clearly uncomfortable.

"Would you tell me why?"

"Greta is the name I give automatically before I know who I'm giving it to. This has gotten me out of a few dangerous situations in the camps."

"So, you didn't trust me; is that it?"

She gave a sigh of frustration. "To be honest, it didn't take long to see that there would be no problem giving you my true name. But by then there was no good opportunity. So I let it be." She continued her furtive glances.

"Are you nervous about something?"

"A little."

He tilted his head in a way that suggested he was waiting for her to explain.

"I don't want people to think I am saying things to you that I shouldn't say."

"You mean, to the *spy*," he said in a wry, irritated tone.

She shrugged.

"That's funny," he said.

"Not to me."

"Look, Annalise." The name sounded odd to his ears after thinking of her only as Greta. "Do you really think we don't know about the Palestine meetings? If anything, I'm the one who could get into trouble. I'm not supposed to fraternize."

She looked uncomprehending. "I don't know this word."

"It just means I shouldn't have social relations with the DPs, especially one-to-one."

She smiled. "Is that what we're having? Social relations?"

"It seems that way."

✳ ✳ ✳

SHE COULDN'T STAY long. She had to get back to the group. Nevertheless, seeing her—finding her—made Stephen happier than he had been in ages.

Before she left, he said he hoped they would see each other again. She asked, "But what about your *not-fatter-or-something* rule?"

He said it would be okay if they were discrete . . . perhaps had dinner at a restaurant in town. But he couldn't tell if she meant the question as an excuse. Maybe the attraction he felt wasn't shared. She seemed to like him, though, and not in the way some of the other women in the camp liked him. They flirted with him, but he, on his guard, sensed they were looking for a meal ticket, maybe even passage to the States—the jackpot for a lot of them. And how could he blame them after what they'd gone through?

He didn't sense this from Annalise. Could this be part of the attraction—another facet of the self-possession he saw in her? An attraction to her strength and self-sufficiency? Wanting someone who doesn't need—because she doesn't need—to be wanted?

He said he would come and see her again, adding with a smile that it would be easier now that he knew her name and where she lived. She returned the smile but didn't say anything. Just parted with a half wave and went back to her group.

He acknowledged to himself that, while it might have been unrealistic to expect more, her lack of obvious enthusiasm nettled him. The most she gave was the absence of contradiction: He said he would find her again; she didn't say he shouldn't. This would have to do.

He wondered if she really planned to go to Palestine, and if so, how she would go about it. No doubt the Zionists would try to find a way.

85

Really, he didn't know anything about her. He only knew that he badly wanted to find out more.

He returned the next day and asked for her, trying to keep his tone of voice as official as possible. He doubted anyone was fooled about his real purpose.

But she wasn't there. Nor was she there when he inquired the next day. Did anyone happen to know where she was? Working, probably, was the answer. Apparently, her facility with English made her much in demand.

"Well, please tell her that Corporal Wroth stopped by." The woman promised she would.

And still there was no word from her, which sent him into a funk. He had no reason to assume anything about her or about the two of them. This didn't keep him from daydreaming about various romantic possibilities—which, particularly at night, morphed into explicit sexual fantasies. Meanwhile, the worm of loneliness burrowed deeper.

It took over a week, and even then, their meeting was accidental. He had gone to the Feldafing administrative office and was surprised to see her there. And further disappointed that she was not there to see him. His face must have dropped when she explained that she was doing some translation work for Lieutenant Prentice, because she smiled in a shy way that suggested (or so he construed it) she was sorry to have hurt his feelings.

"I've been by to see you," he said. "So, I thought . . ." He could feel his face flush.

"I've been working," she said. "I'm sorry," she added. "I didn't mean to be inconvenient."

"I see."

"Truly."

He wanted to change the subject. "Yes, well, we had talked about meeting again."

"I know. I'm sorry."

"Can we try for tonight?"

She shook her head. "Tomorrow night, perhaps."

"Okay," he said, feeling abashed but not sure why. Over near rejection? Did she take pity on him, was that it? Did she feel a need to

86

say yes, and then perhaps she would cancel once a believable excuse could be found? Is that why she wanted tomorrow instead of today, to have space for an excuse?

He was still feeling bruised and unsure when he set off to meet her for dinner the following evening. They had agreed to meet at a bistro they both knew in town, one of a few that actually had something decent to eat.

He arrived early, but didn't go in, deciding to walk around instead. It was a warm evening, the skies clear. There was every reason to take a stroll, yet he knew the real reason was that he didn't want to be waiting for her when—if—she arrived. He admitted to himself that wounded pride was part of the picture, and also perhaps (if he were to be honest) a dollop of retribution.

And for his display of self-discipline, here was his reward: When he returned to the restaurant she was waiting for him at a table, holding a glass of white wine, and possibly, just possibly, appearing relieved that he came.

It turned out to be a good night. The meal was as satisfying as one could hope for in those days, when more often than not food was to be found in the hands of the occupying powers, rather than on the local market, unless it was the local black market. The restaurant continued to use an old, extensive menu, which everyone knew was fictional. They served what they had, and if what they had was any good, a half decent piece of schnitzel, for instance, it almost certainly had been procured illegally—possibly even from the very camp from which Stephen wanted to escape for the evening—and for several times a reasonable price. For the soldiers, price tended not to be a problem, as they had more money than things to spend it on.

More important to Stephen, Annalise seemed genuinely happy to be with him. She peppered him with questions about his life in the States and about what he wanted to do when he returned home.

He wanted to know the same kinds of things about her. But this was harder, as she sought to answer his questions as tersely as possible and return the spotlight on him. He did learn more about her growing up in both Heidelberg and Munich, one of four sisters. Her father was a professor of chemistry before he was prohibited by the racial laws from teaching. They had lived well until then, and in fact, a resourceful family, they had continued to maintain a relatively happy life even amid the danger, economic strain, and privation of the times.

She said, in hindsight, this might have been their undoing. Their happiness removed some of the urgency and encouraged hope they could weather the storm. They would always need chemists, yes? By the time they considered emigrating, it was too late.

And then, in 1943, actually much later than for most of the Jews they knew, they—her family—ceased to exist. Here Annalise drew an impenetrable line for Stephen, limiting discussion to the basics. Yes, everyone and everything was lost. All gone. As far as she knew, she was the only member of her family to survive. She had registered with all the appropriate agencies that might be able to learn something more, so maybe there was someone. Not likely, though.

As for her own experiences, they were not something she cared to discuss. He knew she had been through more than one camp before ending up in Dachau—she had told him as much the first day.

He said he understood why she wouldn't want to say more, though he bristled at her explanation that, at least in part, her reticence was based on his inability—the inability of anyone who hadn't gone through it—to understand. True, he had not suffered anything comparable. But had he not lost comrades and friends—his best friend, at that, and right before his eyes? Was he not capable of empathy? Yet, if he were being honest, he would have to acknowledge that the inability of others to comprehend his experiences was exactly what he himself feared he would find when he got home.

When they returned to the camp, he accompanied her to the barracks. He asked if she would like to go out with him again. She said yes, but they must find new topics of conversation. Her experiences in the war were to be off limits; she'd said all she intended to say on the subject, maybe forever. Could he honor that? He could, though not without misgivings.

Feeling momentarily emboldened, he glanced around to see if anyone was watching and leaned in to kiss her goodnight. She was not put off, but for the time being her cheek would have to do.

An Imperfect Certainty

~ ~ ~ ~ ~

Chapter 10

Fall–Winter 1945: Off Campus

THEY MET WHENEVER THEY could. He taught her the expression "off campus," which usually meant Dachau town, but on some occasions, when he could arrange it, meant Munich. She preferred to go anywhere that didn't have the name Dachau attached to it, but then, they didn't often have much choice.

And really, Munich was no better. The associations, still bad, were simply different. Munich had been her home. A good home, at least as viewed through young eyes. Even as Nazi policies crowded out their lives, her parents had done a surprisingly good job of shielding her and her siblings. And then, with the shock of someone who looks into a mirror and sees for the first time an aged self, they couldn't. Couldn't protect her, couldn't protect her siblings, couldn't protect themselves.

Yet in spite of Annalise's stated desire to avoid past associations, there were times when she made a point of visiting the scenes of her former life. She would stand in silence near a house, a playground, a shop, a school, radiating a signal to Stephen that the silence must be respected. She craved time away from Feldafing, she said, and what choices were available to her? Where in that area—where in Germany, for that matter—could she go that would not be overwhelming, soul-stifling, if she gave into it? Sometimes she preferred to meet the ghosts head-on, likening it to a smallpox vaccination—an inoculation against memory.

Stephen tried to ease the burden by observing her seemingly contradictory no-war-talk rule. Of course, this too was impossible. The war and its aftermath constituted the entirety of their milieu. A gallon of water cannot be compressed inside a quart-sized jar.

Stephen's concerns over violating the army's non-fraternization rules quickly faded. As long as he was reasonably discrete—as long as he didn't flaunt the relationship—almost everyone seemed willing to turn a blind eye. There was always a chance that some disgruntled DP would cause trouble—would, in effect, denounce him to the authorities. While most officers would not be able to ignore it if such transgressions were blatant, so far no one seemed inclined to complain—least of all Lieutenant Prentice, who, though he never said as much, emanated an aura of tolerance for anything that made people happy so long as it didn't make too many others unhappy. One day, in a different context, Stephen heard him ask: "What better thing can a chaplain do in these miserable times than to incubate a little happiness?"

No, to the extent that Stephen was hamstrung by rules, it was because of the rules imposed by Annalise. The simple act of putting discussion of her war experiences off limits, however often this might be honored in the breach, obstructed the most logical avenues to mutual discovery.

Sometimes revelations were unavoidable. There were simply too many triggers to memory and emotion lying hidden to snare her and force her to violate her own rules. In light of this, Stephen insisted on an amendment: If she displayed a reaction to something, he could ask about it; the vow of silence would be lifted, at least for that subject. Still, their encounters with the physical remnants of her past in places like Munich yielded little real sense of her essence. Only of her loss. However much loss arguably was her essence.

One sensitive topic had more immediate relevance: Palestine. Stephen knew Annalise was under constant Zionist pressure to "make *Aliyah*," as they called it—literally in Hebrew, *to ascend* to Eretz Israel, to go up to the Land of Israel. Here was a subject on which both Stephen and his superiors agreed, albeit for different reasons. His superiors, at the behest of the British, wanted to discourage resettlement in Palestine; Stephen, more narrowly, wanted to avoid losing Annalise.

One day she asked him, "just to know," whether he would ever consider going to Eretz Israel after he left the army. Before he could answer, she pointed out how valuable his military experience could be to "their people." But if she had her rules, he had his: No. He had no desire to live anywhere other than the USA, and to put an even finer point on it, no desire to live anywhere other than New York, New York, USA. He spared her the further refinement of specifying the Bronx.

The conversation had occurred as they were taking a stroll through Dachau town. Annalise became quiet, but it was not a mellow silence. Stephen could see the muscles in her jaw working.

"There's the castle," he observed, with a nod in its direction—a benign probe of her silence, which could not fail to be obvious to her since the sight of the town's most prominent historical symbol was hardly new to either of them.

"You know," he continued the forced patter, "people who never heard of Dachau back home must think of it only as a death camp, even though the town is over a thousand years old. A thousand years old," he repeated. "Now *that's* a concept Americans have a hard time grasping."

"Why are you so definite about Palestine?" she asked suddenly, stopping and turning toward him, her face set, combative.

He wasn't in the mood for an argument. Things had been good between them. But he wasn't willing to give in to her, either. "I have nothing against the Zionists. I'd be surprised if they can really turn Palestine into a Jewish homeland, but I have nothing against them trying."

"*They? Them?*" She was as visibly upset as he had ever seen her. "Who do you think *they* are? *They* are people like me who have lost everything and will stand together to make sure there is no next time."

"I have nothing against them, or you, trying," he said again but immediately regretted adding her to the sentence, a clear signal (which he could tell by the expression on her face, she didn't fail to grasp) that their futures would be separate if she pursued her cause. "I'm an American, that's all I mean to say," he added.

"Once, I might have told you I was a proud German."

"America is not like that. Oh, sure, we have our anti-Semites. But we're not Germany."

92

"Fine. Think that if you want to. And try to think you're not a Jew."

"That's not fair, and it's not what I meant."

"You think because you don't believe in God you have nothing in common with the rest of us. But you do. You have history and how you look and a way of thinking. Believe me, you're not alone in doubting God, especially after what we've been through. All I can say is, if you really want to help your people, Eretz Israel is the way to do it."

Now it was his turn to show anger. "I did help my people, as you call them. I'm here, aren't I? Don't tell me you think you'd be alive now if I and a lot of guys just like me—Jew or not—weren't here."

"Then why did you keep telling Henry how sorry you are? Maybe you don't mean it."

"Shit! What do you know about me and Henry! Where the hell do you get off saying something like that to me!" He turned away, said mostly to himself, "Man you really know how to hit below the belt."

"What?"

"It's an expression. If you don't know it, you'd better learn it." He walked away, leaving her standing there.

THEY AVOIDED EACH other for over a week. He continued to be upset over the Henry remark. But he couldn't entirely shut out the thought that, had he been alive, Henry would have sided with Annalise. After seeing Dachau, Henry might well have agreed that he had an obligation to help his people, and he would have put it this way—used these words—without hesitation or self-consciousness. Well, he was not Henry, however much he loved him. He believed he was capable of enormous sorrow and empathy without completely changing his world outlook from primarily American to primarily Jewish. He believed wholeheartedly his angry riposte to Annalise that America—his country—deserved praise for the sacrifices it made, and was still making, for the victims of Nazism.

When they did see one another again, it was with wounds that were still raw. They avoided the resettlement topic as much as they could. But it was not always easy to do so. As time went by and summer began to

93

be clawed away by autumn, Annalise continued to be subjected to the siren of Palestine, while Stephen was feeling the pull of home.

Not that there was anything definite for him. But the logic of it was that his time abroad must be coming to an end. In both the Europe and Pacific theaters, the thrall of victory was giving way to the gritty realities of aftermath and protracted occupation. Some of the men who had arrived not long before Stephen were being sent home. He concluded he must be nearing the head of the line.

He rented a room at the Gasthaus Bavaria in Dachau town. He and Annalise had frequented the Bavaria's restaurant. Their patronage, supplemented by Stephen's willingness to pay surcharges for extraordinary services (as the owner, Herr Breughel, referred to even the most minor accommodations) yielded meals that were only notionally on the menu. They also yielded a sweet enough deal on one of three rooms that the expansively named Bavaria had to let, giving Stephen and Annalise a ready place to be alone when the opportunity presented itself, as it sometimes did with little warning.

They were gradually becoming more intimate, mostly limited to kissing and touching. He was cautious, unsure what to expect from her. She had hinted at forced sexual incidents in the camp. He did what he could to make her understand that this didn't matter to him. It was in the past. Faced with his own powerful urges, he reluctantly concluded that the best thing—the mature thing—he could do for both of them was give her time.

One day, they were in the room, lying in bed, fully dressed. She seemed relaxed as they talked. After a time, Stephen stroked her face tenderly. He kissed her, lightly at first, then more fervently. She responded, her tongue finding his. He touched her breasts. He lifted her skirt. She parted for him. He slid his fingers into her and was excited to find her wet and beginning to move rhythmically.

"Touch me too, please," he said, pressing toward her. "No, under," he said, loosening the waistband on his trousers and undoing the button fly. He guided her hand. She hesitated for a moment, but perhaps concluding that this was a step she was ready to take, she followed his lead.

He returned to moving his finger inside of her, felt the heat within her rise when he swirled it in a crescendo around the little knot he discovered within, until she shuddered and a moment later he released, startling her with his wet surge. She began to pull her hand away but left it there after seeing the pleasure he took from the slip swirl of her fingers on the head of his penis. She continued for a minute, until the drying semen created a tug of friction.

They continued at this level of intimacy for the next few times they were alone together. He said he hoped she would soon trust him enough to make love completely. She said trust was not a problem. Someday soon, she promised. "When I don't look like a skeleton." He kissed her and said she was already beautiful as far as he was concerned.

She did appear increasingly healthy. She had gained weight. The apparition of former beauty Stephen saw when they first met had given way to corporeal reality. Her eyes, not long ago remarkable for providing the only color in a wasteland of ashy skin, now were remarkable for their radiance instead of their contrast. Her hair, too, was growing, coming in dark auburn, tinged with the russet he first saw as stubble. The overall effect was the paradox of looking younger with the passage of time.

He was as sympathetic as a hungry young man could be, trying to understand her holding back as residue of wartime trauma. She would have said residue didn't begin to describe what was left. He tried to reassure her by saying he had fallen in love with her. It was only a slight exaggeration out of the passion of the moment. But it was also true that at an uncertain, but recent, point, it had come to him how much longer his days felt when she was not part of them.

DESPITE STEPHEN'S OUTWARD confidence, anxiety about making love was not only on Annalise's side. Stephen alternated between intense desire and fear of embarrassing himself. He fretted over his inexperience. The only real opportunity he'd had with a woman—a French prostitute in a Dijon brothel—ended in disaster.

He had been goaded into visiting the brothel by several of his buddies, including the more sexually experienced Henry, who needed no encouragement to go along. To Stephen he said, "Oh, come on. You have nothing to lose but your cherry." The idea hardly fit Stephen's stubbornly romantic fantasies of what his first time would be like. But it irked him that Henry could lord it over him in this area, and romance took a back seat to the pressures of the moment.

Five of them went to a house in the red light district that had been recommended by one of the veterans. "Madame Louise will get you fixed up right with a clean girl," he'd said.

Madame Louise did not disappoint. In charmingly accented English, she invited the men into a neat but threadbare parlor and asked them to take a seat. Then—in what Stephen had always imagined the procedure to be—she brought out several girls, each of whom immediately began flirting and encouraging the men to choose her.

Nervous and the last to choose, Stephen nevertheless ended up with a pretty peroxide blonde with an easy smile. He judged her to be about his age, perhaps a year or so younger. She introduced herself as Michelle and asked what he would like to be called. He was about to respond with his real name. However, since he assumed she had given him a false one, he followed a mischievous impulse and told her it was Henry.

He quickly discovered the introductions were at the limits of Michelle's English. Still, as she led him upstairs, he had no doubt she could make herself understood well enough.

They walked down a dimly lit hallway. A runner underfoot dampened the sound of Stephen's boots. Michelle stopped before a room on the right and motioned him inside. She closed the door behind them, gestured toward a narrow bed, and then quickly, expertly disrobed. Stephen stood wordlessly, marveling at the sight of her naked body, until she laughed, not uncharitably, and pointed to him. "You now."

While he undressed slowly (after overcoming the impulse to turn his back to her), she went to a small table near the bed. From a blue-and-white ceramic ewer she filled a basin with soapy water, placed it on a chair next to the bed, and waited for him.

At last he stood there, all of him fully erect and still in his army-issue socks, at a loss for what to do with his hands. He stared as she straddled the basin, twisted the water out of a washcloth, and proceeded to clean between her legs.

"You now," she said again after dipping and wringing out the cloth. She held it out and motioned him closer to the basin. "*Ah, Je vois que vous êtes un Juif,*" she observed in a neutral voice, as if she were merely cataloguing him. In less trying circumstances, Stephen, who did not speak French, might have asked if she could repeat what she said in English. Or he might have simply comprehended the word "Jew." However, she didn't seem to expect a response.

In any case, at that moment there was nothing he could say—nothing he was able to say. In fact, there was nothing he could feel but absolute mortification. Because, with the first touch of the washcloth, he shot hot semen at her abdomen.

He was afraid she would laugh. She didn't. In a sympathetic voice she merely said, "Is okay. Not for to worry. Is much happen. Problem *non.*"

He assumed she would be willing to give him a chance to recover so he could try again. But he couldn't face the empty time that would have to pass between them. He walked over to his clothes. "Maybe another time," he said slowly as he began to dress, hoping she could understand. Looking quickly at her face and then away, he thought she did.

But she appeared confused after he finished dressing when, instead of moving to leave, he merely stood there, his eyes wandering around the room while he considered how to kill enough time to not be the first to return downstairs.

Before she could say anything, a door could be heard opening in the hall. In what Stephen thought was possibly the evening's only moment of mercy, however tinged with awkwardness, he heard one of his comrades thank the girl he was with. Taking his cue, Stephen did likewise. Yet, once again uncertainty about the correct protocol provided a supplement to his mental catalogue of indelible chagrinned moments, as he added a courtly air to the occasion by bowing at the waist before he said, "*Merci,* Michelle."

* * *

WHEN AT LAST Annalise gave herself to him, it was still with some reserve. It was an easy Sunday afternoon. They were in bed, kissing, touching, stripped down as far as their underwear. It took all the discipline he could manage to pull back from her and confront what he believed to be the specific barrier to her affection. "I know you were raped in the camp. I don't care. I'm not that monster."

She blinked hard. "I know you're not," she said, in an unusually reticent voice. "But there are so many things you'll never be able to understand. Never," she repeated with a finality Stephen had not heard before. He wondered at first whether she was withholding something she might have expressed if not for the limitations of her English. But he quickly dismissed the thought. More likely she simply chose not to elaborate, and perhaps she had decided that she never would. Only much later would he understand just how complicated the whole thing really was, and by then it would be too late.

"There's more," he went on. "It's not only that I would never hurt you." And it was at this point that he said it: "I love you."

She began to cry—another thing he had never seen her do. Free-flowing salt tears that he kissed away. He tried to reassure her. Still, the tears washed down onto his lips, silent tears that seemed without end, relinquishing some of the control that had kept her alive and kept something of the essential her.

At last, spent, she held him like a lifeline. She began to kiss him, his brow, his eyes, his cheeks, his lips—to kiss his lips and to bite them, too—how could so much be contained?

When they finished making love, Stephen propped himself on an elbow as sunlight found the window like a stop on an ancient calendar. In the full light he gently traced the outline of her breasts and her abdomen, which had become less obviously concave, then circled lower. He stopped at the raw ridges and scars of cuts and of what appeared to be cigarette burns, and who knew what else? He parted her pubic hair and tracked the outlines of a mean scar that had been obscured before then.

She shivered and moved his hand away. "*Hässlich*. It's ugly."

He lay back and drew her to him and thought he had discovered something in himself real and mature, a depth of feeling beyond what he had thought himself capable. "Not to me."

Now it was all Annalise.

An Imperfect Certainty

Chapter 11

Fall–Winter 1945–1950: Their New World Order

H E WROTE HOME ABOUT her. It was a difficult letter to compose, lacking as it did any real foundation. Until now he had been reluctant to say much, fearing there was no way to express his thoughts about her without sounding like an overwrought schoolboy. He had been resigned that what he told them would simply have to remain out of joint until he could catch them up properly.

Now Stephen felt a need quickly to bring his parents into a picture that had not been drawn for them in anything but the sketchiest of outlines. He kicked himself for not doing so earlier, in small bites, as things occurred. He could have gotten them used to the idea. Now instead of a taste, he had to give them the whole meal at once.

Annalise was not the only reason for the less frequent or forthcoming correspondence with his parents. After Henry died, Stephen lost heart when he thought about writing. After Dachau, he didn't know what to write—how to do justice to what he had seen. He thought often about all the things in his life that had changed completely while his parents nurtured images of the boy who went away. He was always mature for his age—responsible—but what he had experienced since leaving home made his own thoughts of that earlier time a picture of callowness. And then, he would still have to show up at their door without Henry.

His parents responded—separately, a signal in itself.

His mother said she was pleased for him. But she changed the topic abruptly to discuss the prospective joy of his homecoming, and this part of the letter was clearly circumscribed. It contained nothing to suggest a realized vision that he might not be alone when he returned.

His father's letter was similarly guarded. Yet apparently there occurred a final, resolute thought he could not omit. In a postscript he gently expressed the hope that Stephen would have the presence of mind to remember that he was living only temporarily in a world that had little relation to his existence at home. He should therefore "temper his judgments and decisions accordingly."

Well, Stephen thought, at least his father comprehended the essence of the larger problem. It would be interesting to discover whether he expected a different Stephen to return home.

His father went on to remind that many women made homeless by the war were hoping to find new homes in America as the wives of returning servicemen. Reading this made Stephen smile at the thought of telling his parents that he had an opposite problem: the siren for his beloved of, not America, but Palestine. And Annalise had never declared to him what she would do if forced to choose.

* * *

THE COMPLEXITY OF their separate, yet simultaneously entwined, dilemmas came to the fore when Stephen happened to see Annalise in an intimate discussion with a strange man. The two were sitting together on a bench outside her barracks. They were leaning in so that from Stephen's vantage point it appeared that their foreheads were almost touching. When they were distracted by a woman Stephen recognized from the barracks, he took the chance to slip away unobserved.

That evening Stephen and Annalise met for dinner. All day Stephen had wondered about what he had seen and about how he might broach the subject without appearing to accuse her of some wrong. He was more curious than jealous, save for the occasional flash of unwanted visions. Monogamy between them was by then assumed, if never made explicit, and she had never given him reason to believe otherwise.

Stephen told himself that the presence of the strange man on the bench was not, in itself, out of bounds, particularly since the bounds had not been clearly marked. He believed he was bigger than that. The image of their apparent intimacy, though—their faces so close together—ran counter to his desire to be magnanimous in his interpretation.

"You're quiet tonight," she said after they were seated at their usual table at the Bavaria.

He decided to ignore the opening, said he didn't realize it, and went on to make small talk about the trivialities of his day. What he did do—what he decided he'd limit his probing to—was to slip into the conversation mention that he had been in the area where Annalise and the man were sitting.

When this drew no response, he forced himself to let the matter drop. Minutes later, as their meals arrived, his self-control was rewarded when Annalise volunteered that she had met that day with a new Zionist representative, this one from the nascent military force, Haganah. She added that she would not compromise Stephen's position by identifying the man. "But this doesn't mean I'm not angry at how your army is mistreating Zionist supporters here—you would think they would want to be rid of us."

Stephen puffed out his cheeks. Placing his fork on the table, he said, "You are determined not to understand our problem with Palestine. Is there anything you can say about your meeting with the Zionist?"

"I should say no, but it affects me, and so maybe you, too, and I'm angry."

He nodded and waited for her to go on.

"The man told me I'd have to remain here longer than I thought."

"I can't say I'm sorry to hear it, but why?"

"I don't know, exactly," she said with an annoyed wave. "What I think I understand is that with the British clamping down, the Zionists— the ones who bring people in on *Aliyah*—have to concentrate on moving people who have greater need, like the ones who are in immediate danger of being harmed. Also, maybe men who have experience fighting. So, I'm stuck here."

"Stuck with me, huh?"

She made to slap him lightly. "You know that's not what I mean!"

The smile left his face. "It's the same thing, though, isn't it? Eretz Israel first, me second."

"You know I love you, Stephen," she said, earnestly.

In fact, he was not sure she did, but he said, "I know. Just not as much as you love your cause."

"You could still come with me. You will be needed, and we would be together."

"Let's not refight that war."

* * *

OVER THE NEXT two months, as autumn settled in, transitioning from crisp, clear days to the oppressive gray weather that Annalise insisted was the true explanation for such German characteristics as depression, grim intensity, and, ultimately, desperate expansionism, and as Stephen's duties became more of a boring routine, they spent ever more of their free time together.

They traveled as far and as often as time and available transportation would allow, took to hiking the Bavarian woods, and stole away as often as possible to the room at the *gasthaus*. The dull prospect of separation hovered with a growing sense of inevitability. They tried to avoid the subject. Still, the hours spent away from one another increasingly became a time of sadness and both present and anticipatory longing.

One day, as November was drawing to a close, Stephen encountered Annalise in the camp and asked her to meet him for dinner and to stay the night. Although they had spent their nights together with growing frequency, something in Stephen's manner must have worried her as she pursed her lips and looked at him askance.

"What do you have to tell me?"

"Not something I can discuss here. Can you meet me?"

She nodded and said she would, but her facial expression when they parted struck Stephen as being especially taut.

That evening, as he approached the restaurant, Stephen could see through the window that, unusual for her, she had arrived first and taken a seat at what had become acknowledged by Herr Breughel as their table. He slowed his steps to watch her. She was fidgeting with the tableware, picking up a knife and studying it as if it would somehow be revelatory, then repeating the action with her fork.

"What is it?" she asked briskly after he bent to kiss her and took a seat in his customary place.

"I didn't think it was that obvious."

She gave a laugh of disbelief. "You have always been obvious, you know that. You were obvious this afternoon. Thank goodness they didn't make you a spy. You would have been executed the first day."

"And here I always thought it was Henry who was easy to read."

"I wouldn't know about that, but you are." She sighed audibly. "So, tell me—but I think I can guess."

He nodded. "They're sending me home."

"When?"

"A few weeks. They have to confirm space on the ship."

The waitress came. They ordered beer and sat silently for a time. The restaurant was beginning to fill. A boisterous party of six, happy to leave the penetrating damp for a good fire, contrasted starkly with Stephen and Annalise's gloomy atoll.

"What would you like to eat?" he asked.

"I'm not hungry." She laughed as if she had caught herself by surprise. "I don't think I've said that in years."

With sudden resolve, Stephen leaned in and covered both of her hands with his. "Come with me," he said. He rushed on before she could respond. "I love you; I can't stand the thought of leaving you; come with me; we'll get married." He expected the objection and cut it off: "You don't know about going to Palestine, and you don't know when you'll know."

She shrugged. "It will happen sometime."

"And if it doesn't? What will you do?"

"Stephen, we knew we would have to face this one way or another."

"And now we have to. Before, we didn't know when. Now a clock is ticking. And I'm worried about you. If the Palestine business were to fall through, what kind of life would you have here? This country—Europe, for that matter—will be a graveyard for who knows how long."

She looked past him. "I've been through enough to know I can survive."

"Look at me, Annalise. We can have a good life together. I know we can."

When the expected rebuttal didn't come, he said, "Does your silence mean you'll consider it?"

"How are you so sure, Stephen? This life together in America, how can you be so sure?"

"Because it's not complicated for me—this part isn't, anyway. I adore you. More than anyone I've ever known or imagined. I want to marry you. I want to have children together someday."

She surprised him by echoing what his father had written. "It worries me that you have no doubts about this. I'm worried that we have come together in a place that won't exist for us when we leave. I'm worried that there will always be things you will not know about me, or understand. I'm afraid that when we get to your home, you will regret."

"I won't."

"Well, maybe I will."

His demeanor shifted, from eager and doubtless to sober as he relinquished her hands and sat back, pausing before he declared, "I'm willing to try."

She was quiet for a moment as she looked down. When she faced him again, it was with fresh resolve. "I don't think that is enough. It is not like putting on a new shoe. We don't even know how we would live . . . where we would live. And if it didn't work, then what?"

"Now, you see? This is where I'm confident."

"More than I am, apparently."

Ignoring the remark, he said, "And you don't have to worry about how we would live. I know I can get a job. You could, too. There have to be opportunities for people who can speak both German and English as well as you do. And we could live with my family until we find our own place. They'll love you as much as I do. I'm sure of it."

She smiled weakly. "More things you're sure of. Maybe your mother and father wouldn't be so happy to have you bring me along, like baggage."

"Don't be silly. I know them. They'll love you."

When she didn't respond, he redoubled his effort, a salesman becoming more determined in his pitch. "What do I have to do? Get down on my knees and plead?"

With a laugh that brightened her eyes she said, "Please don't."

"Too late. Look, here, I'm doing it." His chair scraped the floor as he pushed it back. People around them looked over in time to see him fall forward to one knee and take her hands.

"Stop," she said, coloring. "Everyone is watching."

"Good. That shouldn't be too much for a Dachau survivor to bear. Marry me, Annalise. Please."

She looked around, blushed obviously at the smiling audience. "Please get up," she whispered.

"I will if you promise to answer—to say yes."

"I'll promise to answer, that's all."

He returned to his chair, said in a post-histrionic voice, "Don't forget. I can get down again."

She let a moment pass, surveyed the room, observed the audience losing interest, and then smiled at him suddenly. "And if I said yes, you wouldn't be so surprised that it would make you think again?"

"What?"

"I had a memory of learning English. My favorite teacher was from London. He loved Oscar Wilde and had us read everything he wrote. The part that comes to me now is the one where he says that when the gods want to punish us they answer our prayers. Would that happen to you if I said yes?"

"There's an easy way for you to find out."

"Not easy. Not easy at all." She put her hands in her lap and studied them.

Stephen didn't take his eyes off of her, his face set, determined now to have his answer.

After what seemed to him ages but could only have been a moment or two, she looked up. She reached, stroked his cheek with a butterfly touch. "From the day I met you, and long before I realized that I loved you, I had fantasies about a life together. I would have moments of seeing us together that came to me—how do you say?—out of the blue.

Silly, isn't it? How could I have known? And then, slowly, the things I imagined began to come true. It made me afraid."

"Of what?"

"It's difficult to tell you this, but I feel I must. I was afraid my imaginings were coming from a bad place."

"Bad?"

He was about to go on, but she put a finger to his lips. "Not evil. But wrong . . . possibly foolish. Afraid I had no way to know if I was confusing feelings for you with a deep need to have another life, which you maybe could give me. It is as if I were a child with a present wrapped before me. I don't know what is in it, its cost, or its value. I only know I want it.

"And yet at the very time I could imagine being together with you, I didn't want to think about the future—in the camps I got so used to avoiding the pain of such thoughts. At first, when I had visions of us together, it gave me pleasure. I made myself stop. There was too much risk. Tonight, I wanted to hear you put an end to my doubts, even though I know my fears will never completely leave."

"And now you've heard."

"Yes."

"Yes, you've heard, but have I put an end to your doubts?"

"I think . . . I think as much as you can—as much as I can. I don't believe I can say more than that."

He reached across the space between them and lightly stroked her cheek with his fingertips. "It's enough for me."

She took his hand, opened it gently, and kissed the palm.

"Will you come with me?" he asked.

She said, softly, "Yes."

"Will you marry me?"

"Yes to that, too." She laughed suddenly, a sound less brittle than before. "I don't believe they'll let me come with you if we don't get married."

He smiled, wanting to hold her close but first needing to ask, "What about Palestine?"

"For now, that becomes part of the future I won't think about." She paused and added, "Part of me is still able to hope. Maybe someday you will change your mind and we will make *Aliyah* together."

She drew her fingers to her lips, kissed them, reached over the table and grazed his. It occurred to him that she wasn't sealing a bargain, his first thought. Rather, he saw it as a benediction. On him. On her. He took her hand and kissed each of the fingertips that had performed the ritual, ignoring the curious stares of others in the room.

✳ ✳ ✳

THEY MARRIED ON December 15, 1945, three days before beginning the voyage to New York. Space on a ship had been found suddenly, leaving little time for planning—or for second thoughts on the profound nature of the things being embarked upon or left behind.

It was a small civil-nondenominational ceremony quickly arranged with the assistance of Lieutenant Prentice, the Feldafing chaplain. Prentice was eager to help, reminding Stephen of his desire to "incubate happiness" whenever the opportunity arose.

Stephen bought simple gold bands. He had hoped to find something unique, but there was no time to search. Meanwhile, Annalise settled on a modest, pale ivory dress, which she hoped would do double duty for the wedding and introductions when they arrived in America. Stephen wore his uniform.

It was not until they were at sea that they had time to reflect individually on the many significances of the journey. For Annalise, it was the sudden comprehension with nothing but ocean in sight that she was leaving behind not only years of despair, but ties to any surviving family or friends, as well as leaving things taken for granted in the essential being of nation and culture.

For Stephen, there were the profound changes resulting from recent, intense experience—of loss and destruction, of awakening to the excesses of humanity, of sometimes wrenching personal discovery and transformation forged by the things he had seen and done. But there was also the comforting prospect of reembracing the familiar, however transformed it and he might have been in his absence. There were these things and more for Annalise, amplified in almost every way but minus the prospective comfort of the familiar, which was replaced by the fraught anticipation of newness and adventure.

Stephen sent a telegram to his parents, informing them of the wedding and providing the details of the sailing and expected arrival. He asked that he and Annalise not be met at the dock, giving as an excuse expected red tape involving Annalise's immigration status. The real reason was that he wanted to control the timing and circumstances of their first meeting. He had no doubt she would be received warmly. He was less confident about how his mother and father might adjust to her once the excitement over their arrival faded. His concern on this score would prove to be exaggerated. Still, they were to face a raft of problems they had not anticipated on that romantic evening at the Gasthaus Bavaria.

* * *

THEY ARRIVED IN New York just after the start of the new year 1946. They splurged on a night downtown at the Plaza Hotel. An impromptu honeymoon, Stephen called it when Annalise expressed misgivings over the extravagance. "It's just one night. We deserve at least this much," he said after explaining that he'd saved enough from his army pay.

The next day, they took a taxi to Stephen's parents' apartment—which was how he thought of it now that he was a married man. Somehow it was no longer his home, even though they would have to live there until they could get settled.

Stephen wore his uniform, neatly pressed for the occasion. As planned, Annalise wore the simple dress she was married in, though she made it less formal with the addition of a stylish silver-and-onyx necklace she happened on just before leaving Germany.

As they started up the stairs to the Wroths' apartment, Annalise stopped suddenly.

"What is it?" Stephen asked, looking back at her from two steps above.

"I think . . . I think it might be better for you to go to the door alone."

"What?" Stephen shook his head as if he must have misunderstood. "Are you joking? Why would I want to do that?"

"To give your family a moment with you to themselves. Just for a moment," she repeated with a smile. "I'll upset their world soon enough."

"Absolutely not! You are the center of my world now. I want them to understand that from the start, which they will, I'm sure of it."

"We should have talked about this before," she said. "It didn't hit me until we got here."

He was about to reject the idea out of hand, but he paused to consider that, despite his family's certain protestations that they want to meet Annalise at once, they might be pleased to know that their new daughter-in-law was thoughtful enough to take their feelings into account.

"I don't mean for twenty-four hours, Stephen," she said with a laugh. "I'll take a walk around the block or something while you hug everyone."

"Well, you can't just show up at the door by yourself like some mail-order bride!"

"I won't. You can come get me in, say, fifteen minutes. Just enough time to hug everyone tight. I know I would appreciate that in their situation."

"And what? That would make you a *special delivery* mail-order bride? There's no need to be nervous, you know. Besides, it's cold outside."

She laughed again. "There's every reason to be nervous, but that's not why I'm suggesting this. Don't make such a big deal. You can even tell them why we're doing it this way."

He shook his head and smiled. "All right. Fifteen minutes, then. I'll meet you in the lobby. Don't be late."

When he reached the apartment door, he paused and took a deep breath. It was as grand an entrance as he ever expected to make. Not that he looked very different—at least he didn't believe he did—though he allowed for changes that might not be obvious to him over the past eventful year and a half. He had witnessed things no one should have to see. He was home with a wife, and without Henry. He had killed and—

110

not the same thing—murdered. The latter would remain secret, but the other things were known to his parents. A second deep breath was to remind himself of this and to prepare for the moment when even these known things were capable of overwhelming when compressed into the first instant of presence before them.

He rang the bell and listened to the immediate commotion inside.

* * *

STEPHEN HAD PLANNED to attend college when he returned home. He dreamed of having the full-ticket Joe College experience, possibly at one of the Ivies, living on campus, maybe joining a fraternity. He could count on his parents to help to pay for it. College for their children, daughter Barbara included, was always high on their list of goals. Stephen was willing to work part time if necessary, and there was the new GI Bill as well.

And then he showed up at home with a wife, who would have to be provided for. A severe postwar shortage of housing and jobs made it necessary for them to lodge with the parents for what turned out to be an extended time that tried everyone's patience. Brother Robbie sacrificed his room for the couple while he prepared to go off to college. In the meantime, Robbie slept on the living-room sofa or sometimes had to move in with a mortified Barbara, who as a result spent every possible moment out with friends.

One bathroom.

Yet, in coping with the new arrangements, they all had the benefit of having gotten through tough times and stunted expectations. All of them had known privation of one kind or another, whether in the maw of the Great Depression, coping with war and wartime shortages, or in Annalise's case, enduring experiences unimaginably worse.

Stephen's father, contemplating the situation generously, spoke of helping out financially if the young couple could find an apartment of their own. He even mentioned the possibility of moving the whole family to the suburbs. For a variety of reasons—chief among them the housing shortage, which was made worse by explicit or implicit refusals in some neighborhoods to sell or rent to Jews—what began as a temporary living arrangement started to appear distressingly without end in sight.

The biggest day-to-day challenge turned on the sudden presence in tight quarters of two women of the house. Stephen's mother did her best to welcome and accommodate Annalise, but it was difficult for her to surrender control over what had been her exclusive and precisely managed domain. Annalise was not the unworldly girl she might have long imagined as a daughter-in-law—the guileless, fresh-faced, recent virgin who would need wise instruction in the proper running of a home. Such expectations might have been fanciful in the best of circumstances, but given Annalise's background, some friction was inevitable.

The situation wasn't helped by Annalise's bouts of depression. To her, this new world was even more disorienting than she had expected. On the surface, it was an idyll she might never have dared imagine in the camps. And yet, in its warmth, order, and sense of protection, it was eerily similar to the one she inhabited among her own family before the terrors of Nazism engulfed them. Her reluctance to speak of her wartime experiences had the effect of placing large swaths of *her* off limits, sometimes straining the desire of the others to be sympathetic. Stephen tried to smooth these edges, but there were, after all, many things about Annalise that were off limits to him, as well.

Stephen enrolled at City College. Early on he declared a major in journalism and worked hard to accelerate his coursework. By mid-1947 some pressures began to ease, temporarily. Annalise was in demand as a translator, so there was some money coming in. Fortunately, this coincided with finding an apartment near Tremont Avenue, not far from Stephen's parents. After graduation from City, Stephen spent a few months doing odd jobs while he looked for work on a newspaper or magazine. Finally, he was taken on as a cub reporter at the Daily News, where he joined the scrum of a journalism career.

By then Annalise was pregnant, a development received by all with both joy and concern over how they would live. A daughter, Sandra, was born in September of that year. Sandra was followed by Jacob Henry in February 1949, and Ben in April 1950.

~ ~ ~ ~ ~

Part II

The Wroth Family, 1967–1978

Richard Samuel Sheres

Chapter 12

April 1967—Hey, Hey LBJ!

AT TWENTY, SANDRA WROTH still tried to lord it over her brothers, Ben, almost seventeen, and Jacob, just turned eighteen. She hadn't had much success since early childhood, so even she was surprised that more recently, at least in matters of social conscience, she had regained some of the lost authority.

She was a beautiful young woman, with rich chestnut hair and looks that favored Annalise's in all important respects. Stephen's contribution could be seen in a softening of Annalise's sharp facial features. She was a nursing student and a woman of causes, joining campaigns for civil rights and against the Vietnam War with natural ease and fit. And determination—once in, determination was the quality that took command. In this above all, Sandra was Annalise's daughter.

Sandra knew, of course—the entire family did—about the grit Annalise must have had simply to survive. However, the telling of it was mostly by Stephen, who portrayed the history as well as he could while leaving out key details, such as the rape (or rapes—Stephen himself preferred not to press) in Dachau.

For her part, Annalise seemed content to let Stephen be the keeper and deliverer of the narrative. It was sufficient. For anyone who had not actually experienced what she went through, it would be difficult, if not impossible, to possess more than rudimentary understanding. The boys pressed for more lurid detail, as boys will. When it was not forthcoming, it didn't diminish the awe they had gained over the years for their mother's ordeal. To the contrary, leaving blanks for their imaginations to fill only enhanced it. Not that any of this affected the typical, fraught day-to-day interplay between mother and children.

Politically, socially, like many of her contemporaries, Sandra came of age in 1960. During the election campaign she made it a point to wear her biggest and shiniest "All the Way with JFK" and "JFK for President" buttons when Nixon's motorcade passed on the Henry Hudson Parkway, near the Wroths' home in the Riverdale section of the Bronx. Her enthusiastic recounting of the event made Annalise, who supported JFK, laugh.

Stephen, by that time an editorial writer for the *Herald Tribune* and a supporter, albeit unenthusiastic, of Nixon (*"Kennedy's just too inexperienced, and his father's a crook and a philanderer"*), merely rolled his eyes and let some air out of Sandra's balloon by asking whether Nixon was able to see the buttons as he whizzed by. The balloon didn't remain deflated for long, however, as Sandra said with conviction, "He *could* have."

Beyond Sandra's somber declaration a couple of years later that after college she would be joining the Peace Corps, it was the fight against racism that consumed her—not without personal cost, as the boys in her class discovered that pursuing this inheritor of her mother's classic beauty was not worth the constant hassle of dealing with her righteous causes.

So, potential boyfriends came and went—mostly went—until in 1964 it appeared she might have broken the curse with a boy who was a year ahead of her in school and headed south for Freedom Summer. It might have worked out for them if Stephen and Annalise had not put their collective feet down and refused permission—despite tears, threats to go anyway, and not very veiled accusations of closeted, retrograde racism—for Sandra to accompany him.

In the end, freedom rides might not have made it onto Sandra's résumé, but just about every other activity closer to home did, including sit-ins, teach-ins, pray-ins, and just about any other hyphenated "in." Increasingly, that résumé included a hefty antiwar commitment. Barely a surface at home over which she held any sway was not covered by a peace sign or slogan, a favorite being "We Won't Fight Another Rich Man's War."

On this particular late afternoon, on the 4th of April 1967, Sandra's dedication was paying off in the form of an invitation—which she took

116

it upon herself to further extend in a "Don't You Dare Say No" command to Ben and Jacob—to hear the Reverend Martin Luther King speak in Morningside Heights.

Ben didn't need much in the way of compulsion to attend. Revolution was his métier—or so he proclaimed often after discovering the word. Those who knew him well probably would disagree. They would say his true métier was contrariness. In the nomenclature of statistics, he strived to be a permanent outlier. Ben might never admit it, but the worst thing someone could do would be to agree with him. Word that King was finally about to come out strongly, publicly against the war would represent a huge victory for Ben's antiwar views, though it might well propel his participatory ardor elsewhere.

Physically, too, Ben was something of an outlier. In a household full of handsome people who were of larger than average stature and inexplicably dignified presence in even undignified circumstances, he was wiry, overfull of jittery energy, and bound to have his say, appearances be damned.

For Stephen, echoes of Henry at this age were inevitable.

As for the older son, Jacob, it fell to him to negotiate between Sandra's constant nagging at his better angels and Ben's thematically varied nipping. He accomplished this by finding his place in the calm water between the wakes. He prided himself on being reliable in a crisis and took satisfaction in a teacher's characterization of him as "reliably thoughtful."

Jacob had a statuesque presence desirable in an archetypal first son. He presented a neat melding of his parents, with well-defined features, gray-green eyes, and rich chestnut hair, which, until it fell from fashion, was particularly well suited to a pompadour. His coloring, slightly swarthier than his parents', contributed to a robust appearance.

Always a good student, Jacob followed in Sandra's footsteps to the prestigious Bronx High School of Science, from which he was soon to graduate with high, though not the highest, honors—and not in the sciences, but in the dramatic arts, a late-blooming affinity.

For a short time, the three siblings were able to take the same city bus to school, with Ben, whose test scores were not good enough to get into Science, peeling off at DeWitt Clinton ("that reform school," as Sandra referred to it). Meanwhile Sandra and Jacob continued down the long block that separated the schools—a journey sometimes accompanied by taunts from Clinton's less than luminous scholars.

At five p.m., the three alighted from the bus and walked toward the Kingsbridge subway el at 231st Street and Broadway. All day Sandra had been recounting (ad nauseam as far as the brothers were concerned) the triumph of securing an invitation to hear King. It didn't matter that, as Jacob reminded her, the event was open to the public and seating was first come, first served. King's Southern Christian Leadership Conference, the SCLC, had still seen fit to reward her contribution to the cause with a note of invitation, sent in a nice envelope with a five-cent stamp, and this set her apart.

She abandoned her usual denim-based uniform for a skirt, an upgrade she was unable to prevail upon Ben to match. His boots and bell-bottom jeans were nonnegotiable; the only concession she got was the substitution of a plain, button-down shirt for his tie-dyed tee. For his part, Jacob took less convincing to wear a reasonably well-pressed pair of chinos and a light sweater.

"I'm hungry. I want to get a slice," Ben declared as he veered toward the pizzeria across the street.

"You just had lunch," Sandra said.

"Yeah, four hours ago," he called back over his shoulder. He dodged a taxi and completed the crossing walking backwards, almost tripping when his heel hit the curb. "Sandra, come on, we won't be late. Jake, tell her."

"I'm in," Jacob responded. "Come on, Sandy, be cool. Ben's right for a change. It won't take long to scarf a slice."

Sandra's face set. "I want to be early. I want a good seat."

Jacob shook his head and laughed. "Oh, for crying out loud, we're gonna be so early, we'll fall asleep and miss the speech." He took her arm and guided her. "We'll compromise. You can eat yours on the train."

She frowned disapproval but followed Jacob. "I'm going to hold you responsible if I don't get a good seat."

"Hold Ben responsible. Come on. I'll even buy. That ought to get your cheap little heart racing."

Ben had practically finished a slice by the time Sandra and Jacob walked through the door. "We'll take two to go," Jacob told the flour-coated man behind the counter.

"Make it three, I'm still starved," Ben said, yanking a tissue-thin napkin from a metal spring-loaded dispenser and applying it to his mouth.

* * *

THEY WERE EARLIER than even Sandra planned when they got off the train at 125th Street to walk the few blocks to the Riverside Church, where King would be speaking. The church was far more imposing than the quaint name would suggest. Commissioned by John D. Rockefeller, Jr., built to Neo-Gothic Cathedral scale based on Spanish and French examples, and with ornamentation rivaling some of the world's best, the church struck the three sufficiently to make them stop and look up. They had driven past it a thousand times on the highway below, paying it no attention. To them, it was merely part of the Westside landscape, just as was the neoclassical Grant's Tomb, the church's neighbor—another landmark they had never visited.

The pews were already half full, which rated a "See?" from Sandra, who seemed barely contained at the prospect of being in King's presence.

"Hardly half full" was Ben's interpretation. "How many seats do you need, anyway?"

With a trace of importance, Sandra presented her invitation to a young Negro volunteer. She appeared slightly deflated when the boy paid it little mind and motioned all of them forward.

"Easy, girl," Ben said, patting her arm as he moved into a row midway down the church's long nave. "Martin's a great man, but he hasn't been elevated to sainthood yet."

"And he won't be, dear ignoramus brother. He's a Baptist preacher, not a prince of the church."

"Well, anyway," Ben retorted, unperturbed, "the point is . . . "

"Thanks. I get the point."

Jacob asked, "Do you think he'll really go for it—make this his big statement against the war?"

"I hope so. He might as well. Everyone knows he's against it. He led the antiwar march in Chicago last month, right? It's about time for him to say something, and this would be a perfect place."

"It's more than about time," Ben chimed in. "I mean, how bad do things have to get before he speaks out? Like you said, Sandy, he's a preacher. So, let him preach."

"I agree, obviously," Sandra said. "But it's not simple for him. He doesn't want to weaken his voice on civil rights."

"And he might," Jacob said, evenly. "There's still a lot of support for the war, and people who follow him on race but not on the war may get turned off."

Ben said, a little too loudly for the staid couple in the pew in front of him, "Well, screw that! *Let* them get turned off! Besides, do you know how many Negroes are being killed in Nam? What a waste. They ought to be back here shooting Mississippi sheriffs."

"Oh, really, Ben, for Christ's sake!" an exasperated Sandra said. To the elderly man and woman in front of them who had turned around, she added, "I apologize for my idiot brother, who among other things doesn't seem to realize how contrary what he just said is to everything about Dr. King."

The couple, seeming slightly mollified by the apology and the realization of Ben as a shoot-his-mouth-off kid, faced forward again.

"Okay, okay, maybe I was over the top on that one," Ben said in a lower voice. "But anyway, no one who supports the war supports him on race. I mean, if you don't give a crap about killing Vietnamese, why would you care about how they treat Negroes in Selma?"

"Really?" Jacob said, leaning across Sandra, who sat between him and Ben. "So, no one who supports the war in Vietnam could also support civil rights at home? I don't believe you."

"That's what I think," Ben responded with debate-ending finality and folded his arms across his chest.

Jacob had started to sit back, but once more leaned across Sandra, pinning her against the back of the pew. "Just for your information, bright boy, you personally know at least two people here who would take issue with you."

"Who?"

"Well, how about Dad, for one."

"Yeah, big surprise there!" After a beat: "He's here?"

"He will be, if he's not here yet," Sandra interjected. "He's working, covering the speech."

"Anyway, so what?" Ben asked.

Jacob said, "The so what is that you know he still supports the war. And he wants to see racial justice, too."

"And who's the other loser here who feels that way?"

"Maybe you're looking at him."

At this, Sandra blinked hard and stared into Jacob's face.

"Okay, don't get your panties in a twist. I have problems with the war, but I also understand why we're there."

"Really?"

"Yes, really."

Ben smiled, barely suppressed a laugh, at having Sandra run interference for him.

"You can't be serious," she said. "With all the boys we've lost and all the Vietnamese people—especially civilians—we've killed or maimed, I don't understand how you can be."

"This is probably not the time or place to give you all the reasons to support the war. So let me just give you one or two—if you and Ben aren't so hard over that I'm wasting my breath."

"Do you know that General Westmoreland is asking for even more troops, even more bombing?" she interrupted.

"I can see I'm going to get really far," Jacob said.

The familiar voice called over from the aisle: "Good evening, *meine kinder*."

"Dad!" Jacob exclaimed. "I'm outnumbered, I think I need your help."

Stephen laughed. "I don't know what the problem is, but you've always held your own." He had put on a little weight in the twenty years since he returned from Europe, but as he said frequently, not nearly as much as he would have if he had stopped smoking—and he knew, because he had tried, several times. He still had most of his hair, a little thinner, a bit gray at the temples. Annalise said he shouldn't try to cover it up; she liked it that way.

"Where are you sitting?" Sandra asked.

"With the other scribes." He nodded toward the area reserved for press. Stephen had only recently found a position on the editorial pages of *The Wall Street Journal*. He had been out of work since *The Herald Tribune* folded the previous year, following newspaper strikes across the city. The strikes pushed several papers to, and in some cases, such as the *Trib's*, over, the precipice. He was still angry at the unions, not for having unjustified complaints but for not knowing how to negotiate or compromise. "Do they appreciate even now how many jobs—including many of their own—they destroyed?" he would complain. "Where's your mother?" he asked now. "I thought she was coming with you."

"She had a rush translation job," Sandra said. "Anyway, she probably wouldn't hear anything from King that she doesn't already believe."

"Well, I wouldn't be here either if I had a choice. I have a pretty good idea what I'm going to hear. How's tricks, Ben?" he asked. "You look like you've got your mad on."

"Okay."

"Sure?"

"Yeah, Dad, just okay." More to himself he muttered, "I'd be better if I thought you would listen to what King has to say."

"Beg pardon . . . I didn't get that."

"Nothing."

Stephen shook his head. "Looks like they're getting ready to start. I'll see you later. Do you want a ride home after?"

"That would be great," Jacob said.

"Which car do you have?" Ben asked, as if that would be the key to his decision.

"The new one," Stephen called back to them.

"Now, where were we?" Sandra said with a just-kidding look at Jacob.

"That ass Westmoreland," Ben said, not having caught the look.

Jacob leaned in. "I don't suppose you ever stopped to consider that he knows what he's doing—that he's a professional soldier who knows what it will take to win this thing."

"What?!" Ben slapped the pew in front of him, fetching a hard stare from the man sitting there. "Sorry," Ben said without contrition. The man's wife urged him to scoot over a few seats. Ben had already returned his attention to Jacob, extending a pointed index finger in his direction. "You can't really believe he knows what the hell he's doing."

"I have to give him the benefit of the doubt, at least for a little while longer."

"*Why* do you have to give him the benefit of the doubt?" Sandra asked, still wearing an expression that said she was completely perplexed by what she was hearing. "How many people have to die before you stop giving him the benefit of the doubt?"

"What, you're waiting to be one of them yourself?" Ben interjected. "You could be called up soon," he added.

"I already have been."

Sandra and Ben stared. "But you haven't even graduated high school," Sandra said.

"Yeah, but it's just a month from now. Besides, it's only for a pre-induction physical."

The church was nearly full by this time. A standing-room-only crowd was assembling in the rear. In the pulpit, a mike check.

"Do Mom and Dad know?" Ben asked.

"Yep."

"So, what do they say?

Jacob blurted a laugh. "What do you think? Mom did the very un-Mom-like thing of bursting into tears and saying she wouldn't let me go. Dad said I would have to answer my country's call to duty or something like that, which got Mom to give him a look that could have melted glass."

"Anyway," Sandra cut in, "you'll get a college deferment."

"Maybe, if I'm accepted."

"You will be."

A wave of applause reverberated through the church as Dr. King appeared and waited to be introduced.

"I've already been turned down by Juilliard, no surprise."

"Shh, later," Sandra said, turning to face forward with an acolyte's focus. Then, "Wait, what? Juilliard did what?"

"We'll talk about it later, he's about to speak."

King stepped up to the pulpit. He was dressed in his usual sober fashion: dark suit, tie knotted carefully into the spread collar of a stark white shirt. He waved briefly to the crowd and began by thanking Clergy and Laymen Concerned about Vietnam for inviting him to speak. He noted that the organization's executive committee had recently concluded that "a time comes when silence is betrayal." He had to speak, he said: "My conscience leaves me no other choice."

Sandra leaned over to Ben and whispered, "I hope he explains why he's waited this long."

As if King himself had been listening, he soon got to that point, describing how promising programs on poverty and racism had been undermined by the war.

But it was the eloquence and what Sandra afterward called the fierce truth of what followed that got all three of them to their feet:

> *We were taking the black young men who had been crippled by our society and sending them eight thousand miles away to guarantee liberties in Southeast Asia which they had not found in southwest Georgia and East Harlem. And so we have been repeatedly faced with the cruel irony of watching Negro and white boys on TV screens as they kill and die together for a nation that has been unable to seat them together in the same schools.*

"Right on!" Ben exclaimed as King talked about the poisoning of America's soul and excoriated the nation's hypocritical support for corrupt, brutal governments. The Vietnamese "must see Americans as strange liberators," King said.

However, when King compared the testing of new weapons on the Vietnamese to the Germans' tests of new medicines and tortures in the concentration camps of Europe, it drew a muttered, "Well, that's a bit much" from Jacob.

When King urged his audience to counsel young men concerning military service with the alternative of conscientious objection, Ben leaned in and pointed at Jacob. "He's talking to you, brother; he's talking to you."

* * *

AFTERWARD, THE THREE gathered outside to wait for Stephen. Sandra's expression was otherworldly, as if she had witnessed the archangel of her future. "That was fabulous. Inspiring."

Ben looked at Jacob and declared, "You have to admit, if that speech didn't make you antiwar, nothing will."

"Don't make it sound like I'm pro-war," Jacob responded.

"It sure sounded like it before the speech. Remember? You and Dad agreeing that you can support the war and still believe in civil rights?"

"That part's still true. And just because I have questions about the war doesn't mean there aren't good reasons for us to be over there."

Sandra, who had come in from wherever her glory-infused mind had taken her, said, "Name one."

"Communism."

"Oh, shit, I don't believe it!" Ben exclaimed, slapping his forehead.

"Dr. King is right," Sandra interjected. "You should be a conscientious objector."

Jacob shook his head. "Have you heard *anything* I've said?"

"I think he's afraid to piss off Dad," Ben said.

"Bullshit!"

"Then why do you keep on with this communism crap?" Sandra asked. "You sound just like him. You know you don't believe it."

"Jesus, Sandra, I don't know any such thing. All you have to do is look at a map. You've got the Soviet Union, you've got Red China, and you've got communism trickling down into Southeast Asia. These are things King conveniently overlooks. And we may have faults, but don't tell me we're worse than the commies."

"And what about King's points about the inequalities right here? I almost cried when I heard him say Negroes are dying to give Vietnamese freedoms they themselves don't have at home."

"And don't forget about the genocide policy we're carrying out against them," Ben chimed in.

"What? We don't have a genocide policy against the Vietnamese," an incredulous Jacob said.

"Not against the Vietnamese, stupid. Against colored people."

"What are you talking about?" Sandra asked, suddenly allied with Jacob.

"I read it."

"Read what?"

"About how poor people, especially Negroes, join the army more than other people. So a bigger part of the Negro population is dying . . ."

"Wait, wait," Jacob interrupted. "That may be true, but you're saying this is a government plot to thin out the Negro population? Are you nuts, or what?"

"That's what I read."

Sandra rolled her eyes. "Oh, well then it must be true. Obviously."

"He's here." Jacob nodded toward the curb as Stephen pulled up.

"He's got the Merc," Ben said. "I've got dibs on the shotgun seat."

* * *

THE DRIVE HOME didn't begin promisingly, as Stephen, his eyes split between the road ahead, rearview mirror glimpses of Sandra and Jacob in the back seat, and brief turns toward Ben next to him, heard Ben declare that if Jacob couldn't do the smart thing and arrange to fail his induction physical ("I know guys who could tell you how"), then he had to be a conscientious objector. "That's all there is to it."

"What are you talking about?" Stephen said, clearly irritated. His reflexive pull on the steering wheel as he turned his head toward Ben made the car drift out of lane. The car next to him swerved and emitted a harsh horn reprimand before it sped ahead, the driver's middle finger raised like a semaphore flag.

"Good move, Dad. I'm . . ."

"You're what? Ben."

"Nothing." Followed by a muttered, "Trying to keep my brother from getting killed in a useless, immoral war is all."

"Do you know *anything* about democracy?" Stephen asked, looking over at Ben and nearly drifting out of his lane again. "Whether the war is useless remains to be seen, though you should remember that defeatist talk like yours—and yours, too, Sandra," he said, eyeing her in the mirror—"risks creating a self-fulfilling prophecy. Positivism and

126

negativism each have their own trajectories. And the war most certainly is not immoral. If anything, it's the North and its communist allies who are immoral. They're the ones denying the South Vietnamese the freedom to choose democracy."

"You call that democracy?" Sandra said, before adding, "Sounds like someone has just written tomorrow's editorial."

"Not perfect, but yes. They're working on it. And what about *our* democracy, Sandra? You may not like it, but when Jake reports for his physical, he's fulfilling his civic duty as determined *democratically* by the people of this country and the lawmakers they voted for."

"Oh, you mean democratically—like when rich men were allowed to buy their way out of the draft during the Civil War. Maybe we can buy a substitute piece of fodder for Jacob."

Jacob, who had remained quiet, now sought middle ground through humor, starting as if in the far distance an operatic basso profundo thrum of "The Ballad of the Green Berets."

> *Ta rum, ta rum*
> *Fighting soldiers from the sky*
> *Fearless men who jump and die*
> *Men who mean just what they say*
> *The brave men of the Green Beret.*

Now Sandra joined in, lowering her vocal register to fit with Jacob's, the crescendo rising with each line.

> *Silver wings upon their chest*
> *These are men, America's best.*

(A sarcastic "yeah, right" from Ben.)

> *One hundred men we'll test today*

(Jacob: "Big finish!")

> *But only three will win the Green Beret.*

"Okay, okay," Stephen said, piercing hoots of laughter. "It's corny. But you know what? It's also true."

"Like you would know," Ben said. The remark was met with abrupt silence in the back seat and from Stephen, who stared ahead as if focusing more intently on his driving.

Ben craned his neck to seek the source of the sudden quiet. He was met with a disapproving look from Jacob.

"Maybe I would," Stephen said, evenly. "Maybe I would know."

"Well, it's not like you talk about the war . . . your war," Ben amended in a defensive tone.

"I suppose that's true."

"Why not?"

They exited the highway in Riverdale and stopped for a light. Stephen looked at Ben, said in a carefully modulated voice, "Because it's painful, that's why. And because if you haven't lived through it, there's no way to make you understand."

"A lot of people at least have tried. In books and movies, for instance."

"Movies," Stephen echoed as the light turned green. "I hope you don't mean movies like *The Longest Day*, where famous actors get shot and fall down in big theatrical heaps."

"Haven't seen it," Ben responded, sullenly, though he had.

They stopped for another light. Sandra leaned forward, said more soberly now, "Maybe we don't want Jake to have to learn it the hard way. I know the rest of the song, Dad. Want to hear it?"

"The Green Beret song?"

"Yes."

"Not particularly."

"You should. My dear mature-acting, responsible brother should too."

As the car began to accelerate, Sandra began to sing again, this time emphasizing the lyrics, which she spoke with only a hint of melody:

> *Back at home a young wife waits*
> *Her Green Beret has met his fate*
> *He has died for those oppressed*
> *Leaving her this last request*

"And . . . so . . . on," she said, giving a staccato strike to each word, not a trace of humor this time. She had begun to cry softly. And then, with forced sarcastic brightness: "Hey, Hey, LBJ! How many kids did you kill today?"

"Come on, Sandy," Jacob said, quietly, as they pulled into their driveway.

128

"Jerk!" she said, pushing him and using the cuff of her sleeve to swipe at a tear.

"Mom's home," Stephen said with a nod toward the green Ford Fairlane he had pulled up behind.

"Anyway," Jacob said as he started to climb out of the car, "I may still get a deferment. Juilliard is the only place that's turned me down so far."

* * *

THE NEXT DAY, Stephen drafted an editorial for *The Journal* that criticized King for oversimplifying the issues and questioned his priorities. "Dr. King is right," Stephen concluded. "We could lose this war. What he fails to acknowledge is, we can still win it. The eloquence—and, no doubt, the sincerity—he brings to the debate should not be allowed to derail this fact."

~ ~ ~ ~ ~

Chapter 13

April 15, 1967: The Mobe

"IF THIS DOESN'T END the war, I don't know what will!" Ben exclaimed to Sandra in an adrenalized rush. They were standing in the Sheep Meadow in Central Park, two among many thousands. "I mean, just look at this, would you! Fucking *far out*, man!" he said to a boy of about the same age standing next to him. The boy had shoulder-length hair and a patchy blond beard, and was holding a handmade sign that said *Drop Acid, Not Bombs*. Ben looked admiringly at his fringed deerskin jacket.

They were waiting to be addressed by the antiwar leadership, including King. Afterward they would march to the United Nations. The event was part of the Mobe—the Spring Mobilization. A parallel Mobe was being held in San Francisco and included King's wife, Coretta.

"How many of us do you think there are?" Sandra asked.

"Must be half a million at least," the boy in the fringed jacket offered.

"At least," Ben echoed.

Sandra appeared doubtful.

"All I know is it's fucking a lot, man," the boy said, his excitement building with each declaration. "And hey, you know, there's even a group of Nam vets with us today. And we're gonna burn motherfucking draft cards at the UN! Talk about far out!"

"Yeah, I'm burning my card," Ben said.

Looking askance, eyebrows forced into a high arch, Sandra said, "That's great, but what card? You haven't registered yet."

"Well no one has to know that, do they, Sis?" His tone suggested she must be an imbecile. "I'll torch something that looks like my draft card. I mean, it's not like I won't burn the real thing when I get it."

The crowd began to surge, jostling Ben and Sandra forward. A forest of posters and banners made it difficult to see or move. *Get the Hell OUT of Vietnam! Peace Now! Stop the Bombing!! No to U.S. Murder! March with U.S. for Peace!*

Ben pointed to a rising cloud over several of the marchers. "Look at that bunch lighting up," he said with a laugh.

"I wish they wouldn't," Sandra said, and then had to repeat it in a raised voice to counter an increasing decibel level.

"Little grass never killed anybody," Ben said. "Smells sweet," he added, stretching the word. *Sweeeet.*

"It's not that. It makes us look less serious, less responsible, like we're really just looking for an excuse to party. And especially when we're shown next to the pro-war people, who *do* look serious."

Ben responded with a dismissive wave.

"They're out here today, too, you know, the pro-war people," Sandra added. "I heard someone say fights have broken out. I heard a group of vets and union hardhats grabbed one of our banners and stomped all over it. Besides, get real—there are still more people in the country who support the war than oppose it."

"Well, fuck them where they breathe!" Ben yelled. "Let anyone try that crap with me, and I'll stomp the shit out of them."

Sandra gave him her best "Yeah, right" look.

"I will!"

A cascading shushing sound went up as the Mobe organizers began to speak. Sandra and Ben were among those having trouble hearing above the din and distortions in the sound system. They joined in on the applause lines anyway, and before long the throng began to move and gain momentum.

"I wish Jacob could see this," Sandra said.

"Too late. He's gone over to the dark side."

"I haven't given up. I still think he might be persuaded not to report. Being here to soak up these good vibes would have helped."

"You're kidding yourself, Miss Sis. He's the good son, don't you know it?"

"As far as Dad's concerned, maybe. He's definitely not doing what Mom wants."

* * *

STEPHEN WAS HOME alone when the phone call came. He had fallen asleep over his book and was startled by the ring. Some kind of commotion in the background as well as a head full of cotton from what he liked to call *nappus interruptus* made him have to ask three times for the man on the other end of the line to repeat himself.

Finally, he made out that the caller was a police officer named Paul Rizzo, who said he was phoning from the 17th Precinct.

Stephen's "where's that?" preempted the more logical question of why the police were calling.

"Mid-Manhattan. East 51st Street."

Now jogged alert, Stephen took little time to comprehend that whatever the reason for the call, it had to involve Sandra or Ben. He knew they had gone to the march. Jacob was playing basketball. Annalise was out shopping in Yonkers.

Rizzo went on without prompting. "Mr. Wroth, we have your son"— he paused, possibly to read the name—"your son, Benjamin, in custody."

"In custody? What for?" Though he asked with as much shocked innocence as he could muster, he had a good idea what he might be told.

"Disorderly conduct. Maybe other things. It's not clear yet. It's a zoo around here, as you can tell from the noise. He was at the peace rally outside the UN. Got into a scuffle with some pro-war activists."

"Is he okay?"

"He's not hurt."

Stephen exhaled more of a breath than he realized he was holding. "That's a relief, the important thing. Is he being charged?"

"I don't know. Can you come down to the station?"

"As soon as I can."

"He'll be here," Rizzo said, and immediately hung up.

He'll be here. Real cute, Stephen thought. He held the phone for a few seconds to be sure Rizzo had actually ended the call.

Stephen grabbed his jacket. It occurred to him that it might not be the worst thing if he took a little time getting downtown. He assumed no serious offense had been committed or Rizzo wouldn't have referred to the incident as a scuffle. It wouldn't hurt to let Ben stew for a bit. And what about Sandra? Where was she? He hadn't had a chance to ask. If she was in custody with Ben, perhaps someone else was handling her case and hadn't had time to call. On the other hand, letting them stew might not accomplish anything. Knowing Ben and Sandra, they would be busy proselytizing and forming alliances with their fellow detainees.

He had just closed the front door behind him when the phone rang again. He fumbled with his keys and almost gave up, thinking he couldn't get to it in time, when he was able to insert the key and turn the bolt. He reached for the phone with a stretch.

"Dad?"

"Sandra! Where are you?"

"Downtown. Near the UN." Her voice was urgent, worried. "Have you heard from Ben?"

"In a manner of speaking," Stephen responded, sternly. "He's been arrested."

"You're kidding. Why? For what?"

"I thought you were together. Frankly, Sandra, I was hoping you might have a restraining influence on him."

"We got separated. There were so many people. You should have seen it!"

"Yeah, well, I'm on my way to see Ben now. Come home. I'll see you when I get back."

"But where is he?" Sandra asked.

"A station house on East 51st. I'm not sure what the cross street is."

"I'll meet you there then."

"Sandra, just come home, would you?"

"I want to see Ben." She hung up before Stephen could respond.

* * *

133

GETTING TO THE police station was a pain, but it was easier than finding a place to park. The march was long over, but protesters were everywhere, clogging the streets, cutting between parked cars, and even more than usual flouting pedestrian rules. Discarded posters and picket signs littered the streets. More than once Stephen had to stop short and lean on the horn.

"Chill out, man!" one boy yelled.

"Chill out yourself!" Stephen called through his rolled-down window. "Goddamn . . ." He was about to add an appropriate epithet, but he let the opportunity pass as he stumbled over what to call the kid. Hippie freak leaped to mind but remained unspoken. "Stupid ass probably would have taken it as a compliment," he said to himself.

He was getting more and more frustrated as he crawled past double-parked cars and garage signs proclaiming "Full," and wondered where all the cars had come from if the protesters had marched from Central Park.

At last, after cruising the streets for over half an hour, Stephen spied someone pulling out of a space. He made a beeline for it and stopped short, just ahead of the new, precious gap between parked cars, in order to parallel park. "Go around, goddammit!" he yelled to the driver behind him, who ignored Stephen's waving arm and blinker and sat on his bumper. By now several more cars had backed up behind them and started a chain-reaction honk. "I'll be damned if I'm giving up this space because of this asshole," Stephen muttered.

The driver barely missed Stephen's bumper as he stomped on the gas and gave him the finger. Stephen pointed emphatically to the vacant spot just in case the drivers farther back were as imbecilic as the first one.

"Thank you," Stephen mouthed to the woman now behind him who gave him enough room to back into the spot. By this time, he didn't care that the space he was squeezing into was too close to a hydrant. He'd risk the ticket.

Fueled by a cocktail of anger and irritation, he quick-stepped the five blocks to the police station. The place was still a hive of cops and milling protesters, some of whom continued to carry protest signs and repeatedly offered a "sorry, man" to people whose faces were inadvertently slapped by them.

"Get those damned things out of here!" a sergeant bellowed. "I don't care if they're pro or anti, just get them out!"

Some young people seemed to be leaving the station in the company of adults. A good sign, Stephen thought. If charges were being brought, they were apparently sufficiently minor to allow the kids to go home.

"Dad!" Sandra called out. Like most of the protesters, she was disheveled. The skin on her face had a dried-sweat sheen. "What took you so long? I tried to see Ben. The cop behind the desk asked if I was the person responsible for him—a scary thought, but maybe I should have said yes."

With Sandra at his side, Stephen made his way to the raised dais where the desk sergeant was half listening to a distraught mother make a tearful case for her son. The obviously exhausted sergeant explained that she could see her son again as soon as he was arraigned. *Not encouraging,* Stephen thought.

Stephen gave his name and told the sergeant about the call from Rizzo, whom he made a conscious effort to refer to as Officer Rizzo.

"He's gone off duty," the desk sergeant said, and directed Stephen to a nearby room. There, he and Sandra were told to sit. They found places on a hard, scuffed wooden bench.

Stephen tried to get a better picture of the situation from Sandra, but she said she didn't know what happened after she lost sight of Ben.

After several long minutes, an officer approached and asked, mid-stride, "Who's here for Benjamin Wroth?"

Stephen identified himself and was told Ben would be up from holding shortly.

"Does that mean there are no charges?" Stephen asked.

"We'll talk then," the officer answered as he turned to go.

"Where's he off to?" Sandra asked.

"Beats me. Though not as much as I'd like to beat the two of you," Stephen added less seriously than the words suggested.

"Me?" Sandra asked indignantly. "What did I do?"

Stephen ignored the question.

"Oh, I called home and spoke to Mom," Sandra said.

"So, she knows."

"Yeah. She's pretty upset."

"Well, no reason she should be the only one spared."

At last, just as Stephen was getting ready to remind someone about Ben, he appeared, held by the elbow and guided brusquely by the officer who had told them to wait. Ben's lip was swollen. There was a smear of dried blood on his cheek, as if he'd tried to wipe his mouth with his sleeve, and another on his shirt.

"What happened to you?" Stephen asked, standing. He held Ben's chin and turned his head gently from side to side.

"I got into it with a pro-war cretin. He started it."

Stephen noticed the cop's face turn angry. Maybe he wasn't going to be as objective as Rizzo appeared to be over the phone. He thought about taking a tougher tone, but he was preempted.

"This might be a smart time for you to keep your mouth shut and listen," the cop said to Ben. Turning to Stephen, he added, "Your son is being released into your custody."

"Does that mean he's not being charged?"

"Not with the disorderly. He gets to slide on that one. As for the draft card burning, the Feds will have a say about that."

"Hold on a sec," Stephen said in obvious confusion. "What draft card? He's seventeen. He's not registered yet."

Stephen could see Ben's so-there smirk, but the smirk didn't last long as the cop produced an envelope and removed a partially charred card. "This is it," he said, matter-of-factly. "It was pulled out of the pot before it burned completely." He held it out to Stephen and said, "His last name's on it, where it's not burnt. Wroth, right? Unless it's yours," he said to Stephen with a smartass smirk.

"But he doesn't have a card," Stephen repeated, sticking to his argument even as it dawned on him what Ben had done. "He turns eighteen later this year, so it can't be his."

"Look, fact is, I don't care whose card it is. Burning a draft card is illegal. We have someone who's prepared to testify he saw Benjamin place the card in the pot. But that doesn't matter either, since according to the arresting officer, Benjamin readily admitted doing it. Anyway, listen, that decision will be made by the Feds. It's their law."

* * *

"SAY AGAIN," AN irritated and distracted Stephen said on the walk back to the car. The face Ben was showing to the world suggested he was more embarrassed at being seen with a parent than he was contrite over anything he'd done.

"I asked if you think anything will come of the draft card burning," Sandra said.

"Oh, I don't know. Probably not. The law is fairly new, and I haven't heard of people being prosecuted." He turned halfway toward Ben while continuing to walk. "It would serve you right if you were, though."

After a few more paces, Stephen stopped short and turned around. "Jacob's draft card," he said over a rigid index finger. "It wasn't enough that you burned someone's draft card, but Jacob's? Does he know you took it?"

"'Course not. But what's the diff? He doesn't need it. He's already been called up."

"You told me you'd burn some lookalike piece of paper," Sandra said, with a suggestion of betrayal in her voice, as if to say, "You couldn't trust me, of all people?"

They had stopped dead center on the sidewalk, and now passersby, some clearly annoyed, were forced to divide, like a stream running up against rocks.

Ben shrugged. "You should both . . ."

"You tell me to mellow out or any crap like that," Stephen interrupted, leaving the possible consequences unspoken.

Stephen turned and resumed walking to the car. Ben and Sandra stayed a few paces behind, and Sandra, appearing miffed, gave Ben a wide berth.

As they neared the car, Stephen halted suddenly. "Goddamn, I don't believe it!" he exclaimed, yanking the ticket that had been left sandwiched between the windshield wiper and the glass. Another exasperated "Goddamn" followed.

"What's it for?" Sandra asked.

"Being too close to the hydrant. What am I, one foot over the line? Damned meter maids."

"Who's the criminal now?" Ben crowed as he climbed into the back seat, well out of range of any corporal punishment.

~ ~ ~ ~ ~

Chapter 14

May–June 1967: Annalise Displaced

FROM THE MOMENT HE walked through the door, Stephen could sense he was in for an argument. The house was quiet, but he was alert to a kind of harmonic disturbance in the atmosphere. He wasn't sure anyone was home until he walked into the living room and found Annalise sitting in an armchair, reading under the only lamp in the room that was turned on. He bent to kiss her cheek. "Skimping on electricity? Where are the kids?"

"Scattered," she responded, enunciating the twin Ts.

Wary, he suppressed a waggish impulse to mimic her enunciation. "Scattered where?"

She put down the copy of *Time* she had been reading and sighed impatience with the effort it would take to explain her catchall for *off doing their own things*. "Ben's playing basketball. Sandra's at a political meeting of some sort. Jacob . . . he's just out with friends, I think."

And here he thought he found the nub of the atmospheric disturbance, not that it was unexpected. He tested her anyway. "No doubt friends who are trying to convince him not to report for duty."

"Don't start all that again, Stephen. He's been called up. He's going. You've won. He's only got a little while before he leaves. He's going," she said again.

"I haven't won anything," he said, resisting the good sense to let the subject rest. He walked over to the bar to pour himself a whiskey. "And

Jacob is simply doing his duty as a good citizen, just as I did. Want one?" he asked, holding up a glass.

She shook her head no and returned to her magazine. Her anger extended beyond the fact of Jacob's going. She'd made it clear that Stephen's righteousness rankled, as did his presumptuous final word as head of the household. Didn't he know it was a new day? Their children knew it, or behaved as if they did, though perhaps this didn't extend fully to Jacob, who apparently was more willing than the others to fit into the traditional patriarchy.

These things came to a head when Jacob took his oath and Stephen insisted that the family be there to show support.

Jacob said he didn't need the event to be witnessed. "It's no biggie," he'd said. "You remember the routine. You hold up your right hand and get it done. 'I, Jacob Wroth, do solemnly swear that I will support and defend the Constitution of the United States against all enemies foreign and domestic.' And presto! I'm a soldier!"

"It certainly is a big deal," Stephen said. "I don't take it lightly that you are putting yourself on the line for your country, and neither should you." He said he himself had sworn the oath almost exactly twenty-three years earlier, and it was one of the most—maybe *the* most—consequential events in his life. Almost everything since had in some way flowed from the decision. "Not least," he added with a smile, "your presence on this earth."

"I understand my obligation, but you have to understand that this is different. This war is not like the one you took part in."

"That doesn't make it unimportant."

"Okay, not unimportant. But not essential to the country's survival, either. No one doubted your war was necessary. The country was united behind you. That's not true now. Listen, I'm not trying to get into a debate over whose war was—is—more worthwhile. I just mean that it's more complicated now. Mom, Sandra, Ben—I get it that they oppose the war. I understand they may not want to come see me take the oath. It's a matter of principle for them—or it is for Ben and Sandy anyway; Mom may just be afraid for me."

"Principle? What principle? What principle is more important than having the support of your family when you go to war?"

140

"If you make them attend, they'll resent it, and I don't want that to be the memory I take with me. Besides, for all I know, I'll be posted in Brooklyn."

Stephen said he was sorry if it had to be that way, but he would raise holy hell with anyone who wasn't planning to be there.

Over Jacob's continuing objections, Stephen was as good as his word when Sandra and Ben said they didn't want to witness the event. In the end, Sandra gave in and said she would go, but everything about her demeanor was sullen and rigid.

Ben held his ground. Stephen, who occasionally threatened à la *The Honeymooners*' Ralph Kramden to turn Ben's rear end black and blue but who had never come close to actually doing so, said, "I mean it, Ben. You will support your brother."

"I am supporting my brother. I'm trying to keep him from getting killed. Mom and Sandra are, too. You're the only one who doesn't give a fuck."

Which drew a slap across the face hard enough to leave an hour-long welt.

But Ben didn't yield. The others went to the swearing-in; he made himself scarce.

A similar row over a going-away party was barely avoided when Jacob made it plain that friends were treating him to a hail-and-farewell, and parents were not welcome. He did want Sandra and Ben to be there, though, even over Sandra's proclamation that she would do so wearing a black armband and over Ben's predictably one-up threat to attend waving a North Vietnamese flag.

"Black armbands if you insist," Jacob said. "But you show up with a North Vietnamese flag, Ben, and I promise, you won't have to rely on Dad to kick your ass."

Now Annalise looked up from her magazine. "He shouldn't have to go," she said to Stephen in a simple, arid tone of voice. "If we had been more responsible parents—more aware of what was going on—we would have insisted that he apply to a safe school, so he could have a deferment."

"You're not being fair, Annalise. We thought he was going to. Hell, we thought he *did*," Stephen said, drink in hand, as he lowered himself into a leather easy chair. "He wasn't exactly straight with us. There were five applications, remember? Juilliard and the two other prestige schools, and the two state schools that should have been safe. I distinctly recall writing checks to them for the application fees. You know as well as I do that he had already received his induction notice when he confessed he never mailed in the state school applications. We got that nose-in-the-air story about how he'd decided—without telling us, mind you—that if he couldn't go to one of the elite schools, he'd just as soon not go at all. Don't tell me you don't remember this."

Annalise shifted uncomfortably in her chair and averted her gaze. After a moment, she said, "I'm not blaming only you for this. I said we should have been more responsible parents. We should have supervised him more closely."

"Maybe we should have. He's always been mature for his age. Maybe we gave him too much credit. He's old enough . . ."

"Old enough for what?" Annalise interrupted.

"Old enough to have the good sense to know that you don't apply only to schools you have little to no chance of getting into, especially with the army waiting in the wings. Anyway, look at the bright side. He'll serve his two years . . ."

"One of them in Vietnam."

"We don't know that yet."

Annalise stared at him, her expression skeptical bordering on contemptuous.

"And if he does go to Vietnam," Stephen continued, "it will be to serve his country—that's the point. And when he finishes he'll have the GI Bill as a reward."

"I need to watch the news," she said, ending the conversation and walking over to turn on the television.

Stephen frowned at the abrupt conclusion that left them where they'd started. Moreover, not only would her ire be fueled by reports about Vietnam (in color, no less, on their new Zenith), but probably by reports on Israel as well. As if their feuding over Vietnam were not enough.

* * *

142

ANNALISE HAD NEVER entirely put to rest her regrets about not going to Palestine in 1946. She took great pride in what Israel had accomplished against heavy odds, and particularly regretted that she was not a part of the big moments, including the creation of the state, the war of independence, and the Suez crisis in 1956.

Stephen's reminders that they had become generous financial contributors, as well as his defensive assertions that they were playing their part by providing vocal support for Israel in the United States, Israel's essential benefactor, did little to stem Annalise's conviction that these things were poor substitutes for putting herself on the line in Israel—which Stephen took as an opening to ask why, if she felt this way, she couldn't understand why Jacob had to go. He knew it was a weak argument the moment it left his mouth.

"It's not the same," Annalise responded. "When you talk about Vietnam, you do so to justify the need to defend U.S. *interests*." He understood her emphasis to diminish the importance of the word. "Israel's *interest* is in not being murdered."

She occasionally expressed a yearning to live on a kibbutz and regret that she had been unable to raise her children in such a noble environment of social cooperation. The regrets grew in tandem with the family's material prosperity.

Since the beginning of the year, Arab attacks, particularly by Syria, had become more intense. In mid-May, Israeli Prime Minister Eshkol warned that Israel would retaliate if the aggression continued.

But it was Egypt's actions that really got the pot boiling, first by moving troops into the Sinai Peninsula and then by demanding that UN peacekeepers there withdraw.

"What are they there for if they're just going to leave when they're needed?" a disgusted Annalise demanded of the unwary TV news anchor after the UN secretary general, U Thant, agreed to do precisely that.

"Settle down, would you?" Stephen had said. "According to some of my colleagues on the international desk, the whole thing is probably just more of Nasser's saber rattling, and probably intended more than anything to impress his Arab allies."

"I think your friends are—what's that expression you like to say?—singing Dixie."

"Whistling. Whistling Dixie."

"Well, anyway, they either don't understand the differences this time or they don't care, which I'll bet is the real answer."

"That's not fair, Annalise. The U.S. was Israel's first supporter."

"Actually, it was the Soviets who recognized the state first."

"All right, split hairs if you want to. The U.S. was the second to recognize Israel. Happy? But the U.S. is the only one to truly support her. The Russians haven't done anything but cause trouble. All they care about is keeping tensions high everywhere in the world, whether it's the Middle East or Southeast Asia. Causing trouble is the only leverage they have."

Arms crossed tight over her chest, face set, Annalise assumed the visage of a portrait that might have been titled "Lady Unconvinced."

"Why do you always look at things only from America's point of view?" she asked.

"I don't."

"Yes, you do. Isn't it possible that the U.S. is wrong about Vietnam?"

"It is possible, but it's not wrong. Besides, the U.S. is my . . . our country. I hope you're not going to turn into one of those Americans—particularly one of those American Jews—who forgets that."

She glared at him. "No, Stephen, I'm one of those Jews who remembers that I'm a Jew, and what that has meant. Unlike you. Maybe you don't remember Henry after all," she added as she marched out of the room, ignoring the resentful objections that followed her.

She came back for another round when, a few days later, President Johnson condemned Egypt for closing the Straits of Tiran to Israeli shipping. She refused to apologize in the face of Stephen's smug, "You see?"

"Do you see?" she crowed when Johnson subsequently warned Israel not to initiate an attack.

Yet Israel's astonishing total victory two weeks later, when in six days it smashed its enemies on all fronts, had a strange effect on Annalise. Her initial response was, as Stephen had no doubt it would be, rapturous. "And Jerusalem!" she cried in joy. "Jerusalem is ours!"

The rapture was quick to fade, however, and not only because such highs are impossible to sustain. Nor was it a question of bouncing from one psychological extreme to another—or at least not only that. Mood swings had been a defining characteristic for her ever since they first met. What Stephen witnessed was a transition to a sober, wistful Annalise, full of regret.

It took some prodding for her to open up to him, and to explain that the source of her sadness was having to watch Israel's success from afar. She had failed to be there for the hard work of years building to this moment. Now she said it felt wrong to exult in the victory. It was as if she were taking credit for someone else's work.

It only made matters worse that her emotional lows now coincided with Jacob's imminent departure. As far as she was concerned, she had missed the noble fight, while her beloved son was to risk his life in an ignoble one. Nothing Stephen said, or could say, convinced her otherwise, or lessened her desire sometimes to pound her fists on his chest.

~ ~ ~ ~ ~

Chapter 15

Late September 1967: RVN-Bound

THE NOTE FROM JACOB, arriving on a Saturday and hastily addressed to "The Wroth Family," was about as succinct as a potentially life-altering message could be:

> *Things moving fast. In case I don't get a chance to phone, just informed our deployment moved up to tomorrow, so may be in RVN by the time you read this. Write or call when I can.*
> *Love you all (and yes, I'll take care),*
> *J*

Stephen read the note aloud, then passed it to Annalise with the formality of evidence at trial.

"Isn't it curious," Annalise said quietly as she passed it to Sandra, "I have this strange urge to cross myself."

Sandra held the note at arm's length, gave it a perfunctory read as if to verify its authenticity, and passed it wordlessly to Ben, who had no similar impulse toward reserve.

"Idiot!" he said. "R V N," he said, stressing each letter with as much derision as he could impart. Just in case his point was missed, he added with an impressive sneer, "The great *Republic* of Vietnam—what a joke. The *Republic* is worth Jake coming home in a body bag, I'm sure."

"Stop it, please," Annalise said, her voice flat and toneless. She took the note from Ben, held it to her breast for a moment, and returned it to

146

Stephen. The circle having closed, she walked silently to the kitchen to prepare dinner.

* * *

"DID YOU REALLY have to?" Sandra said to Ben later, in his room.

"Have to what?"

"Upset Mom like that."

Ben shrugged. "What can I say? I'm pissed off. You should be too."

"Right now, I'm more sad than angry."

"Well then, let the anger bloom, Sis. It's the only chance of getting him home alive. You think LBJ, McNamara, Westmoreland, or any of those assholes will care that you're sad? How many 'Dear So-and-So, I regret to inform you that your kid is mincemeat' letters do they have to sign off on every day? Here's a news flash for you, Sis—we're all sad, but sad don't mean shit. Anger means . . . no, no forget that—anger won't cut it anymore either. What we need is rage! We need rage! Throw-a-rock rage! In a couple of weeks that's what our so-called leaders will get—a full dose of rage. Just wait and see how many of us freaks show up for the Pentagon Mobe." He was alluding to the mass protests planned for October, culminating in The March on the Pentagon To Confront the War Makers. "We will take the Pentagon—really take it over—if we have to."

"Get off it, Ben! That's a fantasy. And it's not that I'm not angry—or enraged—or committed," Sandra said, clearly miffed, her tone resentful. "I'm the one who got you involved in the antiwar movement in the first place, remember?"

"Yeah, well, that was then. It's like ever since you started nursing school you've pretended to be this remote—detached, that's the word—this detached woman, above getting your hands dirty."

"I am not detached! Not everyone has to blow off everything else in their lives just because of the movement. Going to nursing school is a big thing for me. It took a long time to figure out what I want to do with my life, and I'm not going to screw it up. I believe I can be a good nurse—someone who makes a real difference for people. And you know, in the end, it might be the only way I can do something real for Vietnam vets."

"Except stopping them from becoming vets in the first place."

Anyway," Sandra went on before Ben could get on a roll, "after the draft card-burning business, no way Dad lets you go to Washington. He'd throw a fit."

"Listen to Saint Sandy," Ben said with a laugh. "Like there's any way in hell he'll keep me from going. I don't give a shit what he says. I figure if I'm old enough to be drafted . . ."

"You're not."

"I will be soon. He may have persuaded my soft-headed brother to live up to his warped idea of patriotism, but no way I do that, just no fucking way."

* * *

A WEEK LATER, a letter from Jacob informed the family he had arrived safely at Tan Son Nhut airbase.

> *You may be interested to know, Dad, that our transport was a lot easier than the one you've told me about when you went to France. That's the wonder of jet travel for you. And it wasn't even a military plane. It was a 707 chartered (stolen, someone joked) from Pan Am. We even got to make a refueling stop in Hawaii.*
>
> *Don't get the wrong idea. It's not like the trip was cushy. The plane was jam-packed with sweaty GIs, and that stop in Hawaii lasted for all of six hours. We weren't allowed to leave the base. They did fly us over Pearl on the way out. I could see the Arizona memorial. I guess they wanted to remind us we're fighting for something important. I hope we are.*
>
> *They say there are about half a million of us here or on the way. I can't imagine that won't be enough to get the job done.*

"Why do I get the feeling Jake is writing only to Dad?" Ben said to Annalise, the thin airmail sheets fluttering in his hand.

She was in the garden, preparing belatedly for fall. She had taken up gardening only recently. Ben was just happy to see it didn't involve new chores for him. To the contrary, the harder and dirtier the work, the more

148

Annalise seemed to reserve it for herself. She was particularly aggressive about pruning and weeding. "I don't think that's true," she said now. "It's addressed to all of us."

"No, it's not," Ben said, his voice rising. "If you mean, does it say "Dear family," yeah, it does. But you know what I'm talking about. The whole thing is soldier to soldier. Listen to this . . ."

"I already read it."

"Well, maybe not closely enough."

I expected to find a lot of activity here, but Saigon is nuts crazy. Soldiers are everywhere, of course, both our guys and ARVNs (Vietnamese), plus uniforms and get-ups I haven't got a clue about. Every place is a bar, I think. As you'd expect, a lot of drinking and carousing goes on. (Tell Mom I'm being responsible!)

"See?" Ben exclaimed, triumphantly.

"See what?" Annalise said. She was on her knees, wrestling with a milkweed stalk that was threatening to become a tree.

"You don't say things like tell Mom if you're writing to Mom." Ben continued reading, skimming for something more to his point. He read quickly, barely aloud.

The first thing that hits you is the heat. Everybody warned us about it and said we'd get used to it. I hope so. Right now I feel like writing this letter will sap an entire day's energy! It's incredible! It takes about two minutes for all my clothes to be soaked through.

"Right, okay, general stuff, the weather and so on," Ben said. "Oh, okay, here—tell me this isn't meant only for Dad:"

Before I left home, we were talking, and you were remembering how negative the grunts could be. You said something about bitching instead of fighting being the main occupation.

So let me tell you, it didn't take long to see what you meant. Especially the guys who've been here awhile, there's nothing they don't complain about. I have to say, though, it's more than

149

typical griping. I'm surprised at just how pessimistic the guys are, particularly the ones who were drafted, but even the enlistees. Sometimes I'm surprised none of the officers step in and stop this chatter, but then I overhear them saying the same things to one another. There's a lot about not knowing why we're here or how we can win. No, check that. The chatter isn't so much about how we can win. It's more about wondering what winning means. I imagine for you it was pretty clear: Get to Berlin (or Tokyo) and get an unconditional surrender.

But no one here talks about "occupying Hanoi," even though we might be bombing the hell out of the place. During our indoctrination sessions (excuse me, make that orientation meetings—I think only the communists can use the word indoctrination anymore), an officer said victory means getting the North Vietnamese to respect the territory of the RVN. I haven't met anyone who sees that happening anytime soon.

Love to all. My platoon should be rotating into the field soon. I'll write when I can.

Jacob

"There, you see!" Ben said. "It's a letter to Dad that we're allowed to read."

Annalise sat back on her haunches and wiped her brow with her sleeve. The aggressive milkweed stalk lay dead at her side. "Oh, Ben, for God's sake, let it go."

A FEW DAYS later, Ben's righteous pique got a boost when Sandra received a letter of her own from Jacob. The letter was determinedly upbeat, full of vivid description and commentary about life in a place he said was more exotic than she could imagine. After cautioning that he couldn't write at length, he tumbled into a travelogue featuring humidity that would put a sauna to shame and which was made worse by the fumes of every conceivable kind of combustion engine.

The fruit and vegetables would be amazing if it weren't for the Clorox solution bath you have to give them to counteract the night soil (that's the polite term for human waste fertilizer, as I just learned). The street vendors sell "cute" star fruit (really—they look like stars) and something particularly loved by the locals called durian. The Americans call it garbage fruit, and that's putting it as politely as night soil. You wouldn't believe the stink. Imagine a case of cantaloupe festering in a hot room for a month and that wouldn't begin to describe it. The more it stinks, the more the locals like it, and the more they're willing to pay. You'd be amazed at what a prized (forgive the expression) durian goes for. I gag when I pass a hawker selling the stuff. And hawker is probably the right word. When you cut the thing open, it looks like snot on a rock. Also, did I mention that everyone hawks up here, all the time. Great globs of phlegm all over the place.

Okay, I suppose that's more than you wanted to know about hygiene and durian! On a brighter note, don't be surprised if I come home with a Vietnamese bride. I've never seen more beautiful women.

Only once did Jacob allow himself to drift into duskier territory. Adopting a tone similar to the earlier letter, the one Ben said was to Stephen, he wrote about how confused he often felt. He didn't elaborate beyond attributing the confusion mostly to having to learn the ropes quickly.

"A little more on that subject would be nice," Sandra said when she showed the letter to Ben. "I guess he reserves the serious detail for Dad, mano a mano, so to speak."

"Yeah, well at least you got a letter," Ben responded. He was sitting crosswise on his bed, his back propped against the wall and his attention focused on bouncing a basketball off a well-worn spot across the room.

"Maybe he's afraid you'd only lecture him," Sandra offered.

"He'd be right."

~ ~ ~ ~ ~

151

Chapter 16

Late November 1967: Quicksilver

❝YOU LOOK BEAUTIFUL TONIGHT,❞ Stephen said as he watched Annalise smooth her pale aubergine cocktail dress. It occurred to him only after he said it that it was one of those increasingly rare moments when a compliment could be given with spontaneity and full investment, and with a déja vu sense of early days between them.

They were getting ready for a party hosted by an editor at the *Journal*, Andrew Swanson, in honor of a retiring financial reporter. Andrew was several years Stephen's senior both in age and in tenure at the *Journal*. They had shared a few working lunches, water cooler sports postmortems, and after-work bull sessions at the editors' favorite hangout. They were not particularly close, but there was enough mutual liking for these occasions often to end in pledges to get together with the wives.

Annalise was checking herself in the full-length mirror on the back of the bedroom closet door. The dress was shorter than any she had worn before, and she was trying to reach a verdict. Stephen came up behind her and kissed the nape of her neck.

There was uncertainty in his movements, the product of the repeated rows, most rooted in their differences over Jacob. The kiss required a conscious decision to risk rejection that could sour the evening. He was relieved when she touched the hand on her shoulder and responded with a sincere, unfreighted, thank you.

Looking into the mirror, she said, "I have yet to get used to seeing so much leg. I hope I'm not becoming one of those deluded older women who thinks she looks attractive in her daughter's mod clothes."

"Not a chance."

The mirror reflected her smile. "Not a chance I'm deluded or that I'm an older woman?" She turned around and sealed the truce with a kiss on the lips light enough not to smear the freshly applied lipstick.

"Not a chance I'm delusional enough to think there's a good answer to that question. I also like your hair," he added. "It looks good shorter."

She thanked him for this, too, and for not remarking on—or perhaps, even better, not noticing—the recent color rinse masking the sprouts of gray.

Relieved and encouraged by the serendipitous truce, Stephen kissed her again, with more conviction but still some reserve.

"My lipstick," she cautioned.

"You can reapply it."

Another kiss, with more mutual heat.

"The dress, too," he whispered.

"The dress?"

"It can be reapplied, too."

She smiled. He unzipped.

More kisses soon led to fewer articles of clothing—removed with some care, her dress, his shirt and trousers. He unhooked her bra, slid the straps down her arms, let the bra drop to the floor. The remaining articles came off fast, with less care.

Still standing before the mirror, he cupped her breasts and knelt slightly, kissing one nipple, then the other. Then kissing harder, sucking, tugging gently. He could hear her breath quicken. She reached down, a little awkwardly, to touch him, held him, rubbed a thumb over shaft and head until he, fearing he might come too soon, knelt lower, beyond her reach. He removed her panties, inserting fingers at the waist and sliding them to the floor. He began to kiss and lick, parted her with his fingers, following with his tongue.

They fell to the bed, for the moment all that had divided them cast aside in a mania of lips, tongues, teeth, and trails where nails drew white and once or twice unnoticed red.

In full voice she came before he completely entered her, then he a moment later.

For a brief time, they lay quietly, side by side. He was feeling mellow—happy and grateful for the moment out of time, a respite from the mounting antagonisms over Jacob that had marked their lives.

She looked over to the clock on the nightstand. He propped himself on an elbow. The scars he had traced with his finger that first time, so long ago, were still there. Much fainter, white instead of mean red, less an overt symbol, not so much a source of self-consciousness. Silently he ran his finger along that same trail, until she shivered, and the last of their fever spike subsided.

* * *

THE DOORMAN HAD their names on a list when Stephen and Annalise arrived at the apartment building on 46th Street and Park Avenue. "It appears senior editors do quite well at *The Journal*," Annelise whispered as they took the elevator to the eighth floor.

"Probably not *this* well," Stephen responded. "I have the impression Andrew comes from money," he added, with the further smiling emendation, "And who would be better placed to grab inside stock tips?"

"I like this saying 'comes from money.' It's very expressive. It makes me think of a goddess rising out of a sea of dollar bills and gold coins."

A middle-aged Negro woman in an old-fashioned, heavily starched black and white uniform, met them at the door. She took their coats, draping them over her arm, and ushered them into a foyer with a black and white checkerboard marble floor that perfectly complemented the uniform. Several smartly dressed men and women could be seen sipping drinks and chatting. There was a promising energy in the room.

"I wonder if the maid is always here or just for the night," Annelise said in Stephen's ear. "Either way, it must be nice."

He smiled. "Careful, your capitalist aspirations are showing."

She returned the smile. "Where better than here?"

"There's Andrew," he said with a nod. "Come on. I'll introduce you."

"Besides, I'm curious, not envious," she added, taking the guiding hand.

Well over six-feet tall and completely bald except for a neatly barbered ear-to-ear semicircle fringe, Andrew bent slightly at the waist as he greeted Annalise. The gesture gave him a courtly, patrician appearance.

"No rock 'n' roll, eh?" Stephen said, as on the stereo Benny Goodman's orchestra kicked off "Don't Be That Way."

"Staid crowd tonight," Andrew responded.

Stephen laughed. "I'm afraid I come from a more rowdy journalistic tradition."

"Still good, though, isn't it? Goodman's 1938 Carnegie Hall concert. Harry James, Gene Krupa, Lionel Hampton, the whole gang. Do you know it?"

"I do," Stephen said.

Turning to Annalise, Andrew said, "I understand from Stephen that you two met in Germany."

Annalise's gracious "Yes, I was very lucky" failed to conceal the slight discomfort Stephen was able to detect in her face. He understood that the fact of their meeting in Germany was not significant (she made no secret of it), but she would feel cautious not knowing how much Stephen had disclosed about her and what she might say freely.

"Andrew's wife also is German," Stephen said.

"Yes," Andrew nodded enthusiastically. "Helga. I'm sure you'll have much in common. If I can find her, that is," he added, scanning the room obviously.

"Don't go to any trouble," Annalise said. "I'm sure we'll run into one another."

"Perhaps Germans attract," Andrew said, smiling.

"Now there's a frightening thought," Stephen responded with what he hoped would be taken as polite ambiguity. He and Annalise made for the opposite side of the living room, where a small bar had been expanded to accommodate the party. Along the way Annalise drew not a few admiring glances from the men, as well as some looks that were perhaps more critically judgmental from some of the women.

"You seem to be the belle of the ball," Stephen whispered.

"The what?"

At such times Stephen was taken aback to find Annalise unfamiliar with a common expression. Her English was good when they first met, and had become superb over the years. A quirk was that when she didn't know a word or phrase and asked about it, a slight Germanic inflection crept in—a whisker of *V* in the word *What*, for instance—as if to remind him how far she'd come with her adopted language. "The most beautiful woman at the party," he said.

She smiled. "I doubt it, but thank you."

She asked the bartender for a glass of white wine. Stephen asked for rye and soda, which seemed the drink of choice of the men in the room. He was happy to see her enjoying herself—happy that, for whatever reason, their bedroom truce seemed to be holding. It was certainly not something he could take for granted.

In recent months, as the tone of Jacob's letters became more frankly grim, and as Ben's eighteenth birthday approached, they had spent long stretches of time where only the quotidian demands of home and family broke the silence. On several occasions the mood was such that one or the other of them removed for the night to the convertible sofa in the guest bedroom.

Jacob's letters now were almost always addressed explicitly to the family as a whole, as he explained there was no time to write to people individually. They arrived sporadically; sometimes almost daily, sometimes weekly or less frequently in batches that posed a minor dilemma as to the order in which to read them. Last first? Or, perhaps with the discipline of one per day, as they were written, beginning with the oldest. Anxious for the most pertinent news, they usually chose to begin with the most recent.

Many of the letters were composed in the field, rather than in the rear areas where one might think Jacob would have more time to write. In one letter he explained that when he was on patrol he was often too wired to sleep even when sleep was possible. He wrote whenever he could snatch a moment, often at night with a flashlight under his poncho, and often in the rain—the proof of which was frequently evident in mud smears and water stains on the sheets of paper and the envelopes—using empty C-ration or ammunition boxes for a composition surface.

Conversely, it was when he got back to base that he caught up on his sleep.

At first, Jacob tried to be upbeat. His prose tended toward travelogue. Seldom did he write of specific hardship or discomfort, only very rarely did he mention casualties. Gradually, more honest, explicit accounts came forth. Like someone who, perhaps unconsciously, drifts from being shy when raising an embarrassing subject to providing every lascivious detail, Jacob began to complain about interminable, exhausting patrols, during which for weeks they were subjected to nothing but torrential rain or broiling, sultry sun. ("I'm a bug under a magnifying glass.") He wrote about mud, ravenous mosquitos, filthy uniforms that were more suitable for burning than laundering, more mud, and—surprising to all concerned—hunger. He complained about the insufficient calories in the C-rats and asked that packages from home include food: Spam (which he had always hated but he now requested almost reverently), tinned sardines and tuna—anything that would survive the trip and the weather. He said he lusted after Annalise's apple strudel but would settle for her oatmeal raisin cookies, noting that it didn't matter if they fell apart in transit, the crumbs would still be good.

All of these accounts, singularly and cumulatively, had profound, but differing, effects on the recipients back home. Annalise read every word, trying hard, though usually unsuccessfully, to disassociate the words from the person of Jacob. When the two merged she became frantic over his safety. Nevertheless, she persevered in her reading. Sandra and Ben took each letter as evidence of Jacob's (and Stephen's) folly, as one more argument against the war in general, and against Ben, himself, having any part in it.

Like the others, Stephen feared for Jacob's safety, but like Annalise, his personal experience in war made him less shocked at what Jacob described. Except in one respect, which was the source of greatest discord within the family and defensiveness on Stephen's part: No matter what horrors Stephen had witnessed in his war—sometimes *because* of the horrors he had witnessed—and no matter how critical he might have been about the feckless ways in which his war was conducted, he never considered his war to be unnecessary. Particularly in the time following Henry's death and the liberation of Dachau, if anything, he became more resolutely convinced of the need to win it.

Thus, it was with growing anxiety that he read Jacob's increasingly explicit professions of confusion, when, after weeks in the field, going from one hamlet to the next, he would wonder openly (and in ways Stephen was always surprised were not censored) what was being accomplished. Jacob was guarded about his own role, but his negative references to the government's obsession with body counts as almost the sole measure of success left little doubt. When the objective (Jacob underlined the word) was to kill VC—"good ole *Charlie*"—or flame Charlie's village, or destroy a bridge, what did it mean when, the next time out, the bridge had been rebuilt and Charlie seemed as plentiful (or as elusive) as ever—and "how the hell do we even know which papasan, mamasan, or babysan might *be* VC, anyway? What's the point of what we're doing? What's the point of the guys we're losing?"

* * *

STEPHEN INTRODUCED ANNALISE to several colleagues. They caught sight of the retiring honoree, a man named Paul Roby, who waved them over.

"He looks very young to be retiring," Annalise whispered.

"He is young," Stephen said under his breath as they started in Paul's direction. "Patrician. Tons of money. Retiring's not quite the word. He's moving on to play somewhere else. Until he becomes bored with that," Stephen added with an edge of disdain just before they came within orbital earshot.

Stephen introduced Annalise to Paul and the others with him, a wizened copy editor named William (not Bill if you please) and his wife, Carol, and an advertising department exec named Ralph, whose new fiancé, Mary Kate, hung on his arm, her left hand conveniently turned outward at an angle that ensured the facets of her ring refracted the most light possible. Stephen had met the first wife (or was it his second?) and was struck that Mary Kate was not only the requisite younger woman, but younger in a way he imagined nearly identical to the way the first wife must have looked.

158

From the moment Stephen had caught sight of them, the members of this particular group put him on guard. He knew well that, in an office that tended toward a pro-war point of view, these men stood out as being notably hawkish. Not that Stephen necessarily disagreed with them, but the last thing he wanted at the moment was to disturb the fragile equipoise so recently achieved with Annalise.

It didn't take long after introductions were made to arrive at the danger zone, when William, the copy editor, announced that Stephen (not Stephen and Annalise) had a draft-age son. "We've just been talking about the draft," he added.

"Almost," Annalise said. "Almost draft age."

"Ah, right, you already have a son in the service, don't you?" Paul asked.

"Yes," a cautious Stephen replied. "The army," he added, hoping Paul would let it go at that.

"He's in Nam, isn't he?" Paul said.

"Yes, he is," Stephen got in before Annalise had a chance to give a more elaborate answer.

"Good man," Ralph opined. "Good man," he repeated before adding, "We need men like him to win the war."

Stephen agreed but just as clearly didn't want to go down this road. Thus, he was relieved when, through a cloud of cigarette smoke, he spied Andrew and his wife across the room and excused himself and Annalise, pleading a need to pay respects to the host.

"Helga, this is the Stephen I've been talking your ear off about, and his charming wife Annalise," Andrew said as they drew near. "And dear guests, this is Helga, the fabulous, glamorous Teutonic wife I was telling you about."

Stephen agreed that Helga was glamorous. She was a Marilyn Monroe bleach blond type, but it was done well, somehow unnaturally natural. She had sharp features and bright olive eyes. Her cocktail dress, of obviously fine quality, accentuated an hourglass figure.

Stephen took the proffered manicured hand. Helga gave him a warm smile, as she did also with a slight turn to Annalise.

Stephen thought it a genuine smile. Also genuine—did anyone but Stephen notice?—was Annalise's frisson of recognition, which she covered quickly.

"Small world, eh?" Andrew said.

"I assume you don't mean only that we have German wives," Stephen said with a laugh. "I'd imagine that's actually a pretty large world."

The women joined in the laugh, but it struck Stephen that the levity was forced, especially on Annalise's part.

"Not generic German," Andrew clarified. "Displaced. Displaced Germans."

Helga said, "Oh, don't worry, Andrew. There are plenty of us too." Her English was clear and colloquial, but so was its provenance, much more so than with Annalise, who had managed to scrub away most of her linguistic roots. "I'm sure we have better things to talk about," Helga added with a lightly dismissive wave.

"I'm sure," Annalise echoed from what appeared to Stephen a strangely oblique posture, which favored Andrew more than Helga. "I hope you won't think me rude," Annalise said, "but would you point me to the powder room? I'm a little desperate, I'm afraid."

"Of course," Andrew and Helga said in unison and then laughed at the synchrony. "Just down that corridor, second door on the left," Andrew said, pointing.

Annalise thanked them and turned to go.

"Are you all right, hon?" Stephen asked after her.

"Yes, fine, just in a rush."

"When nature calls," Andrew said with a smile.

"True enough," Stephen said, affably. "I think I should make myself available just in case," he added, hoping no offense had been given.

"Of course," Helga responded.

Andrew waved his hand to indicate the rapidly growing number of guests. "What we need is a nice quiet dinner, just the four of us."

IN THE BATHROOM, the door securely latched, Annalise took a deep breath. Grasping the sink on either side, she locked her elbows and leaned in toward the mirror. She took another breath and stared at herself as if for the first time, focusing in the bright light on how the flaw—the black speck in her left eye—slightly distorted the field, like an air bubble trapped in a glass marble.

As she continued to stare, the image in the mirror changed, went back twenty-plus years, and now she was her hollow-cheeked self, standing in a gray-plank barracks, dim naked bulbs dropped from the ceiling on single cords. In the background, a pot-bellied stove gave off barely detectable heat.

Not Dachau.

Months before.

Buchenwald.

And a soldier approaching, an officer, one she hadn't seen before, young, junior (but how much did the seniority really matter)? He was smiling. Not cruelly this one, almost pleasant, as he prepared to lead her to a walled-off area she knew well—had been led to how many times? She was no longer keeping count. There they would do it quickly, or slowly, or savagely, or sometimes, rarely, with a regretful tender face staring down at her.

Just barely, casually in her field of vision behind the young soldier, standing near the stove, was a woman who arranged these liaisons, who was in fact known by Annalise and others like her as "the arranger." The woman, also an inmate but of a different caste, a sharp-featured brunette with a figure still—improbably—shapely, and who somehow was past the point of being used as Annalise was being used, or at least it seemed so, gave the officer to Annalise as one might lend a book from a library. For reasons she could only guess, Annalise had become a favorite of the woman, who tried to assign her cleaner, less loutish men (or, again, so it seemed) and who had once told her that it was good that they should work well together, as that way they just might both survive.

The vision, clear as air now, was upset by a knock on the bathroom door followed by Stephen's sotto voce inquiry, "Are you all right?"

To which she responded in as steady a voice as she could, "Fine. I'll be right out. Go mingle. I'll find you."

After a moment, she unlocked the door and tried to push to the back of her mind the only part of the vision she was incapable of erasing completely—that of the arranger, the woman who she was as certain as she could be was now a blonde who went by the name Helga Swanson.

* * *

STEPHEN WAS WATCHING for Annalise as she scanned the room looking for him. He gave a slight wave, and she smiled. He was perplexed, both by the anxious visage he caught as she had looked for him and the relief he read into the smile.

"Are you okay?" he asked yet again.

"I'm fine." She took his arm.

He gave a sidelong glance, whispered in her ear, "You can't kid a kidder."

"Really. My insides went a little wobbly, that's all. I'm fine now. Let's socialize."

He refreshed their drinks, then led her to friends and colleagues he wanted her to meet.

Outwardly, she had regained her usual charm. Yet he couldn't help noticing that everywhere they circulated it was as if she were nudging him outside the conversational range of Andrew and Helga.

* * *

ANNALISE WAS QUIET on the ride home. She responded to Stephen's comments on the party with set pieces that encouraged no flow from Stephen's end, but more importantly required no thinking from hers that would crowd out the guilty thoughts already filling her head. Guilty not so much for the visions that had returned—with enormous effort over the years she had been able to reach the point where, on those occasions when memories of her war insinuated themselves, she was able to resist blaming and punishing herself—but guilty because this part of the history, the Buchenwald chapter, had been withheld from Stephen. There were moments when she had considered

162

unburdening herself to him, but those moments had escaped, and unlike her own memories, which she allowed to become less painful with time, the prospect of making the revelation to Stephen became ever more difficult.

Finally, when they stopped for a light, Stephen looked at her evenly. "Are you going to tell me what happened back there? It was something to do with Andrew and Helga. I could see it."

"It was nothing, Stephen. I told you."

"I wish I could believe you, hon, but I know you too well. In any case, I hope you're leveling with me, because if I know Andrew, there'll be dinner for the four of us in the near future."

~ ~ ~ ~ ~

Chapter 17

January 1968: Beyond Your Command

S ITTING AT HIS DESK two days after New Year's Eve, Stephen was staring ineffectually at the op-ed he was trying to edit for the next day's edition. He was still regretting the quantity and variety of alcohol he had consumed on the occasion, as well as a quantity he didn't want to guess of Lucky Strikes (continuing the brand loyalty established during his war). He had waved off Annalise's recent remark that if he insisted on feeding his smoker's cough, the least he could do was switch to a filtered brand. When he practically heaved up a lung the following morning and then again today, it didn't seem like such a bad idea to begin thinking of ways to quell his body's increasingly manifest rebellion. He was, after all, solidly past forty now.

His mood wasn't helped by the piece he was editing—yet another military expert advising that setbacks in Vietnam not be allowed to derail an all-out effort to achieve victory. "We're closer to winning than many of the war's misguided detractors think," the expert wrote.

It wasn't so much that Stephen disagreed with the thrust of the piece as that he was tired of the subject. Whether at work, at home, or in the world, as the troops liked to refer to any reality that wasn't theirs, he couldn't escape the multi-front carping. And as much as he might agree with opinions on the right, and to feel derision for the frothy views put forth by the so-called flower children and their supporters and sponsors, he was simply getting bored listening to, and editing, essentially the same arguments repackaged as fresh brilliance.

Moreover, if opponents of the war were right that the country was "mired" in Southeast Asia, Stephen was certain that the country couldn't be any more mired than he was at home within his own family.

Ever since Ben and Sandra thumbed their noses at him and Annalise and joined October's massive march on the Pentagon, Stephen had stewed over the loss of parental authority that he saw not only with his own kids but all around him. This wasn't a particularly big problem with Sandra. Disobedience regarding the October episode aside, her protesting ways were taking a back seat to completing her nursing program. Besides, she was over twenty, already beyond the age when several of her friends had moved out on their own. His sway over her increasingly was reduced to pathetically banal declarations beginning with the phrase, "As long as you're living under my roof." Fortunately, such declarations were seldom necessary.

But Ben. What to do about Ben?

As far as Stephen was concerned, Ben was getting completely out of control, and for once, Annalise agreed. They both saw Ben's disobedience in going to Washington as the crossing of a line that exposed any remaining illusions of authority. Not that they hadn't tried, but they were running out of punishments and incentives. Stephen's temperament and traditional views on filial defiance ("I wouldn't dream of so blatantly disobeying my father") kept his outrage within easy reach.

The most recent provocation involved Ben's grades. After repeated assurances that his studies were going well, or at any rate, well enough, Ben failed half the subjects in the first semester of his senior year.

For Annalise, once again, the overriding issue was the specter of the draft. She waved the report card close to his face. "What's the matter with you!"

Ben shrugged and said he was thinking of dropping out anyway.

"Dropping out and being drafted! Are you out of your mind! Do you know how many boys have been killed over there so far!" She visibly blanched at the inadvertent release of fright over Jacob.

A recounting that night of Ben's derisive response to Annalise sent Stephen into a fit of his own. "Ben said *what*?" he asked as if he had not heard correctly.

"He said I was the one who was out of my mind, that I must not understand a thing about him if I thought after all his protesting of the war he would allow himself to be drafted."

"Meaning?"

"I suppose that he'll run away first. He'll go to Canada or something."

"The hell he will!"

"Let me finish. He didn't actually say that. Only I don't know what else he could mean. I've never heard him talk about becoming an official objector, if that's what you call it, or about going to jail to avoid the draft. So what's left?"

She let Stephen stew for a good ten minutes before she said, quietly, "Stephen, I'd never tell him this, but I'd prefer he went to Canada if the other choice is having both my sons in Vietnam. I suppose Jacob would finish his tour before Ben went over. Even so, Ben would be in danger and we would spend another year in fear."

"That's impossible, Annalise," Stephen responded, at least better containing his anger now. "Not only is it cowardly and immoral—especially when Jacob is doing the right and honorable thing—it would kill his future. Doesn't he realize that? Doesn't he realize what it would mean to be a fugitive for perhaps the rest of his life? To give up everything here—his family, his friends?"

* * *

NOT LONG AFTER this conversation, Stephen violated his ideals of privacy and went snooping in Ben's room. He rationalized it with fear over what Ben might be hiding about school and the draft—fear that was given additional impetus when Annalise stumbled on a hash pipe and a roach clip hidden in a flower pot inside the garage.

"Did you find anything?" Annalise asked after Stephen had given her a litany of excuses for what he had done. He had assumed, without ever having really tested the assumption, that her experience of living in Nazi Germany would have made her staunchly on the side of Ben's personal privacy. If so, this was trumped by her terror over Jacob and Vietnam, as well as by the discovery of the drugs paraphernalia (drugs tools, as she put it). Thus, she surprised him by accepting his explanations in the spirit of a sermon to the converted.

"No, not really."

"No? Or not really?"

Stephen blew out his cheeks. "A letter." It was not something he wanted to reveal, and not only because of the privacy issue, but also because he knew how she would react. But now, on impulse, he decided the letter was too important to withhold, even if it upset her and started a row.

"Who from?" Annalise asked.

"Jacob."

"You read a letter to Ben from Jacob?"

"It wasn't really concealed," Stephen said, his tone defensive, uncertain. "I found it in his desk drawer, which wasn't completely closed. At first, I wasn't going to read it. In fact, I glanced at it and put it back without reading it. But it was obviously Jacob's handwriting, and a few words caught my eye. I told myself I'd just scan it to make sure there wasn't something important we needed to know." He shrugged. "One paragraph led to another."

"And?"

"And what?"

"What did you discover?" she asked, impatiently.

He started to summarize, maneuvering around the points he was most concerned about—about how they would affect her, beyond any ethics of privacy—involving Jacob's regrets over having gone to Vietnam. He recognized at once that he was doing a bad job of it and decided there were bigger things at stake than whether he would have to fend off another assault from his wife.

"Stephen, you're not making sense."

After taking a deep breath, he said, "Maybe it would be best for you to read it yourself."

She didn't hesitate. The expression on her face told him he had only succeeded in heightening her fears.

He followed her upstairs and led her to the desk. "Here," he said, handing her the letter. "If you're cornered, you can always say I was the purloiner."

"The what?"

"The thief."

"Oh." She sat heavily at Ben's underused Formica-top study desk. When she unfolded the letter, a photo dropped into her lap. It was a small, glossy, black-and-white Polaroid shot of Jacob, dressed in fatigues and giving the camera a sardonic smile. He was standing next to a larger man, also in fatigues, also smiling in a way that might have seemed intended strictly for the benefit of the camera. She held the photo out in front of her and squinted for a different perspective, or as if she feared getting too close. She turned it over, read "Me and Al Oct '67."

"Al," she said aloud.

"It'll become clear when you read the letter."

She laid it in front of her and smoothed it open, taking care to avoid dislocating the creases.

> *Ben,*
>
> *I'm sending this one only to you. You can share it with Sandy if you want. I think it would only cause a fight if I sent it to Mom and Dad.*

"Well," Annalise said, looking up. "Ben didn't try very hard to hide it, did he?"

"I know. Either he's placed trust—apparently unwarranted—in our respect for his privacy or, consciously or unconsciously, he wants us to read it."

With an audibly anxious sigh, Annalise continued reading.

> *I'm upset right now. Very upset. So take that into consideration. Also, what I have to say may seem a bit garbled—a bit out of whack. Make what you can of it. I need to blow off some steam.*
>
> *First of all, I'm okay—not injured anyway. I just returned from what seemed like an endless patrol. I won't go into details of where, just in case the censors are doing their jobs. (Then, again, they may be as useless as everyone else in this man's army.)*

We were out for almost a month. To put what happened in perspective, you have to understand what it means to be humping in the field for that long, and that these are things people back in the world haven't got a clue about.

Let me start with basic fucking exhaustion. The terrain is impossible. You probably get to see the wide shots of rice paddy on TV. Looks beautiful, I'm sure. What they don't show is how hard it is to slog through the stuff. I'm in the best physical shape of my life, but my legs wobble like Jell-O after a day out. Don't forget, it's me and my 65-pound pack and my M60 (I'm the squad's machine gunner, remember?) that I have to hump. If it's not paddy, then it's long grass or hills—well, you get the idea.

Seems like every other minute we catch some kind of movement and have to hit the deck. It might be nothing. Maybe a breeze. But it could be Charlie.

And while you're looking around to see the source of the movement, you sure as shit better be looking at where you're planting your feet. Otherwise you might step on a mine and lose your legs, arms, head—you name it. Or fall into a tiger trap. Charlie is very clever about covering these up so you can't see them until it's too late, and also clever about the nasty things that might be waiting for you if you fall in. A couple of months ago I saw a guy land on bamboo sticks all sharpened to a mean point. He screamed as he fell—you know what's going to happen to you before you land—then screamed again as the stakes went straight through him like some giant monster had picked him up with a fork. That guy was lucky. He was impaled through his heart, so it was quick. If the stakes had missed his vitals, it would have taken a lot longer, and I don't need to tell you, it's not a pretty death.

Of course, there are lots of other evil things waiting. Lots of simple booby traps, for instance. Walk through a tripwire and Boom! Maybe a grenade goes off, and so does your dick.

Oh, and punji sticks. Talk about simple and effective! It's the sharp bamboo thing again, but this time you don't need to fall into a pit. All you need is for the stick to pierce your boot. The tip might have poison on it. But they don't even need to be that sophisticated.

All they have to do is put a little shit on it (I mean literally). Believe me, in this heat and humidity your foot's sure to become infected in no time. I personally know guys who had to have a foot amputated. All things considered, they may have been the lucky ones—at least they got to go home. There are lots of self-inflicted wounds for that purpose, by the way. I'm told it doesn't hurt so much if you're stoned, which at least half the guys here are, all the time—makes life bearable but doesn't do much for buddy reliability.

Did I mention it gets hot and humid? Hot and humid as hell, actually. Everything rots here. When the rains sweep in, I swear, you're never dry. Sometimes my feet feel like they're going to rot away. The only advantage to the big rains is sometimes they uncover the traps so you can spot them. Small comfort. When it's not raining, everything can turn brown, which creates different problems.

There are forests here, too. Good for hiding Charlie. So, as you've probably seen on the tube, the military uses napalm to clear them out. Napalm—sounds nice, like a hand cream, doesn't it? Ha Ha. Don't let the name fool you. It's nothing but jellied gasoline that sticks to everything it touches. Sometimes the targeting is a wee bit off and our own guys are turned into crispy critters. Ditto for when our asshole officers call in artillery on our heads.

I have never felt so alone . . . so abandoned, as when I'm out on patrol.

Stephen watched as silent tears tracked over Annalise's cheeks. She swiped at them before they could hit the letter.

We're supposed to be resupplied as we go, of course. Guess what? We're not, or at least not regularly. And if the genius quartermasters have to choose what to send us? Well, ammo, of course. Food? Even crappy C-rats would be welcome. I think I've written to you about this before, but we actually go hungry here. Dry clothes? Ha! By the time we return from patrol our uniforms are falling off. We're lucky if there's enough material left to cover our balls.

I could go on, and I probably will when I get up for writing another "travelogue," but I haven't even got to the part that's got me so upset.

So, let me tell you the story of . . . well, I won't use his real name, just in case. Of what I don't know, but just in case. I'll call him . . . Oh, fuck it! What's the difference? His name is Al. (I've enclosed a snap.)

It's a funny thing here. You can easily get to the point where you're afraid to make friends. Afraid they'll end up boiled in oil or some damn thing. On the other hand, sometimes you make friends really fast, like you don't know how much time you've got and you're both in the same shit soup, so nothing is held back, and before you know it, you have a buddy you'd lay down your life for. That's how it happened between me and Al.

Here's another funny thing about being in this shithole, and it's actually a good thing: You get to make friends with people you wouldn't give a second thought to back in the world. Al's a good example. He's from Texas. (I found out by accident that his name is really short for Alferd—not a typo. He said if I ever called him that, he'd brain me.)

We had absolutely zero in common. His father is a welder on oil rigs, and also a preacher, the kind who speaks in tongues or some such shit. NO FUN ALLOWED. No drinking, smoking, dancing, not even singing unless it's a hymn. The only Jews Al knew about were from the Old Testament. Because of that he had good things to say about us as "People of the Book," but always ended by saying we're going to burn in hell anyway. It became a joke between us.

I could go on for hours about our differences. I'd mention bagels and lox and he'd look at me like I was the one speaking in tongues. The amazing thing is that we still found a kind of comradeship that I really can't put into words. I suppose we were connected by our feelings about this place and all of its weirdness. There was trust between us that, especially here, is worth more than gold.

If I've been mixing up my verb tenses in telling this story, you've probably guessed the reason. Al is in my thoughts, but he's not in this world anymore.

Here's the short version. One day not long ago, we went out on patrol. We were dropped by chopper into an area we were assured by the intel guys had been secured. Not to get too far off track, but you need to understand two things: First, a "secured" area means we've swept every hamlet around, which means we've killed just about everything that moves. Pregnant woman? No prob. Grandpa? No biggie. Anyone could be VC, even little kids, so we've learned not to take chances.

Which brings me to the second point: There really is no such thing as a secured area. It's no accident that when the choppers come in to drop off troops, they barely touch down before the pilots haul ass out of there, because if they linger they'll get their "secure" gonads shot off. The military brass and the politicians talk about places being "pacified." Don't you believe it. Unless by pacified they mean we've scorched everything—people, plants, and animals—that ever lived.

On that day, at first, it looked like the J2 guys might have been right for a change. We walked in patrol formation, and nothing bad happened. But that's the thing about Nam. Nothing happens, until it does.

About two miles from the drop zone, Al stepped on a punji stick. He was a big guy . . . heavy . . . so when he stepped on it, it went through everything and came out between the laces. You could see by the discoloration at the point that the stick had been dipped in something or other. Actually, deluded guys that we are, we thought Al might have caught a lucky break. If the stick hadn't gone clear through ("clear through"—got that? I'm talking like a Texan!), we reasoned it might have had more time to do its nasty business.

After Al stepped on the stick, there was a commotion, but not as much as you might expect. We're used to stuff like this, and usually a lot worse. We got Al settled down, got him to a small clearing, and called in a Medevac chopper.

So, here's how it goes. We wait for I don't know how long, but not really too bad considering, and here comes the chopper with a nice big red cross on its nose. We clear a perimeter to make sure Charlie's not lurking. The chopper lands (well, more like hovers a few feet off the ground—the pilots are very good at that). So far, so good.

And then, one of the guys near me drops. Bullet clear through (that Texas-ese again) helmet and head. Just that one shot. Everyone's yelling "Sniper!"

And then more shots, from all over. The chopper scrams. We don't know where the fuck these guys are, so we return fire everywhere out beyond the perimeter (some perimeter we'd set, huh)? This is where my M60 helps. I was already set up, and I let loose a sweep of suppressing fire.

After a pretty short while, the incoming fire stopped—don't know why, whether they'd done their day's work or we hit a bunch of them. The chopper touched down again, and the guys were able to get Al aboard. (Amazing how fast this can be done when you're afraid someone is going to shoot you. And I have to tell you, this Medevac pilot was brave. I've seen lots of them where, if they see there's any kind of incoming in the landing zone, they're outta there, which as I said, this guy was, the difference being that he came back as soon as he thought he was clear.)

Right, so Al's aboard, the chopper's lifting off, and we're not taking fire. My gun sweeps might have done some good, and in the meantime, we've called in the air cavalry and you can hear the rotor thwumps in the distance.

The chopper rises to, maybe, fifty feet off the ground. And then a single rifle grenade, perfectly placed, goes through the open door and explodes. For a second, the chopper just hovers, like a bee that's been stung by a wasp—just for that second. And then, when the frozen second is done, a huge explosion—a fireball of chopper and fuel.

All of us on the ground were stunned. I couldn't believe it. Somehow in the course of maybe less than an hour we'd gone from safe drop to uneventful patrol to punji stick to . . . this. There wasn't enough left of my bud from Texas to bury. I'm sure his preacher parents got some nice letter from the army about what a hero he was.

I'm writing this now like I'm some kind of news reporter. Straight up. But I don't want you to get the wrong idea. You don't know how

173

much Al's death got to me. Later, when we finally got to the rear, all I wanted was to be left alone. I'd go off by myself and just sit. Without realizing it, this strange liquid stuff would fill my eyes and begin dripping down my cheeks. If someone came along, I'd turn away and wipe my face on my sleeve. And then I'd think, amazing that with all I've gone through, I still have some ridiculous need to be the macho man. No crying for this GI!

So, why am I writing this now? Why am I opening up now, when I haven't done it before?

Because I'm not just sad. I'm angry. Really, really angry—more angry than you'll ever be able to comprehend. You know when people talk about something leaving a bitter taste in their mouth? I can tell you, it's not just an expression. I can taste the bitterness all the time, and nothing covers it up.

The simple fact is, I don't know why Al died. I don't know why any of us has to die here.

Everything we've been told about why we're here is a big fat fucking lie. Everything we're still being told about why we're here is a lie. We're keeping Communism at bay? Bullshit! All I can imagine is that there are a bunch of Russkies and Chicoms laughing up their sleeves at the sight of their number-one enemy pinned down in this giant swamp, squandering lives and treasure like there's no limit to it.

LBJ says we're winning. Really? If this is what winning looks like, I'd sure hate to be losing. And winning what, exactly? Oh, yeah, I remember—body counts. We're killing more than we're being killed, though it sure doesn't feel like it or like it makes a difference.

And democracy? We're fighting for democracy here? What a sick joke. These fucking people wouldn't know democracy if it hit them over the head with a fifty-pound ballot box. Believe me, there is nothing, absolutely nothing we can do to bring democracy to Vietnam.

Remember when we all went downtown to see King speak? All of a sudden what he said really means something to me. The idea that we've got all these Negro boys over here "fighting for democracy" when they can't even piss in the same bathroom as white people at

174

home . . . well, that has to be the sickest joke anyone ever thought up. It's no surprise black people back home are angry. The surprise is they don't shoot every white they see, just like everyone over here, black or white, would like to frag their stupid, incompetent officers (not that I know anything specific, dear censors).

I admit, I bought into this shit. Yeah, I went to the protests with you and all that. But really, I had no idea. I bought into what we were being told, and even when I didn't, I accepted that I had to serve my country. Now I know that I would have served my country a lot better by resisting being shipped over here.

I was a coward. There! I said it! And not a coward as I'd ever thought about being. It turns out I can face the bullets and the tiger traps. Not that I'm not afraid, but it's fear I overcome here every day. No, I'm a coward because I was too afraid to do what you and Sandra do—confront Dad. When Dad would talk about fulfilling my duty in a democratic society, I found it was easier to go along—to be the good boy—than it was to go my own way, to think for myself and be my own man.

I've thought a lot about this. Do I blame Dad? Yes. But only to a point. The fact is, whenever I thought about resisting the draft, I became afraid of the consequences. Not only would I be defying him and placing myself outside the main part of so-called patriotic America. I would be ruining the ideas I had about myself. Could any of the plans I had for the future—or of how I saw myself when I looked in the mirror—be squared with a record as a draft dodger?

I'll tell you one thing: Not applying to a school I was sure I could get into was the biggest mistake of my life. I mean, what the fuck was I thinking? I can't tell you how much I'd like that deferment now. What I think about now is getting home and warning people.

So I'm going to start with you, little brother! I know you're already against the war. But let me be clear: If there's any way in hell you can avoid joining me over here, do it! The easiest way is to stay in school. Not that I don't have questions about the morality of that, too. One of the first things you see in this shithole is that it's full of people whose parents don't have enough money to educate them out of the draft. So the worst of it over here is being shouldered by poor people, especially (King again) poor Negroes who really ought to be home fighting for their rights. But you probably still have the deferment option, so moral or not, take it.

Stay cool (and study, dick-brain)! I'll write again when I can.
Jake

Stephen was quiet while Annalise finished reading. He watched intently for her reaction, taking note of the places she paused or read something again. From the day he met her in Dachau, a defining characteristic had been self-control. Not that she wasn't capable of showing anger, or any other emotion for that matter, but he never had the impression that she wasn't, on some fundamental level, in control. And it was precisely this control that had the ability to unsettle him.

Now he couldn't read her face; it was turned away as she gazed out the window at bare branches and a raw-steel sky. At times while she was reading—and she'd read the letter slowly, as if needing to let each word ferment—he saw her hands tremble. And when she did look up, it was away from him.

"When was the letter sent?" she asked, absently, before checking the first page.

"A few weeks ago."

She continued to stare out the window. "It doesn't seem like Ben has taken the advice to heart." She turned toward Stephen. Her face was blank, empty of expression, making it appear she was talking through, rather than to him.

"I know."

"He hasn't taken his schoolwork any more seriously than before. He hasn't done anything to show he cares about graduating and going on to someplace that might get him a deferment. In fact," she said more directly to Stephen, "I have a sickening feeling that he doesn't want a deferment—that he wants to stand up and tell the draft board to go to hell."

"Well, I hope he at least understands that draft boards don't look kindly on being told to go to hell. Maybe he doesn't realize what that would mean."

"Or he does, and this is the rebellion he's choosing. It could be that's why he throws the idea of running away in our faces so often."

"Well, you know how I feel about that."

Annalise stood. She refolded the letter along its creases and placed it in the drawer as she remembered when Stephen had removed it.

"I should have fought you," she said now, forthrightness returning to her face and voice. But it was a calm sort of forthrightness, determined and self-possessed.

"Annalise . . ."

She shook her head. "I should have fought you for our son's sake. For both of their sakes."

"No, Annalise, you . . ."

But she wouldn't let him finish. "I'm not going to stand here and argue about Jacob. It's too late. All we can do is pray he returns in one piece. But I want you to promise me something."

Annalise paused to find the words she was looking for. Stephen remained silent.

"About Ben," she continued. "I want you to promise that whatever he does—whether he goes to jail or runs away to Canada or anywhere else—I want you to promise that you will support him."

She didn't wait to hear his answer before she left the room.

~ ~ ~ ~ ~

Chapter 18

January 1968: Terms of Sacrifice

ANNALISE MIGHT HAVE RESTED slightly easier had she known Sandra had taken up her cause. As soon as Sandra read Jacob's letter, which Ben shared with her immediately, she began a panicked campaign to ensure Ben found a deferment.

"I don't get you!" she said to him, barging into his room without knocking and raising her voice to be heard over Jefferson Airplane's booming victory refrain, "We got a revolution." Once again Ben was demonstrating determined nonchalance by thudding a basketball against the wall. It would have surely brought a vigorous complaint from either or both of his parents had they been home.

Now it was getting to Sandra, too. "Could you stop doing that? And could you turn down the stereo?" she added, brushing off the Airplane's repetitive proclamation that "we're volunteers of America."

With a facial expression that suggested his own irritation with Sandra, he continued bouncing the ball off the wall until she caught it on a rebound. "This is important, Ben," she said, as she cradled it against her body.

Ben stared at her in annoyance. He pushed the hair out of his eyes. He had to do this often since it had grown almost to shoulder length. Like his adolescent skin, now sprouting a scraggly beard, his hair always appeared oily, no matter how often he claimed to wash it. "Yeah, I know," he said. "I'm tired of thinking about it."

"Well, you gave me the letter," she protested.

"I didn't think it would turn you into Mom. I thought we were on the same wavelength." He motioned for her to give the ball back.

She ignored the request. "We *are* on the same wavelength. None of us wants you to go to Vietnam."

"There's no chance of that. So what's your problem?" He opened his arms to receive the ball again.

"But *how* are you going to avoid it? Yes, I know, you can run away. What I don't get is why you'd want to run away if you don't have to. It's not too late to get your grades up. You're not failing *that* badly, are you? Though God knows why with as little work as you've done. All you'd have to do is squeak by. Just enough to graduate. Then you could get into some school—Jesus, *any* school as long as it got you a deferment. You saw what Jake wrote. Not getting a deferment was the biggest mistake of his life. Why do you have to make the same mistake?"

Ben pushed himself forward to the edge of the bed and planted his feet on the floor. "One, it's probably not true that I can get in someplace. It may be too late to bring up my grades enough. They're worse than you think. Two, I hate school, or haven't you noticed? I don't *want* to do the schoolwork. I want to be done with it."

"You'll hate Vietnam a lot more."

"Three," he said, shaking the hair out of his eyes, "I also agree with what Jake said about the system being unfair. I'm against the war, and I'm against using a rich man's loophole to get out of it."

"Yeah? Well I agree with Jake, too—especially the part where he says you should do it anyway."

"What can I say?" He shrugged.

"I hope you realize that running away will make things *mucho* difficult for you. Or maybe you don't realize it. Have you actually thought about what life will be like as a fugitive? Having to live on the run aside, how will you live? Dad will cut you off, that's for sure."

"Let him."

She rolled her eyes.

"So he'll cut me off. I'm not a retard. I'll figure something out."

"Anyway," Sandra continued, inspired to make a final frontal assault, "where did you get the idea that running away is the brave thing to do?

179

You really want to take a stand? Why don't you apply for conscientious objector status?"

"For the same reason Jake didn't. I'm not a C.O. I don't think all wars are stupid or immoral, just this one. Besides, they're making it really hard to qualify."

"Okay, then how about going to jail?"

He laughed. "You mean like Cassius Clay . . . uh, excuse me, Muhammad Ali?"

"What's so funny about that? Ali is sacrificing a lot for his beliefs. Now *he's* really brave. The point is, you'd be exercising your conscience. Besides, jail might be bad, but it's not Nam."

"If I go to jail, the government still wins. That's the problem."

"I don't understand. How is the government winning?"

He shook his head as if she were a simpleton. "It's winning because it gets to punish the people who are against it. It's a dumb way to resist."

"Tell that to King or Gandhi."

"Yeah, next time I see them."

"What a jerk." She turned to go, slamming the door behind her and ignoring the protest that she still had his ball.

~ ~ ~ ~ ~

Chapter 19

January 1968: The Unblinking Tube

A T THE END OF January, the family was gathered around the kitchen table for dinner—an event which, to Annalise's regret in particular, was becoming increasingly rare. Sandra's nursing program was intensive and demanding. Stephen was busier than ever at the office. Ben was . . . who knew? Trying to corral him was nearly impossible. Even Annalise, whose schedule tended to be flexible, found herself ever busier with translation work. As for Jacob, his absence was a palpable presence. When the family did manage a meal together, Annalise insisted on setting a place for him. "My Elijah," she would say with a grim smile.

They were about to watch the *CBS Evening News*. Having a TV in the kitchen was a recent thing. It required overcoming longstanding objections from Annalise that the kitchen table was meant for eating and meaningful conversation. Stephen, who agreed with Annalise and who for years joined her in resisting the kids' pleas for mealtime TV watching, finally surprised everyone when he broke down and came home with a new set.

Stephen justified the purchase by saying that, with so much going on in the world—and with so much covered in near-real time by the networks, increasing competition for what he considered to be the real press—it was harder and harder for him to keep abreast of things. Staying on top of current events had become even more important lately, as his responsibilities had expanded to include a growing international portfolio. He appeased Annalise by saying that during family meals the TV would be reserved for "edifying watching," and a springboard to discussion. The TV sat on a new rolling metal cart with a gold-tone finish and clear plastic wheels, the wheels being another selling point, as he assured Annalise that if the discussion failed to materialize, the unit could be easily rolled to a new location and the experiment abandoned.

By and large, the box's more noble purpose did emerge, although not without some unintended consequences, the most important of which probably could have been predicted—the family being subjected to ever more ubiquitous, graphic, and frightening reminders of the war. Often, the reporting on the war led not to intellectually stimulating discussion, but to angst-filled silence in which no exchange of views was needed; each knew perfectly well where the others stood. Of course, the real common denominator was Jacob. And now, increasingly, Ben.

In a way, Stephen was in the most awkward position. He not only had Jacob's safety on his mind, but as the only supporter of the war (though not without growing reservations he kept to himself), he found it hard not to become, reflexively, defensive when the reporting was negative, which increasingly was the case.

Just recently this dilemma had landed on him particularly hard with reports of a sudden attack on the American base at Khe Sanh. Any complacency one might have been inclined to feel over the progress of the war was jolted when the initial attack killed eighteen marines outright, wounded forty more, and managed to hit the ammunition dump, practically wiping out the base stockpiles and turning the sky into a random fireworks display that continued for days.

"Jesus Christ! That can't be dumb luck, can it?" Stephen demanded then, addressing the universe in the guise of the Zenith. "They'd better find a way to relieve those poor bastards," he muttered, using coarser language than Annalise, who had left the kitchen to talk to a neighbor at the front door, tolerated at the dinner table. "Not to mention the public perception disaster if that base is lost," he added.

"Oh, yes," Sandra said. "It's the P.R. we should be worried about."

"You know what I mean," Stephen responded.

Annalise returned to the table carrying a bowl of Jell-O salad and took her usual seat next to Jacob's. For all her fear-based passion over the war, she seemed to work hard at not joining the debates about it that broke through mealtime reticence. The role she had established for herself on those occasions was one of referee, whose chief function was not to adjudicate on substance, but rather to keep arguments from violating implicit rules of civility and decent language. It was a wonder to Stephen that she could keep her emotions in check; he concluded it must have something to do with fear of what might happen if she let them out.

"I do know what you mean, Dad. That's the trouble," Sandra said. "I look at those poor kids and I think about their families, like us, back home. I already know we're not winning a war we shouldn't be fighting in the first place. What you're worried about is that too many people may come to understand this."

"Don't be so naïve, Sandy. What the people at home believe has a real effect on the battlefield. I'd hate to think what my war would have been like if the people on the home front had a steady diet of the things we see every night. I guarantee, the pressure to call a truce would have been enormous. And I also guarantee, letting the Nazis and the Japs off the hook like that would have been an unspeakable disaster."

A derisive laugh erupted from Ben. "I think we've got the reverse of that problem. What'll we say if the Vietnamese demand *our* unconditional surrender?"

"For crying out loud, Ben, be serious."

"I am being serious. What? When something like Khe Sanh happens, you don't think our noble leaders don't start freaking out over what happened to the French at Dien Bien Phu?" Ben followed this with a possible impersonation of LBJ, complete with finger jabbed into an imaginary chest: *I don' wahnt any damn Dinbinfoo!* "It's true!" Ben insisted, cutting off his father. "I heard that's what he told the Joint Chiefs."

"Once again, Dad, I don't know why you don't get this, but these are not the Germans or the Japanese we're fighting," Sandra offered.

"That doesn't mean they aren't our enemies, or merely, quote, misguided or misunderstood people, as some of your hippie friends might put it."

Sandra ignored the taunt. "Well, they're not bad people, or anyway not any worse than most. They're human, that's all."

"The Vietnamese are *revolutionaries*, Dad!" Ben put in. "Christ! You'd think Americans would understand people wanting their own country."

"And the South Vietnamese?" Stephen asked, obviously straining to keep his cool.

"They didn't get a choice either. How'd we have liked it if some foreign country decided during our Civil War that we *should* be two countries, north and south, and sent their army to enforce it?"

"Well, son, not to split hairs, but the British pretty much tried that with their navy."

"So? What's your point?"

"One of my points, snotty kid, is that I'm tired of the antiwar people making it sound like we're the bad guys and the North Vietnamese are poor, saintly victims."

"I repeat, what's your point?" Ben said, his rising voice placing him in jeopardy of Annalise's reproof. "You think the NVA and the Cong do bad things? You think their tiger traps are any worse than the napalm we drop?"

"What I think is that someday you'll come to understand that the world is not a logical place, that things are not black or white, and that there is real evil in it—that there are people who are truly bad, not just *misunderstood*." He let the word ooze. "We may not be perfect, but compared to many others—and for sure next to the North Vietnamese— we look pretty damn good."

The sound that emanated from Sandra could only be interpreted as her own version of derision. However, the words that followed before Stephen could object were more conciliatory. "Someday, Dad, I think *you'll* come to understand that even if the U.S. is better than most, it is still capable of things as horrible as any. Think slavery. Think American Indians. And yeah, think Vietnam."

"Right on!" Ben said, his amen to Sandra.

"Don't you mean groovy?" Stephen responded, the sarcasm registering just low enough on the obnoxiousness scale to not demand retaliation and to permit an undeclared truce. But there was more to it.

184

The main reason the family was able to keep these arguments cum debates from boiling over (in addition to Annalise) was its observance of an unspoken rule that they must agree to assume Jacob to be okay, as if to say or even to think otherwise would place him in greater danger. (Superstition being what it is, at other times, a reverse proposition seemed to be observed: Like carrying an umbrella to ward off rain, worrying about him forestalled harm.)

As for Khe Sanh, it was on the northern border, an outpost, far from where they knew Jacob to be (or so he said). Anyway, these were marines up there, not army troops like Jacob, so the family could breathe a little easier.

But then came Tet, which scared the bejesus out of everyone.

~ ~ ~ ~ ~

Chapter 20

January–February 1968: The Way It Is

"ARE YOU GOING TO talk to me?" Stephen asked Annalise. They were alone in the living room. He had just mixed himself a martini and was sitting on the sofa in after-work mode—tie loosened, the knot dropping about an inch from the collar, sleeves rolled midway up the forearm.

"There's nothing to talk about."

He was certain this was not true. He recognized the signs. One sure hint to the extent of Annalise's angst was silence, something akin to but not quite brooding as she seemed to climb into herself. For some reason it was a behavior she never owned up to. If asked, she would snap to denial, as if to admit to being troubled would be to show weakness.

Stephen knew such quirks well by now, even as he remained unclear about their origin. Was her denial of internal turmoil a habit developed during the war, or earlier? A survival trick, perhaps, from the days when to demonstrate weakness was to provoke a beating, or worse? It might always have been integral to the Annalise he understood to be tough and self-contained. But how could he tell for sure when she wouldn't so much as admit to the behavior in the first place?

There was another tic, another giveaway to the anxiety, another tell. Annalise would scratch at the number tattoo on her forearm. Although she usually tried to conceal the mark with long sleeves, she wasn't obsessive about it; it was just something she preferred not to call attention to, a subject she preferred to avoid, especially with strangers.

Stephen was aware, even when she perhaps was not, that something was bothering her when she scratched at it.

Leaning against the arm of the sofa, he began to place his glass on the end table, close to a stubborn ring from a previous such placement. Another sign Annalise's mood scale had shifted: she neither looked reprovingly as the coasterless glass neared the table surface, nor approvingly as he caught himself and raised it before it made contact.

Whatever was behind the mood, as far as he was concerned it was not benign. It took passive-aggressive form, and the object, admitted or not, was to hurt him and make him feel guilty—to make a certainty of the holy hell that would befall him if anything happened to Jacob. It would be easier on both of them if she would just get on with it and fight. Fighting ultimately took less of a toll than her stewing, which only encouraged him to play a passive-aggressive game, too.

When the North Vietnamese chose the end of January, the beginning of the Lunar New Year, Tet, and normally a time of truce, to launch a mammoth offensive across all of the south, the entire family counted the hours and minutes to hear from Jacob. As the enemy, enduring unimaginably huge losses, swarmed over territory U.S. leaders had promised was secure, every day that went by without confirmation Jacob was safe was a day of anguish and unspoken recrimination.

Symbolically, at least, the low point was reached when the enemy breached the U.S. embassy compound in Saigon. True, they were driven back. But what kind of U.S. military success was this? The family, Stephen included, wanted to know how Johnson and his advisors could look the public in the eye and tell them the war was being won when anyone could see the enemy remained capable of inflicting so much punishment, so much damage, seemingly at will?

And where was Jacob?

Typically, soldiers would place phone calls home over the Military Affiliate Radio System, known as MARS, which operated on the amateur, or ham, radio network, thus avoiding onerous long-distance bills. These calls worked not as typical phone conversations, but as one-way radio connections, complete with each person having to say "over" after speaking. Refraining from the normal habit of stepping on each other's sentences took some getting used to. The ham operator acted as intermediary, placing a call via the telephone company's local operator, who phoned the recipient to advise that a MARS call was coming in. This meant that the call often needed to be scheduled in advance to ensure someone would be home.

Shortly after arriving in-country, Jacob told the family that he would do his best to call every Wednesday at ten in the evening, New York time—nine Thursday morning for Jacob. He was trying to avoid the busiest times, over the weekend. He warned that there was no guarantee he would be able to make the call as scheduled, and that the family was not to take the absence of a call as an indication something was amiss. Despite Sandra's skeptical "Yeah, sure!" they tried to heed this admonishment and keep fears for Jacob at normal, simmering levels when they didn't hear from him.

Until Tet. Until two weeks passed without contact either via MARS, a splurge on a normal overseas call, or a letter. With each report of chaos in Vietnam, nerves tightened. Minor annoyances were amplified.

Calling the family together, Stephen proposed a schedule that, as much as possible, would have someone at home to accept a phone call at all times. For once, there was no discord, at least over the plan. Actually arranging coverage around busy schedules was challenging. Sandra suggested hiring a phone sitter for times when all of them had to be away. No one said this was excessive.

They were asleep when the call finally came, at just after three in the morning, the ringer on the phone turned up to its most shrill. Startled awake, Annalise lurched over Stephen's slower-to-rouse body, stretching for the phone on his nightstand. For a moment she lost ground as Stephen tried to raise himself. With a "dammit" and a final lurch, she grabbed the handset and held on as the telephone base fell to the floor with a crash of bells.

"I'm here; don't hang up!" she yelled.

An operator, her voice calm, efficient, and mercifully compassionate, told Annalise not to worry. She instructed her to stand by and then turned the call over to the ham operator.

Annalise swung her legs over Stephen so that she was now sitting on the edge of his side of the bed. Her knuckles turned white with the chokehold she had on the handset. Stephen pushed himself upright with his back against the headboard.

"Okay, hold on," the ham operator said. At the same time the extension in the kitchen clicked, Sandra or Ben obviously listening in.

Annalise took deep breaths while she waited. When at last a young voice came on the line, it wasn't Jacob's, and Stephen could hear her breath catch.

"Is this Mr. or Mrs. Wroth?" the voice asked, followed with "Over."

"This is Mrs. Wroth. Who is this?" She hesitated before she remembered to say "Over."

"Mrs. Wroth, I'm a friend of Jake's. I . . ."

There was a momentary garble, as Annalise stepped on the transmission by speaking before the caller finished. "I'm sorry. Over," she said, catching herself.

"My name is Carlton," she heard as they got back in sync. It was a young Negro man's voice, soft with a Deep South politesse. "I'm in Jake's platoon. He asked me to call and tell you he's okay. Over."

"Oh, thank God. Why didn't he call, himself? Over."

"He's still out in the field, ma'am. Over."

"I see." Annalise appeared momentarily flustered, not certain what to ask. After a pause: "Well, why aren't you with him? Over."

"I caught a little wound, a bit of shrapnel. Nothing too bad, but I had to be treated here in Saigon. Jake asked me to call. Over."

"Thank you, but . . . when was this? When did you see him? Over."

"Yesterday. Or maybe it was the day before. Sorry, ma'am, it's been a little crazy here. Over."

"But Jacob was okay—not hurt—right?" she asked, turning to look at Stephen and holding the handset far enough from her ear that he might hear. "Over."

"When I saw him, ma'am, yes. Over."

"Can you give him a message? Over."

"Maybe. If I see him. Over."

"Um, well, tell him." She paused to collect her thoughts. The pause was just long enough to suggest the connection might have been broken.

"Hello?" Carlton said. "Over."

"I'm here. Over."

189

At this point the ham operator cut in. "Mrs. Wroth, I'm afraid you'll have to wrap this up. We have a long line of callers, as you can imagine. Over."

"What? Oh, yes, okay. Thank you, Carson . . . no, Carlton. Tell Jacob we love him and to be safe. And you be safe, too. Are you still on? Over?"

"I think we've lost him," the ham said. "Over."

"Oh. Well, if Carlton comes back, could you tell him . . . tell him . . . tell him to tell Jacob we love him and want him to call so we can hear his voice . . . Over." She added in a rush, "And to be safe."

"Yes, Mrs. Wroth. I'll tell him if I can. Sorry, I have to go now."

The line went dead. The kitchen extension clicked off. Annalise stared at the phone, as if more might be revealed.

Stephen touched her back. He could feel the muscles tense. "At least we have word he's okay," he said.

"A day or two ago." She let out a short, surprised laugh. "I nearly said over," she explained to Stephen's curious look. "Yes, a day or two ago he was safe."

* * *

IT WAS ALMOST another two weeks—each day the fear rising exponentially—before they actually heard Jacob's voice, and then only for a few moments. He was all right, he said. The "good guys" were regaining the initiative, making the enemy pay.

Shortly thereafter, a letter from Jacob arrived for Ben, delivered via a friend who was instructed that it was for Ben's eyes only. It was short, written in a hurried scrawl, and more pointed than any of Jacob's other communications. It said, simply:

> *Dear little brother,*
> *This message is only for you 'cause it would set off nuclear war between Mom and Dad. It's just this: I hope you've gotten that deferment by now, but WHATEVER YOU HAVE TO DO—WHOEVER YOU HAVE TO PAY OFF OR KILL—STAY THE FUCK*

190

AWAY FROM HERE. I MEAN IT. Don't be a schmuck. Don't do something stupid.
    That's it. Gotta go. "Duty" calls.
    J

And now here they were, together, on the 27th, antepenultimate day, of February 1968, a leap year, waiting for Walter Cronkite's special report. He had gone to Vietnam after Tet to see for himself about the war. Word around Stephen's newsroom that afternoon was that he would take the highly unusual step of offering his opinion on what he found.

"Well," Stephen said now, with a sigh, "if anyone can be counted on to be objective, it's Cronkite."

"Good old Uncle Walter," Ben said, his tone ending on the faintest hint of mockery, an inflection that had so thoroughly suffused his speech that it could be hard to know what he really thought about anything. Whatever the listener's interpretation—in this instance via Stephen's well-practiced ear—Ben had a decent shot at plausible deniability.

Stephen cocked his head in annoyance. "I know you're a big deal revolutionary and all, but isn't there anyone who qualifies for your approval?"

"Mao!" Sandra said with a laugh.

"Probably right," Stephen said.

Annalise put a finger to her lips. "Shh. It's starting."

Cronkite's face came on the screen, his expression solemn, almost mournful, as if he had taken it upon himself, or perhaps had it thrust upon him, to decide the outcome of the Vietnam War. He began by saying that neither side had clearly won the Tet assault. Further standoffs might be coming.

Khe Sanh could well fall, with a terrible loss in American lives, prestige, and morale, and this is a tragedy of our stubbornness there; but the bastion no longer is a key to the rest of the northern regions. . . .

"No kidding, Walter," Stephen interjected. "The problem is, it never was. It was a screwy decision to build the base there in the first place."

"Ooh! Stop the presses! Criticism of the war from Dad!" Ben said.

"Shush," Sandra said. "I'm trying to hear."

We have been too often disappointed by the optimism of the American leaders, both in Vietnam and Washington, to have faith any longer in the silver linings they find in the darkest clouds.

"Right on!" Ben and Sandra shouted in unison, fists pistoned into the air. They laughed at the spontaneous synchronicity of their reactions.

"It's about time someone like Walter called a spade a spade," Sandra added.

"Shush. He's talking about what comes next," Stephen said.

. . . our realization, that we should have had all along, that any negotiations must be that—negotiations, not the dictation of peace terms. For it seems now more certain than ever that the bloody experience of Vietnam is to end in a stalemate.

"Or worse, for us," Ben interjected.

This summer's almost certain standoff will either end in real give-and-take negotiations or terrible escalation; and for every means we have to escalate, the enemy can match us . . .

"Got that right," Sandra said.

And with each escalation, the world comes a little closer to cosmic disaster.

Stephen shook his head. "I agree things haven't been going well . . .

"Understatement," Ben interrupted.

"But," Stephen continued with obvious effort to keep his cool, "I'm not so sure we can't still win this thing."

As Cronkite continued, the posture of each member of the Wroth family increasingly mirrored his gravity, as if this judge alone were capable of rendering a wise verdict. All of their chairs were pushed back from the kitchen table. Each of them leaned in, fully focused, as if each in turn had the power to affect him as he was affecting them. Now there were no more shouts of exultation or disagreement. If warranted at all, these things could be reserved for later.

To say that we are closer to victory today is to believe, in the face of the evidence, the optimists who have been wrong in the past. To suggest we are on the edge of defeat is to yield to unreasonable pessimism.

"See?" Stephen said. "He's not giving up."

To say that we are mired in stalemate seems the only realistic, yet unsatisfactory, conclusion. ——

192

"That's what he's really saying," Sandra rejoined.

On the off chance that military and political analysts are right, in the next few months we must test the enemy's intentions, in case this is indeed his last big gasp before negotiations. But it is increasingly clear to this reporter that the only rational way out then will be to negotiate, not as victors, but as an honorable people who lived up to their pledge to defend democracy and did the best they could.

This is Walter Cronkite. Good night.

There was now no rush to comment, as they seemed to spurn the family's long-held tradition on any subject of instant analysis, instant debate. It appeared for a moment that Ben would crow. But he managed rare restraint and stopped himself mid-syllable. In this unexpected airlock, seconds seemed like minutes, though it could not have been much more than half a minute before Stephen mounted a subdued defense of his isolated bastion. "It seemed a little too pessimistic to me. He means well, but I'm not sure he really appreciates the astonishing firepower our forces can bring to the battle. I suppose we should be grateful he didn't end with his usual signoff, 'And that's the way it is.'"

"But that *is* the way it is, Dad," Sandra said, a look of astonishment on her face. "He got it right. There won't be a winner. We have to find a way out of this mess."

"I don't believe this shit!" Ben said, self-restraint already a dim memory.

"Language," Annalise admonished.

He stood and glared at Stephen.

"What is it you don't believe?" Stephen said, barely containing his impatience. "Tell me what you don't believe, O great know-it-all son."

"What Sandy said!" Ben looked around, apparently flustered by the very idea that someone could challenge the supreme logic of what he had just heard. "How can you not scope on to the truth of Cronkite's words?" he said at last. "How much more obvious can it be? I mean, Uncle Walter himself has only just caught on to what the rest of the world has known for ages. Pham van Dong—you know, the North Vietnamese premier . . ."

"I *know* who Pham is," Stephen interjected.

"Okay, then maybe you don't remember what he said a couple of years ago. He was being interviewed—by *The Times*, I think, if that does it for you—and he asked how long we wanted to fight. Two years? Ten years? Twenty years? You know what he said?"

"What did he say, Ben?" Stephen asked in a tone of weary patience. "Just tell us."

"He said they will accommodate us! However long it takes, they will fight us for as long as it takes. That's what he said, and that's the truth. Isn't that what Uncle Walter is saying in his own words? Christ! I don't believe you!"

"Calm down a little, Ben," Annalise said. "We may agree with you, but you're talking to your father. A little respect, please."

"You mean respect, like when you give Dad the stink eye for risking Jake's life? Like we don't notice? Like we're stupid? You mean that kind of respect?"

"Stop it, Ben," Stephen said coldly.

"I do no such thing," Annalise protested.

"You should try checking the mirror every once in a while."

Sandra, adapting to the situation a sober, direct, calm approach to crisis derived recently from her nursing classes, said simply, "Cronkite spoke to me, Dad, he did, and I hope to most other people. I'm really sorry he apparently couldn't convince you."

~ ~ ~ ~ ~

Chapter 21

April 1968: Fight or Flight

B EN WAS WALKING UNDER the Jerome Avenue el with Ted, a friend from school. It was an April Tuesday, mid-morning, the air cool but the sun bright with a tease of unambiguous warmth in the afternoon. The two were laughing as they approached the corner candy store to buy cigarettes.

They were dressed alike in the improbable military surplus store fashion that they and many of their antiwar friends had spawned. Both wore olive green tees under long-sleeve army shirts. The uniforms differed only in rank, Ben displaying the two stripes of a corporal while Ted had scored the insignia of a master sergeant. There was no starch in this man's army. The shirts were unbuttoned and untucked, the sleeves rolled tight at mid-forearm to accentuate a masculine bulge of muscle and vein. (Popeye arms, Sandra scoffed—"gristle and gore.") The tees were tucked into frayed and faded jeans, which in turn were tucked loosely into surplus army boots—bloused, as Stephen's wartime compatriots would have described it, though the offense here was compounded in that the vets from Stephen's war considered blousing one's trousers a privilege to be earned.

As they exited the store, Ben was tamping the new cigarette pack into his breast pocket, not looking where he was going, when he bumped into an equally oblivious woman. Their startled excuse-me's were quickly followed by laughter of mutual recognition.

"Sandy! What are you doing here? Do you know Ted?" Ben asked after a beat.

Sandra looked over with an expression of uncertain recognition. "We may have met. Cutting class, I presume," she added, addressing both boys.

"Something like that," Ben responded. "Why are you here?"

"Same as you, I guess—well, not cutting. Buying smokes."

"Cool. You can stop bumming them off of me."

"I'm over at Montefiore. Doing an all-day practicum on the glamorous subject of urinary catheterization."

"Better you than me," Ben said.

"Too bad. I was hoping to practice on you. Seriously, why aren't you in school?" Her face suddenly filled with maternal worry. "You're not screwing up again, are you? I mean, we have talked about this."

Ben looked around, obviously uncomfortable at the prospect of having to explain to Ted. "You mean you've talked about it," he said after a beat. "Look, I'll see you at home, okay? Ted and I are late."

"Late? For what?"

"Not now, Sis." Ben motioned to Ted that it was time to leave.

"What *are* we late for?" Ted asked when they were out of earshot. "You never told me your sister was a stone fox," he added when he got no response.

"Yeah, well, fuck you."

* * *

THAT EVENING, JUST before dinner, Sandra tapped on Ben's door. Getting no answer, she peered in. His back was to her, his ears covered by headphones tethered to the stereo. The music leaking from them was loud enough for her easily to identify the singer as Janis Joplin.

"Ben!" she shouted, placing her hand on his back.

He jumped at her touch. "Jesus! Try knocking, why dontcha?" He sprung the headphones around his neck.

"So, what was going on today?"

196

"Well, *Mom*," he said, stressing the sarcasm, "it's really none of your business."

"Oh, come on, Ben. I thought we'd agreed that you'd get serious and graduate."

"No, Sandy, you must be taking lessons from Mom and Dad in hearing what you want to hear. *You* said I'd get serious, remember? That's what you wanted. I said I was sick of school."

"Great, asshole! You turn eighteen next week. Doesn't that ring a bell?"

"Lots of them, but none of them sound like school bells."

"Christ, Ben, can't you just get your shit together for a few more weeks?"

"Too late, Sis."

"Why too late?"

"Because I'm already a dropout, that's why."

She gave him a look of incomprehension. "How can you be a dropout? You can't quit without Mom or Dad's permission, and no way they'd give it."

"Let me show you the paint-by-numbers picture, Sis. I haven't been going to school for weeks."

"But . . . phone calls home, letters, truant officers, something."

"All easily intercepted, darling sister. Besides, get with the times. You really think truant officers give a shit about high school seniors? It's over. Period. On my birthday next week, I can make it official, without Mom or Dad's permission. So just stop hassling me already, would you?"

She sat heavily on his unmade bed. "You really are an asshole. You're going to be called up. You know that, right?"

"Oh, for fuck sake, Sandy, I already have been called up. I got a letter ordering me to report to Whitehall Street for my physical."

"Well, bright boy, what are you going to do?"

"Go down there, of course," he said in a tone that suggested she hadn't a brain in her skull.

"You mean actually report? You've lost me. What about all this stuff about there being no way the army is going to get you?"

"And it won't."

197

"Oh, shit, Ben! Would you please stop it! What the hell are you talking about?"

He smiled broadly, his most smug smile, and put the answer into a slightly off-key tune. *You can get anything you want, at Alice's restaurant.* "Get it? Arlo Guthrie?" he asked to her continuing confusion.

"Okay, yeah, the song, I got it. Arlo Guthrie. 'Alice's Restaurant Massacree.' Very clever. You're telling me you're going to get yourself arrested on some dumb littering charge so the army won't take you because you have a record? Is that it? That's your stupid plan for getting out of the draft?"

"Not exactly. Look, I've said all along that I'll beat feet if I have to. But there's no sense bookin' before I go for the physical. There's always the chance I'll flunk it."

She shook her head from lock to lock in disbelief. "You look pretty goddamn healthy to me."

"I've been doing some stuff."

"What the hell does that mean?"

"Well, like I've been eating mucho salty things. I figure if my blood pressure is high enough, they won't want me. And grass. I've been smoking a lot of grass. Hash, too. And I've dropped a tab or two of acid. I thought of using smack, but that's a little *too* heavy."

"That'll keep you out, is that what you figure, genius?"

"Ah, yup."

"And if they do believe you're a druggie, you're sure they won't send you to jail? That would be funny, wouldn't it? Not being willing to go to jail on principle but going anyway on a drug bust. Or maybe they'll send you to rehab. And *then* Nam."

Sandra stared at him, waiting for a response. Ben stared back, as if confident he'd finally convinced her he had the situation in hand.

"What makes you think I won't tell Mom and Dad?"

"Because I know you're not a rat fink. Anyway, like I said, what can they do? And you wouldn't want to *force* me to run away if I didn't have to, would you?"

"Well, good luck," she said, finally, rising and turning toward the door.

"It's cool, Sandy," he said to her back. "Really."

"How is it cool?" she asked, turning to face him, her voice swimming in resignation.

"You know the good thing about deciding to bug out? It's something I can do anytime. I flunk the physical, I stay. I pass it, I go. It's that simple."

~ ~ ~ ~ ~

Chapter 22

April 1968: O Canada!

O NCE HE GOT TO the interstate, Ben was on his way, nonstop, courtesy of a drowsy long-haul trucker who was looking for someone to talk to all the way to Buffalo. That was the price of Ben's passage, and measured in words per mile, he soon thought it might be a steep one.

That morning, he'd left a note for Sandra in a place that was sufficiently inconspicuous that it wouldn't be the first thing she saw when she awakened. Otherwise, she might do something stupid, like try to stop him. He needed the head start. The note couldn't have been more to the point:

Sorry for the no notice but it's time to haul ass.
The army says I'm fit, so I had to split. Like that? I'm quite the poet.
Tell Mom I love her.
I'll be in touch when I've figured things out.

* * *

The driver—"Frank-short-for-Francis with an 'i,' not an 'e,' like a girl," a fiftyish product of Erie, Pennsylvania, with a two-day growth of salt-and-pepper beard, dungarees stained with blobs of who knew how many days' worth of meals-to-go, toad-skin hands produced by years of handling rough freight (crates of machine tools that day), and an ability

200

to keep up a patter as voluble as it was banal—soon revealed himself to be standing on a tight-assed pro-war, anti–civil rights platform that made Ben wonder why he would bother to stop for a hippie-go-lucky-looking kid such as himself.

Ben had intended to trim his hair before he reached the Canadian border, but all he could manage before he stuck his thumb out for a ride was to stuff some of it into an upturned collar. In any case, he was not about to question the good fortune of his long-haul benefactor's questionable judgment, and passed the miles expressing, not agreement (he had *some* principles, he told himself), but either ambiguous silence or meaningless interjections (*Oh, right, uh-huh, I get it, that must have been tough*).

His plan was to find a place to crash for the night in Buffalo and make the border crossing the following day. An antiwar activist he met at a rally had given him the addresses of two communal houses on the verges of state university property. He was to ask for a guy named Larry in one ("looks like a mass murderer but don't be put off by that; he's a nice guy"), and someone named Willie in the other ("Negro kid, prelaw student, looks more stoned than he is, but that's still plenty"). Ben opted for Willie, reasoning that he could preserve his minimal cash with an offering of pot, which he had in better supply and the remains of which, unfortunately, he would have to jettison before he got to the border if he didn't get to toke it first.

His logic turned out to be sound, at least for that night. Willie, who it seemed might topple over from the size of his afro and the thick black plastic, long-tined comb stuck in it like an axe in a tree stump, was so welcoming that at first Ben thought someone must have introduced him in advance of his arrival. It quickly became obvious that Willie was simply hospitable, and all the more so under the influence of Ben's offering. He told Ben how he put his pre-legal skills to good use in what amounted to a "bitchin' underground railroad" for draft resisters and evaders, as well as for soul brothers suspected of shaking one Molotov cocktail too many.

"More deserters coming through the pipeline, too, which is cool by me," Willie said before Ben told him that he was an evader who hoped never to fall into the deserter category.

"Bullshit!" a guy called angrily from across the room. Ben judged him to be a little older than Willie, maybe late twenties. "Gonna get us in trouble. One thing to be runnin' away from the draft, but the Man don't put up with no deserter helpers. You sure you no deserter, honkie?" he added, which confused Ben because as near as he could tell, the guy was white. Further confusing evidence was given by Willie, who waved the guy off, saying, "Who you calling honkie, honkie?"

"I am, brother, I am. What? My skin not dark enough for you?"

Now Ben was really confused, since on closer inspection he would have guessed the guy's roots to be closer to Norway than Ghana.

"Don't pay him no mind," Willie said. "He's just a pain in the ass."

Space was found on the living-room floor for Ben to spread out his sleeping bag. "You lucky, man—got some *room*," Willie said, stressing the word with a smile. "Night before last, folks practically be sleeping upright."

It occurred to Ben that as deluded as the white black guy might be, Willie was strange in his own way. He came across as bright and educated (he was prelaw at a real university, after all), but the way he slipped in and out of dialect made him sound like someone determined to appear fresh out of the ghetto—and maybe that was the explanation. Maybe he was halfway between worlds.

Ben thanked him and called out a general thanks, just in case it was needed, to a guy and a girl who at that moment shot up the staircase in a frenzy of high-spirited grab-ass, both nearly slipping on a threadbare runner. Ben figured them to be actual residents of the house.

After Willie left him to get settled, Ben stood for a moment to take a breath and get his bearings. The house was an old Victorian that had clearly seen loftier times. From what Ben could see of it, it was still solid, with heavy dark wood everywhere; cluttered and worn, but not dirty.

His sleeping bag and a tightly stuffed backpack were all he had. He was dressed in his army pseudo-uniform, which was becoming increasingly satirical under the circumstances. He took off his boots, but the pants stayed on, the only way he could feel confident about waking up with his money and happy weed where they should be.

202

* * *

HE AWOKE EARLY the next morning, apparently the only one up at that hour. During the night another body had crashed on the floor near him. He couldn't tell if it was a man or a woman, then realized the sleeping bag was being shared by two people. Ben rolled his sleeping bag and took his things down a long hallway to what seemed to be the only bathroom, at least on the main level of the house.

The bathroom floor of chipped black and white octagonal tiles was cold under his bare feet. He hung his backpack behind the door and pulled back the floral bedsheet that was being used as a shower curtain. Lacking a rod, it was tied with twine to eyehooks placed haphazardly along the ceiling. The tub was fairly clean, if he overlooked a clump of dark hair in the drain and rust spots where the spout continually dripped.

He stripped and stepped in. He had trouble adjusting the water temperature to get it somewhere between scald and freeze, twice having to leap as far away from the stream as possible. The only soap was in four small shards that had become caught by the hair in the drain. He decided a good soapless rinse would suffice.

He had barely adjusted the water to a reasonable temperature when he heard a rapping at the door, accompanied by a girl's urgent voice. "Anyone in there?"

"Out in a sec," he responded over the splashing water.

"Could you step on it, please? Gotta go bad."

"Okay, okay. Hold your horses." He was about to turn off the water when the door opened with a sudden thud, trapping his backpack against the wall. "Hey!" he called.

"Sorry, I'm desperate. Just stay where you are behind the curtain," the girl responded. He heard the crack of the toilet seat dropping hard against the white porcelain bowl, followed almost simultaneously by a hissing torrent. A scald-producing flush and a minute later he heard, "Thanks, man. Sorry to barge in like that." The door slammed shut before Ben had a chance to say it was no prob. He peered out from behind the curtain to make sure she had in fact gone before he stepped out. He had forgotten to bring a towel and took the only thing available, a damp washcloth hanging next to the sink that had been used as a hand towel. Hearing new footsteps near the bathroom, he dried himself as well as possible.

He pulled on his pants and decided to finish dressing back in the sleeping area. The sleeping bag that had contained two heads now had only one, clearly a man's—a towhead, as far as he could tell in the dim light. He was snoring steadily.

The aroma of fresh coffee drew Ben toward the kitchen, where an avocado green Sunbeam pot was perking away, mini-geysers of gradually darkening water popping off the glass knob top with increasing urgency. The white Negro from the previous night was standing at a chipped Formica counter, keeping vigil over the process. He gave Ben a hard look as he picked up the still perking pot and began to pour a cup. Ben readied himself for more words, but he was surprised to hear a contrite "Sorry 'bout last night, man. I was kind of pissy."

"It's okay," Ben said after a pause, relaxing a little.

"Got some more joe here if you want."

Ben considered passing on the offer and taking off early but thought it might be good to have something hot and caffeinated in his stomach. He dropped his gear off to the side, then noticed a girl sitting at a round, beat-up dining table that had been hidden by the open door. She was cradling a mug in both hands, Japanese-style. She was pretty, with emerald eyes, a head full of wild russet curls, and an endearing, slightly shy smile revealed when she said, "Sorry to crash your shower like that."

He returned the smile. "How do you know it was me?"

The girl—he could see now she was perhaps his age or a year or two older—laughed and said, "Your hair's still wet."

Which drew a self-conscious laugh. "I guess it didn't take a genius to figure it out, huh?"

She smiled again, showing slightly uneven teeth, which Ben thought somehow sexy. She returned her attention to a map laid out on the table in front of her.

"Going somewhere?" he asked, taking a weak stab at keeping her engaged.

The antagonist from the previous night came over and handed Ben a cup. "Hope you don't take anything in it," he said with a casual smile, "'cause we ain't got nuthin'."

"It's okay. Thanks."

"Peace, my brother," he said, turning back to the counter.

Ben was still uncertain about what to make of the guy, who in morning light appeared if anything even whiter but seemed no less intent on being taken for black. *He can't have more than four percent Negro in him,* Ben had thought when they'd met; now he doubted the number was that high.

"Canada," the young woman said, answering Ben's question.

"Me, too," Ben said, hoping he might have found a travel mate, and an attractive one at that. "Ben Wroth," he added, extending his hand to her and then, an afterthought, to the white black guy.

"Martha," she said.

"Jerome," the guy said and added, "Sorry again 'bout last night. It's just me and Willie, we got different ideas 'bout deserters."

Ben noticed Martha starting to fidget and wondered if there was something she was trying to conceal. She made an unlikely deserter.

Jerome went on, apparently not noticing. "You be evading the draft—dodging, or whatnot—and I'm down with that. Don't really have nuthin' against deserters neither 'cept Uncle Top Hat, he *really* don't truck with 'em, and it's trouble we don't need here, if you know what I mean."

Ben nodded. Martha stood, still cradling the mug, which he could now see was a cup that had lost its handle. She was tall—at any rate probably taller than Ben by a good three inches—and lean, small-busted but not flat. "Good to meet you guys," she announced, making ready to leave.

"You wouldn't be looking for a travel partner?" Ben ventured.

"Thanks," she said, and his spirits rose, then immediately fell when she added, "But I'm with my boyfriend. He's the one still conked out on the floor."

"Oh. I guess you were the ones sharing the bag when I woke up this morning."

"That was us alright," she said with a smile. She drained the mug and folded the map neatly along its original creases.

"I've always envied people who can do that," Ben said with a nod toward the map and hoping to keep the conversation going.

"That's what Neil—he's my boyfriend—says. But it's bullshit, you know? I tell him all it takes is patience, of which he has zero."

"Maybe it's a guy-girl thing."

"Maybe." She gave a small shrug and headed for the door.

"Pretty damn cute," Ben said to Jerome after she'd gone.

"I s'pose. Different strokes and all that. She a little on the white side for me."

* * *

THE OPTIMISM BEN felt when he woke up dulled after Martha declined the suggestion that they travel together. Now he faced the prospect of completing the move to Canada alone, a word to which he had never attached much meaning. Second thoughts had leached in during the ride to Buffalo with trucker Frank. Some of the bravado he had nurtured over the preceding weeks started to fade.

So far, he was guilty only of failing to show up for induction—an offense he presumed to be minor and correctable were he inclined to change his mind. But he had no such inclination, which now placed him in the position of having to, as his father liked to say, annoyingly, fish or cut bait.

He went to look for Willie to thank him for the use of his floor. Passing the living room, he noticed a blonde guy, presumably Neil, the boyfriend, on his knees rolling a sleeping bag. "Hey, man," he said to Ben as he tightened a strap and stood. He was tall, in good shape, too, Ben observed; he had the look of a college athlete.

"Hey," Ben responded.

"You the one headed for Canada today?"

"How did you know?" Ben asked, wanting to say something.

"My girlfriend told me. I think you just met her, in the *bathroom* as I understand it."

Ben laughed. "Yeah, man, I meet the best chicks that way, 'cept they turn out to be someone else's."

"Ha. I know the feeling."

Ben doubted Mr. Joe College did.

"Where in Canada? Toronto, right?"

"Right."

"That's what I figured. How are you getting there?"

Ben held up his thumb.

"Well, listen, we're driving there in my car. If you like, you can come with us. Share the gas, maybe."

"Yeah, sure." Ben brightened. "It's not very far—shouldn't take much gas," he added, smiling but wondering if he had said the right thing. He didn't want to appear ungrateful or cheap; then again, he didn't want to seem like an easy mark.

"No, I guess not," Neil said, amiably. "Martha suggested I ask you. She said you seemed like a good guy."

"She did? That's nice of her. I'd be grateful for the ride. And the company," he added.

"Cool. Done deal. Can you be ready in about half an hour? That's assuming Martha can get her shit together by then. She can be like molasses in the morning."

"I can leave now," Ben responded.

It took almost an hour for Martha to get ready (she explained a lot of that time was spent waiting in line for the bathroom), although Ben could detect nothing different in her appearance, which was still fine as far as he was concerned.

They carried their things to the car, a dusty-green Buick Skylark that drew an unconscious pat of appreciation from Neil as he opened the trunk.

"Indiana, huh?" Ben said, noting the license plate.

"Naptown," Neil said. "Indianapolis," he added in response to Ben's questioning look.

"You both from there?"

"Born and bred," Martha answered with a sidewise laugh that Ben took as slightly depreciating the place.

Neil closed the trunk firmly and walked to the driver's side, while Ben and Martha opened the passenger side door. Martha pushed the seatback forward so Ben could climb in. As he bent over to get into the back seat, Ben experienced a pleasurable instant when his face passed close to Martha's breasts, which were clearly braless, the outline of her nipples made visible by the morning chill.

Ben asked whether they had driven straight through to Buffalo from Indianapolis. Martha said they had stopped for a couple of days in Cleveland to see friends.

"Surprised you bothered stopping in Buffalo then," Ben said.

"We talked about it," she responded. "You're right, it didn't make much sense. It sounds funny, but we both felt there was something important about spending a last night on U.S. soil. I mean, we don't know when we'll be back."

"Plus," Neil said as Ben got settled, "we thought it would be a good idea not to have fogged up brains when we deal with whatever it is we'll have to deal with at the border."

The car's interior smelled of incense, patchouli oil, and stale marijuana. "This a sixty-five?" Ben asked.

"Sixty-four. I treat her right," Neil responded as he turned the key in the ignition. "Nice," he added appreciatively in response to the mellow roar from the perfectly tuned pipes.

"You think we'll have trouble at the border?" Ben asked.

Ben must have looked concerned over what he might be getting into, because Neil seemed to want to reassure him. "Nah, I don't think so. We need to be careful is all. You're a dodger, right?"

"Yeah, but I'm only a couple of days overdue. I doubt I'm on anyone's dragnet list yet," he added in a voice that sounded weaker in his ears than he would have liked.

"Probably not. Never can tell, though."

Martha turned in her seat to face Ben. "The thing is," she began, but then said to Neil, "Kill the engine. We need to talk about this."

Martha twisted again to face Ben, who moved to the center of the back seat to make it easier for her. "What Neil's not telling you is he's a deserter. He . . ."

"Yeah, man, that's right," Neil interrupted, looking at Ben in the rearview mirror. Ben thought about the discomfort he sensed in Martha when the subject of deserters came up with Jerome. "That's because the army fucked me over," Neil continued. "I actually enlisted because they promised I could be a signals tech and that I'd be sent to Germany. Now

208

they tell me, 'Sorry sucker, but we need you in Nam and blah bullshit blah bullshit.' But listen, man, that's my prob, and if you want to find your own way across the border, we're cool."

"Nah, I'll stick with you guys," Ben responded, and then wondered if he hadn't been too quick—whether he wasn't overly relieved to have found traveling companions. "Far as I know from what I've heard," he added, now looking at Martha and wanting to impress her with his confidence, "the border crossing is pretty much no hassle. I mean, the Canadians are cool."

"Well, yeah," Neil said, turning in his seat. "But it's not the Canucks I'm worried about. It's the Law on our side of the line."

Ben smiled. "Probably not a bad idea to air out the car, then."

Martha rewarded him with a laugh.

"And if we're going to clean out the car, we might as well take a toke or two first and then hit the local House of Pancakes for lunch," Neil added.

"Right on!" Ben exulted with a fist pump and a laugh. "The less we have to dump before crossing, the better. Thought of pissing away good weed hurts my heart. I figured it would take longer than it did to get to Buffalo, so I have more left than I planned on."

"Us too," Martha said. "You know, we shouldn't just toss it. We should give some of the excess to Willie. It'd be a kind of far out tribute to his underground railroad station."

"Good idea," Ben and Neil said in unison. "I can see it now," Ben added, spreading his arms, "Big neon sign: 'Willie's Underground Railroad and Dope House.'"

Martha returned a couple of minutes later sporting a Cheshire cat grin. "That was one grateful dude," she said, getting in and slamming the door.

Neil offered a coda by restarting the car. In a sign the stars were aligning to justify the new mood of joyful defiance, the radio began pumping out "White Rabbit."

"Yeah, Baby!" Ben exulted with a laugh. "Feed your head!"

~ ~ ~ ~ ~

Chapter 23

April 1968: Unbidden Reprises

STEPHEN'S BODY JERKED AT the nearness of the shot. He cried out as a splinter of cobblestone lodged in his eye. He sensed where the next shot would strike and tried to scramble away. When it came it grazed his leg, leaving a blood trail visible through his pants. But that pain was nothing compared to the fire in his eye, which made him flail like a madman. The little control he had left over his body was devoted completely to staying out of the line of fire.

It was Henry who pulled him to safety, whose face loomed in his good eye. "Oh, thank God. Thank you."

But it was not Henry's face he saw as he lurched upright in a ropey tangle of sheet and blanket. Rather, it was the disorienting face of Annalise. "Nightmares again," she said simply, her voice reassuring in its matter-of-factness, in its comprehension.

"Épinal," he said. The air in the room was arid, his voice raspy. "Goddamn but it seemed real. I was trapped next to the statue, the one in the center of the town square. Henry saved me. Riggs—I told you about Riggs—he was there, too; off to the side, just standing there, not helping."

"A dream," she said, touching his shoulder. "Only a dream."

He nodded. Of course, a dream. Henry never saved him in Épinal. And Riggs wasn't in the division then. Henry had his own troubles there. Stephen said aloud, more to himself than to Annalise, "His gun jammed.

210

And I couldn't save him, either." After a pause, he repeated it, the sad reality: "I couldn't save him, either."

"I know," she said softly.

He was awake now. It was only in the last few weeks that the dreams had returned. He thought he had them licked. This time, Épinal. Or a variation on Épinal, one of many nocturnal variations on his war. He could never account for them all, and there were always permutations like Riggs showing up. But the basic ones, the ones that served as a sort of armature on which to hang them, he could almost catalogue: Dream No. 1, Épinal firefight; No. 2, Aschaffenburg/Henry, Murch, and Riggs; No. 3, Dachau/Horrors & Atrocities; No. 3-A, Dachau/Executions of SS; No. 3-B, Dachau/Greta-Annalise.

One night, he dreamed he actually participated in the Dachau coal yard executions. In a rabid frenzy, he was shooting as fast as he could, contributing to the bloody heap of Germans, until his rifle jammed. Upon waking it took time to sort out the strands—to recall that although he didn't take part in the incident, he experienced spikes of guilt over helping to throw the army investigators off track. And of course, the jammed gun must have been inspired by Henry.

He realized he was hardly alone in having such nightmares. At occasional Thunderbird Division reunions he heard many of his comrades allude to them. Most would not describe them in detail.

And he was the one who couldn't save Henry, not the other way around. It didn't take a genius to figure out that was what the dream came back to: Henry pulls Stephen to safety, and Stephen fails to return the favor. Well, the last part was true. He did fail, didn't he? In ways both real and imagined, he failed to save Henry.

"My turn for nightmares tonight, apparently," he said. "One of these days maybe we'll both be able to stop."

"I'll get you a glass of water," Annalise said. "Maybe you can go back to sleep."

He leaned back against the headboard. He thought he knew the trigger for the latest round: Jacob's letter—his desperate letter to Ben, his recounting the loss of his Oklahoma friend. Was it Oklahoma? No, another convergence—Murch was from Oklahoma. Texas, maybe. What was the friend's name? Al, right. Not Alfred. Alferd, but don't call him that.

After reading Jacob's letter, he wondered what Jacob's nights would be like. Would he spend them revisiting Al's fateful step on the poisoned stick or the fireball that claimed him? Were there conversations between them that were unrevealed in the letter but which, like his own with Henry, were capable of placing the events in a context suitable for continual nighttime distortion and variation?

He took the glass from Annalise, thanked her, sipped just enough to wash the burrs from his throat, and set the glass on his nightstand. "It wasn't you tonight, anyway," he said, stroking her arm. "That's something, anyway."

* * *

HER NIGHTMARES HAD never gone into remission as Stephen's had. They weren't constant, but they never stayed away long enough for her to declare them gone, vanquished. There was little symmetry in their experiences. He called out in his sleep; she rarely did. He explained his dreams to her; she almost never explained hers to him. She did confide that she thought of her dreams as being more accurate than his. To his uncomprehending look, she said, "I don't know the exact word. It's a little like replaying a movie. When I wake up I don't say to myself, oh this or that never happened or didn't happen the way I dreamt it. I think, yes, that's the way it happened. And then I try to put it out of my mind."

"I suppose you meant mine are more representative or metaphorical compared to your movie rewind."

She said yes, that was probably right. But while she was willing to concur in the diagnosis, she refused to talk about the specifics of the symptoms.

Whatever the triggers to their respective nightmares, there was little doubt as to the origins of their increasingly frequent arguments. To the skirmishes over Jacob they now added the ones over Ben.

"All I asked is that you not write Ben off," she had said a fight ago.

"And I didn't. I haven't had a chance to write him off if I'd wanted to. We haven't heard from him, remember?"

"We haven't heard from him because he knows how you'll react."

"Sandra hasn't heard from him either. Ben would contact her if he wanted to contact anybody. Maybe he's written Jacob. It has nothing to do with me."

She ignored the defense. "We haven't heard from him because he knew how much you'd hate him if he ran away."

"That's not fair, Annalise. Hate him? Why would he ever think a thing like that?"

"Because he's dramatic."

"Look, I think it's wrong to run away. I made that clear. But hate him?"

"Maybe that's a little strong," she admitted. But she stood her ground. "At the least he'd know you had no respect for him—that you wouldn't help him."

"That's not hating."

"I said that may have been too strong. But don't you see how he would come to think of it that way?"

"No, I don't. You're also not being fair because I'm not the one who put him in the situation he's in. I didn't think he should evade the draft. I didn't think he should run away. That's all true. But Ben's the one who put himself between a rock and a hard place. He could have stayed in school. He could have gotten a student deferment. But what did he do? He lied to us repeatedly, about everything. He chose to drop out and run away. He's old enough to take some responsibility for his actions. It's unfair to place all the blame on me."

But Stephen understood that she did blame him, fair or not. Anyway, the argument wasn't only about Ben. There was a compound effect. Every argument was also about Jacob. Jacob was in Vietnam, full stop. As far as she was concerned, the fact that he was in mortal danger was completely Stephen's fault. Only what she thought of as his blind patriotism was to blame. Jacob heeded the warning that it would displease Stephen if he chose any other course. Ben got the same message but defied Stephen anyway.

The day they found out Ben had run off, Annalise reiterated where she stood—updated her position so there would be no doubt. She told Stephen that as sorry as she was that Ben had gone, and as much as she

213

regretted that he didn't do the smart thing and find a deferment, given a choice between Vietnam and Canada . . . well, there was no choice.

She dismissed Stephen's concerns over the lifelong consequences Ben would face at home. "He could recover. I know what it's like to be a refugee. It's not an impossible existence, as you can see. Especially"— she emphasized the word and raised a hand to ward off any objection— "if the choice is life or death. I only wish my own family had the . . . I don't know . . . whatever it would have taken to become refugees about ten years earlier."

"The difference is that Ben is a legal fugitive. Something would have to change that."

"I asked you to promise you would support Ben if he left. You never actually answered. So let me tell you, Stephen: I will support our son, whatever it takes, and you will too, or I will never forgive you."

* * *

ANNALISE'S DREAMS CYCLED on with a vengeance soon after Stephen's had run their course. Stephen asked about them, as always. He suggested it might help to talk. As almost always, she said it wouldn't. The exception was when she dreamed about her family. When she was overwhelmed by guilty dreams of survival, of selfishness in surviving, of failing to perish with them, she sometimes told Stephen about it. He comforted her; she was sometimes comforted by the expiation. At least until the next time.

About her other ordeals—in particular her life in the camps, her life before she met Stephen—she said nothing. There was a clear link—an obvious prompt—to the latest dreams, but in the absence of context that might have been provided by a regular true recounting of them—and the consequent growth of a carapace over discussion of the Dachau period, in dreams or not—there was no reason for Stephen to have made the connection: his casual announcement that, following up on the Christmas party, he had arranged for them to meet Andrew and Helga for dinner the following weekend.

That night Annalise had a vivid, explicit dream about Buchenwald and the woman she was increasingly sure was Helga—"the arranger"—

whose real name (or the name she knew her by) was Margit. In the dream Annalise was given the relatively less objectionable assignment of pleasuring a decent-looking young German officer—a man from whom in another time that seemed impossible now she might have happily received an invitation to go dancing.

It was an enduring mystery to Annalise that in this version of hell, with misery and misery's only relief, death, all around them, Margit was able to affect an air of conviviality with their captors. Her precise words on this occasion, spoken with a smile as if she were a shopkeeper—a baker offering bread, a milliner suggesting a hat, a bookseller recommending a title—were, "I give each of you the pleasure of the other." Once, when Annalise remarked to Margit on the seeming ease of her countenance, Margit stunned her with an enraged slap across the face. "This is how I survive, you stupid girl."

The rebuke was startling but not enduring. Annalise observed to herself that Margit was not a good enough actress to play the part of the happy arranger as convincingly as she did without being able to draw on something of her true self. If anything, Margit's outrage may have revealed just how close to the bone Annalise's remark had cut.

Annalise (Greta, as she introduced herself when the young officer asked her name) led the man to her private area. She gave him an authentic-looking smile—an arrangement of her features quite different from a true smile, but this learned behavior was something only she was aware of, and she guarded the secret as one of the few ways she had of preserving something of her core, not to mention, perhaps, her life.

She closed the makeshift wooden door and latched it with an eyehook, which mostly functioned as a signal of privacy to her client, since in reality it was a worthless barrier to entry. No one except perhaps a more senior officer would dare to barge in anyway. That day it didn't take long for such minor details to become irrelevant.

The first sign of trouble occurred when she began to take off her skirt, a sarong-like garment that was easy to deal with. She looked up, startled by his command: "You can leave it on. I don't want to stick myself in you." His demeanor, pleasant a moment before when the two of them were with Margit, was now a compressed snarl. To her surprised

215

look at the abrupt dropping of the veil, he explained, "Who knows what vermin might be hiding in that Jew cunt of yours."

It was only later—after—that she imagined the response she would have wished to give: that the only vermin in that place were the likes of him. Of course, it really was a fantasy; making it a reality could only have resulted in her end.

"We'll do it this way," the officer said as he placed a hand on her shoulder, pushed her to her knees, and undid his pants. Before she could even set herself and find her balance, before she could take a breath, his prick, stiff and fungally ripe, was jammed into her mouth. "Now, suck on it like the best sweet you ever had," he commanded through clenched teeth as she gagged, the reflex only made worse as he grabbed the back of her head and clamped her to him.

She tried to recover, tried with every particle of self-discipline, as if her life depended on it, to gain control. It helped momentarily that he began to soften in her mouth—the erection that had been so stiff now, with surprising suddenness, losing its procreational essence. "Jew whore! Suck!" he commanded again, this time with a slap that made her ears ring, frustration added to the growing rage.

She tried. Petrified, she worked her mouth in every way she could. At least his softening had helped with the gag reflex. But the softer he became, the more urgent became the hand behind her head pulling her to him, and the louder the commands until, finally, he pulled back and slapped her hard enough to knock her off her knees and onto her bottom.

It had all happened so fast, so disorientingly fast. She tried to focus, was afraid she might pass out. Her ears were ringing even worse than before.

What she would remember, dream about still, was the total vulnerability to this maniac's whims as her revulsion was displaced by fear. "Look what you did!" he yelled as he stood there, his member drooping. "This is your fault, you worthless cunt!" He drew his hand back to slap her again. Only the fact that she was sitting on the floor and out of easy reach made him pause.

It was the voice at the door—Margit the arranger's voice, asking with controlled fear if everything was all right—that saved her. She was sure of it. As if another switch had been thrown, the man tucked himself in, straightened his uniform, and drew himself up as though he had suddenly remembered the need to maintain the dignity of his office.

"Fine," he called in a clipped voice that made clear nothing further would be said. He opened the door suddenly, yanking the eyehook from its mooring and startling Margit, almost knocking her down as he charged out. "Someone else next time," he called over his shoulder. One might have taken him for a dissatisfied customer who was only slightly let down by a shopkeeper's recommendation.

Still sitting on the floor, Annalise retched. And then she wept.

~ ~ ~ ~ ~

Chapter 24

April 1968: Knowledge of a Kind

"MAMMA LEONE'S?" ANNALISE ASKED in a tone perhaps more incredulous than she intended.

"That surprising?" Stephen said with a smile.

"I didn't get the impression Andrew and Helga . . . well, I just assumed they would go for something a little fancier. I was looking forward to a good French restaurant."

In fact, she had been dreading any restaurant that included Helga as a dinner partner. Stephen explained that Andrew and Helga had been given hard-to-get tickets to *Cabaret* for their anniversary. Andrew suggested it might be fun to eat at a kitschy Italian tourist palace in the theater district like Mamma Leone's. "We won't starve, that's for sure," Stephen added, alluding to the restaurant's reputation for outsized portions. "I have to admit, I would have thought a place like Sardi's more their style."

Yet as she obsessed over the coming encounter, Annalise concluded it might be better this way. Better a large, noisy restaurant than an intimate one. Such a place might be an ally in obscuring things if things needed to be obscured, lost in a din. It seemed a safer prospect than some place that held the possibility of every nuance being open to scrutiny.

In the days leading up to the dinner date, Annalise was sometimes able to convince herself she was mistaken about Helga. Perhaps it wasn't the woman she remembered after all.

These hopeful spells were fleeting. Most of the time Annalise thought it absurd that she could mistake Helga-Margit for someone else. She had a good memory for faces. However much Margit might have aged (and she must have been a decade older than Annalise), however much her face might have filled out with prosperity or gone under the plastic surgeon's knife, there was a reason Annalise's breath had caught upon meeting her. The most she could hope for—a long shot—was that Helga's memory wasn't as acute as her own.

In a strange way it wasn't the prospect of seeing "the arranger" again that was the cause of so much anxiety. After all, it wasn't as if she needed prompting to relive her nightmares. What Annalise feared was having to reveal her secrets to Stephen. At this moment she felt foolish for not having done so—confessed them, as it were—a long time ago. He mostly knew how she had been used in Dachau. He was deeply moved by what she had experienced. Would he have been so much more upset to hear that it had all begun earlier, in Buchenwald? Stephen was a good man. He might have been all the more sympathetic. But telling him now really would amount more to a confession than a revelation.

She tried to analyze the reasons for her reticence—tried to face them squarely, particularly in light of the recurrent nightmares. One possibility: She suspected there was a limit to a man's forbearance where a woman's honor was concerned. Stephen was a good man, yes, but he was a man. What she recounted of her Dachau experience had, naturally, emphasized the involuntary nature of the acts, including the rapes, plural—over time she had expanded the narrative to include more than the one rape she had originally implied. Then, again, the passage of time added an element of uncertainty. Could she have only imagined that she had expanded the narrative, or could she have actively created a false memory? It was even possible that for reasons of his own *he* continued to think only of a single incident, distilling many into one.

Would he understand Buchenwald? Understand the absence of choice she faced? She had only one thing to offer in the camps. She was no chemist who could help with explosives, no artist who could be used as a forger, no violinist who could play at candlelight dinners for the camp commandant. Would she have been allowed to survive by working on some assembly line? Perhaps. For a while. But she had her looks. She had her youth. These dictated an occupation, which could not be rejected in any case if she wanted to live. A false choice to be sure.

Burying a secret under the sediment of time was risky. The gamble could pay off. The secret could become fossilized while life at the surface proceeded.

Of course, much would depend on the psychological makeup of the concealer. Would Annalise be strong enough to build and maintain the layered barriers to memory? For as long as she lived? If things went her way, the accretion of sediment holding the secret in place might be an uneventful process. Ferns might turn into shale without interruption.

Then again, there might well be geologic shifts. Fissures. Helga-like heat vents that would need to be either released or capped. And that is where Annalise's strength of mind—the ability to keep the pressure under cap—entered the picture. But the longer the time of compression, the greater the potential for explosive release.

Surely she should understand that this could be Helga's dilemma as well. Had Helga revealed her past to Andrew? If so, did she assume Annalise had been similarly forthcoming with Stephen?

And what if she were, belatedly, to tell Stephen the truth—perhaps even do it prospectively, before the dinner out? He wouldn't leave her; she was sure of that. The irony was that during the past year she had had episodes of being so angry with him over Jacob and, more recently, fair or not, over Ben, she had fantasized about leaving *him*.

No, it wasn't that. Rather, it was being afraid of the feral consequences of broken trust. When an unfaithful partner is punished, it can be as much for the act of concealment or dishonesty as for the act of wandering carnality.

Now, more than two decades into their marriage, she decided there would be no voluntary unburdening to him. She would keep her secrets unless forced by Helga to reveal them. She hoped she was worrying for nothing.

* * *

ANNALISE WAS QUIET on the drive downtown, passing the time looking out the window.

"Anything wrong?" Stephen had asked into the silence.

"Just thinking about Ben," Annalise lied. At almost any point since Ben ran off, the statement would have been true. At that moment her thoughts were all about Helga.

"I'm sure we'll hear from him soon," Stephen responded in a reassuring tone of voice. "I think we can count on it." He switched on the radio to fill the void.

Sinatra was playing in the background at Mamma Leone's. They checked their coats. "Better music than the last time I was here," Stephen remarked with a nod to the atmosphere. As if on cue, "You Make Me Feel So Young" was replaced by a scratchy Caruso rendition of "O Solo Mio."

"Spoke too soon," Stephen said.

Annalise, glancing around distractedly, said, "What?"

"Never mind."

Andrew and Helga were waiting at the table, cocktails before them. Andrew stood and extended his hand as Stephen apologized for arriving late, blaming the city's impossible parking situation. He had offered to drop Annalise off at the restaurant while he hunted. The offer was declined with alacrity.

When she saw Helga, Annalise had the same frisson of recognition as the first time. However, confirming the impression proved more difficult than she expected. For one thing, there was no reciprocal sign of recognition on Helga's part. The lighting was low, and once the women were seated—side by side, opposite their husbands—most of the views were in profile. Nor could Annalise tell from the voice, which was huskier than she remembered, though this could be explained by aging and the effects of heavy smoking. With long, perfectly manicured fingers that also would bear little resemblance to them in a previous life, Helga proceeded to light one cigarette off another. Was this typical, or was she nervous?

As the men dug into, and the women nibbled at the edges of, the garlic bread on the table, Stephen and Andrew kept the shop talk going, seeming oblivious to the polite, ornamental contributions of their wives. And as the patter continued through the shrimp scampi, the linguini with red sauce, the sausage and peppers, and finally, the slab of tiramisu, plate of cannoli, and espresso (the women grazing, the men feasting), Annalise, with great if only temporary relief and yet unsatisfied curiosity, had just about given up on a definitive sign of recognition.

A second round of espresso for the men followed in something of a rush as Andrew consulted his watch. Annalise (self-consciously using a phrase she always thought silly) said she needed to go powder her nose. There would be no respite from the strain of the evening, however, as Helga pronounced this a good idea and stood to join her.

By this point, with the evening almost over, Annalise was breathing somewhat easier with the idea that it might be better that answers to her questions not be found. If Helga was indeed Margit, she had given no clue, either deliberately or out of lack of recognition. Their talk on the way to the ladies' room was limited to agreement that after the meal they'd just consumed they would never eat again.

It was the bright light in the ladies' room, illuminated by theatrical mirrors outlined by many bulbs, that enabled Annalise to arrive at a state of certainty. In the twenty-plus years since the war, Helga's appearance may have changed, but the birthmark strangely located on the underside of her jaw brought everything back. The assignments. The degradation. The occasional gestures of kindness.

Still, as they stood next to one another and chatted about nothing to their reflections in the mirror, there was no sign that Helga shared Annalise's recognition. They wiped their hands and threw the towels into a wicker basket.

Annalise made for the door and held it for Helga. And then . . .

With a quick, furtive look around, Helga eased the door shut. For all of her mental preparations, Annalise had not imagined anything like this, as Helga took both of her hands in her own and looked hard into Annalise's face. Her searching expression could have meant a thousand things but meant only one. Helga said not a word.

Finally, with a nod and a gentle squeeze of Annalise's hands, Helga opened the door and walked through it, leaving Annalise to follow.

~ ~ ~ ~ ~

Chapter 25

April 1968: Baldwin Street Blues

ALL THREE OF THEM—Neil, Martha, and Ben—reacted at first with shocked, relieved silence at the ease with which they were able to cross the border. For Neil in particular, the final approach on the American side seemed to be filled with the kind of terror an acrophobe must feel on his first skydive. As they sat in line with three cars ahead of them, Martha had to ask him more than once to stop pulverizing the bones in her hand.

There was no doubt Neil had the most to lose if the border agents apprehended him. The open question was whether he had remained ahead of whatever bureaucratic maw was responsible for digesting and spitting out the names of deserters. "I hope our little stopover in Buffalo didn't make me a day late," he said amid one of his bone-crushing grabs.

Ben hoped so, too. As the car rolled forward, he had a flash of panic over whether he had made the right decision in sticking with Neil and Martha. He was fairly sure it was too soon for his name to appear on any wanted lists. But what if Neil were to be detained and questioned? Worse, what if Neil were to be arrested? Might that not cast suspicion on him?

Thus, when the U.S. officer gave them a cursory scan and asked if they were carrying contraband—a question even Neil could answer with a steady voice since they had either smoked or given away anything in that category and "deloused" the car, as he put it, and considering the frequent assurances Ben had received from friends supposedly in the know that the agents were more concerned with what was coming into the country than what was leaving—and when the officers on the Canadian side gave them a greeting that was almost friendly, the three looked at one another in wonder, as if their parachutes had opened after all.

"So, how does it feel to be in a foreign country?" Neil asked the others, his voice now waxing victorious.

"Ask me after I've calmed down," Martha said.

"You?" Neil responded, in an incredulous voice. "You were my rock."

"Yeah, crushed into gravel," Martha laughed, holding up the hand with feigned deformity.

Neil looked in the rearview mirror at Ben. "You're pretty quiet," he said.

"I'm still amazed at how easy it was."

"You sound more sad than amazed," Martha offered.

"A little, maybe. I was thinking that going back to the States might not be so simple."

"Ah, come on!" Neil said. "Don't kill the buzz. Have you ever been to Toronto? It's a cool city. It'll make you forget all about what you're leaving behind."

"I've never been anywhere outside the U.S."

"Me neither," Martha said with a note of camaraderie. "Well, Tijuana once, but I don't think that counts."

"*Oh I theenk si eet does, señorita,*" Neil said, his José Jiménez shtick energized by continuing high spirits. "Hey, Ben," he went on in his own voice, "I never asked you, where are we dropping you off? Do you have a place to go?"

"Not really."

"Come with us then," Martha said.

"A flicker of annoyance passed across Neil's face. But he said, "Yeah, definitely, come with us."

"Where?" Ben asked. "Do you have friends in Toronto?"

"Not exactly," Neil responded.

"Meaning?"

"I have some contact info for the American Ghetto."

"What's that?"

"That's what they call it," Martha offered. "It's an area downtown, near the university. There are supposed to be a lot of refugees like us there."

"You've read the *Manual*, right?" Neil asked Ben.

"The what?"

"Man, you really came here cold, didn't you?"

"Ah, cut the guy some slack, wouldja?" Martha said, giving Neil a playful shove.

Martha craned to look at Ben. "*The Manual for Draft-Age Immigrants*," she said in a helpful tone of voice. "It's kind of a how-to on getting settled. It's new, and you can forget Neil's superior know-it-all attitude. We only know about it because we lucked into a Canadian guy in Indianapolis."

"There's a thing called the Toronto Anti-Draft Program—the TADP for those of us in the know," Neil added, which drew another shove from Martha. "Yeah, yeah okay, I'll be nice," he continued. "They do all kinds of things to help you get settled. That's our first stop."

* * *

IN DOWNTOWN TORONTO they got out of the car and asked directions from a slightly spaced-out young woman with stringy blond hair and an armload of books. She told them to look for the place with a yellow door and a picture of a bird on it.

"Dove of peace sort of bird?" Neil ventured.

"Yeah, man, I suppose," she said, continuing on after rebalancing her books.

"We probably should have asked someone else," Neil said.

But the TADP office with the dove on the bright yellow door wasn't hard to find, and before long they were standing in a short line to talk to one of the volunteer counselors. A bewildered-looking kid in front of them was writing furiously as he was being given advice on cheap places to eat. "Be cool, my man," the counselor said with an easy smile and handed the kid a mimeographed sheet. "It's all here," he added, pointing to the list.

Neil nodded toward the kid and rolled his eyes for Martha's benefit.

"Oh, like you already know all this stuff, right?" Martha whispered.

At that moment, a young man, apparently another counselor, came around a corner and beckoned them to a beat-up, castoff oak desk. Introducing himself as Mark, he smiled and motioned to a pair of matching oak chairs in front of the desk, their seats buffed shiny by years of occupants. Mark looked around for a third chair for Ben.

"No sweat, man," Ben offered. "I'm good standing."

"So, let me guess," Mark began, "you all just arrived, and you need to scope out the scene."

"That's about it," Neil answered. "We're up on the *Manual*," he added in a transparent effort not to appear like a know-nothing tourist.

"That's good," Mark said, evenly. With the efficiency of a pro, over the next half hour he went through a checklist of things the newcomers would need, beginning with their immigration status. "For lots of people this is where the reality hits that they've landed in another country, not just another American state." Mark explained that there were several steps they had to take to get what he called landed immigrant status. He said he would go through the information quickly just to give them the lay of the land, but they shouldn't worry if it didn't sink in immediately—there was a lot to digest, and they could begin the process after they got settled.

"Your case may be a little touchy," Mark said to Neil, who looked surprised to be singled out and asked Mark why he would say that without knowing anything about him.

With a laugh and a determined "I've seen it all before" look, Mark said, "Let me guess. You're the deserter in the group." He tapped his head. "Your hair, man, your hair! An army cut if ever I saw one, but grown out enough to know you haven't been on active duty for a little while. Am I right?"

Neil nodded.

"No need for panic," Mark continued. "We can work it out. It's probably no surprise to you that the army is getting tougher on deserters and dodgers both, but deserters face the harsher penalties, so we'll want to make sure your safety net in Canada is as strong as possible. Anyway, first things first. We'll see if we can get a roof over your heads. I assume you don't already have something arranged?"

Soon Neil, Martha, and Ben had what Mark blithely referred to as his special O Canada! Starter Kit, which consisted of a place to stay, local maps, advice on restaurants, stores and basic services, and phone numbers in case they got into trouble. Also, the lyrics to the national anthem. "Just in case." Mark laughed. "Who knows? You might be out watching the Maple Leafs and all of a sudden be overcome with gratitude to your new home.

You'll really get to know Baldwin Street," he went on. "That's one of the main hangouts for newcomers. Kind of ground zero for the antiwar set—you'll see, the whole area's plastered with posters and leaflets. Also some good music hangouts and places to buy stuff—clothing collectives, that kind of thing. Check out The Yellow Ford Truck. It's kind of a modern trading post in the Ghetto," he added, pointing to a spot on the map.

They were given directions to a TADP-run hostel on John Street. "It's not fancy, but it will let you catch your breath," Mark said. "Some folks stay for a pretty long time," he added. And a final piece of advice to Neil and Martha: "You didn't hear it from me, but if you want to stay together, when you get to the hostel tell whoever is on duty that you're married—only if the subject comes up, don't raise it. It's just that one or two of the house-minders are surprisingly old fashioned. It'll save a hassle."

"We're almost married," Martha said with a smile.

"Yeah, almost," Neil said. Something about the way he said it rubbed Ben the wrong way, though it didn't seem to register with Martha.

* * *

AT THE HOSTEL, the newlyweds were given a small room to themselves upstairs. Ben was assigned a bunk in a four-man room on the ground floor. Only two people were living in the room at the time, and no one was there when Ben poked his head in. He had been told that the lower bunks on the left and right were taken; he chose the upper one on the right, dropped his pack, and threw a sweatshirt on the bunk to stake his claim.

The room echoed off a linoleum floor and hard furniture surfaces; only the mattresses were capable of soaking up sound. There was a small turquoise-and-beige tile bathroom and two closets, each one capable of holding a minimal amount of clothing, though neither was full. Ben assumed he would have to share, not that he had much to add.

There were two stray chairs in the room. Ben pulled one up and sat heavily. The euphoria he experienced when he crossed the border and the relief he felt at the help received from the TADP had subsided in the spartan space of the room. He reminded himself that things so far had gone as well as he could have hoped. Here he was, less than forty-eight hours into his new life, and he had managed to get to Toronto with two new friends and find a place to stay. He had already succeeded in making his point about the war and the draft. By any measure, things were going well.

And yet . . . also here he was in a land where he no longer had the distinction of being The Rebel. Literally overnight he had lost a feeling of specialness. He had joined the majority as far as the war went, become almost a member of the establishment. He could, and would, continue his antiwar activities. But here in Toronto he would be to a large extent preaching to the converted.

Suddenly he was overwhelmed with a sense of being alone. He could hear feet shuffling and furniture scraping along the floor in the bedroom over his head as, presumably, Neil and Martha rearranged the space. Worse, after a short time he thought he could hear a heavy rhythmic beat from the bed that could only mean they were having sex. A couple coupling while he sat in an empty room.

He found himself resenting Neil. He might not be able to articulate his reasons at that moment, but he was certain Neil was not serious about Martha. She deserved better. And while he resisted following this train of thought to its conclusion, he probably wouldn't have denied the suggestion by an astute observer that he, Ben, could make her happier.

He thought about calling home. Just to let them know he was safe. He wanted to talk to Sandy, not either of his parents—he wasn't ready to deal with them.

There was a pay phone in the hall, but he needed to convert some of his money to Canadian to use it. He decided to call collect. Surely whoever picked up would accept the charges. Well, maybe not his father. Sandy and Annalise might be angry, but they wouldn't shut him out. Hard to tell with Stephen. Anyway, even if they declined, they would know he was alive. It was worth a try. He could always hang up.

In any event, no one answered, and Ben returned to the room.

A small gift—at least there were no erotic sounds from the floor above. Outside, it was beginning to cloud up. He swung his legs onto the bed and quickly fell asleep.

It was full dark when the need to use the bathroom awakened him. It took a minute to map a path in his head. He had no idea of the time. His parents had given him a watch for his seventeenth birthday, a handsome stainless-steel Timex with an expansion wristband. He seldom wore it, however, and forgot to bring it. Now he wished he had.

He opened the door and winced at the bright light in the corridor. Sounds of life could be heard from a couple of rooms. He considered knocking on a few doors to introduce himself, but this degree of initiative was beyond him at the moment.

He returned to his room and cracked open the blinds. The street was still active, with headlights and taillights moving in and out of view. At least he hadn't slept through the night.

He was hungry. With a small burst of enthusiasm, he went upstairs to see if Martha and Neil wanted to catch a bite. He heard a stereo in the adjacent room, but a feeling of emptiness returned when neither Martha nor Neil answered his knock. He thought the least they could have done was ask if he wanted to grab a pizza or something.

Well, fuck 'em, then. He remembered the list of restaurants he had been given at the TADP office. He'd check for nearby places and go off on his own.

It took almost no time for the swagger to fade and be replaced by the previous deflation. He closed the door behind him, checking to make sure it was locked. He had considered taking his pack but was sick to death of living with it on his back. Taking only his money, he left it on his bunk.

He decided to call home once more before he left the building. Surely by now someone would be there. The fact that it might not be Sandy who answered gave him cold feet. He was in no mood for the inevitable confrontation with his father. Still, after dithering for a moment, he placed the collect call; this time the operator was able to complete it. Even better, it was Sandy who picked up and accepted the charges. "Where *are* you?" she asked. "We've all been worried to death."

"No need," Ben said with more confidence, his mood lifting upon hearing the familiar voice. "I'm in Toronto. I found a place to stay."

"Toronto!"

"Yeah. Where else would you expect?"

"I don't know. I guess I didn't really think you'd do it. Listen, let me find Mom and Dad. They've been crazy worried."

"Wait! I don't want to speak to them yet. Is Dad worried, or mad?"

"Worried, dopey. Well, maybe a little of both."

"That'll change. Count on it. As soon as he realizes I'm not dead, it'll be a hundred percent mad. Anyway, like I said, I don't want to talk to them now. And I have to get off," he added, though he didn't.

"Ben, listen to me. You can still come home. It hasn't been that long. Nothing has really changed."

"And that's the problem, Sis. I'd still be facing the same choices. If it's all the same to you . . ."

"It's not."

"Either way, I'll see it through here."

"You don't sound very sure," Sandra ventured. "Are you there?" she asked into a sudden silence.

"Yeah, I'm here. Yes, I'm sure."

~ ~ ~ ~ ~

Chapter 26

May 1968: Née Wroth

WALKING DOWN THE STREET with Martha, Ben presumed a certain proprietary closeness. He resisted an urge to take her hand, but he was close enough to her side that the crowd's jostling permitted more episodes of physical contact than were necessary. If she saw the contact as intentional, she didn't seem to object.

They were among a stream of protesters that grew block by block as they headed for the U.S. consulate to renew demands to stop the war. The energy of the stream was palpable, growing in proportion to its size. Fresh impetus was provided by a broad North Vietnamese offensive, widely referred to as Mini-Tet, in which well over a hundred cities were attacked with rockets and mortars. The U.S. responded with high explosives and napalm.

"Look at that Negro guy over there," Martha said with a nod toward a wiry young black man carrying a placard saying, "No Vietnamese Ever Called Me Nigger!"

"You got that right, friend!" she called to him. He rewarded her with a Black Power salute. "It feels good to be hitting the streets again," she said to Ben.

Martha wasn't very much taller than Ben, but the few inches caused him to tilt his head back slightly to look at her as they walked. "There's been too much bullshit jawboning among ourselves," she said. "I know we've been busy getting settled here, but I was starting to wonder if we were ever going to get out and protest."

"Absolutely," Ben declared with an antiwar zeal that also reflected Neil's absence. A week before, Martha and Neil had moved out of the hostel to a small apartment nearby. Both of them had arranged to meet up with Ben for breakfast before joining the march. Ben wasn't disappointed when only Martha showed and made a lame excuse for Neil. She had never confided in Ben about their relationship, but over the weeks since they had arrived in Toronto it had become increasingly clear to him that something was wrong. Which gave rise to fantasies both sympathetic and erotic, the common thread being Ben in the role of rescuer.

Once, after hearing muffled sounds of argument coming from the room above, Ben drifted into reverie about charging up the stairs and demanding that Neil open the door so he could see for himself that Martha was safe.

There were variations: The obvious one, Neil refusing, Ben having to force the door, finding a tear-streaked Martha in retreat (to bed, other side of bed, corner); cut to Ben kissing away tears, Neil somehow having been dispatched from sight. Or, Martha gratefully kissing Ben, at first tentatively—Neil after all being not yet cold in the vault of convenience. (Ben's fantasies had limits. It wouldn't do to set up Martha as being flighty in her affections.) Then, having surrendered to the inevitable, they kissed with more passion.

The fantasy and its several permutations soon became staples of self-induced orgasm. Once, reality intruded when his approach to climax was disturbed by squeaking bedsprings overhead, which he tried, and failed, to appropriate for his own erotic purposes. He finally gave up and switched the fantasy to an old girlfriend.

Martha might have been only a couple of years older than Ben, but it seemed a gulf in experience and maturity. Ever since he had met her and Neil, he had settled into what he had begun to think of as a little-brother role. It bothered him. They were the ones who knew where they were heading and how to go about it. They had the car. They knew about the TADP. They were generous about including him, but the decision was always theirs, by definition keeping him in a dependent position.

232

At the coffee shop that morning, his fantasies took on a modest realization when, faced with a quietly remote Martha, he ventured to ask if anything was wrong. At first, she waved off the question. But when Ben ventured further, suggesting that he sensed of late that Martha was unhappy (was she, really?) and that the source of the unhappiness seemed to have something to do with Neil, she rewarded him with a tepid "maybe."

"You know you can talk to me about it, right?" he said with a smile and a stab at casual levity, pronouncing "about" in exaggerated Canadian: *aboot*. "I'm a good listener."

"I know you are, and I appreciate it, I really do." She reached across the table and gave his hand a pat.

"Just so's you know," Ben said, hoping it would prompt further confidences. When none were forthcoming as she concentrated on stirring her coffee and staring into the whirl, he tried a different tack. "How long have you two been together?" he asked, an awkward, innocent-sounding reset even though he knew the answer.

"Couple of years."

"So, it's serious between you."

"I guess you could say that." She looked up from her coffee, gave a quick puffed-cheek exhale. "On my part anyway, or so I'm beginning to see."

Ben was quiet for a moment before asking, "Do you want to tell me about it? Like I said, I'm a good listener."

She shrugged. "Not really."

Ben covered her hand with his own, felt a frisson, an outpouring of horny solicitousness. "It's okay. Whenever you want."

"It's not such a big deal, really," she said, looking at him more directly. "I don't even know exactly what's wrong. It's mostly a vibe I'm getting from Neil that he's less interested in me than he was."

"That's hard to understand," Ben said, and immediately feared he would come across as pandering. "In my opinion. For what it's worth," he added.

Martha took a deep breath, shrugged, and said, "We should go."

It was a disappointing closure. Having worked himself up to a point of urgent, desire-fueled sympathy, Ben's mission to rescue Martha had become more important than mounting another antiwar demonstration. He reeled himself in, though. "Right, we should go. Anyway, if you ever want to talk again . . ."

"You're sweet," she said, and they were off to end the war.

* * *

THE FOLLOWING WEEK was marked by further disappointment, as no additional insights were revealed, either (predictably) when he met Martha and Neil together for dinner one night, or (more significantly) when he ran into her alone as he was coming from the TADP office. The latter occasion was not a complete loss, however, as she took note of his downcast mood and said, "It's too nice a day to look so sad."

Ben told her he was worried because he hadn't had any luck finding work. He had gone through the list of possible openings provided by the TADP the day they arrived. The only jobs he was qualified for were as sales help in local stores or doing manual labor, and all of those jobs were filled. "I'm bummed, man, you know?"

Martha nodded sympathetically. "I guess there are just too many of us here looking for that kind of work. Not many doctors or accountants in our antiwar crowd. Now, if there were a market for picketers," she said with a smile.

Just when Ben thought he could take some comfort in her commiseration, she added, "I was lucky, though."

"You mean you found something?"

"Nothing great. Waiting tables at Reuben's, that deli off Baldwin. I start tomorrow. Neil hasn't found anything yet," she added, providing commiseration of a sort. "I think Reuben's might need someone to bus tables, if you're interested. It's not exactly a dream job, but it's something."

Ben's lack of enthusiasm for the suggestion was offset by the idea of working with Martha, until she laughed and said, "I mentioned it to Neil, but he said he wants to hold out for something that requires half a brain."

"Can't blame him for that."

"I guess. But beggars can't be choosers."

"I'm not a beggar yet," Ben said, glossing over the problem of his dwindling bankroll and fighting off the annoyance of hearing one of his father's bromides on Martha's lips.

A week later he decided to wander over to Reuben's and maybe take that job after all. He returned to the hostel more deeply depressed and still jobless after being told that the busboy gig had been filled. Probably by Neil, he thought bitterly.

It didn't help that his two roommates were working. One, an eighteen-year old from Denver named Calvin, had cadged a job at The Yellow Bus. The other, Stan, a twenty-year-old from Detroit, was a skilled carpenter; he had no trouble finding work. In fact, between abundant work hours and steady girlfriends, Calvin and Stan were rarely around, to the point where Ben, who at first liked having the room to himself, felt ever more lonely. The least they could do was give up the bottom bunks if they weren't going to sleep in them, he complained to the empty room.

Now he sat, depressed, recounting his cash one more time in hope of having overlooked something. He was jolted to find that the recount totaled less than he thought. After a third count provided minor, relative relief that he had accurately counted his inadequate funds to begin with, he fell asleep.

* * *

LATE THAT AFTERNOON he was awakened by a hard rap on the door. When he shuffled over, bleary-eyed, it turned out to be one of the hostel managers, a guy named Marvin. Ben's first thought was that he was late with the rent—which was true, nominal though the rent was—but Marvin had come by only to pass the message that the TADP office had called to say that Ben should call home, and that it was important. "Something about your Dad, I think. I'm not sure."

"That's it?" Ben asked.

"That's it. I guess whoever called didn't have a number for you here."

But how did his parents or Sandy know to call the TADP? He had only made the one call home when he arrived, and he was sure he hadn't given the family the satisfaction of having an easy way to contact him.

Ben's concern that something was wrong at home quickly descended into fearful projection. Beginning with the mystery of how anyone knew to call the TADP, he cooked up a stew of ideas that took him from worry over what had prompted the call (his first thought, which he forced himself not to dwell on, was that Stephen had been stricken in some way, perhaps a heart attack), to irritation that he could be found—the latter mitigated by the thought, which he also resisted, that it would feel good to hear a familiar voice.

Well, he would call (collect, of course), but he'd take his sweet time. Whatever the problem was, there wasn't anything he could do about it from Toronto. He was on his own, independent, and not obligated to his parents' whims.

A half hour later he was still pondering the right time to call—sufficient to respond in what his parents would consider a responsible manner, but not so soon that he would appear needy or subservient—when there was another knock on the door. "Marvin" came the response to Ben's query.

"Hey, man, have you by any chance made that call?" Marvin asked when Ben came to the door.

"I was about to."

"Okay. It's just that I got another call from the TADP, so I guess maybe it's important."

"It's cool, man. I'll do it now."

"Do you want to use the phone in the office?"

"Pay phone's fine, man."

Beneath the bluff performance, Ben's stomach began to churn. Thoughts he had deep-sixed suddenly shot to the surface. Something must be seriously wrong for his parents to have tracked him down. Twice.

He hoped Sandy would pick up, but the voice that answered before the first ring finished was Stephen's. "Ben! We've been trying to reach you!"

"I just got the message. What's up? Are you okay? The guy who gave it to me said something might be wrong with you."

"With me? Who told him that? No, not with me. It's Jacob."

"What?!" Ben's voice went up an octave. In the background he could hear an ill-defined commotion, shards of voice slicing through, a cut from Sandra, another from his mother. Of all the possibilities he had considered and dismissed, none came and went more fluidly than the most obvious one of bad news about Jacob. Throttling the phone and trying to steel himself for the worst, he got something marginally better.

"Jacob's been wounded," Stephen said.

"Wounded," Ben echoed. "When? How? How bad?"

"Bad enough."

Ben was unprepared for the stretched quality of his father's voice, which seemed stripped of its normal confidence. He was also unprepared for the instant deflation of the reassurance he had automatically expected to hear of Jake's wounds being slight.

"Three days ago," Stephen continued. "We only just got word."

"What . . ."

"He was hit by a mortar. In Saigon while he was on leave, no less."

Ben resented what he interpreted in Stephen's voice as irritation over the absurdity of fate that Jake could be wounded in Saigon, when he had never been hurt in the field. Well, it figured that his father would act as if he himself were the one who had been wounded!

"All we know," Stephen continued, "is that he's in the hospital and that the wounds are serious. There's no prognosis, in any case nothing they were prepared to say. Hold on. Your mother wants a word."

Without a chance to absorb anything he'd been told, Ben heard Annalise's voice—not the desperately plaintive voice he might have predicted, but also not the stoic, measured voice he might have expected as an alternative. Rather, it was something more straightforward and businesslike: "Can you come home?" she asked without a preface. "Come home, Ben."

"Mom, I don't know. If I try to cross the border they might, you know, arrest me."

"I'll bet they wouldn't," Annalise said. "I'll bet they wouldn't arrest you."

237

"Why do you say that, Mom? You have no way of knowing."

"Pass me the phone, please," he heard Stephen say. A moment later: "Listen to me, Ben. We don't know what's going to happen. But we need to be a family right now. You understand that, don't you?"

"Jesus, Dad, of course I understand. But it's not going to help anything if I'm sitting in some jail."

"I've been thinking about that. I may have some contacts who can help. I won't know until tomorrow. Where can I call you?"

"I don't need your help. I don't want it."

"You may not want it, but you apparently need it if you're concerned about getting home."

After a pause, Ben said, "I can give you this number. It's a pay phone in the hall."

"You don't have a private number?"

As insignificant as the question might have been given the present circumstances, or however innocent (though Ben rarely allowed for innocence in anything Stephen said), Ben was stung by it, as if he were being upbraided for failing to establish himself with something as basic as a telephone. If he had hoped the absence of contact with his parents would create a vacuum they would fill by assuming he must be making it on his own (he wasn't asking for anything from them, was he?), he now thought he'd blown it by revealing the glaring deficiency of having nothing better than a pay phone.

"All right, give me the number," Stephen said. "Better yet, why don't you call me here. Tomorrow evening. I should be able to find out something by then. By the way, those people I talked to at the . . . what do you call it? The Toronto draft resisters or something? You need to correct your name. They couldn't find you under double-u. They have it as Roth, without it."

"I'll call tomorrow," Ben said. He hung up before his father could press him on the elision that occurred when he deliberately registered as Roth.

* * *

JAKE WAS WOUNDED—only wounded, Ben said to himself, assembling a narrative he could cope with as he walked back to his room. Only wounded. That was the main thing. He was in Saigon, in the hospital. Lucky he hadn't been wounded in the field. So far, so good. He'll get better. They can't tell how long it will take, but he'll recover and then he'll come home. A hero, no less. Man, will he ever be a pain in the ass to live with! And then he remembered that he wouldn't be there for Jake's homecoming.

At any rate, this was how the story played out when Ben related events to Martha and Neil at a nearby all-night diner. He was relieved that they could meet up. He needed to talk it out with someone. That the choice of confidants was as limited as it was embarrassed him. He who had always made friends easily had somehow managed to restrict his Toronto inner circle to two people he had met by chance in Buffalo. And of the two, really it was only one he cared for, or who cared for him . . . possibly. Had Martha answered his call he would have been content—happy, actually, despite the circumstances—to meet her alone.

They were sympathetic, of course. Both steered him toward the optimistic version of events, reminding him at each pivot point in the story that the little he knew so far about Jacob's situation sounded hopeful: He was wounded, yes—even seriously—but in the absence of further details Ben should not assume the worst. Take a deep breath, they said. Things may look better tomorrow.

Only at one point did it seem Neil might depart from the supportive role Ben needed him to play, when he started off on a diatribe against the "fucking war." Martha, sitting next to Neil and opposite Ben, gave Neil a tap on the forearm, which was all it took for him to change course, though the tap itself, with its suggestion of how well the two understood one another, did not fail to ignite a passing spark of jealousy in Ben.

* * *

HE CALLED HOME the following evening. He had mentally prepared himself for the inevitable lecture from Stephen—steeled himself against the Sanctimonious Father who always knew the right thing and everyone's part in it.

The lecture never came. What he got was a Stephen who sounded thin, exhausted, played out.

No, the news about Jacob wasn't all bad, though it was still sparse. He had regained consciousness, at least intermittently. A piece of shrapnel had barely missed his spine; he probably would not be paralyzed. However, his right leg was hit in several places; it was uncertain that he would keep it. And the fragment that missed his spine damaged a kidney. Fortunately, the other one was unharmed.

"We don't know how long it will take to get him home, Ben. But the recuperation will be long. He'll need you—I'm sure you realize that—we all will."

Ben had rehearsed what he would say to the request for him to come home. It amounted to, come home to what? Arrest? At best, to being drafted.

But his rehearsals had not allowed for the response he received. Stephen told him he had managed to find sympathetic contacts through his office. What it came down to was Ben hadn't been gone for very long. The army would probably hold action against him in abeyance if he reported promptly. They could overlook his being overdue. Yes, he would have to serve, but given the circumstances surrounding Jacob, the army would probably delay Ben's entrance on duty for some time, and if it could be demonstrated that his presence were necessary to assist in Jacob's convalescence, the army almost certainly would try to find some local assignment, something he could commute to from home.

"And then?"

"And then what, Ben?" Stephen said, not trying to hide his irritation.

"What would happen after Jake gets better?"

"Listen, Ben . . ."

"What then, Dad?" Ben persisted.

"I don't know what you expect. They won't promise anything once Jake is recovered. Why would they? Presumably, restrictions on where they could send you would be lifted. It's a pretty damned good deal, Ben. You're lucky I was able to get it. Frankly, I don't see how you could expect more."

"Can I speak to Mom?"

"She's not here right now. You can call back. Don't change the subject."

"I'm not. I want to know what she thinks. And how she's doing. About Jake, I mean."

There was a pause before Stephen said, "So-so. About what you'd expect. She's upset. We all are."

"But only you pushed Jake to be there."

Once again, the expected righteous response didn't come. Stephen said, simply, fatigue in his voice, "You should come home."

"I'll think about it."

"Don't take too long. It wasn't easy to get these assurances. It won't keep." Into the silence Stephen added: "I love you, Ben. This is your chance to put things right, maybe the only one you'll get. I hope you'll take it."

~ ~ ~ ~ ~

Chapter 27

May–June 1968: The Mend

THEY ALL WAITED NERVOUSLY to actually hear Jacob's voice. He sent a telegram saying he was improving and would try to place a phone call in the next day or two. Given the often-devastating associations between telegrams and war zones, for this apparent good news to sink in it first had to overcome the leg-weakening trauma of its mode of transmission. The shock-and-reprieve was absorbed by Annalise, who was able to spare the others by leading with the good news. None of them were spared the anxious speculation over why Jacob didn't just telephone in the first place.

When the call came (this time not via MARS, but instead a spare-no-expense overseas connection), Annalise, who had tried to be within steps of the phone at all times, answered and held out the receiver for Stephen and Sandra to listen. "I'm on the mend," Jacob said after the excited greetings trailed off.

"He sounds tired," Annalise said, covering the mouthpiece while she listened for more.

"Of course he does," Stephen whispered.

No matter. It was *his* voice.

"I'm sorry I couldn't call sooner," Jacob said. "I could never seem to get the timing right. The first days were tough, but I'm definitely doing better."

"What about your leg?" Annalise asked.

"My leg? Oh, Christ! No one's told you! I'm happy to say I still have it!" (Another lurch in Annalise's gut, another reprieve—couldn't anyone begin with the good news?) "It hurts like hell sometimes," Jacob went on, "but the docs say that's good. It shows I have good nerve function or something. Anyway, Mom? Dad?"

"Me, too, little brother!"

"Hey, Sandy! So listen up, all of you! My war is over! I have to get well enough to travel, and I'll be on my way home."

"How long?" Annalise asked, new energy in her voice. "And what about your kidney?"

"I've only got the one now, but it seems to be up to the job."

There was a pause to take this in. "We're just happy things are moving in the right direction," Stephen said.

"How long?" Annalise asked again, this time in chorus with Sandra.

"I can't say for sure. My leg needs to be stronger. Couple or three weeks maybe. No one is willing to be pinned down. I'll have to spend some time recuperating when I get back, but I'll be home. That's the main thing. Has anyone heard from Ben?"

"He knows," Stephen responded. "We're trying to get him home, too."

"That would be great. Okay, I've gotta go, folks. You know the army—get 'em up, move 'em out! I'm getting a little winded anyway. It's tough work being a patient."

"I'm grateful to hear your voice," Annalise said. "What a relief!" she added just as the connection ended.

"He did sound tired," Sandra said.

"That's to be expected, don't you agree, Nurse Wroth?" Stephen interjected with a thin smile. "He's been through a lot."

"We should call Ben and tell him to hurry home," Annalise said.

* * *

FOR STEPHEN, BEYOND the obvious reassurance of hearing Jacob's voice, the call had the benefit of making Annalise easier to live with. From the moment they received word of Jacob's wounding, an undeclared truce took effect. It was as if, having argued so often over the

243

prospect of Jacob being drafted and then enduring the reality of it, there was nothing further to say. Instead, they both walked through the house with all that had gone before sealed airlessly inside them, along with fears of what might happen if the seal were broken.

But if nothing was said, nothing was released, either. Passing one another in narrow corridors, they took pains to avoid physical contact, as if the slightest brush would set off a chain reaction of recrimination and resentment. And really, was there any point to Annalise reminding Stephen for the umpteenth time that he was responsible for anything that happened to Jacob (or to Ben, for that matter)? Would there be any point to Stephen defending himself on this score?

Of course, the logic of such restraint would be for nothing if the news from the Saigon hospital had been worse.

They continued to urge Ben to come home. Without doubt, Jacob would need help until he fully recovered, and the arrangement Stephen had been able to broker with the government wouldn't hold forever.

Ben stalled. He talked in generalities about the importance of coming home to support the family, to help his brother. Not that he otherwise needed to come home, mind. He was doing just fine in Toronto. If he came home, it would be to do his bit.

But all the conversations remained stuck in the conditional. *If* he were to come home, not when. Stephen fumed. "The next time the selfish little twit proclaims how important family is and how much he cares about his family, I swear, I'll reach through the phone and throttle him."

"Maybe that's why he's acting the way he has been," Annalise rejoined.

"All I'm saying, not that it matters, is that it's not enough to proclaim love of family. He's needed here. I've arranged it so he can come home. So where's the proof any of us means a damn to him?"

For Annalise's part, there was growing ambivalence about his return. His coming home still held the prospect of military service, and hence, of Vietnam. He might be deferred, but deferred didn't mean exempted. In any event there was nothing in stone. An "inclination" not to prosecute was not a promise and had no legal standing.

As she reasoned it, if anything, the deal would make it more likely that Ben would eventually be put in harm's way. The army had a bottomless appetite for soldiers in Vietnam. It would already have given Ben a break. Why would it go further out of its way? Besides, wasn't it she who had declared that if the choice were Vietnam or Canada, she would prefer the latter? The important thing was that Ben was safe. Stephen might worry about what this would mean for some vague future when he returned home. But hadn't most of the damage already been done? For Annalise the essential point was that Ben would have a future.

In the meantime, there was much to do to prepare for Jacob's homecoming. Sandra might be an actual nurse, but Annalise left no doubt that she would be in charge of his convalescence. She would sleep by his bedside if necessary. As she once slept by his crib when he was sick. It only remained for her to wait and prepare.

~ ~ ~ ~ ~

Chapter 28

June 1968—A Visitation

THE WAIL WAS SO loud, so piercing, it caused a passerby, a neighbor walking his dog whom Annalise barely knew, to rush up the rough slate steps to her front door, tripping and gashing his shin in the process. The white-whiskered black lab he had dragged up the steps stood next to him, panting from the exertion. Hearing nothing now from within, the man tried the bell but couldn't hear from outside if it was working.

The pitiful cry again, suggesting nothing so much as a declaration of eternal war against the fates for their treachery. The man pounded on the door hard enough to bruise the bone under the meaty part of his hand. "Hello!" he yelled. "Does someone need help?" Getting no answer, he tried the door. Unlocked, it gave faster than expected, and he tripped for a second time, over the threshold, and all but fell into the house.

When he looked up, Annalise was standing in the entrance hall. She stared at him, through him, not really seeing or comprehending. She clawed at her hair; if it were longer she would be holding fistfuls of it.

"Are you all right?" the man asked. He stood there, still holding the leash with which he had half-hanged the poor old Lab when he fell. He asked again. "Are you okay? I'm Martin Gold, your neighbor down the street. I heard a cry."

Slowly she looked at him, some small shadow of recognition returning to her eyes. "Yes," she said, her voice as vacant as her stare. "Yes," she said again, a response not clearly matched to the question.

"You're sure you're okay?"

She nodded, began to say yes, stopped short. "No." There was a canary-yellow piece of paper at her feet. She looked down, made a half-hearted effort to pick it up.

"Here, I'll get it," the man, Martin, said. He only had time to read the first line as he handed it to her, only the words, THE SECRETARY OF THE ARMY HAS ASKED ME TO EXPRESS HIS DEEP REGRET . . . After a beat, the significance of what he had just read obviously sinking in, he said, "I think you should sit down."

"No."

"Really, you should. Let me help you." He let go of the leash and went to Annalise, taking her arm gently and guiding her to a chair in the living room.

"Your leg is bleeding," Annalise said with a nod to it as she sat.

"I fell. It's okay, no big deal." He looked back to the dog and called for him to lie down, which the dog, now identified in the command as Ovaltine, did with an arthritic groan.

Martin turned to Annalise. "Is there something I can do for you? Someone I can call?"

Wordlessly, Annalise handed him the telegram.

"Should I read it? Do you want me to . . . read it to you?"

Getting no response, he scanned the text and began to read aloud, slowly, as if prepared to stop if this was not what she wanted. He was a kind-looking man, in perhaps his mid-forties. He had dark brown eyes and nearly matching chestnut hair, which was showing streaks of gray. His face was clean-shaven to a gloss that suggested a beard might have been present as recently as minutes ago.

He began: THE SECRETARY OF THE ARMY HAS ASKED ME TO EXPRESS HIS DEEP REGRET THAT YOUR HUSBAND . . .

Annalise's eyes shot wide. "What?"

REGRET THAT YOUR HUSBAND, STAFF SARGEANT JACOB A. WROTH . . .

"Give that to me, please."

"Of course," Martin said, handing her the message.

She looked at it, then shook her head to clear it. "This doesn't make sense," she mumbled, as if Martin were not there.

Now he looked confused as well. "Your husband isn't in the service, is he?"

She shook her head and began to read again. HUSBAND . . . SEVERE WOUNDS . . . ATTENDING PHYSICIAN . . . UNABLE TO REVERSE SUDDEN DECLINE INTO CARDIAC ARREST . . .

"Not my husband," Annalise said, the expression of confusion heightened but some normalcy returning to her voice. "My son is in Vietnam. He was wounded, but . . ." She looked down, read it again, looked up, confusion now diluted with, what? Hope? "He's not a staff sergeant, either. And his middle initial isn't A. It's H." Perhaps an error, then. Something sent by mistake.

"Very strange," Martin said, at a loss. "Who should we call?" he added.

"You're very kind," she said.

"It's nothing. You've had a huge shock."

"Your leg is still bleeding."

He gave the shortest, surprised laugh. "Now that really is nothing. Is there someone I can call for you?" he asked again. "Your husband, perhaps? I think I'd recognize him. He's the one who drives the Mercury, right?"

"Yes, that's Stephen."

"Okay, why don't we begin by calling him. I can do it for you if you'd like."

"No. I'd better do it. It would be shocking enough without hearing it from a stranger."

"Well, I'll stick around to make sure you're okay."

"Thank you very much, but you really don't have to. I have to pull myself together."

"I'm sure you will, but I'd like to stay. No offense, you still don't look right. Besides, there's a chance I may be able to help. Clearing up your questions, that is."

She looked up at him, her expression curious, tentative. Perhaps it would be too soon to clear them up. At the moment the only thing standing between her and catastrophe was ambiguity, the possibility of the mistake. The moment of not knowing. May it last!

248

"I'll explain after you speak with your husband." He looked over to the still-open front door where the dog was laying, graybeard snout resting on his paws. "I can tie up Ovaltine outside if you'd prefer."

"No, no he's fine. The least of my problems, you might say. Ovaltine," she added as if a distant echo.

"Um, if that's a question, he was supposed to be a chocolate Lab."

"Tell me how you can help. Maybe it will affect what I tell Stephen."

"I have a good friend in the Pentagon, a colonel, who might be able to clear up the message."

She nodded, looked away, then back, and spoke aloud the thoughts of a moment before. "This is one of those times when you're not sure whether clearing things up is what you want. I want to believe there's been a big mistake, but . . . in my heart . . . I don't believe the answer will help. And I'm afraid."

She stood and walked over to the phone, dialed, and waited what seemed a lifetime through the slight friction that accompanied the return of the dial to its point of origin after each digit. Finally, an answer. A receptionist. Or possibly a secretary. Annalise's request to speak with Mr. Stephen Wroth. "He's not in," Annalise said to Martin after a pause, cupping her hand over the mouthpiece. Into the phone she said, "It's his wife. Tell him to call home. It's urgent."

"Is there anyone else?" Martin asked.

"My daughter, but I'm not sure where to reach her. My other son is . . . away. If I can, I probably should figure out what's going on before I call them anyway."

✳ ✳ ✳

BUT REALLY, SHE knew—had known for weeks now, had sensed it—a premonition based in pregnant fact: Not long after the phone call from Jacob, when he said he was coming home, there was another call in which he said he'd had a minor setback. He was running a low-grade fever. They needed to learn what was causing it. They suspected something in the injured leg. No cause for worry, Jacob said. It would just delay him by a week or so while the docs worked it out.

When a week went by with no word, Annalise began to fear for Jacob in a way she had resisted since that day he poked the malevolent gods by saying he would be coming home. Then, as more days went by without news, she became fearful to the point of obsession. In her life she had witnessed too many worst cases coming to pass to allow for optimism. The bright side had been ground out of her as an option. In her mind, in the absence of proof to the contrary—and proof in hand, at that—the worst case could be relied upon to carry the day. Her nights were sleepless and devoted to pacing and to satisfying sudden nervous hungers.

For Stephen's part, he shared more of her fears than he wanted to let on. He forced himself to focus on reason: There was no real cause for worry. If the army doctors in Saigon knew anything, it was how to treat battle wounds. But embedded in his fears was the knowledge that beyond the reality of whatever might happen to Jacob, there would be the need to deal with Annalise.

✳ ✳ ✳

"WHERE HAVE YOU been?" she asked, the query sounding perhaps more accusatory than intended in front of Martin. Stephen appeared taken aback, his confusion no doubt heightened when he came through the partly opened front door, had to step around a patiently waiting dog, looked at a vaguely remembered neighbor, and finally was asked the question by his wife who appeared to be the simultaneous embodiment of anger, fear, and grief. "I called your office," she added.

"I was out, at a meeting. From which in any case I drove straight home. And I'm early besides. What's going on, Annalise?"

In an obviously awkward position, Martin introduced himself briefly, reminding Stephen that he was the neighbor from four houses down, and took a stab at explaining his presence. He quickly changed course at the prospect of being the one to deliver the news and left it at saying only that he was walking by and thought Annalise might need some assistance. It would probably be best if she filled Stephen in herself. To Annalise, Martin said, "I have your number. I'll call if I learn anything."

"Thank you," Annalise said, oblivious to Martin's response that it was nothing as she turned to Stephen. Martin slipped out the front door, a slow but obedient Ovaltine behind him.

"What's going on?" Stephen asked again, his tone this time registering more foreboding than confusion.

"We're trying to figure *this* out," she said, thrusting the telegram at him, the impulse toward blame momentarily overriding fear and grief. She watched as Stephen absorbed the message, his breath catching obviously, and then the confusion settling in. "Your husband, sergeant . . . what is this?"

"I'm praying it is a mistake."

* * *

ALL THAT REMAINED, then, when the officer, an army captain with an apologetic demeanor, came to the door, was for Annalise, Stephen, and now a blindsided Sandra, too, just home from school, to break down and weep. The final, gossamer hope obliterated. There was no keening this time, just a sickening realization by everyone that the errors in the telegram were in the fine points, not in the heart of the matter.

It was left to Stephen—his hands shaking, voice quivering and cracking—willing himself to hold it together, to deal with the captain, who apologized for the errors, as well as for the manner in which the news was related. He explained that he had received a call from a superior officer in the Pentagon, who, the captain said, looking at his notes, had been alerted to the situation by a Mr. Martin Gold. His superior ordered him to find out what had happened and report to the Wroths in person "forthwith." The expression on the captain's face—including a quick pursing of the lips—suggested that he might have regretted using the robotic army jargon.

"We are extremely sorry for the loss of your son," he said now, and added again, "and also for the terrible way you learned about it. The army takes full responsibility."

"Who cares about your responsibility!" Annalise cried suddenly. "Your responsibility? Your responsibility was to keep my son alive!

Screwing up the way you told us about . . . about," she paused, unable to continue. "It's just . . . how do you say? . . . icing on the cake."

"The captain is trying to apologize, Annalise," Stephen said, his voice low. When there was no response from her, he said to him, "As you can understand, we're very upset. We realize what's happened is not your fault."

"Do we?" Annalise demanded. "Whose fault is it then? This goddamn useless war! My son is dead, and you, Stephen . . . you . . . all you can think to do is apologize because this man might be offended! You're both disgusting!"

"I'm sorry," a flustered Stephen said to the officer after taking a deep breath and running his hand across his hair.

"I understand," the officer replied. "Once again, the army offers its sincere condolences to you and your family. Your son is a hero to this country."

Annalise pushed past Stephen. "He is not! He is no such thing!" Her face was inches from the officer's. "To his country he's nothing but another casualty, and fit for spitting on like the other veterans if he'd returned home. He was hit by a mortar in downtown Saigon. If he's a hero, it's because he's a hero to me! He chose to go to that godforsaken place against everyone's advice—everyone but my husband."

"We'll let you know as soon as possible about a funeral for your son," the captain added, turning to go.

"Yes, leave!" Annalise said to his back. "Go find out why this stupid country took my son's life!" She lurched forward, following the officer out the door and onto the porch. Stephen went after her, interposed his body to restrain her. "You killed him!" she yelled over Stephen to the officer's retreating back. "You and your worthless, incompetent doctors." She hugged herself tightly, as if she could compress her entire being into the tiniest space, a black hole from which no light would escape. Into this space that already contained her family in Germany and her own past of suffering and degradation, and to which she now had to add Jacob. The harshest blow in her harsh world.

Sandra came up and hugged her from behind. "Come on, Mom," she said, tears flowing. "This won't help."

"No?" Annalise pulled away, looking at Stephen. To Sandra she said, "Tell me what will then. Tell me what will help, Sandy. Even better, tell your father, the great patriot. Tell him what will help."

Stephen reached for Annalise, but she spun away and marched back into the house, slamming the door so hard that the flower pots on the porch shook, and leaving him and Sandra frozen in place.

"We have to tell Ben," Sandra said after a long moment. It was a warm evening, the air growing thicker. Her voice had a distant quality, as if she were speaking from inside a bell jar.

Stephen nodded, the features of his face fallen. "I'll call him."

"Tell him he has to come home," Sandra said, more determined now to get the words out. "Home for the funeral." At these most final, definitive, and absolute of words she broke down in great roiling sobs, which were beyond Stephen's power to ease as she shook off his embrace and followed Annalise's path inside.

~ ~ ~ ~ ~

Chapter 29

June–July 1968: Morning Coffee, Creamed with Dread

“OF COURSE I ASKED him to come home,” Stephen, feeling put upon, said to Annalise and Sandra. “Why? What did you think?”

It was the morning after they received the unwanted clarification. Annalise had just put on a pot of coffee to help counteract the sleepless night that followed.

They were bracing to receive neighbors, friends, and coworkers who would be just now getting word of the family's tragedy and would soon phone or arrive with flowers, bagels, Danish, casseroles, coffee cakes, pans of lasagna, and awkward sympathy, all of which at the moment seemed to Stephen likely to make the unbearable more so.

“What did he say?” Annalise asked. “About coming home.”

“Nothing was decided. He was so distraught over the news. I didn't want to push. He'll want to speak to the two of you today anyway. You can bring it up again.”

“When were you able to get through to him?” Sandra asked. “I didn't fall asleep until almost three, and I don't think anyone had spoken to him.”

“It must have been a little after five,” Stephen said. “He wasn't at his usual number. Eventually someone answered and said Ben was out with some girl, maybe staying with her. I don't know. I finally got a good number to call.”

"Does the girl have a name?" Sandra asked.

"Well, I presume so, but I don't know it."

"You don't have to be snippety."

"You're right. I'm sorry."

"It sounded like I woke her up. I probably did at that hour. When Ben came to the phone it sounded like I woke him up too. So, draw your own conclusions. In any case I had more on my mind than Ben's love life, and he . . . he didn't take the news well. He was as shocked as we were."

Annalise brought the coffeepot to the table and poured. "Does anyone want toast or something in their stomach?" Her tone of voice discouraged a positive response.

"I can make it," Sandra offered with similar lethargy. "Some eggs or whatever, too."

"I'm not hungry," Annalise replied.

"Coffee's good enough for me," Stephen said.

Sandra shrugged. "It's not worth the effort to cook just for me."

"People will be bringing food soon anyway," Annalise said, absently.

"About Ben," Sandra said, looking at Stephen. "Where do you think it stands about him coming home?"

"I told you. I didn't press."

"I meant has anything changed about whether he would be charged or drafted?"

"Ah. Well, I'm not sure about that, either. I spoke to my contact in the office a couple of days ago. He also didn't really know, but he expressed concern that too much time may have passed since the original offer. That's why I was hoping Ben would get off the dime. I get the impression the army expected its generosity to be acknowledged quickly. Still and all, if I had to guess, I'd say they wouldn't prosecute, assuming he reported for duty."

Annalise glared at him. "Today of all days I have no intention of dealing with that subject."

"Sandy asked," he said with a shrug.

"Dad, I hate to bring it up right now, but isn't there something about the army not taking a sole surviving son?"

Annalise visibly blanched at the question, but Stephen said, "I was thinking about that, too, but it's complicated. There is a law, but

255

basically, each branch of the service has considerable leeway in applying it. Ordinarily, I might say the law would apply favorably to Ben. The problem is, technically, Ben should already be in the service. If a decision boils down to the sympathy of some army bureaucrat, he just may not be feeling so generous. There's also the possibility that Ben could be drafted and assigned noncombat duties, but there, too, there are no guarantees."

"Oh, I'm sure your army will demand its pound of flesh," Annalise said, her expression bitter and drawn. As sometimes happened when she was under stress, her native German surfaced, flesh coming out *fleisch*. That it was his army—not the same army that saved her—was not lost on him, but he bit his tongue.

A few minutes later the doorbell and the phone rang simultaneously. Sandra went to the door and accepted a rush delivery of flowers, while Stephen, wary of the multiple invisible snares that might await him, reluctantly went to the phone. He was truly grateful for the sympathies of his friends and neighbors. If only they could be expressed later, and not all at once. As he picked up the handset, he resolved to assign someone the task of screening calls.

"Just a moment," he said. Covering the mouthpiece with his hand, he said to Annalise, "It's Ben."

"Are you all right?" Stephen asked into the phone, followed by, "For God's sake, Ben, you know what I mean! Are you a child who needs it spelled out that I mean are you all right, *considering*? No. No arrangements yet. We don't know the timing of the funeral. It depends on when the army sends . . ." He paused, deciding not to finish the sentence with Annalise hovering. He thought he heard muffled crying before Ben firmed up his voice sufficiently to ask, "What now?"

"We want you to come home, Ben. Whatever plans take shape, you should be here. No, I was just telling your mother and Sandy, it's not clear what will happen as far as your situation goes. You should come home anyway. Hold on a minute. Mom wants to speak to you."

But when Annalise took the phone, Stephen was unprepared for what she had to say.

"Ben? I don't want you to come home. Not until we know for sure what will happen to you." She began to break down. "That's it. I'll talk to you later."

Handing the phone back to Stephen, she added, simply, "Better he stay safe where he is than risk losing my other boy."

* * *

IT TOOK LONGER than expected to get Jacob's body home for burial—providing yet more fuel for Annalise's contempt for the U.S. Army, which to her mind didn't even have the basic competence, never mind the fundamental decency, to ensure proper funerals for its human sacrifices.

Stephen wanted Jacob buried in Arlington National Cemetery. Annalise objected. It was too far away, she said. She wanted to be able to visit him—to comfort him, as she put it.

Stephen suggested a military cemetery in New York. Annalise objected to this, too. As far as she was concerned, Jacob should not rest in a military cemetery, period.

For his part, Stephen was increasingly irritated by Annalise's attitude and having thoughts (thus far not vocalized) along the lines of, *You may fancy yourself the sole grieving parent, but he is my son too.* He suggested it would be fitting for Jacob to be among his fellow soldiers who had given the last full measure of devotion (he was deliberate in his choice of Lincoln's words, though he hoped not to dilute the larger point by having to explain their historical significance). Yes, he wanted Jacob to be viewed by his fellow citizens not only as one, but as one of many, row upon row, so they could understand the magnitude of the sacrifice.

Annalise said this was precisely why she did not want Jacob buried in such a place, because over time, as memories faded, these citizens would come to simply lump his sacrifice together with the groups of soldiers from other wars who were buried there. In response to Stephen's quizzical look, she said she wanted people always to remember that these particular sacrifices in Vietnam were worthless and unnecessary. She wanted the distinction between noun and verb to be preserved: The dead were monuments not to sacrifice, but to being sacrificed by arrogant men. Though left unsaid, Stephen assumed in her mind, and at least at this moment, this group included him.

They settled on burial near his parents and sister Barbara, who had died suddenly of acute leukemia in 1957. The funeral was well attended. Among the mourners was Stephen's brother Robbie, who made a rare trip from Sydney, where he had settled not long after Barbara died. Among the few things Stephen and Annalise could agree on that day was being appreciative and touched by the effort Robbie made to be there.

Most of the people in attendance knew enough about Ben's situation to refrain from bringing it up. One of Stephen's colleagues from the office who was aware that there was another son but not the reason for his absence asked Annalise where he was. The question was innocent. The colleague wanted to express his sympathies. Another colleague jumped in to change the subject, thus sparing her the need to give the one answer she and Stephen could agree on in advance—that he was abroad and unable to find a flight after his was suddenly canceled due to mechanical problems.

Temporarily lost in the swirl of events was curiosity on the family's part, or an explanation on Ben's, about the girl who answered the phone when Stephen called to tell him about Jacob. It took some time for Ben to relate the story of his relationship with Martha, or of her split with Neil, which preceded it.

~ ~ ~ ~ ~

Chapter 30

October 1968: Vortices

THEY SEEMED TO DO nothing but fight now—when they acknowledged one another at all. Each appeared to take for granted that nothing good could come from encounters, only more recrimination and puncture wounds. And although the funeral brought a gratifyingly large turnout of mourners, their presence could never be large enough to conceal the hole created by Ben's absence.

The return of Jacob's body itself might have been akin to ripping a scab from a wound if there had been time for the scab to form in the first place. To the contrary, the funeral and events following closely to it presented to Stephen and Annalise a reality that drowning doesn't require being dragged down dramatically under a thousand feet of water, and not all poisons work quickly. And just as mold may spread from a few spores to become an overwhelming contaminant, their mutual, self-imposed isolation, which deprived each of someone to push back and point out flaws in thinking, created conditions in which there was no impediment to developing a self-aggrandizing—ultimately toxic—narrative.

For Annalise, that narrative only reinforced the obsessive belief that Jacob would be alive if Stephen had been able to see past his misguided notions of duty. Occasionally these thoughts were expressed in an internal diatribe that would only be evinced outwardly by the unconscious moving of lips in German. The silent rant might end with the imagined, door-slamming pronouncement—as outrageous and hurtful as any she could think of—that Stephen reminded her of the Germans of her adolescence who, in their warped, unquestioning self-righteousness, ended up brutalizing her and murdering her family.

For his part, Stephen's quiet histrionics (often mouthed to the bathroom mirror) led to similar places but with opposite conclusions. The roll of his boiling gall was a where-would-you-be-without-me resentment of Annalise's ingratitude to him and his country.

Only once did these narratives clash in the sunlight, and by then it was probably too late to kill off the spores. The fight began with Stephen's angry assertion that "you wouldn't be alive if all American mothers had been like you."

Annalise's response was as simple as it was angry: "You and your army may have ended up saving us, but that was not why you fought. Henry tried to convince you about this—that's one reason you still feel guilty, isn't it? America never would have come into the war just to save us. We happened to be there when you happened to arrive. Besides, Vietnam is *not* World War Two. Nothing changes the fact that *this* war is immoral and my son . . ."

"Our son, Annalise, *our* son."

"More guilt for you then. *Our* son is dead because you couldn't see the difference between that war and this one. *Our* children knew it, and yes, that includes Jacob, who was only trying in his misguided way to fit your definition of a good son."

She was nearly shouting, which prompted him to flash back to their first meeting in Dachau and how oddly poised she had been after all she'd been through. Maybe it wasn't poise she had exhibited after all, but exhaustion.

Afterward, what Stephen thought he could not bring himself to admit in the heat of the moment—amid the *sturm und drang*; yes, the German was what came to mind and expressed it better—was just how much he did, in fact, blame himself for the family's tragedies, and in a larger sense, for what he regarded as profound personal failings.

He remained convinced that he strived with honest purpose to do right by the principles of duty and integrity. He told himself that despite the many sufferings and his own sorrows, he did what was necessary. However much it pained him, he was keeping faith with principles upon

260

which the slim prospects for human survival rested. The world depended on his country, and his country, however flawed, depended upon the steadfastness of its citizens.

Still, when stripped of things majestic, when forced to keep his thoughts within the realm of the quotidian—when brought up short as he sometimes was by Annalise's instruction to get off his high horse—he couldn't shake the wrenching guilt over pushing Jacob into the perilous situation that ultimately had killed him, nor over becoming the focal point of Ben's rebellious streak, which resulted in his flight abroad and might well cost him in any number of ways for the rest of his life.

He expected no sympathy from Annalise. He knew what she would say: For all his manly, principled certainty, he was as naïve as a babe. Where in his tortured dialectic over principle, duty, and grief was his basic understanding that the world is hopelessly corrupt, and that the survival of humankind is more dependent on trillions of serendipitous events and interactions than on godly principles? Nothing is more important in such a context than oneself and the other selves that constitute the family unit. And even if he was right about the importance of good people standing on principle, how did one score the lost potential of a single good person who happened to be his son?

No, to expect relief from Annalise would be like expecting the coal stoker to go easy on the boiler.

But then, two months later and without warning, an incident occurred that caused Stephen the kind of righteous anger that could compete with Annalise's, and all but ensured that the downward spiral of their marriage would accelerate.

~ ~ ~ ~ ~

Chapter 31

December 1968–January 1974: Closing Time

THE HOUSE WAS ENTICINGLY warm when Annalise came in out of the late December air. Struggling to wrangle an armload of groceries and presents and maintain her balance, she managed to close the front door with her foot.

Festivities of the month were no longer really observed, Hanukah having succumbed to the absence of children to celebrate it, and Christmas—always observed as a secular celebration of the season—even more than usual now a matter of ambivalence and social obligation. And between Annalise and Stephen, nothing now could be more obligatory than the gifts to one another, presented without feeling and intended to do nothing more than mask the state of their existence, or perhaps keep things from becoming worse.

The presents that filled Annalise's arms that day were for friends and various colleagues and clients. Her heart might not have been into shopping, but shopping did have the benefit of distraction.

She was drawn toward the sound of crackling fire in the living room. A muffled whump of logs shifting was followed by the soft rustling of embers.

Stephen was sitting in front of the fireplace with his back to her. The only other light in the room came from a lamp on a nearby table. A book was open in Stephen's lap, but his gaze was on the flames. Next to him was a bag of pine cones, which he liked to toss into the fireplace to watch the brilliant explosions of teal, cerulean, and hot red.

He didn't bother turning around as Annalise said to his back, "I'm home." She began placing some of the wrapped gifts on a table, which sat where once, in a time long before the family's dark troubles, they had tried out a Christmas tree.

"I'm home," she said again. This time he nodded.

She brushed invisible particles from her skirt and began rearranging the presents on the table by color and size, moving them a fraction to the left or right and back again, a kaleidoscope in search of perfection.

"When were you going to tell me?" Stephen asked, still facing away from her.

She froze in place as he said, "Were you ever going to tell me?"

He turned, first twisting in his chair, then picking it up and swinging it around so he could face her.

"Tell you what?"

"I had lunch with Andrew today. Imagine my surprise."

She stared at him for a moment, then began to turn away. She didn't complete the turn, however, but rather came back to her original position facing him. Her expression blank, her features fallen, she waited silently.

He preempted the defense she might have given. "I suppose as the years went by it must have become more difficult for you. Here we were starting a family, and then having one. It would have been a difficult conversation. Kids, Mommy was in Dachau. When you're older maybe I'll explain something about what it was like. Oh, you *are* old enough? Well, maybe it's time to explain that Mommy was raped, and so forth.

"But then it would have gotten harder, wouldn't it have? Harder to say, 'Oh, I forgot. It wasn't only one incident. Or even two or three. And it wasn't just Dachau, kids. There was a place called Buchenwald, too. Kids, have you ever heard the expression 'comfort women?' That's what the Japanese used to call them. It was sort of like that for your mom.'"

Annalise remained silent. She held Stephen's gaze, waiting for the next lash. When it didn't come, she began to say, "Stephen . . ."

But he interrupted. "Do you know the funniest thing about this afternoon, Annalise? Well, funny is a strange way to put it, I suppose. Anyway, the right word will come to me. For now let me just say it was

263

funny to see Andrew squirm. Poor guy. He thought I knew. You know what else he told me? He told me he knew about Helga from the beginning. Apparently, she thought it was important to be honest about her past. Go figure! And all of a sudden, the strange looks I thought I had observed between you and Helga made sense."

"Stephen . . ."

"Were you ever going to tell me? Oh, right, I almost forgot. Time passing and all that."

"That's true. It became harder as time passed. You can understand that, can't you? I don't remember you telling the children about your experiences in the war. I wonder how they would react to your act of murder—that terrible man Murch. I wonder if they would understand. But maybe it's only the sarcasm you were going for."

"And before time passed? What was your excuse then?"

"I was afraid you wouldn't understand—couldn't understand. Even now I wonder. Do you understand that I did what I did to survive? Or should I have chosen death? Because that was the choice; there was no other. I ask if you can understand, but really, you should be able to—you were there. You saw for yourself. You saw what people went through. You know what people did to survive. Some worked in the factories making the bullets and bombs used to kill your comrades. I've never heard you question their choices. Some were sonderkommandos helping the Nazis kill us more efficiently. The only thing I've ever heard you say about them is how cruel the choice was they had to make. Women used what they had, Stephen. Some lucky ones worked at sewing uniforms for the Wehrmacht. Other women had to use . . . other . . . things. And believe me, this was not done willingly. You have no idea—*no* idea— how much I hated myself. Or how much I still hate myself, even as I stand here justifying my actions."

When he didn't respond she went on, her voice softer. Where it had been rising with indignation, now it went over to sorrow, tears not falling from her eyes, but audible from her throat. "When you have your nightmares . . . about Henry, and what you did and didn't do, or about the things you saw, the things you saw and kept to yourself . . ." She paused without completing the thought, then said, "Tell me, in which direction was your great moral compass pointed when you decided to overlook—no, not overlook, what's that word . . . whitewash, yes . . . I like that word, it's very descriptive . . . whitewash—the executions carried out by your fellow soldiers at Dachau? You didn't think I knew about that, did you?

"But nobody made you do the kind of things I had to do—the kind of things that still make me wake up wondering if I shouldn't have chosen death. Killing Murch was one thing. You don't feel guilty about that . . ."

"I . . ."

But she wouldn't let him go on. "Mostly you were afraid you'd be caught. And I know it's like that with what you heard your soldiers do to their prisoners . . . or however you learned about it. Let me tell you something. Guilt weighs less when it's not over something you actually did, but about something you know someone else did.

"What is it men like to say? Death before dishonor? But when men say it they usually have something else in mind, like death before surrender—that kind of dishonor, very clean. They have a different standard for women. And as much as the good angel says in my ear I was right to choose life *and* dishonor, you have no idea how many times, when I wake up to the nightmare, I am convinced I made the wrong choice."

Stephen took it in. For a moment it seemed he might soften. But he was in no mood to give quarter. He desperately needed to even the score for the dense weight of pain she had inflicted over Jacob. In this moment justice had no part in it. Fairness had no part in it. Kindness was exiled. Resetting an equilibrium was what mattered, even if it was a parity based on recrimination. At any other time empathy might have won out. Not now.

He said, "Or maybe the real issue was you were afraid I wouldn't rescue you and take you to America. You remember America, don't you? The country that took you in? The country that, when it called, you apparently didn't think you owed anything? My friend Henry died trying to save people like you."

If he expected her to stagger, he was quickly proven wrong. Now it was her turn to bristle, as she looked at him in disbelief. "Henry might have died to save me, but I'll say it once again; the U.S. Army wasn't there for that reason, and neither were you—and you know it. What I just told you is the truth, all of it. I loved you. I was afraid you wouldn't love me if I told you everything at the start. And America? Have you forgotten that I didn't want to go to America? I wanted to go to Palestine, remember? I came to America because above all I wanted to be with you.

"And I'll tell you something else, Stephen. Whatever you think of me now, I won't have you using me or Germany or Henry or anybody else as an excuse for what America has done to my children. Don't lecture me about choices. You made choices, too."

* * *

THEY HAD REACHED a limit. Shortly after this fight (the holiday fight, as Annalise called it without irony), they separated. Soon thereafter they made it permanent. Each had been driven to divorce by anger that had gradually come to bubble and cling to their insides like boiling pitch.

For Annalise it was all about blame for Jacob. Any chance her anger might have diminished was lost when Stephen accused her of hiding her past. Much as she would not want to think of it this way, her memories of Jacob constituted a store of ammunition—a reliable source of hurtful vitriol when she needed something to counter Stephen's attacks, whether actual, anticipated, or imagined. Tragic outcomes she might have attributed to being star-crossed were instead viewed as deliberate. In this context Jacob's death was not merely the unwitting result of Stephen's misguided patriotism. When Annalise wanted to hurt him, he became guilty of tying Jacob to the tracks.

Likewise, Stephen, who perhaps could have been willing to let his anger be softened by time, found that he, too, had a reliable source of fuel. Without realizing it they had become like two armies with large reserves of poison gas at their disposal. Neither particularly wanted to use it, or to be first, but once one side fired, the other was bound to respond. If he was a murderer, she was a whore.

Before things reached this stage they had actually made an attempt to resolve their problems without resorting to lawyers. The attempt quickly broke down in recrimination; the only thing they were able to agree on was that they shouldn't meet again *without* their lawyers. (Not surprisingly, this was also the lawyers' advice.) And once the lawyers took control, the divorce headed for a donnybrook as they fanned every ember they could.

Neither Stephen nor Annalise could say exactly what triggered a move toward reason, but they both somehow managed to conclude at about the same time that the lawyers were only making a sad situation worse. Going against, needless to say, advice of counsel, they determined that there was no reason to let the lawyers be the only ones to benefit from their misery. They agreed to try again on their own.

The transformation was both gradual and remarkable. Paradoxically, it was perhaps the very intensity of what they had experienced—and the sheer exhaustion of it—that changed the breakup into something that was, on the whole, respectful.

Each of them pulled back from the assertions of willfulness on the part of the other. On some fundamental level, they seemed to view themselves more charitably as victims of extraordinary circumstance. If ever there was a mature moment between them, it was when they arrived at an implicit agreement to work at limiting further damage to Sandra and Ben and, almost as an afterthought, themselves.

Not that this removed bitterness from the equation or prevented the occasional flare-up of vituperation, but these became less frequent over time. Gradually, Stephen allowed himself to become more understanding of Annalise's withholding of her wartime experiences from him. As time passed, it all seemed increasingly remote, the sting diminished.

It was harder for Annalise. Try as she might, she could never completely forgive Stephen for Jacob and Ben, and it was this very inability to forgive—Stephen's simply knowing how she felt even without her articulation of it—that for him remained the greatest source of resentment and sorrow. Often, he imagined himself rearguing the case with her, not fundamentally changing, but rather tweaking, the arguments in his defense. As far as he was concerned, he punished himself enough on this score for both of them.

In October 1973, with Israel's fate hanging in the balance following a surprise attack by combined Arab forces, Annalise determined that if ever she were going to commit to Israel—and make amends for failing to do so in 1946—this had to be the time. Shortly thereafter, viewing public announcement of her intention as additional impetus to go through with it, she declared to family and friends that she was making *Aliyah*—emigrating to Israel. A few years later, she was joined by Sandra, who by then was married and had a daughter.

Under the terms of the divorce, Stephen had agreed that Annalise should keep the house. She didn't sell it immediately when she moved to Israel. She rented it out for a substantial figure, sufficient to permit Stephen to stop paying alimony, which for his part he had paid without need of a court order. He was grateful to her for this. The timing was perfect, as he had recently suffered a number of reverses in the stock market. Later, when it was clear that Annalise would not be returning to the U.S., the house was sold for a significant profit, and this, too, was shared, again even though there was no requirement that she do so under the terms of the divorce decree. The reasons for such cooperation were never made explicit. Stephen assumed they had simply arrived at a mutual, simultaneous wish to limit the bloodletting.

~ ~ ~ ~ ~

Part III

I Beseech you, in the bowels of Christ, think it possible you may be mistaken.

Oliver Cromwell

The Families Wroth and Roth, 1978–

Richard Samuel Sheres

Chapter 32

1978: The Repatriates

BEN AND MARTHA RETURNED to the States in 1978. They could have come back sooner. In 1974, shortly after President Ford pardoned Nixon, he announced an amnesty program called "Earned Reentry." Ben and Martha credited Ford's stated desire to "bind the public's wounds," but with Watergate fresh in mind, neither trusted government promises. Two years of public service would be required of those taking part in the program. This could be reduced for mitigating circumstances. Or increased in some circumstances? They wanted to know. Who could be sure?

Besides, there was no rush. What they wanted was not so much to return as to have a right to return without fear of government retribution. In the years they lived in Toronto, they had made something of a life. Increasingly, Toronto was home—actually felt like it as memories of their prior lives took on a remote daguerreotype quality. They had earned veteran status in the exile community. It was where their friends were, where their regular supermarket was, where they went to the dentist. They never moved more than a mile from the neighborhood where they first landed.

For the first three-plus years after Neil split for Vancouver, they lived together in the apartment Neil had shared with Martha. About Neil, Ben had to resist the temptation to tell Martha he told her so. While he actually hadn't told her so in so many words, he silently credited himself with the foresight to realize that Neil was not, as she would put it in Midwestese, a keeper.

Ben supported them, barely, while Martha pursued a licensed practical nursing program, a career choice made as much for its

271

portability as its intrinsic merits. After waiting tables at various local eateries, Ben settled on one, a popular pizza place called Pie-Eyed, where he worked his way up to assistant manager.

* * *

ON BEN'S SIDE, following Jacob's death and Stephen and Annalise's breakup, Annalise and Sandra tried to maintain a semblance of family life. Sandra in particular became a fairly regular visitor and supplier of things from home he needed or was unable to afford.

Like Annalise, Sandra was content to have Ben safe in Canada. No doubt the negative consequences of his actions that Stephen warned against would arise in some form, even if Ben and Martha were able to return to the States without legal jeopardy. The legal issues aside, Sandra fretted over the kind of existence that probably awaited them. Ben wasn't getting any younger, and what prospects did he have with no formal education beyond his senior year of high school? He had few skills beyond those of assistant managing a pizza joint.

For Stephen, visits to Toronto involved considerable equivocation. He was unable to develop an affinity for Canada. He had never been there before Ben moved, and now he found it almost impossible to separate the country from his family's diaspora. In his heart, he still resented Ben's flight, both for what it represented philosophically and because of the turmoil it caused in all of their lives. Nevertheless, he continued to pay occasional visits, mindful that, after losing Jacob and Annalise, he did not want to lose Ben, too.

It was different for Martha, whose parents back in Indianapolis were unforgiving. When she left for Canada, her father made the somber, Biblical declaration that she was dead to him. At the time she was not overly concerned. She took for granted that he was given to histrionics, particularly when his definition of patriotism was at stake. To her mind, she was guilty of nothing more than running off with Neil, and later, of taking up with Ben. But guilt by association was enough for her father, an early member of the John Birch Society. As far as he was concerned, the only thing LBJ did right was to try to stop the Red Tide in Southeast

Asia. "If that's where your sympathies lie, with a draft dodger," he said to her, "then we're done with one another."

Time proved he meant it. As the war wound down and public opinion coalesced against it, Martha expected him to soften. It didn't happen, nor did the will he exerted over the rest of her family diminish. Neither her mother nor her younger brother and sister ever visited. The only contact with them occurred in the form of occasional, furtive phone calls and letters postmarked from another city. These became less informative with the passage of time and the diminution of common bonds and frames of reference. For Martha, the pain of separation remained acute.

Nursing provided a natural bridge between Sandra and Martha. If the usual stuff of friendship—music, books, television, movies, politics, scandal, and of course, the war—failed them, they could always fall back on the good, bad, and ridiculous of the medical profession. Even before Martha graduated from her program they could reliably commiserate over low pay, long hours, and bureaucracy that would make a communist proud. They told each other tales of doctors who were variously heroic, stupid, incompetent, genius, boorish, or philandering.

Life improved for Sandra after she married one of the Montefiore Hospital doctors, a pulmonary specialist named Ethan Shulman, to whom she attributed only the positive among these characteristics. Ethan shared Sandra's opposition to the war and admired the courage shown by Ben and Martha in fleeing to Canada. When they were able to cadge time off together, they were happy to make the journey to Toronto. They brought bagels, "appetizing" from Zabar's, pastrami and salami from Katz's, and other bounty of what Ethan called NuYawkalia. "My mules," Ben called them with a laugh. Courier service is what Sandra called it. She didn't mind the role.

Ethan was a barely practicing Jew. He embraced only the major holidays, which nevertheless still made him more observant than a determinedly secular Sandra. But he did care deeply about his cultural heritage. He was a keen supporter of Israel who occasionally talked about emigrating there. It took some time for this to be endearing to Sandra, but Annalise immediately found it a winning attribute.

The cross-border activity slowed somewhat when Sandra became pregnant. She gave birth to a girl they named Deborah, which Ethan insisted on pronouncing DebORah—"You know, like the Biblical general." They gave her the middle name Jordana, which Sandra chose for its J-tribute to Jacob.

* * *

BEN MIGHT HAVE risen further at Pie-Eyed, to co-manager or manager. But every time it seemed he would succeed, he did something to set himself back. He would go through phases of being sullen or rude with customers. Or he would run a string of absences or late arrivals for his shift and offer only the kind of banal excuses people make when they don't give a damn. He wasn't feeling well, he'd say, with little effort to sound the part or provide convincing details. The first time or two the excuses were received by his boss, an easygoing guy, with sympathy; and subsequently, with more I'm-not-stupid-you-know suspicion. Sometimes Ben would pin it on Martha, limiting explanation to a statement that she wasn't feeling well and he had to care for her.

And then there was one incident that almost got him fired on the spot, when he got caught divvying the tips in his favor. The dawn breaking that there really might be limits to his boss's forbearance and that this episode really could cost him the job, he pleaded poor math skills. For some reason, the plea was accepted.

The fact that these offenses tended to occur in waves that began at about the same time a string of good performances was being acknowledged and possibly rewarded both angered and worried Martha, who thought the self-sabotage obvious even if the reasons for it were less so. She posited that, since his episodes seemed also to coincide with her earning ever greater accolades in the nursing program, his behavior could be attributed to resentment, which he served up with more than a jot of passive aggression.

"Are you *trying* to get yourself fired?" Martha demanded after the tips episode.

He denied it in a childish "it's not my fault" tone she might have recognized from his high-school days had she known him then.

Certainly, his parents and Sandra would recognize it, just as they would recognize the other adolescent-gauge fights he started.

"Excuse me if I'm not supporting you to Neil's standard," he protested when a probable promotion was undermined by a string of absences. Though disappointed about the lost promotion, Martha had not actually said anything that would logically prompt such an outburst. Later it occurred to her that saying nothing was as inflammatory as saying something caustic. The whole thing was internally driven, a tantrum in search of an opportunity.

Something close to the heart of the matter appeared the morning after Martha received her nursing degree. At that point Ben had managed to accumulate enough good performance days to put him back in his boss's good graces. He was sitting in the kitchen, at the tiny drop-leaf table that served as a dinette. Martha, wanting to show gratitude for Ben's support as well as confidence in him, came in and hugged him from behind.

A mug of coffee sat on the table in front of him. His second joint of the day, smoked down to the roach, was threatening to burn his fingers.

"Want one?" he offered on the inhale.

"A little early for me."

"What else do you want to scold me about?" he asked with a look of disdain as she poured a mug of coffee for herself and sat opposite him.

Caught by surprise at his reaction, she was about to respond, the set of her mouth signaling she would give him a fight if he was looking for one. But she caught herself and reached to touch his hand. "What I came in to tell you is, first of all and once again, how grateful I am for making yesterday possible. I want to remind you that I know you've sacrificed to support us. And I want you to know I'm ready to do the same for you."

He'd been holding the last toke in his lungs. The exhale emerged as a combined cough and barked laugh.

"I mean it," she said, again taken aback at the reaction.

"Support me while I do what?"

She stared at him. "Whatever you want."

"You haven't been paying attention, or you'd know I don't have a fucking clue. You know why I fucked up every time they were going to promote me? Because I didn't want to top out too soon."

"What the . . ."

He laughed again as he added, "Hit the limit of my ability."

"That is such total bullshit!"

But really, it made some sense. Strip away the thespian self-pity, factor in the morning joint, and there was still a part of him that was in some way arguably damaged. Early in their relationship this had been obscured by his outward anger over the war—in this single realm of antiwar activism he could keep himself on track. At the time she was unable to see that to no other area of his life could he bring commensurate dedication and discipline. He hit a low point after Jacob died and he didn't attend the funeral. Focused anger grew into unfocused rage.

No doubt he was immature. She recognized this from the start. But the expected emotional growth never came. What did come was greater frustration as the war's bitter conclusion became increasingly inevitable and his crusade a touch passé. In 1973, with fifty-eight thousand Americans dead, sixty percent of the country had come around to believing the war was a mistake. Martha found this gratifying. Ben found it irksome and depressing. "Six out of ten think Nam was a mistake? You think that's good? I think it means that after all the country has gone through—never mind what the Vietnamese have gone through—with nearly sixty thousand dead and who knows how many wounded and MIA, with the treasury bankrupted, with thousands of families like ours ruined, nearly four out of ten fucking stupid Americans still think it was worth it! That's what I see, the asshole forty percent."

Martha, ever the leveler: "We're clearly in the majority now. That's something."

But Ben being Ben, he didn't need to win so much as he needed to be in a continual state of opposition. In Toronto, on the war he was in the majority, leaving him marooned in a community in which to protest was not to rebel.

Martha figured into this too. In a sense she became a surrogate cause—first, as he engaged in a guerrilla war against Neil for her affections, and then by replacing Neil when he'd gone. Basic White

Knight Syndrome. In retrospect, she believed she should have seen it coming.

She wouldn't give up on him, though. Whatever the underlying cause or motivation for his behavior—and she would maintain, charitably, didn't we all operate on hidden premises?—she was grateful. She wasn't doing well herself when Neil cut out. Ben was sweet, indulgent, caring, and a surprisingly sensitive lover. These qualities were under assault now as he berated himself as a failure. He was prone to whining. Blame for just about anything gone wrong was spread widely, and only in an outward direction. Whatever the predicament, as far as he was concerned, none of the reasons redounded to him. The negatives became more pronounced as he turned to drugs and alcohol.

She shrugged off fellow students' warnings against taking Ben on as a lifelong project. "Aren't all men lifelong projects?" But in more sober moments she was afraid this could in fact be the outcome.

She was determined not to let it happen. But she was also determined to stick with him, and not just out of gratitude, but out of genuine affection—sometimes love, though this was less certain. After taking it all into account, not long after she finished her degree, she decided to go all in. A month later she and Ben were married. Marriage was a curable condition, wasn't it?

When Sandra gave birth, it fueled baby envy in Ben and Martha. In spite of Martha's concerns over Ben's behavior and drug abuse, they tried to get pregnant, but without success. The barrier turned out to be what the doctor called a tipped uterus, a reparable condition. After rethinking the timing of a pregnancy in favor of more stable jobs (and, Martha hoped, a more stable Ben), they came to consider the problem as a good thing in disguise.

* * *

IN JANUARY 1977, Jimmy Carter took the step that convinced Ben and Martha it would be safe to return home, when he issued a proclamation pardoning people who had been convicted of violating the Selective Service Act by evading the draft. Technically, the proclamation didn't apply to Ben, since he had never been convicted.

Nevertheless, for the first time he could be comfortable about possibly returning to the U.S.

They made the move a year later, settling in a small apartment in Yonkers. Seven years after that, having had her tipped uterus righted and having nearly given up after two subsequent miscarriages, Martha gave birth to Michael Jacob Roth.

~ ~ ~ ~ ~

Chapter 33

December 2004: Michael

E YES CLOSED AGAINST THE makeup being applied to his face and the nearly constant harassment from his comrades-in-arms, Sgt. Michael Roth, USMC, son of Ben and Martha Roth, grandson of Stephen and Annalise Wroth, was getting ready for his star turn on national television. Lighting and sound technicians milled about, while the marines joked that they had placed the real star, one of the network's top news anchors, on the BOLO list. (Be On the Lookout, Michael translated for the makeup woman.)

"So, how come they want to interview the ugliest marine who ever put on dress blues?" one said with a metallic laugh as he threw a makeup puff at Michael.

The woman flinched and shot the man a would-you-please look.

BY THE TIME Michael had joined up, two years after Nine-Eleven when he turned eighteen, everything had changed. Whatever the poll numbers, no one doubted there was a solid consensus that no matter what happened, the Vietnam experience would not be—must not be—repeated. Of course, the reality was that a new generations had grown up—people who didn't think about Vietnam in the first place, or as ancient history if they did. On Nine-Eleven the country was attacked, savagely, on world TV. The U.S. military was once more a respected, almost worshipped, institution—one of the few things Americans could agree on.

Even so, there was no unanimity in the Roth household in 2003, when Michael announced to Ben and Martha his intention to enlist. "I knew it," Martha said in a tone that suggested she could never outrun the fates as Ben looked on in stone-faced silence. "I knew you would want to join."

Michael moved to console her. But she held him at arm's length and did the unimaginable: Tears in her eyes, she managed to say she understood. "And as much as I hate to say it, I believe it's the right thing to do." Then she hugged him to her.

After a long moment, she blotted her eyes with the cuff of her shirtsleeve. "Of course, I'll worry about you every second you're away. That goes without saying. But a response to those savages is needed. There's no draft, thank goodness. It's up to people to volunteer when the country is in danger. And after watching the towers come down, who can doubt the country is in danger?"

Michael thanked her for understanding. "I was all ready for a big fight with you."

"You haven't got past me yet," Ben interjected.

"I knew it was too good to be true," Michael said. His voice contained a note of condescension, as if to add, *What else could I expect from you?* "I don't have to get past you. I'm over eighteen. I don't need your permission."

"That's too bad, because you don't know what you're doing. Neither does the country. We're about to fight the wrong war. Again. Iraq? You want to go fight in Iraq? Our stupid-ass president doesn't even know what country to attack. All he knows is he wants to hit something. Wants to finish his daddy's work. So he and Cheney, his vice-presidential puppet master, the real decider, drum up a war. At least W's daddy had the sense to put together a coalition and not try to colonize that sandy shithole."

"I could be sent to Afghanistan. Don't forget that. Or is that off your table, too?"

"But you won't be sent there. I guarantee it. They'll need the big numbers in Iraq. Besides, it might have made sense to go into Afghanistan when we did, to clean out the terrorists. But when do we get out? *How* do we get out? Cheney and his puppet haven't thought about that, I'll bet."

"What about the WMD? Isn't that a good enough reason?"

"The only so-called weapons of mass destruction worth worrying about are nukes, and I promise, they won't find any."

"Shit, how can you know? You can't know that! CIA thinks they're probably there."

Ben gave a contemptuous snort. "CIA. Yeah, right."

"Well, I'm joining up. I'm going. I'm not you, that's for sure."

Ben drew himself up. "Meaning?"

"Meaning maybe people had it right when they said the guys who ran to Canada were really just cowards."

Ben turned rigid. Balled his fists. He started to respond, but the words that came forth were disjointed, as if, in trying to line up several points, he overwhelmed himself and couldn't decide which one to lead with. At last, he turned and walked away, the only response left to him the bang and rattle of a slammed door.

"That wasn't fair," Martha said. "What your father did was the right thing, and it took courage."

"Maybe. But I gotta tell you, I've never heard him say anything he thought was worth fighting for."

It hadn't been easy for the network to gain "unencumbered" (it had asked for unrestricted) access to the place, the place being the National Naval Medical Center, more often called the Bethesda Naval Hospital, and more specifically to the Wounded Warrior Center. A disillusioning year and a half after the Iraq mission was declared accomplished, the brass was divided over whether the program would be remembered for the superb quality of wounded warrior care or a reminder of how many wounded warriors there were to care for.

281

The program was to feature a few carefully selected patients who would describe their experiences of being wounded, medevac'd, and helped against long odds to recover. Michael was proving to be one of the best subjects from both the network's and the military's point of view. In the face of grievous, but (important for TV) not repulsive, wounds, he appeared to be indomitable. He was young, but not callow, popular with his comrades (*You go, Mikey, OORah!*), and handsome in an everyman telegenic way, with startling-blue eyes, sandy hair grown long enough to test the rules, and an unforced smile. He came across variously (but not erratically) as optimistic or somber, outgoing or reserved. He was articulate but not so eloquent that the average viewer could not relate to him.

The counterpoint was the network anchor, Frank Jessup, who fit an evolving TV mold—tall, near-white, old enough to have sufficient gravitas and the beginnings of avuncularity, still young enough to appeal to the youth demographic, handsome enough in a nonthreatening, gender-neutral way. He had experience going for him—the wisdom and media savvy not to pretend to expertise on subjects—military service, for example—on which he had little knowledge. As a young reporter in 1988, he had watched the Democratic presidential candidate drive a tank to burnish his national security credentials. What the public fixed on instead was the candidate's doofus helmet, which made him look more like Snoopy than Patton. Jessup was forever after alert to the fatal damage that could be done by a single, ill-considered image.

"Nervous?" Carolyn, the anchor's assistant, asked as she positioned Michael for the cameras. Her tone suggested she had a quiver of calming arrows at the ready.

"A little."

She cocked her head, shot him a comically quizzical look.

He laughed, mimed being choked. "Only a little more than for my first firefight."

"Everyone is the first time. Don't worry. Frank is very easy to talk to. You've met him."

Michael nodded.

"Well, then you know. The last thing he'll want to do is embarrass you." She smiled at him. "Wouldn't do to embarrass a wounded hero, would it?" Spying Jessup, she added with a flourish of faux drama, "And here comes the star now."

"Nope, Michael is the star," Jessup said, extending his hand. He had dispensed with his usual suit and tie in favor of a more casual war correspondent look—khakis and a powder blue shirt with sleeves rolled precisely to mid-forearm, Rolex exposed. "Carolyn's got you totally prepared, I presume," he said with a smile.

"Yes sir, totally on point."

They went over the outline for the interview. Jessup reminded that they were taping, not live. They could pause at any time. Some of the tension seemed to ebb from Michael's face.

An audience of hospital staff and patients stood on the periphery of the set. Ben, Martha, and Stephen had arrived, as well. Martha waved. They exchanged fleeting, nervous smiles.

As the taping began, Jessup looked into the camera and started reading from a teleprompter. "We have chosen this center for our program because it is here that soldiers must learn to take back lives shattered by modern weapons of war." His voice was resonant, reverent just short of cloying. "We will take you through this advanced facility and introduce you to the remarkable people, technologies, and equipment responsible for this amazing transformation."

Visible behind Jessup was a thicket of rehab equipment—treadmills, stationary bikes, stair climbers, whirlpool baths, weight machines, walking courses, parallel grab bars, and a cat's cradle of ropes and hoists. The season was on display, as well. Artificial Christmas trees, both life-size and tabletop, with colored lights and dripping tinsel dotted the area. A large Hanukah menorah sat on a table in one corner of the room. In a less conspicuous space, as if to denote its more recent celebratory aspirations, multicolored foil letters spelled out Kwanza.

"We begin today with Michael, a young marine sergeant who has gone through his own personal hell, and who, with the help of many people you will see and meet, can yet hope for a full, nearly normal life." The camera cut to a close-up of Michael, who nodded, his visage focused, determined, sufficiently vulnerable.

"When did you arrive here at the Naval Center?" Jessup asked.

Michael's answer, unhesitating and succinct: "December 13th, 2003."

"You remember clearly, then."

A shy smile. "Yes and no, sir."

To Jessup's questioning turn of the head, Michael continued: "I remember when I arrived, but not much about when I was wounded. It was a mine. I stepped on a mine."

"And it took your legs." The camera drifted from Michael's face, past the fresh USMC Semper Fi tee shirt, to the two stumps, neatly bandaged and covered with compression socks, jutting like bowsprits from his wheelchair.

"Yes, sir. There isn't much I remember besides what people told me. I know they stabilized me in Eye-raq, and that they almost lost me a few times. They had trouble stopping the bleeding. I was airlifted to a hospital in Frankfurt. When I got well enough, they got me on a plane to Andrews. And then here."

"But we should tell our viewers that you know the exact date you arrived for another reason."

"Yes, sir. December 13th was the day we captured Saddam Hussein. Pulled that Eye-raqi monster out of his spider hole," Michael added with a smile, which widened as cheers and applause could be heard off camera.

"So, Michael, it's taken a whole year here for you to recover, and you'll still have more to do when you leave. That's a long time."

"Yes, sir, it is."

"Many of the people we've spoken to describe you as a hero."

Michael gave the by now oft-heard military-humble response. "No, sir. The guys who didn't make it home at all are the heroes. I was just in the wrong place at the wrong time. And now I'm lucky to be here." The smile again, this time involving the blue eyes.

"Explain. You have this terrible injury, you're facing a lifetime of disability and, I assume, lots of pain. Explain to our viewers why you believe you're lucky."

"Well, sir, I'm alive, and there are guys all around me hurt much worse. When I look at them and see they haven't given up . . . well, to tell the truth, I'd be ashamed to look at the dark side."

"But you must have dark moments."

"Sure I do."

"And you've overcome them."

"So far." A slight smile, more tentative than before.

"Could you tell us about it?"

Michael started, stopped short of a frown. He began to raise his hand in a way that suggested he might want to pause the interview. The last thing he wanted was to discuss his dark moments. So far he was rolling along, saying all the positive things he wanted to say. He was happy to give credit to the people who had helped him. But he didn't want to be the subject of TV melodrama—to be exploited or have his experiences cheapened.

He wanted to keep the discussion in the physical realm—the things, like his legs, that could be easily seen and understood, the things the average person could relate to. By all means, show him struggling to take those first steps on his new legs. Show the grimace. Show the doubts in his face that he could take one more step. Show the PT people urging him on, playing to the marine can-do, and how they caught him when he stumbled but demanded he give it one more try. These were the moments of success and inspiration.

But then, there were those other times. Like the group therapy sessions, where the men could speak their minds. But only to a point. Only about the predictable kinds of things it was acceptable to say among a group of war fighters, the things you could admit to the others. *I'm afraid of letting my buddies down.* Or, *I feel like I did let down my buddy/squad/platoon/the Corps.* Or, *I'm afraid I'll lose my girl.*

Some anger and resentment were permissible, too. *Yeah, damn right I smoke—it's the only comfort I've got, so don't go telling me I need to quit. Same with my drinking.* Or, *I can't stand my mother's crying or my father's bullshit bravado ("You can tough it out, son"), which is even worse when it's really just an excuse for him to go on about his time in 'Nam. ("I may not have been wounded, but that doesn't mean I don't know hardship.")*

You could complain about the clueless relatives, might get a knowing laugh about them—the ones who would tell the shot-blinded nephew they hardly knew about how they loaded ammunition palettes for five days straight in Korea. *("Darn back's never been right since.")*

These were the kinds of things you could say to a group. You could even make the occasional admission of fear.

But not weakness. And not fear as weakness, but rather as something to be overcome.

Weakness—and regret—were reserved, if at all, for the one-on-ones. Where you could let loose, tell the shrink how the chickenshit officers really fucked you up good—how they hid in their bunkers while out where the action was you were being turned into a gimp for life. Then the smug pricks would show up for the cameras to pin a Purple Heart on you and watch you smile in showy gratitude. Hey! Look at the bright side—a Purple Heart tag on the car so the cops won't give you a ticket! OOrah! But your future—your life—it's really over, isn't it? That's the truth.

Of course, you could hide stuff from the shrinks, too. Hide the real stuff. Like how maybe not dying isn't all it's cracked up to be. How maybe you'll off yourself. Eat your gun. Fire for effect.

"So far, so good," Michael said, hoping Jessup wouldn't press. The camera captured a distant smile. "With a lot of help," he added.

"You've had to learn how to walk again."

The smile, more natural this time. Back on safer ground. "Got my titanium legs. I move pretty well on them, too. You'll see when I put 'em on. I'll race you."

A blurted laugh from the anchor. "And I wouldn't bet against you! Later we'll show our viewers how you learned to use your new legs. It really is remarkable. I understand your parents are here today. Is that your mom and dad, off on the side?"

The camera panned to an unlikely looking couple. The man, wiry, intense, with unruly hair turning silver, caught off guard and clearly unhappy about it. The woman, taller, striking, big-boned, smiling politely, shaking long, bottle-enhanced red hair out of her eyes.

"Yes," Michael said. "That's Martha, my mom, and my dad, Ben. My grandfather, Stephen, my dad's dad, is here, too. Now, he's the one you should be interviewing. He's a Second World War vet—a true hero. Fought from France to Germany. He's seen it all."

Jessup sent an almost regulation military salute in their direction and turned back to Michael, who was disappointed not to get Stephen into the shot. "Let me scratch the surface of another area we'd like to explore in this program," Jessup resumed, "one that goes to the heart of the U.S. effort in Iraq. Michael, when you look back on your experience of the past few years, and look forward to what I hope will be a long life—when you consider everything from Nine-Eleven to boot camp to this place here—what do you think? Has it all been worth it? Has this war, and your sacrifice, been worth it?"

Michael frowned slightly, then forced a weak smile. The question seemed to catch him out, as it once again veered into restricted territory. He was told the interview would concentrate on his experiences, not questions about policy that could get him into trouble with his superiors or cause friction within his family. It was the kind of question that had given his family continual grief. Hesitating obviously, he started to respond, but Jessup interrupted him. "You could start with a simple yes or no."

"Oh," Michael said without enthusiasm before pausing, reflecting, looking away from the camera. A one-word answer would make things even worse. There was nothing simple about it. Stephen, whom he loved and admired, had asked him something similar. At the time the best Michael could do was, "Maybe. Probably."

Besides, what did it matter what he thought about the big picture? He was no policymaker. He didn't have a PhD. He didn't work in some think tank trying to figure out the world. It wasn't that he didn't care about these things. But what did he know beyond his tiny piece of the action?

Yeah, some of the guys he served with thought they had it all figured out. As far as he was concerned they had no problem drawing a map of the world from the wrong end of the telescope. True, when he was feeling low, Michael sometimes berated himself for not having their powers of comprehension. But he was also capable of reminding himself that having an opinion isn't the same as truly knowing something.

His country called. He answered. That was enough, wasn't it? That's what his grandfather did. He didn't regret it, did he? If Michael thought only about how the war affected him, personally, it would probably make him feel bitter or sorry for himself, and he didn't want that.

287

"Your parents and grandfather may want to answer as well," Jessup added on impulse. The camera caught his father's expression of unhappy surprise at being featured again, and the frame cut back abruptly to Jessup. "You told me earlier that they weren't on the same page when you enlisted," Jessup continued. "If I've got this right, your mother supported the decision, but your father was against it."

"Has it been worth it?" Michael echoed, avoiding the still worse terrain of his parents. "Yes or no?"

"Okay, yes or no," Jessup confirmed with a nod. Then, appearing belatedly to recognize the depth of Michael's discomfort, he said, "Or let me put it slightly differently. Knowing everything you do now, with perfect hindsight, would you do it all again?"

Michael nodded that he understood, his lips pursed, no help found in Jessup's reformulation. The pause verged on television producers' bane, dead air, before he settled on, "Well, it has to have been worth it. Doesn't it?"

~ ~ ~ ~ ~

Chapter 34

January 2005: Pieces Falling to Earth—The Thereafters

"**W**ELL, IT HAS TO have been worth it. Doesn't it?" When Sgt. Michael Roth concluded his hospital interview with these ten ambiguous words, neither he nor his interviewer, Frank Jessup, had given much thought to the impact they would have. Yet they soon became the distilled essence, appropriated by all sides, of the Iraq war debate.

Pressed by reporters for followup interviews, Michael declined, fearing anything he said would be misconstrued or deliberately twisted. He could end up appearing brave, tragic, or foolish—and he fretted over the possibility that he was all of these things. Besides, did it really matter what he thought?

Supporters of the war, believing the mission—overthrow of the depraved dictator Saddam Hussein, neutralizing of Iraq as a regional threat and possible source of weapons of mass destruction, or WMD, and opportunity to spread the blessings of democracy—had indeed been accomplished, took Michael's words at face value, with no hint of doubt or sarcasm.

Opponents, who had been showing signs of flagging in the face of an onslaught of Bush Administration boosterism, now had something to latch on to and appropriated every bit of doubt and sarcasm the other side forewent. Superimposed over TV images of Michael, his stumps protruding from the wheelchair, was the spin: Has to have been worth it? Hardly. Yes, sergeant, just look at what we've accomplished: a region in chaos, a depleted treasury, thousands killed or, like you, maimed. And those WMDs? It seems they weren't there after all, were they?

The more Michael saw the clip played and heard himself quoted by the various factions, the less he, himself, was certain what he had meant.

For Ben and Martha, it was a bittersweet moment. All of America could see how fine a son they'd raised. The pride was offset by the reality of daily existence away from the cameras and a worrisome future.

No one who knew anything about Ben and Martha's history could fail to appreciate the exquisite irony of Michael's situation. The draft dodger's son a war hero who paid the price. Maybe paid the price of the father's rehabilitation into society as well, though the groundwork already had been laid by a solidifying consensus that Vietnam was a disaster best pushed to the rear of the country's consciousness.

Jessup, at first pleased with himself for having ended the interview on the perfect sound bite—one that elevated Michael's answer into the realm of what Jessup once described at a journalism workshop as lofty ambiguity—was soon embarrassed by sniping from colleagues-cum-competitors who said what he had actually done was leave the story's lead on the cutting-room floor. Meanwhile, self-anointed Keepers of the Craft charged that Jessup's failure to clarify what Michael meant was precisely what was wrong with the media: Be satisfied with the innocuously meaningless phrase just so long as the ratings are high.

Still and all, the network was happy with the high ratings and wanted to give Jessup another bite at the apple. Moreover, when word got around that Michael's father had been a draft dodger who met his mother in Canadian exile, Jessup tore the hide off his producer and assistants who missed this angle and became determined to interview the whole family together. It would be perfect, he exclaimed. He would have the wounded hero son of draft dodger parents all in the same room and available to deal with the ambiguities of the first interview.

It only remained to convince the parents to do it. And good luck with that after they dropped out of the original program. They had been on board until the moment Jessup had the camera swing unexpectedly in their direction during Michael's interview. What followed was a "What the hell were we thinking?" epiphany as they envisioned becoming the unpatriotic foils to their son's patriotic sacrifice, in the process dredging up all the things they had tried not to dwell on since they came home.

* * *

MICHAEL WASN'T KEEN on doing a followup interview, either. It was during the churn and turmoil after the initial interview that he came up with the phrase he believed perfectly described the essence of his problems and the difficulty of explaining things to Jessup. The interview had centered on his experience in recovering from his wounds. What it ignored was what Michael thought of as "the thereafters"—not the physical recovery as such, which at any rate he could credit largely to others, but the things he would have to contend with for the rest of his life.

In hindsight, when he thought about the day he was wounded, Michael had the odd feeling that the actual event—the event most people fixed on—wasn't so bad. There was the flash of recognition when the mine went off that something traumatic was happening to him, but this was immediately wiped out by his body going into total physical shock, his organs nearing collapse, and his being drugged to the max by the medics.

It was not until he reached the hospital in Germany that the first round of thereafters began to sink in. Even then he was distracted. First, he had to get through the pain. Getting the meds right in the first place was a challenge. Pain management, they called it. Bullshit! Like most facile phrases, this one did more for slick brochures than the patient's reality.

They upped the OxyContin when even the high dose he was on wasn't doing the trick. The result was a bad case of pharma-psychosis, with a dose of Tourette's thrown in for good measure as he bellowed and thrashed. Doctors, nurses, and orderlies at his bedside were transformed into fucking Eye-raqi camel jockeys who were conspiring to finish him off. *(Just like I knew they would, but nobody goddam listens to me!)* Never mind that he only survived because his Iraqi translator absorbed most of the blast. Ice chips and glycerin pops to

291

soothe his sandblasted-raw throat were transformed into poison to be spat out. *(Fuckers! If they can't get me one way, they'll get me another!)*

His upper body remained amazingly strong. It took three orderlies to put the IV back in when he yanked it out. After the third time, they tied his arm to the bedrail with gauze strips and put gauze mittens on his hands to keep him from scratching fissures into himself or them.

All of this before the more rational "here I am" thereafter in which he could begin to imagine his legless future, wonder about what he might be able to do with his life, worry about who besides his family might love him. If he were an airplane, the Jessup interview would have captured only the landing, the Mission Accomplished moment, not the lumbering takeoff that barely cleared the tree line, the time in the air that was all chop and roll, or the thereafters.

His physical challenges were obvious, the psychological ones less so as he wore a convincing mask. Yet there was a daily struggle simply to rouse himself out of bed. Sometimes it took more than one of the PT people to force him out. And then they forced him into their contraptions. Forced him into positions and therapies in which he would fail far more times than he would succeed. The ratio of failure to success eventually reversed, but the rate of progress at first was almost imperceptible.

On the day of the interview, he was the face of America the Indomitable, his struggles to walk on his new legs blithely past, over with. The Corps was happy. The navy bigshots were happy. Actually, Michael was happy—a willing participant, caught up in the moment. *It has to have been worth it.*

✻ ✻ ✻

AND NOW THIS, a year later. After the interview. After the high fives. After the fist bumps. No legs. The What Nows. The Thereafters, lurking.

Has to have been worth it, doesn't it?

~ ~ ~ ~ ~

Chapter 35

March 2005—The Interpretation of Dots

L OOKING AT THE STILL-GLOSSY black-and-white photo with its quaintly scalloped edges, it occurred to Stephen that the photo was doing a better job of aging than he was. Better for that matter than the others captured in the image, most of whom were long gone.

There he was, in full uniform, standing with the young soldiers who would define so much about his life both before and after the frozen moment. The camera captured him smiling. But he couldn't have been as carefree as he looked, could he? Perhaps it was the naive beginning— maybe that was the explanation.

Who took the picture, anyway? What he remembered was the camera itself, an old reflex box, not the identity of the photographer. Likely it was shot by the odd man out, the member of the group who didn't make it into the photo, or at least not this iteration of it. It might have been taken by Henry; it would explain his absence. Too bad—it would be nice to see the two of them together. The scumbag Murch was there, and Riggs wasn't, so it had to have been before Aschaffenburg.

He wondered if Riggs was still alive. For all the angst Riggs caused at the time and for many years thereafter, Stephen was surprised not to know. Odd, he thought, that if Riggs was dead, the only person on earth who knew about Aschaffenburg would be Annalise, assuming she never told anyone. Probably she hadn't; she was always discrete.

One thing was certain: None of the people in the photo could have comprehended what was coming.

He reminded himself that he shouldn't dawdle. He was supposed to be getting ready for his day. But his eye had stopped at the photo. It was always there among a group of significant photos, nicely framed and placed deliberately as spurs to reminiscence. There were his parents, formally posed, in sepia tones with hints of color added after the fact by the photographer. Photos of his brother and sister, too, as well as of Annalise and the children in happier times. Over time the photos blended into the background and rarely caught his eye as intended. However, today he paused to remember and to permit one remembrance to spawn another. It was the kind of indulgence he had come to savor as time earned.

At first he would resist such random captures of his attention, particularly when they resulted in failures to remember what he'd set out to do. They said being easily distracted—what he thought of as a grasshopper mind—came with age. But of course, it could also signify something much worse: *The old man must be losing it, can't keep his mind on something for more than a blip.* Eventually he proclaimed the hell with it and gave in to the pleasure. Memories, most of them comfortingly clouded by time, as if viewed through a caul, were the reward for living long, and god knew there were enough negative things about the achievement.

As for having difficulty remembering things, he believed this was not necessarily the failing it often was portrayed as being. Rather it was merely that the old had so much more material than the young to work with! The older one got, the more new experiences were relatable to things already experienced in one way or another.

Nearing his eightieth year, Stephen was grateful for his relatively good health. Considering how long he had practiced the vices of his generation, heavy smoking and a love of hard spirits, he might even omit the "relatively" qualifier. He traveled. He attended plays, concerts, ball games, and museum events. Sometimes he had to wrestle with a cantankerous, seemingly whimsical prostate and the occasional need to use a cane. He would dispute that the cane was really necessary, saying it was a convenience when he was temporarily undermined by a disloyal hip or knee. The medications he took regularly, to control blood pressure and cholesterol, he regarded as merely precautionary.

He tried to maintain an active social life, though it required effort to overcome the discriminatory tendencies of a youth culture unwilling to expend much energy trying to appreciate the experiences of the aged—or at any rate as much energy as he was willing to expend to stay *au courant* on those of the young. He tried to make new friends as old ones died off at what seemed an alarming rate. Restocking the pond, he called it. Well, it would be tough to be the last man standing, if it came to that. Striking up friendships with his contemporaries was easy (low-hanging fruit, the then-current term of art). Many of them were lonely, and befriending contemporaries had the advantage of shared experiences. It was convenient to be able to talk about Nixon or Mao without having to explain who Nixon and Mao were. But befriending people his own age defeated the objective, actuarially speaking.

This morning he was expecting grandson Michael. The two had always been close, but it would be the first visit together since Michael had received his new legs and was discharged from the rehab facility.

It was a sunny day. Light streamed in from the east-facing windows. Stephen lived in a large corner apartment on the fourteenth floor of a condominium, which also gave him views facing south to Manhattan and southwest across the Hudson to the Jersey Palisades. He had purchased the place about ten years earlier. Before that—after the breakup with Annalise—he lived in a series of rentals, all of them within a mile of the house they had shared.

He came to appreciate ever more the joys of living on a single level and not having to shovel snow. Unlike others his age, Stephen had no intention of moving to warmer climes. He was a New Yorker, through and through—and still a Bronx Man, if further definition were required.

The weather that day was warm enough for Stephen to open the windows, which he liked to do whenever he could. He liked the fresh air for its own sake, but it also addressed one of those geriatric problems he hated: He was losing his sense of smell, and constantly feared that without his realizing it, the apartment could take on the embarrassing shit-and-piss redolence of a nursing home.

He was struggling to force open a stuck window when the doorman called to announce Michael's arrival. He gave the window one more try, then gave up and went to the front door to greet Michael in case he needed help. He considered meeting him at the elevator but then thought better of it. Michael had obviously made it as far as he had on his own. It was a question of finding the sweet spot between being available and being gratuitous—pride may be a vice, and this time it could literally go before a fall, but it's also a great motivator. So he watched as Michael paused unaware of Stephen's presence, gathered himself up, and began the determined walk down the corridor, moving one titanium leg after another, aided by a pair of forearm crutches.

"Impressive," Stephen said, applauding as Michael approached. "I'd offer to help, but if I know you, you'd tell your old Gramps to take a hike."

"Got that right," Michael called. "*OOrah!*" he added with a smile.

"Seriously, Mikey, you're looking good," Stephen said as he reached the apartment door. "I'm surprised by how much progress you've made."

"Yep. Better every day." He was dressed in civvies—jeans and a short woolen jacket over a plaid shirt.

"Come on in. Let me get a good look at you in the light. Amazing," he pronounced as Michael moved toward the window. "My bionic grandson."

"Yeah, it is amazing, isn't it. Especially compared to the peg legs your generation had."

"Hell, it's way ahead of even what the Nam vets had. Watching you walk, if I didn't know, I would have thought you'd only pulled a muscle or something. Come on over to the sofa and take a load off."

"I don't need to."

"But I do."

"Right, you're a geezer."

"What are your plans?" Stephen asked as they got settled. He nodded toward Michael's legs. "Will they let you stay in the Corps with those things?"

"Probably, but I'm not sure I'd like the work they'd find for me to do. I'm definitely not ready to be a desk jockey. So maybe it's time to take my Honorable D and report somewhere else."

"Any ideas?"

"Nothing for sure. I've got a few options, including a couple of private sector companies doing counterterror work. It'll depend on the job, and no matter what it is, I need to make it real clear that I won't take anything out of pity. Either I can pull my weight, or I keep looking."

"Good attitude, but I wouldn't worry about it. Knowing you, even if they hired you out of pity they'd find you indispensable before long. How are your folks, AKA my formerly Canadian children?"

"Okay, I guess. You probably talk to them as often as I do."

"I doubt it."

Michael looked for meaning in Stephen's face, apparently found none.

Stephen laughed. "I didn't intend to sound so dramatic. Just that time goes by quickly between phone calls and visits. Besides, you're living on site—you are still, right?"

"For now, yeah. It's a little awkward. I had to go somewhere when they kicked me out of the hospital. Makes sense for me to live at home for a while. It doesn't hurt that Mom's a nurse. My halfway house, I call it." Michael smiled, and added, "Dad says don't get too used to it."

"But he's not really pressuring you to leave, right?"

"Not at all. He knows me well enough to realize I'm anxious to move on. Ha! Before I started calling home a halfway house I used to call it a commune. Gave the old hippies a hard time! Funny reversal, huh? The straight-arrow marine telling the hippie parents to clean up their act and get a job!"

"You have no idea," Stephen said, smiling and shaking his head. "So, seriously, how are they doing? It's been a difficult time for them, too."

"Not bad. Mom keeps on keeping on. You know what she's like. For a hippie, she's pretty anal. She's had a few tough days over her dad."

To Stephen's questioning look, Michael said, "Oh, I guess you didn't know. He died."

"Oh? When?"

"Over a month ago."

"She never said anything. Did she go to the funeral?"

"No. I mean, it was bad between them to the end. You know I never met him, right?"

Stephen nodded.

"Basically, I think he wasn't quite right in the head. I've heard of lots of people who have gone through the big drama—the 'you're dead to me' stuff—but I can't remember ever meeting anyone who actually meant it. And over something so stupid! I mean, even I, Mr. Gung Ho Marine, think Vietnam was a goat fuck. Excuse my French. Anyway, I always felt bad for Mom. I wanted to help. She never said so, but it crossed my mind when I joined up that maybe I could kind of make amends for her, you know? I thought maybe her dad would call a do-over. Like I said, the guy wasn't right in the head. I mean, you made up with Dad, right?"

"Yes, but it wasn't easy or quick."

"And my mom was just like collateral damage, you know what I mean? It wasn't like she was dodging the draft."

Stephen nodded. "I suppose her father thought that was enough of a sin—to be the enabler, as they say. But the real thing may have been that your mom had the temerity to disobey him." He added a shrug. "We may not know the half of it."

"I guess. Anyway, I'm glad you were able to patch things up with Dad. I've always thought maybe that saved his life."

Stephen perked to attention. But before he could ask Michael what he could possibly mean, Michael threw him another curve. "When I signed on for Iraq, I knew Dad was against the war, of course. But maybe the thing that made him not too mad at me was thinking something like, 'Well, he's like his grandfather'—like you—and maybe . . . I'm not sure, but maybe that he, meaning Dad, was the odd man out, with the two of us supporting the Iraq war." Michael cocked his head. "Why are you looking at me like that? Doesn't it make sense?"

It didn't. None of it, not least Michael's assumptions about Iraq. If he assumed Stephen supported the Iraq war, it couldn't be because of anything he'd actually said. Michael must have made the leap from Vietnam to Iraq, and he was being simplistic in just about every way. Of all the emotions Stephen could have summoned, the one that came now, unbidden, was resentment, even as it was followed immediately by an attempt to bear in mind that such simplifications are the province of the young and his grandson had paid dearly for his convictions.

298

But still, resentment? Yes, because one thing Stephen always hated was being pigeonholed. Simply on principle he hated it when people assumed anything about him. Whether the assumption might be true wasn't the point. In a way it was actually worse if it was true, particularly if the offender had decided things about him by following an illogical path. He supported the Vietnam War? Well, then, he must be a staunch right-winger—probably opposed equal rights for blacks, too! He wrote editorials for *The Wall Street Journal*? Certainly, he had to be a foursquare Republican—straight down the party line. Must have voted for Goldwater. Must have voted for Nixon. Twice. And stayed loyal to him to the end—opposed impeachment, opposed the resignation, supported the pardon; must have hated Carter, revered Reagan, supported the first and second Bushes. The list was endless, and only some of the items were true.

He could explain all of these things to Michael, but he felt flummoxed and wrong-footed, and irritated with himself because of it. The explanation of his true views was complicated. Telling Michael he actually opposed the Iraq invasion would be more than a matter of setting the record straight. It would amount to a rebuke, essentially answering the question posed in the interview, which Michael might well prefer to remain ambiguous. *Has to have been worth it?* Well, not really.

Instead, Stephen asked, "What did you mean when you said I saved your dad's life?"

"Mom believes that."

"She does?"

"Sure."

"She said that?"

"Sort of. Mom says Dad was fucked up when he returned from Canada. Excuse my . . ."

"Yeah, yeah Michael, I excuse your fucking French. Tell me what your mother said."

Michael laughed. "Right. Seriously, she said he was lost. I asked what she meant, and she said that when he ran off to Canada he had a cause, you know? He was doing something he believed in. But when he came home, the cause was gone. I guess you could say he'd won. The war was over. Everyone he knew thought it was a waste. He didn't even have a high-school diploma since he not only dropped out but did it just before graduation for Christ's sake. He had to pick up a G.E.D. What he knew when he came back from Canada was how to run a pizza restaurant, which in my opinion isn't a bad thing to know, but it was nothing to him. And then there were the drugs."

"Did you understand any of these things growing up?"

"Not really. Well, the drugs, I guess, when I learned what drugs were. In school they told us to just say no and showed us crap like the crime-fighting dog, what was his name, McGruff? The funny thing is that drugs never appealed to me, except for the occasional joint, which I don't think counts. But all of a sudden Dad's weird behavior made sense. The stuff he tried to hide. His yelling at me or Mom over nothing, and then how he'd feel bad about it afterward.

"Anyway, a lot of that changed when he went into rehab. A couple of years ago Mom said they had you to thank. For helping to find a good place and then helping to pay for it, I guess, or for helping out with the bills while he was away.

"So he got his shit together. I mean, he does work as a drug counselor now. Like the drunk who goes to work for AA. That's not an accident. Hasn't Mom ever thanked you? Hasn't *Dad* ever thanked you?"

Your mom, yes. Your dad, not in so many words. Maybe he's embarrassed about the things that didn't work out for him. Maybe it only takes my presence to trigger it all. Hell, maybe he's still not over the bad blood between us when he left home, which of course got even worse when your Uncle Jacob died."

Michael shrugged. "I don't know. Maybe the other things—the things you did to help—made up for it. Don't forget, we didn't have anyone else—any other family, I mean."

"Ben . . . your dad . . . was always close to Grandma. To your aunt Sandy, too."

"Yeah, Grandma loves us, for sure. But she lives in Israel, and we didn't see much of her. Hell, she was gone before I was born! And Aunt Sandy and Uncle Ethan moved there, too. I've met any of my cousins maybe once. You were it, Gramps," Michael concluded brightly. "The whole enchilada."

"Except that it's the kind of thing that can cause even more resentment—I mean being helped up by someone—i.e., me—who you think knocked you down. Well, enough of this for now. Are you up for a bite? We can go out, or I can put something together here if you'd rather rest those iron gams of yours."

"Oh, sure, like that's not a challenge! Come on, old man, I'll race you to the elevator."

* * *

STEPHEN WATCHED FROM behind as Michael propelled himself down the corridor. "Tough work," he said, shaking his head.

"I'm making progress."

"I can see that."

"I'm hoping I won't need the crutches much when we go to Israel next month. If we go. You know about that, right?"

"You mean Yad Vashem," Stephen said, referring to the national Holocaust memorial in Jerusalem. "Yes, I do."

They reached the garage. "Nice wheels," Michael said as he maneuvered himself into the front seat of the BMW. "Is it new?"

"About six months."

"Dad always said you liked cool cars. Kind of surprising you'd go German though."

Stephen laughed as he got into the driver's seat. "I didn't want to for a long time. Then I thought, well, shit, I had a German wife!"

"Funny. But what you had was a Jewish wife. This isn't a Jewish car."

"Well, the war's been over for more than half a century. Anyone who had a hand in building this car had nothing to do with it. And those people who think Germans need to be punished in perpetuity? How would you feel if I kept punishing you for what happened at Wounded Knee? Besides, these same people have no problem buying Japanese cars."

"So anyway, you know about the Yad Vashem thing," Michael said as Stephen pulled out of the garage.

"Yeah, I do."

"Fifty years since Dachau was liberated, right?"

"Sixty."

"Sixty, right. Never very good at math. Did Grandma Annalise ask you to come? Is that how you found out about it?"

"No. I've given money to Yad Vashem for Holocaust studies. I got an invitation. They want to get survivors and liberators together before we all fade away."

"And? Are you coming with us?"

"I haven't decided. Probably not. It might be awkward."

"It's not like you haven't seen Grandma since the divorce."

"True, but not for a long time anyway, and even then, just to settle certain things like the house. There's not much between us now, and I'd just as soon not stir up bad memories. We'll see."

"You'll have to make up your mind soon. It's coming up fast. You want to see your Israeli grandchildren, don't you?"

"My daughter and son-in-law, too, for that matter."

"How long's it been?"

"A year or so since they visited here. Longer since I've been there. Three, maybe four years? The older I get, the more it all runs together."

"Come to think of it, Mom mentioned it's more like five."

"Q.E.D. How about the little cafe on Johnson Avenue for lunch?"

"Sounds good. You know, it's strange, but I think Mom's more Jewish than Dad. He doesn't really care about the religion stuff. She'd probably do the *Aliyah* bit if she really were Jewish."

"She's got enough Catholic guilt to compensate. Solid citizen, your mother."

"Yeah, and not Canadian either, ha ha."

"Close call."

They lucked into a parking space. Stephen fed the meter. "You okay getting to the restaurant from here?"

"Fine, Gramps. I wish you'd stop asking."

They were led to a booth. Michael said under his breath, "You're not going to ask whether I can slide in, are you?"

"No, grandson, I'm going to wait until you fall on your behind and all the people in the restaurant will say, 'Why doesn't he help that poor boy? He's just standing there, laughing at him.'"

"Deal."

A waitress brought two oversized, laminated menus. They perused them in silence for a time, until Stephen peered over the top of his and asked, "So, do you want to give me a list of approved subjects?"

"Very funny. Ask away. I'm a marine."

"I'll start easy. Girlfriends?"

"You mean do I approve of them?" He placed his elbows on the table, leaned in. "Shit."

"What's wrong?"

"I have it in for waiters who don't know enough to wipe sticky crap off the table."

"Serves you right for being a smart-ass. I assume that means you're not seeing anyone. All right, here's a more serious question: Do you worry that your injuries will make it hard to find someone?"

Michael smirked, then stopped a jocular response in mid-air. "Yeah, sometimes. But I'm lucky; it's my lower legs that are gone. Everything else works. Dick's fine. That's not true for a lot of guys. Some of them have trouble keeping girls they had before they left—like the contract's been voided. Wives too, for that matter. I don't kid myself. It's going to take a special woman to want to take me on, functioning dick or not." He took the fork from his place setting and tapped a leg. "And I do have problems with these guys. The whole phantom limb thing, for one. There are times I could swear my legs are whole and tingling and itching like hell. And even after all this time, I do reach and scratch the air."

Stephen nodded.

"What's worse is sometimes I get these shooting pains that make me stamp my fake legs hard. Gets lots of attention in restaurants and on airplanes. But when I said I was lucky, I wasn't kidding."

"I know you weren't."

"And not for the obvious reasons, like I'm still here for one." Michael gave Stephen a sudden look. "I'm sorry. I don't mean to bring up . . . bad memories. Jacob, I mean."

"Of course not." Stephen shook his head vigorously. "Believe me, I couldn't be happier that you're here."

They were quiet for a moment before Michael said, "What I really hate? There's a certain kind of girl out there, one who takes on

303

relationships with badly wounded soldiers . . . looks for them, kinda. Amputee groupies. It must be some sort of martyr complex. Some of them are beautiful, too. You wouldn't think they'd need to go wounded warrior hunting. Pisses me off when a beautiful girl who happens to be fucked up in the head comes on to a guy who's in bad shape and gets his hopes up. And then maybe she changes her mind and gives the marine the brush-off. Let me tell you, there's some bad shit I want to happen to that girl."

They stopped to order and remained silent while Stephen stirred his coffee and Michael frowned at his Coke. "What I'd really like is a beer."

"So, have one. It's lunchtime."

"Can't. Interferes with some of my meds."

"Ah, right. Before I forget, when you were talking about living at home you said it was awkward. What did you mean? That you're too old to be there?"

"Not really." Michael shrugged. "Oh, sometimes I guess I feel that way. But we all know it's a temporary thing until my recovery is a little further along."

"What, then?"

Michael smiled. "I'm not sure what I meant when I said it. What occurs to me now is that sometimes I'm concerned about being the cause of tension between Mom and Dad." Michael paused, took in Stephen's questioning look, and went on. "It's one of those things that bubbles beneath the surface, like the differences over my enlisting. I wonder sometimes whether just the fact that I'm around—it's not like I can hide my wounds—doesn't stir things up between them."

"Have you seen . . ."

"No. If your question is whether I've seen them argue or anything, then no. The subject's never come up. It may be in my head more than theirs. But when I come clattering into a room, I automatically imagine that it sets something off."

They were quiet for a moment as the waitress brought the food.

"So, then," Stephen said, breaking in. "Next question." He smiled. "See? You'll have to come around more often if you want to spread these things out. How are you dealing with the fallout from the Jessup interview—with the whole business about 'It has to have been worth it.' That must have stirred things up at home."

Michael took a sip of Coke, frowned at it again. "Not really. But the whole business, as you put it, ticks me off. Everyone went on about what I meant like I was some fucking Buddha with the secret answers. Do you know, not one goddamn person has asked me what I meant by it? You have the talking heads going on about how I must have convinced myself it was worth it because how else could I live with myself and all that bullshit. And another one would come back and say something like, "Well, maybe we should just take his words at face value and stop"—Michael held out a dainty pinky—"*parsing* them.

"And then Jessup got pissed off when Mom and Dad refused to do the followup interview. I have to admit, I was surprised when they agreed to do the first one. They probably didn't know what they were in for, especially when they started to get nasty letters from people about how they were cowards and traitors for running to Canada. One nut job offered to adopt me so I wouldn't have to come in contact with Mom or Dad."

"So, then, allow me to be the first to ask: What did you mean?"

"Ha!" Michael exclaimed loudly enough to make a couple at a nearby table look over. "That's just it. I really don't know."

Stephen sat upright, gave an exaggerated look of surprise. "Seriously? Was it just something you blurted out? Because if it was, I'd have to cast my lot with the subconscious parsing set."

Michael looked down at his hands, then directly at Stephen. "The truth is, the whole *mishigas*, as my Irish Catholic mother likes to say, made me question what I did mean. Maybe you'll say I punted, but I ended up thinking it didn't matter whether I thought it was worth it."

"Not even to you?"

"Not even to me. After those raghead fuckers brought down the twin towers, all I knew was that my country needed guys like me to go after guys like them. It might not be the kind of perfect, clean war you got to fight, but I didn't get to make that decision. I joined up. I served. I took a hit. Period. Case closed."

Stephen was taken aback by Michael's vehemence, and it must have shown in his expression as Michael paused and smiled. "Maybe the raghead thing is a little strong."

Michael leaned in suddenly, said in a lower voice made more intense by the compression of words in a smaller space, "On second thought, to tell the truth, I feel like I've earned the right to call them what I want. And I never saw anything in Eye-raq that would make me think any better of them. Oh, one or two maybe, but for sure not if you're talking about the Nine-Eleven camel jockeys."

"Well," Stephen began, but Michael kept going.

"I know you feel the same way," he said.

"How do you know that?"

"Because you're the only one in the family who knows what it's like to go up against an evil enemy in battle. You think I can talk to my dad about any of this? He buggered off to Canada at the first shot."

"That's how you see it?"

"Well, didn't he? Don't get me wrong. I love my dad. That doesn't necessarily mean I respect him. You're the one I've always looked up to. Don't look so surprised. It's true."

But Stephen was surprised, caught completely off guard, and it was much more than a matter of humility. "I don't know what to say."

And he didn't. He wanted to say *something*. How could he not, considering the overwhelming farrago of things that had just been thrown at him? But where to begin? He shared Michael's views on Arabs? On war? On Ben's character? Why did Michael assume any of these things? Could it be solely because Stephen fought in "his" war, a war now rendered into untouchable myth and popular touchstone by unceasing glorification and the passage of time, a war whose very purpose and conduct had become unquestioned and unquestionable? That was probably where the "perfect, clean war" crap came from. Did Michael just spin out a complete biography of his grandfather based solely on this one distorted thing about him?

And here it was the resentment that crept in again. Even if everything Michael said were true, even if he had reached the right conclusions, he hadn't done so honestly, hadn't done the work. Michael made leaps that

Stephen himself would not have made. He saw the pointillist canvas without seeing the myriad points that created it.

Stephen was surprised to find that his impulse was to defend Ben. He was on the verge of saying something like—something as banal as—those were different times. He might have said Ben had shown a different kind of courage. In the face of Stephen's strong opposition, and under threat of retaliation from the government, Ben picked himself up and headed for parts unknown to him, where he made a life.

But did Stephen really believe this? Could it not just as well have been that an eighteen-year-old kid acted like an eighteen-year-old kid, reveling in defiance and unthinking of consequences?

Yet there it was, whether he believed it or not, the impulse to defend Ben to Ben's son. And the unwelcome thought that the defense was rooted in the same righteous, atavistic rigidity that caused him to support the Vietnam War and push—yes, push, he was able to admit this forthrightly now—his sons into service. Could it be that the same root impulse now was to defend Ben, not so much because the son needed or deserved defending, but because of a deep-seated belief that at least until a certain point—a golden arrival of maturity no matter what the chronological age—sons don't comprehend fathers, and it is they, the fathers, who need and deserve defending? And by proclaiming solidarity with Ben, was he not really asking for understanding himself?

Overwhelmed by these thoughts and a million tangents, Stephen only found it possible to stall—who knew for how long—until he could work through at least some of them. And so, in the run-up to returning the rest of their luncheon to the stuff of inconsequence, Stephen said, "I don't know how to respond to you. So much of what you just said may appear straightforward. But none of it is. Not to my mind, anyway. What is it young people like to say, that they need to *process* this or that? Well, I think that's what I need to do."

~ ~ ~ ~ ~

Chapter 36

April 2005: RSVP Regrets Only

IT WAS MICHAEL'S IMPORTUNING for what seemed like the umpteenth time that caused Stephen to decide firmly that he had no desire to make the trip to Israel—not that he would tell Michael this.

"Don't you think it would be cool to get together with other camp liberators?" he had asked. "You might even know some of them. You could be face to face with the people you rescued, including the person you actually married. Okay, so maybe it didn't work out so well, but you have to admit, the whole idea is pretty amazing. And if all that's not enough, you can't pass up an opportunity to have the whole family together."

Stephen was listening on speaker, a sure sign he was only half listening. Michael's gung-ho might be annoying, but it was also endearing. Given the family's rocky history, it was something of a wonder, and gratifying, that Ben and Martha had succeeded in imparting the importance of family ties.

In a curious way, Michael's enthusiasm was also a source of envy. How long had it been since Stephen had experienced so much passion for . . . well, for anything? He wondered if Michael would reach a point where his enthusiasms were balanced, or perhaps exceeded, by the negatives of his experiences—particularly considering the enormous negative of his lost legs.

Such questions had been much on Stephen's mind since Michael had brought up his startling assumptions about the supposed commonality of their views on war. Years from now, when people no longer debated the Iraq war, when they no longer served up the simple dignity of even having an opinion on it, when the war was reduced to a factoid and completely overtaken by events (R.I.P. Iraq 2003–), what would Michael think then? Would the loss of his legs still make sense? Would he do it all again? Would he be eager to attend a reunion commemorating the capture of Saddam Hussein in the presence of some whole-bodied kid asking, "Who's he?"

Stephen considered himself fortunate, even privileged, to have fought his war. However much it irked him to hear Michael talk blithely about it as "perfect," it was, after all, a war that was not, and probably never would be, considered to be unnecessary or relegated to being a footnote. He could take pride in having played a small part in ending the Holocaust. Kids in the future would still be taught about the Holocaust, wouldn't they? (Alas, there was always a chance that it could be displaced by a worse, more recent, holocaust in the same way the calamitous Second World War supplanted the calamitous First, which otherwise would still be known as the Great War.) In short, if Stephen's passions were capable of waning, what chance did Michael have?

Michael had no idea how much energy it took Stephen to dredge up the past. Or to confront it when someone dredged it up for him while his guard was down. Annalise, Henry, war crimes, murder—all the things he could never completely put a lid on.

"We'll find an occasion to bring us all together," Stephen said finally. "Just not this one."

Michael was nothing if not tenacious: "This is the perfect time, the perfect occasion. Not to be rude, but there's a reason the Israelis want this commemoration now, while there's still a minion left to participate."

"I'll take my mortality under advisement."

"Just don't make me get Aunt Sandy on your case."

Stephen laughed. "The horror! The horror!"

It occurred to him after he hung up that all of the pressure to attend was coming from the kids—Ben, Martha, Michael, Sandra, Ethan, and their kids, the latter whom he thought of as the lost grandchildren, living so far away. The missing voice was Annalise's. Were the kids doing her bidding? Or maybe she would be more comfortable if he didn't come—

perhaps that explained her silence. Probably she shared his ambivalence. After all, he was not the only one with ghosts to exorcise. Sandra had told him over the phone recently that Annalise, herself, had to be persuaded to participate at Yad Vashem, though Sandra conceded it wasn't a very hard sell. Where the Holocaust was concerned, she said, survivors—Israeli Jews above all—readily played the guilt card (or had it played against them). They all had an obligation to keep the lesson alive.

For his part, Stephen believed he had earned the right to refuse this particular invitation. To put it crassly, that's what years of contributions to Yad Vashem bought him. He smiled at the thought that it was like earning reverse reward miles on his credit card—do enough for the cause and earn the right not to fly to Israel.

One regret about the decision involved Sandra and Ethan's kids. The fact that he even thought of them as kids made the point. Deborah would be nearing thirty; the boy, Yonatan—Yoni—was only a few years younger, the family sabra, born not long after Sandra and Ethan moved to Israel.

Stephen felt like a stranger to both of them, though there was some connection to Deborah as the first grandchild. She was born in New York during the period when all of them were making the journeys to Toronto. Yoni spent two summers with Stephen when he was young, but his English then was mediocre, and either because of that or simple childhood reticence, there was not much of a connection.

HE WAS PLEASED to hear Sandra's voice when she called, even as he anticipated that much of the conversation would be a tiresome rehash of the ones he'd had with Michael. He rushed through a summary of what they'd said. He could hear in the background Ethan give a command in Hebrew; he couldn't understand the words, but the tone and cadence suggested it was directed to the family dog. But then, he thought with a smile, with Israelis everything sounded like a command, and an irritable one at that. It was one of their endearing attributes.

To his surprise, Sandra didn't pursue the subject of his visiting, or at least not on a tack he would have predicted.

"What?" he said into a silence.

"What caused the breakup with Mom?"

"Are you serious? Where is this coming from?"

"Belated curiosity, I suppose. I always assumed it was all about Jake."

"What's changed your mind?"

"Conversations with Mom."

"Dangerous," Stephen said, an unconvincing stab at ambiguous levity.

Sandra ignored it. "I'm not saying Jake wasn't an important reason."

"But?"

"But Mom told me not long ago about her experiences in the camps."

"You knew about that."

"I don't mean Dachau," she added quickly. "Buchenwald."

Stephen was quiet for a moment. "When was this? What did she tell you?"

"A few weeks ago. We were sitting at her kitchen table, just the two of us. We were talking about Dachau. It probably came up in connection with the Yad Vashem thing. I knew most of the story. She talked about meeting you. She was wistful. I didn't expect that. Then, without prompting, she told me about Buchenwald, which totally surprised me. Especially when she went into detail." Sandra gave a short laugh. "I don't know, maybe she thought a nurse could be more clinical about it. It didn't work. Listening to a parent talk about sex—if you can call what she went through sex—what can I say? Being a nurse didn't keep me from getting lost in the emotional forest.

"Anyway, as I said, I don't know what got Mom to open up. Maybe it was the Dachau commemoration. Maybe it's that she's getting old. She hasn't been well, you know."

"No, I didn't."

"She had to have a kidney removed. There was a tumor . . ."

"Malignant?" Stephen asked with a start and a flashback to hearing Jacob play down the gravity of his loss of a kidney.

"Yes. She asked us not to tell anyone."

311

"Sounds like her."

"It was discovered by accident. She was complaining about back pain. The good news is they caught it early. There's no indication it's spread. We talked about undergoing chemo just to be sure. Mom said at her age she'd prefer to take the risk."

"I can understand that."

"She's doing well. But I did wonder how much of what she had to say was because of the experience. Mortality confession, you might call it."

"Well, please give her my best."

"Okay, but to come full circle, I was hoping you'd come here and do it in person." Sandra paused for a moment and added, "I gather you don't want to talk about any of this."

"Not really."

"Yeah, but let me finish. After Mom told me about Buchenwald, I asked whether you knew about it. She said you learned about it, but not until a long time after you were married. I got to thinking about whether there might have been more to your breakup than Jacob and Ben."

"There's always more than one thing."

"I get that. But this would have been a big thing, presumably."

"What does this have to do with my coming to Israel?"

"It doesn't, not directly. After talking to Mom, I just got interested." Into a sudden silence, Sandra said in a resigned tone, "You're not going to tell me, are you?"

"I'm not sure what to say, Sandy. It's not something I think about often," he lied. "The fighting over Jacob, Mom's blaming me with no forgiveness in sight—that would have been enough, I believe. I try not to think about it, anyway," he amended.

"But," Sandra ventured, her voice turned tentative, "the other thing must have been important." She added hastily, "I would guess."

The silence again, followed by a sigh. "You might say it was the final straw, or in any case it set things in motion. But not for the reason you probably think." He paused before continuing. "Just for the record, it's not easy to talk to your child about something like this."

"Apparently, Mom was able to do it. Anyway, some child! I'm closer to sixty than fifty."

312

"Not a factor. Come on, Sandy, you know what I mean. You just told me how difficult it was to listen to Mom on the subject. You have grown kids. You know they're permanent children. Anyway, listen, it wasn't that I couldn't understand what Mom went through. Or that I had some kind of macho insecurity about the . . . sex . . . however forced. I'm not entirely sure your mom would completely agree with me about this, but after all and in my defense, I may not have known about Buchenwald, but I knew about Dachau, and I fell in love with her anyway."

"Some people might say you fell in love *because* of Dachau—her knight in shining armor and all that."

"I don't see the psych credentials next to your name."

"It's true, though. What? Sometimes a cigar's just a cigar? Is that what you're telling me?" she added with a laugh.

"There is that. Believe me, I *have* wondered about the white knight thing. I can't swear there's no truth to it or that I'm not in denial, but I honestly don't think so. My generation had to grow up fast. Still, keep in mind that I was all of nineteen or twenty at the time. And I hope your mom doesn't believe the issue between us was what happened at Buchenwald. She never had anything to apologize for on that score.

"What did make a huge difference was Mom's hiding what happened to her, which was made worse by my finding out about it by chance, through a colleague at work whose wife *did* confide in him. It's the kind of secret that undermines a marriage because it's so essential to the life of the person who keeps it. By definition its absence becomes essential to the life of the one who discovers it. After a secret of that magnitude is revealed, everything—every assumption about the relationship—becomes open to question. And on top of everything else that was going on at the time with Jacob and Ben, it was humiliating to find out about it the way I did.

"So, can we drop it now? One reason I don't want to do this Yad Vashem thing is I have no desire to pick at this particular scab, or any other, for that matter."

~ ~ ~ ~ ~

Chapter 37

April 2005: Exigencies

WITH THE EL AL 747 out of JFK at thirty-seven thousand feet, Stephen was cramped, unable to stretch his legs, still hoping for sleep, fairly certain it wouldn't come. Given the prospect of this discomfort for about another ten hours, he was more than a little annoyed at the cost of his last-minute ticket. A passing flight attendant asked if anything was wrong. Stephen shook his head, a little surprised and slightly abashed that his facial expression had so automatically and so obviously revealed his state of mind.

There was no point fretting. He was faced with the true definition of Hobson's choice, meaning not a difficult choice as most people seemed to use the term, but no choice at all. He had to get to his destination quickly, the flight was full, and he was lucky to have any seat.

So much for carefully considered decisions. After all the back and forth about attending the Yad Vashem commemoration, here he was on an urgent journey to Jerusalem—and it had nothing to do with the ceremony.

It had everything to do with terrorism. A bomb. A bus. Shredded metal and splintered glass. A wounded grandson he hardly knew. He saw the report on CNN before he received the call from Ethan. Prior to the call—before he knew the incident directly affected him—he watched with sad, but detached, resignation over this latest of God knew how many misery-inflicting acts, seemingly perpetual and inevitable. On the screen, an industrial-sized tow truck was dragging the scorched, blown out husk of a bus, which looked like nothing so much as a popped kernel of corn.

It was not until Ethan's phone call, consisting of a taut stream of words without a break, that the perpetual and the inevitable became the personal. Stephen cut in, astonished. "Yoni? Yoni was on that bus?"

He wasn't, quite. He was waiting for it at the stop when the bomb went off. Shrapnel, Ethan said. The manifestly ordinary city bus turned into flying bits of metal, vinyl, and flesh. Luckily, it had been only half full. Some, perhaps a third, of the passengers were not badly injured, Ethan said. "It was a miracle, Stephen. But others waiting at the stop, including Yoni" (and here his voice broke) "were caught in the blast."

"He's not . . ." Stephen said, suddenly numb (*when did someone you actually knew get caught up in this kind of news?*) and recalling Ethan's tendency to give his patients bad news last.

"No. But he's seriously hurt; we still don't know how seriously," Ethan responded with another catch in his voice. "He looks like hell. His eyes are bandaged. He may have slivers in them. X-rays weren't helpful. We're waiting on a CAT scan."

"Where is he?" Stephen asked, fighting back memories of a similar call about Jacob (*caught in a blast, probably will be okay*).

"Jerusalem. Hadassah Hospital."

"That's good, right?"

"The best. Even so, there are always limits to what can be done."

"You're there now, I presume."

"Yes, waiting for Sandra."

"How is she coping?"

"Not well. She insisted on driving from Tel Aviv. Not a good idea, and it will probably take forever with all the commotion in the streets. She was going to pick up Annalise along the way, but then she didn't want to be slowed down. I have to go. It looks like some of the scans are back."

"You'll keep me posted?"

"Of course."

"Let me know if I can do anything."

"I will. Oh, wait, Stephen?"

"I'm here."

"You can call Ben and Martha. I wasn't able to reach them."

"I'll call right away." Then, out of the blue, Stephen added, "Ethan? One more thing."

"Make it quick."

"I'm coming over."

* * *

WHATEVER POSSESSED HIM? The simple answer was a desire to support his family, to patch where it could be patched, shore up where it could be shored up, be present and accounted for. No matter their differences, he had always tried to be there when he was needed. Hadn't he? He had always tried to do the right thing. With Jacob, too. It was a tragedy, to be sure, but not one caused by bad intent.

Of course, whatever the intent, he had been wrong. Wrong about the war. Wrong about encouraging Jacob—no, as long as he was facing up, he mustn't shy from saying it as it was: He did more than encourage. He pressured. Today they might soften it, say he was merely trying to be *proactive* or some such thing. Even Henry, never one to defend the status quo, might have approved. But in this case Henry would have been wrong, too.

Have faith in the country; trust the government to do the right and necessary thing. He had taken these lessons from his war. Mostly, the lessons were buttressed by Korea—another war that needed to be fought. And then he applied what he learned. By the time Jacob was of draft age, the lessons had become absorbed, automatic, his words to Jacob made rote. Essentially, he had extrapolated a war too far. Vietnam was neither his war nor Korea.

He had since learned, too late, to be alert to countervailing evidence, had learned the meaning—the anesthetizing power of—that sterile, academic term "confirmation bias." During Vietnam he was, indeed, wide open only to the things that confirmed what he knew—or thought he knew—and closed to those that contradicted what he knew. Who was it, Twain maybe, that said it's not what you don't know that gets you into trouble. It's what you know for sure that isn't so.

316

And the contradictions, the things he didn't see, were rife, beginning with the coming of age of a generation—his children's—that, far from believing, drew strength from rebellion, from basic contrariness. It was a generation willing—increasingly eager—to call out The Man, to bloody The Man. The same Man Stephen saw as his duty to respect and honor even in the face of gross aberrations from what he knew. How, he reasoned, could he not think well of his government when it led the fight against Hitler, Tojo, and later, Stalin (and later still, the rampaging Koreans and Chinese)? He and so many of his generation had been inoculated against those—his children, to be precise—who were eager not to believe and to disrespect.

It certainly wasn't as if the leaders in his war made no mistakes. He never thought that. It was more a question of intentions. Our generals screwed up? Maybe they had. But we weren't inclined to question their motives, their basic integrity. Feckless they may have been, but intentionally? Dishonorably? It's not that we ignored the screw-ups, either. We dealt with them with the few weapons we had in the pre-Internet era, and at a time when being foursquare on the team was what counted. We turned them into the butt of derisive jokes. Satire lived! Sad Sack lived! GI Joe lived!

We were well inoculated against the heresy of the later generation, which maintained that the system was rotten and needed tearing down. It wasn't. It didn't. It needed improving, for sure. But the means and mechanisms to achieve this were in place.

So Stephen believed. Still believed, actually. The belief was shaken now, sometimes badly so. Still, improvement—change for the better— was built into the country's essence. So much so that his children didn't have to think about the dangerous consequences to themselves of their protests. They could be confident that they would not be tortured or killed by their government. The faith vaccine he had received weakened over time, yet it still offered protection; it only needed a booster. That's where the flower children got it wrong. It wasn't the Age of Aquarius; it was the Age of Cynicism and Lost Hope.

He made excuses. Unlike subsequent generations, his didn't have the benefit of revelation. Things were covered up—hidden, obscured, and ultimately ignored by a population disinclined to think the worst. FDR's extramarital affairs? His true physical state? Squelched. The head-slapping paramour parade of JFK (not to mention the inexcusable idiocy of taking up with a Mafia don's girlfriend)? Likewise. If such things had been revealed, the inoculation might have worn off much sooner.

When the sixties came along, he was unprepared for the Age of Revelation that came along with it and continued right up until the present. In the face of alleged government wrongdoing, his generation's impulse was to circle the wagons; to say to the Aquarians, "Prove it."

But prove it they did. Tonkin, Pentagon Papers, Watergate tapes (and gaps). Cheating presidents exposed (impeached even, the hypocrites). Questionable, if not useless, wars.

It was too late for Jacob. For Stephen, it was an open sore. Not the only one, of course. There were still those weeping wounds involving Henry. And Dachau. And Ben. And Annalise. In all of these instances he had strived to do right. He fell short. Woefully short. Justifiable or not. Forgivable or not.

Now, as he looked out the window at a black sky, he hoped at least some amends could be made.

* * *

HE OPTED FOR a taxi rather than a cheaper sherut, or shared service, for the long ride to his hotel in Jerusalem. In about the same brief time it took to decide he was making the journey, he decided he would do so without running the pensioner's usual savings-to-life-expectancy calculation—weighing a purchase against the likelihood of his money running out before he died. Someone joked that the goal is to bounce your last check.

It was a behavior he both resisted and resented for its old-age stereotype, yet which, to his frustration, was becoming increasingly automatic in the face of rising prices and relatively good health. He was determined that whatever expenses he encountered on this trip would be dealt with in a spirit of free-spending generosity and pushed into a folder at the back of his mind labeled "cost of doing life's business."

In the same spirit, before leaving home he gave a significant gift to Ben, Martha, and Michael to lighten their financial burden. The three

Roths (as they continued to spell it with the dropped "W") had already made arrangements for the Israel trip that was to occur in less than two weeks. It was a financial sacrifice for them, and Annalise, Ethan, and Sandra had banded together to help make the trip possible. Stephen was disappointed not to have been asked to contribute. He hoped this reflected an oversight based on his decision not to go, and not a more pointed snub. And then he wondered why he needed to be asked.

When Stephen called Ben to tell him about Yoni, Ben said they would change their tickets to reach Jerusalem as soon as possible, and then extend the trip. Which gave Stephen an opportunity for largesse, as he told Ben he wanted to pay for any additional airfare and hotel expenses. He suggested the American Colony Hotel in East Jerusalem, where he would be staying.

His flight arrived early in the morning of the following day, a couple of hours behind schedule. The delay was typical of EL AL in Stephen's experience, and usually attributed to the need for extra rigorous security procedures. A good thing, of course. In any case, he often felt obliged to respond to friends' automatic questioning of the wisdom of traveling to the Middle East by pointing out that there were a few (very few) advantages to reaching his advanced age, and one of them was the knowledge that sudden death would not mean much in the way of missed opportunities. He could never quite understand it when his contemporaries became more averse to risk, not less. He had passed most of life's benchmarks—birth (not a given for his generation), school, war, marriage, children, career, retirement. There wasn't a lot left. No eulogy would mourn his unfulfilled promise. The first President Bush's birthday celebration parachute jumps should be their model.

In the taxi queue, a swarthy middle-aged driver, disheveled and apparently as sleep-deprived as Stephen, swung out of the car and took hold of his luggage. Stephen had called Ethan as soon as he landed but was unable to get through. He left a message saying he would check in early at his hotel if he could, and freshen up before heading to the hospital.

"You're Jewish?" the driver inquired in heavily accented English into his rearview mirror as they pulled away.

319

Stephen knew Israelis well enough not to be surprised or offended by the blunt question. Still, in his bleary state, he was annoyed by the intrusion. "Yes," he said, finally, after rejecting more convoluted answers.

"Then why are you staying at the American Colony? It's not in a good part of the city," he added. Which Stephen took to mean it wasn't in the Jewish section.

"I've been there before. I like it."

"Why?" the driver pressed as he swerved to avoid an encroaching car.

Clearly, Stephen thought, he should not have expected such a terse response to suffice. The lesson hadn't taken, however, as he said, "Well, because."

The driver noticed Stephen looking at his I.D. placard. "Avigdor," he said, helpfully. "Avi. That's what my friends call me."

So, he was apparently to be considered a friend. The bar must be low. He wondered idly if the friendship could survive a meager tip. "Well, Avi, aside from it being a beautiful old place with lots of history, I like it because it's not kosher. Even tomorrow, Shabbat, I can have bacon with my eggs. I could smoke, if I hadn't given it up."

"The hotel isn't too far from Mea Shearim," Avi offered with a slightly wry expression.

"Yes? Why is that important?"

"Because, that's where the really religious Jews live. They'll beat the hell into you if they smell bacon on your breath." He laughed.

"*Out* of you. They'll beat the hell *out* of you," Stephen corrected, then wondered why he bothered. "Jewish Taliban," he said under his breath.

"Eh?"

"Never mind."

His phone buzzed and he fumbled for it in his pocket, trying to answer before it went to voicemail. "Ethan?" he said after he found he couldn't make out the faint screen without his reading glasses.

"It's Sandy, Dad."

"Hi, sweetheart, I . . ."

"I know. I'm using Ethan's mobile."

"How's Yoni? How are you?"

"I could be a lot better, but the word's not as bad as we feared about Yoni."

"That's a relief." Stephen noticed that Avi wasn't even pretending not to listen.

"He looks bad, but most of the wounds are superficial. Our main concern is his eyes."

"That's what Ethan told me."

"They operated last night. The surgeon said his left eye should be fine. The splinters missed the important parts. He thinks so, anyway. Some of the splinters were very fine, barely visible pieces of metal and glass. He wasn't as confident about the right eye. There could be more lasting damage. We might not know for some time."

"Well, I'm already reassured. The main thing is he'll recover, and at least he won't be completely blind. Are you at the hospital now?"

Sandra said she was. She and Ethan had spent the night.

Stephen told her he would shower at the hotel and then come directly there.

"This was someone from the bus?" Avi asked as Stephen ended the call.

He resisted the urge to tell him it was none of his business. "Yes," he said, which turned out to be enough to keep Avi monologuing on the subject of "we want peace, but how can you have peace with those people."

When they pulled up to the hotel, Avi asked if Stephen wanted him to wait. "I can get a coffee, and the meter will go at half rate," he said. "It might not be so easy to get another taxi," he added, despite the presence of several waiting in queue.

Stephen was about to tell him it wasn't necessary but changed his mind as he concluded that Avi had probably done him the service of providing an intensive refresher on Israeli culture. He likened it to being shot out of a cannon first thing in the morning. Besides, he thought, *the devil you know* . . . "Yes, okay," he said, careful to ensure that his tone wasn't overly friendly.

He grimaced as he stepped out of the taxi and got muscles, tendons, and ligaments properly aligned. Avi went to hand the baggage to the porter. *The devil you know*, he thought again as he moved toward the lobby.

~ ~ ~ ~ ~

Chapter 38

Late April 2005: Inversion

S ANDRA DIDN'T NOTICE HIM at first. She was sitting close to the bed, softly stroking Yoni's arm, taking obvious care to trace a path through the field of small wounds. Without makeup and in the harsh hospital lighting, she seemed to have aged considerably since he had last seen her. She had let her hair go gray and had put on weight.

Yoni's eyes were bandaged. His head was in a cage-like device that looked to Stephen like something out of a torture chamber. He couldn't tell if Yoni was sleeping.

She smiled as he approached, which gave back some of the years. She stood. They moved toward one another and embraced tightly. "Thanks for making the trip," she murmured into his chest.

"How could I not?"

"He's asleep," she said with a nod toward Yoni. "They've got him pretty drugged up."

"And that contraption around his head?"

"It looks dreadful, doesn't it? It's not really so bad. It keeps him from making sudden movements."

"And the prognosis is good, right? That's what counts."

"Apparently. Better than we'd feared. Still . . . my only boy. Worrying is a mother's first duty," she said with a weak smile and moistening eyes.

And a sister's, Stephen thought, recalling how Sandra always took it upon herself to look out for Jacob and Ben. "Where's Ethan?" he asked.

"He went for coffee. I understand Ben, Martha, and Michael will arrive tomorrow."

"That's my understanding as well. Same EL AL flight I took."

"I'm sorry one of us couldn't meet you at the airport."

He waved away the apology. "Don't be silly. The whole point of my coming is to help you, not the other way around. Besides," he added with a laugh, "I would have been deprived of Avi's tutorial on everything Israeli, Jewish, and Palestinian. He was quite thorough."

"Avi?"

"My taxi driver. We're on a first-name basis. And Deborah, how is she?" he added, remembering to accent the "O" in the middle of her name.

"You just missed her. She's doing her *miluim*, her military reserve duty."

"They wouldn't let her off for this? To be with Yoni, I mean."

"They would, but she insisted on returning to her unit. She said she could do more for Yoni there than she could sitting by his bedside."

Ethan came in, juggling a four-cup cluster of coffee cups on a flimsy cardboard tray. He, too, had aged, though not as obviously as Sandra.

"Let me help you," Sandra said, taking a cup. "What army were you buying for? We were just the two of us."

"Now we're three, and it never hurts to have a spare." Ethan extended a newly freed hand to Stephen. He had always maintained a kind of proper formality toward Stephen, which Stephen attributed to the time and circumstances under which they had met, including his divorce from Annalise (with whom Ethan was always close, particularly given their kindred views on Israel), the long-lived repercussions of Jacob's death, and Ben's exile. Stephen perceived a warming trend with Ethan over the years, but they saw one another too infrequently to establish a shift in their formal protocols.

"Has your mom been here yet?" Stephen asked Sandra, once again unsure of the proprieties of asking something so simple. Include the possessive "your" and it implies more than a divorce, but a permanent disjunction—a reapportionment of loyalties—which was close to the truth but sounded colder than necessary in the circumstances. Omit it and it sounds like things are reconciled, warmer—also partly true, a lukewarm peace instead of a cold war. Maybe they hadn't succeeded at much, but separately and on the rare occasions they were together, he and Annalise had managed to avoid further poisoning the well for Sandra, Ben, and their kids.

"She came last night while Yoni was in surgery," Sandra said. "She's staying with a friend near Mount Scopus. I was glad about that. She didn't want to stay at our place—it would be too inconvenient for us, she said, even though I thought she was being ridiculous—and I didn't like the idea of her making the drive back to Tel Aviv so late."

It occurred again to Stephen that he and Annalise hadn't actually seen one another in years. They had spoken on the phone occasionally when something involved one of the children or grandchildren, and had exchanged a few letters, such as when the house was sold. In the meantime, Annalise had remarried. Stephen knew little about the husband, an Israeli-born telecommunications bigwig, who had died a couple of years ago. Stephen sent a condolence card and had a tree planted in his memory. Annalise never acknowledged either.

"How has she been?"

"Good," Sandra answered in a rising tone that suggested there might be more to it. "She's made good progress since the surgery," she added after a pause. "We still worry. It was a close call. I imagine you'll see her for yourself before long."

"So, she'll be coming over?"

"Sometime soon."

"Good," he said, not sure he meant it. It wasn't that he didn't want to see her, just that he'd prefer to be more rested and alert when he did—ready to bring his A game.

Yoni stirred and let out a small moan. Sandra and Ethan went to him, while Stephen held back at the foot of the bed.

"I can't see anything," Yoni said, slight panic in his voice. "What's this?" he asked not for the first time as he felt the cage around his head.

Sandra's touch and calm voice soothed him. She explained again patiently about the cage and reminded him about the bandages on his eyes. "It's only temporary."

In a voice still not fully alert, Yoni said he understood.

325

"Grandpa Stephen is here. From New York," she added to distinguish him from Ethan's father, also named Stephen (but spelled "Steven" with a "v"—the inferior way, Stephen would say with a smile) from New Jersey.

Yoni gave a weak wave. "It took a terrorist to get you over here," he said. His mouth was dry, making him difficult to understand.

"Oh," Stephen said after Yoni repeated it and everyone laughed. "I guess so. Tell you what," he added, "you rein in the terrorists, and I promise to come without the incentive."

"Deal," Yoni responded without smiling.

Stephen stayed past lunch but was fading as he sat in a chair at Yoni's bedside.

"Dad, why don't you go back to the hotel and take a nap," Sandra said. "You can come back when you're refreshed. Yoni may be more awake as well."

"Maybe that's a good idea. It looks like he's fallen asleep again anyway."

Ethan, who himself had been nodding off, stood to accompany Stephen to the elevator. Stephen held up a hand and told him to relax; he'd seen his way in, he could see his way out.

He had taken only a few steps from the room when he saw Annalise coming from the opposite end of the corridor. She was limping slightly, using a cane that she didn't seem to rely upon much, particularly as she led another woman who was walking more slowly.

Stephen smiled at the thought that once he got past the momentary reaction of wondering who the old woman with the cane was, he would know Annalise anywhere. She was still slim—perhaps too much so, suggesting the beginnings of frailty—but the proud steeliness and self-possession in her bearing that were among the first things he noticed when they met some sixty years ago were evident today. Her hair, cut short, was completely, handsomely silver. She smiled with her eyes as she recognized him, which in itself surprised him and encouraged a reciprocal warmth in his smile.

They embraced. It was brief and a little tentative, but notable for what it said about the absence of rancor, which, fortunately for both of them, must have been leaching away imperceptibly over the years. Later, he

326

would reflect with satisfaction that they might have arrived simultaneously at a point of reconciliation. Not necessarily forgiveness, as such, which would probably have required an explicit re-airing of grievances better left dormant, but a point where the very issue of forgiveness receded. It was a viewpoint perhaps enjoyed only by those who had experienced much—endured much—and remained standing.

She introduced her friend, Miriam, who was as plump as Annalise was lean and whose Hadassah-brunette hair also was a counterpoint to Annalise's silver. The two were a study in different approaches to aging—Annalise's dignified accommodation (not surrender) versus Miriam's aggressive, albeit somewhat ridiculous, denial. "I'm staying with Miriam here in Jerusalem," Annalise said.

"How are you feeling?" Stephen asked, his voice solicitous.

"I'm making good progress. We caught the cancer early on, thanks God."

There was a slight inflection in Annalise's voice, different from the original German. Taken together with the plural "thanks God," it seemed to Stephen that she had lost some of the Americanized English she had acquired so quickly. It reminded him that she had been an Israeli longer than she had been an American.

She tapped her cane against the floor. "I'm hoping soon I may be able to call this thing a . . . how do they say in the magazines . . . a fashion accessory?"

Stephen laughed, his own cane having been left at the hotel—a point of vanity to be sure, which he now compromised by admitting his own frailties: "I'm sure you'll soon be back to where you only have to endure routine arthritis and such. I know the feeling. I've been resisting the inevitable joint replacements. Of course, then I'll see Michael, and complaining is out of the question."

"Oh yes, poor boy," Annalise said. "He'll be here tomorrow?"

"Yes, arriving with Ben and Martha."

"You've seen him recently?"

"I have. He's doing well. Getting around quite nimbly."

Annalise turned to Miriam. "This is the grandson who lost his legs in Iraq."

"Oh, yes, poor boy," Miriam echoed. Stephen noticed her English was native British. "At least it was in a good cause," she added.

Stephen nodded, suppressing his automatic objections to the statement and giving Miriam the benefit of the doubt. A polite woman, what else could she say?

But it was what followed that knocked him for a loop.

"Yes," Annalise said, "thanks God at least it was in a good cause." She followed this quickly by saying they really should get in to see Yoni. "I'll see you at Yad Vashem, if not before?" she asked.

But Stephen was distracted, still letting the words "a good cause" roll around in his head like ball bearings looking for a slot. "What?" he asked.

"The ceremony. Yad Vashem. And also the party at my house in Herzliya Pituah."

"Oh, yes. I hadn't intended to, but I'm here, so . . ." he added with a weak smile.

"So *shalom*, then. *Lehitra'ot*—see you."

Watching them go, Stephen wondered why he had thought it necessary to say he wouldn't attend if he had not already been here. It sounded so petulant. Was his desire to hurt her still so potent that it laid in wait, fangs hidden in the weeds, searching for the smallest opportunity to bite? Was what he felt only moments ago an illusion? Had there really been little progress in all these years? She was doing a good thing getting them all together. It hadn't happened in ages. In fact, the extended family had never actually gotten together in one place. Even Jacob's funeral was minus Ben. This event would only take place because of what happened to Yoni. Otherwise, Stephen would have kept himself apart. For what reason? So the rest of them would be conscious of his absence, like tonguing for a missing tooth? Is that what he was hoping for? Was it really so necessary to diminish her in some misguided service of his self-importance?

And then there was the barely considered notion that they might not have been all that conscious of his absence. Enveloped in their own lives or nursing their own grievances, they might have become used to it. Or said another way, to his so-occasional presence. Here he was, succumbing to the churlish instinct to hurt her when he should have been thanking her for making the effort to include him, and to ensure he would be part of whatever family reconstruction was possible.

There was more. As he sat in the taxi to return to the hotel, not quite seeing the city he was passing, the other thing that really bothered him—shocked him, actually—was the simple phrase, "a good cause."

Of course, he, himself, had never told Michael otherwise. It would have been cruel to do so. The closest he had come was to dispute Michael's encomiums for nation-building in Iraq, as he compared this to what the U.S. did for the Axis powers following the Second World War. No, Stephen had said, there was an important distinction to be made. The U.S. began the war in Iraq with nation-building as a key objective—a fool's errand. The very concept is arrogant and can't succeed. There was only one objective in World War II, to defeat Germany, Italy, and Japan, and only after the U.S. had been attacked. "What we had the wisdom and foresight to do was engage in nation-rebuilding. Rather than let the defeated powers collapse, we saw mutual advantage in helping them recover—eventually to become the allies they are now."

Michael replied that he wasn't sure Stephen wasn't just splitting hairs between building and rebuilding. Stephen thought he'd pressed the point as far as he wanted to.

But, increasingly, Iraq was proving to be anything but a good cause. He, Stephen, for most of his life a supporter of America's wars, even he thought of the Iraq invasion as misguided and a waste. So how was it possible that Annalise of all people—she who had spent so much of her life berating him for Vietnam, for Jacob—how did it come to pass that she could think what the U.S. was doing in Iraq was a good cause? That her grandson had lost his legs in a good cause?

It seemed impossible, almost absurd.

~ ~ ~ ~ ~

Chapter 39

Sunday, May 1, 2005: The Large House

THEY GATHERED IN ANNALISE'S house on Wingate Street in the Tel Aviv seaside suburb of Herzliya Pituah. The house, a villa in the Mediterranean stucco and terra-cotta style consonant with its surroundings, was far too large for Annalise alone. It was in fact too large when she shared it with her late husband, whose wealth was sufficient to purchase it outright. Yet, before long she had been surprised to find she had become accustomed to hearing her voice echo off the walls. Just so long as she didn't have to clean the house herself.

It was the natural gathering place for family and friends. Also, it was security—a nest egg and something to leave to her heirs. Not lost on Stephen—or resented by him, for that matter: the irony of his DP camp "rescue" having a more substantial estate to leave behind than he did.

They were all there. Too few of them to fill the house. Still, it was all there was of the Wroth family and its various annexations—which is the word Stephen used good naturedly in years-old banter with Ethan, when Ethan pointed out that Sandra had, after all, agreed to take his surname, Shulman. No, Stephen said, Sandra had used a hyphen, technically becoming Sandra Wroth-Shulman, thus annexing the Shulman family.

Ah but this was a technicality, Ethan typically rejoined—Wroth was honored in the breach since as a practical matter his wife went by the pure form Sandra Shulman. Moreover, his children were documented only as Shulman, so if Stephen wanted to stake a claim on posterity, it would have to be through son Ben, and he would then have to settle for the truncated, W-less Roth. Typically it would be at this point that Stephen would throw up his hands in mock surrender, declare he'd had enough, and say it was easy to see why no one would ever best Israel in Middle East peace negotiations.

After Yoni's discharge from the hospital, Ben, Martha, and Michael moved from the hotel in Jerusalem to Annalise's house. Stephen also moved, but believing the family dynamic was complicated enough, he declined an invitation to join them and instead checked into the nearby Dan Accadia Hotel.

Yoni's rapid recovery contributed to a festive mood. It seemed there would be little or no lasting damage to his eyes. Yoni's crisis aside, the original, bittersweet reason for their gathering, formally the Holocaust Day of Remembrance for Victims, Survivors, and Liberators, was still a few days off.

For Stephen, the time spent with Ben was possibly the most rewarding aspect of his stay so far. In a sense this was odd, because since Ben and Martha's return from Toronto—an astonishing nearly three decades ago—Stephen probably had spent more time with them and Michael than with anyone else in the family. However, with regard to Ben this was a perfect example of quantity over quality. The simple fact was that the essence of the relationship never got much beyond the contentious juvenile-parent time preceding Ben's flight to Canada.

Ben still struggled to find a comfortable identity, as well as to gain a financial footing. Stephen tried to help where he could. Nevertheless, rather than coming closer to Ben, he became closer to Martha, and later, especially after his wounding in Iraq, to Michael. It was Martha who, in Stephen's opinion, had done best at putting the tumult of the sixties behind her. She had matured. She exhibited a practical, can-do spirit, which kept Ben afloat and for which Stephen was grateful.

Particularly during stressful times, such as when, after returning from Toronto, Ben had trouble finding, or keeping, a job, Stephen became the target of his frustration. As far as Ben was concerned, Stephen was the number-one reason his life had turned to shit. No amount of reasoning or trying to convince him to take at least some responsibility for the path he had taken seemed to work. Only Martha was able to stop the rants. She stayed loyal to Ben and held fast to the idea that he was fundamentally good and worth saving, even when any reasonable observer would have understood if she had given up and left. She was the one who finally prevailed upon him to get clean and go back to school.

Stephen thought he detected in Martha's loyalty a kind of penance. At first, he speculated that it might have had something to do with her failure to become pregnant. Or perhaps she was determined to avoid the kind of meltdown that had occurred in her own family. But the loyalty remained after Michael was born, and in any case, he didn't care what motivated her. He was grateful. He credited her with the steady maturity that on several occasions kept him from telling Ben to go to hell and walking away completely.

Once, after a particularly nasty episode of Ben shouting at Stephen and stomping off, Stephen hugged Martha and said with a smile, "Don't ever force me to choose between rescuing you or my son, because you'd win hands down."

She wasn't up for the humor, however. "You'd be making a mistake," she said, and added, "Ben loves you more than you know." Stephen thought it was a nice sentiment that quite possibly wasn't true. But he hugged Martha again just the same.

Now, in Israel, they found time simply to be together without rancor. There were no blowups. The topics of discussion tended to be banal. Stephen didn't care what the reason was. He would take what he could get.

Of all the surprising discoveries Stephen was making about his family, one of the biggest was how quickly he was developing an antipathy toward Yoni. The initial take was that Yoni was a typical kid: young, headstrong, a know-it-all who needed neither the benefit of anyone's experience nor their approval. At first, his obvious disdain for social convention reminded Stephen of Henry.

But Henry was good-natured and not bigoted. In the army, even when he proclaimed a desire to kill Germans, it was because of what Germans had done, not who they were. What most disturbed Stephen about Yoni was his casual, matter-of-fact hatred of Arabs. It seemed the subject could never come up without Yoni making some remark to the effect that if they were all wiped out it wouldn't bother him a bit. And while some of this charitably might be attributed to what Yoni had just gone through, other remarks suggested a deeper dehumanizing animus. A typical remark occurred while they were driving past a group of Palestinians working in the blistering sun to muck out a sewer (they were from Gaza, Yoni was sure—"terrorists casing the infrastructure"). "At least they've found work that matches their mental abilities," he said.

Stephen regarded this as a perfect example of the limits of parental influence: clearly, neither Sandra nor Ethan shared these views. The bigger fear was that Yoni's opinions on Arabs were representative of a considerable, and perhaps growing, segment of the population. If true, it would be especially, ironically poignant given the ceremony in which they were all about to take part. Yoni apparently felt some obligation to add his two cents on any subject. It struck Stephen that he might be wearing some of his bandages longer than necessary to lend sympathy and authority to his pronouncements, particularly on terrorism.

Yoni's impulsive callousness was on view late one afternoon. Stephen, Annalise, and Ben were having coffee and discussing the forthcoming ceremony, when Yoni breezed through. "Lucky survivor, Grandma," he said, popping a grape in his mouth and turning to go. Annalise was about to agree that she was, indeed, lucky when over his shoulder as he left the room he added with a laugh, "You could have ended up a puff of smoke, or a camp whore."

After a moment of shock, Stephen said, "Stupid ass. *He's* lucky somebody doesn't slap him silly."

Ben shook his head in dismay and excused himself, saying he had promised to spend time with Michael.

"He's a kid," Annalise said after they were alone. "He'll learn. Besides, what he said is actually a little funny, considering what he doesn't know, don't you think?"

* * *

THEY TALKED FOR A little while longer, until Annalise stood and said she needed to get some exercise. She had fallen behind on her therapy regimen, and as long as the afternoon heat was past its worst, she wanted to take a walk. In a small surprise to both of them, Stephen asked if she would mind if he came along.

They walked slowly down Wingate, mostly in silence. When they reached the next intersection, Annalise suggested they go right, toward the sea, "though I may not make it all the way there."

After awhile she said, "I'm pleased you came. Whatever the reason."

"I am, too," he said. "Who knows when we'll have another opportunity? Honestly, I didn't realize I would feel this good about all of us being together."

Stephen noticed she was relying increasingly on her cane as they went along. She had been placing only a little weight on it when she left the house. "Is your back bothering you?" he asked. "We could turn around."

"It is, a little. Let's try going a little farther; it's good for me. You seem to be getting around well," she added.

He laughed. "It's an act. If you saw X-rays of my knees and hips, you'd wonder what was holding me up. The orthopedist has me on high doses of ibuprofen, which my regular doctor says will wreck my stomach. Nobody warns you that when you reach our age there are no good choices.

"But listen," he went on. "I don't mean to ruin this moment of harmony, but I have a serious question, and if I don't ask it now I may not get a chance."

She stopped and looked up at him. "No, I won't marry you again," she said with a straight face.

"Well, okay then," he said after they stopped laughing. "But lord knows I never thought we would be able to kid about something like that."

She nodded agreement. "All right. What is this question that will ruin our outing?"

He pointed to a shady spot. There was a bench, which was missing a slat on the back and in need of paint. "I don't know if it's public property."

"I don't think it is," Annalise responded. "*Macht nichts*. Whoever owns it probably won't have two old people arrested."

As they sat down, he recalled another bench, much like this one, all those years ago in Germany, and another important conversation, much like the one he wanted to have now. He began, choosing his words carefully. "When I ran into you at the hospital . . . whenever it was, last week . . . you said something that I haven't been able to understand. You said something about Michael's wounds being in a good cause. Do you remember?"

"Yes, I do."

"Did you mean it?"

Annalise didn't hesitate. "Yes, of course. I was very happy when America finally got rid of Saddam."

"You do understand why I'm curious, don't you?"

"I imagine it's because you oppose the war."

He wondered if she was being coy. "I do. I wasn't sure at first—the weapons of mass destruction and all that. But then the WMD didn't turn up, and the Bush people seemed so desperate to find other reasons to be there—the fictitious connection to nine-eleven in particular, which I never believed. And now add to that the fact that we seem to be making such a hash of the so-called nation-building enterprise, with Iraq ever more out of control . . . well, yes, I do oppose the war. But that's only part of it." He looked at her intently. "For the better part of the last almost forty years, our lives—yours and mine—have been, how shall I say it . . . twisted out of shape by the death of a son . . ."

She began to speak, but he said, "Please, let me finish. I shouldn't have put it that way. It's too passive. 'The death of a son'—it's not something that simply happened, like an accident, or like the sun rose in the east today. It was my fault."

She looked at him, clearly surprised. Something, perhaps charity, appeared in her eyes, but he went on quickly. "It's taken me a long time to be able to say it without reservation. It was my fault. I was wrong about Vietnam, and pigheaded about it, too. I admit I even supported the war long after I had to—I mean, long after sensible people, people who could have given me cover, if you will, to change my mind honorably if I'd been open to it, had come to the right conclusion. That much has been clear for years.

335

"And, yes, I could sit here and explain. I could try to make you understand, if you don't already, why I believed what I did at the time. But the point is, it simply doesn't matter. I pushed Jacob to go to Vietnam. I'm responsible for Ben running to Canada. The part about Ben wasn't intentional, but the irony is, I may have done him a favor, just as you may have done him a favor when you told him to stay there instead of coming home. If I'd had my way, he probably would have ended up in Vietnam, too.

"Let me finish," he said again, his nervousness betrayed by the fact that she didn't seem about to interrupt. "I'm not asking for your forgiveness, or even your understanding. I'd like both, but in the end, it doesn't change anything. I can't forgive myself for what happened. All of my rationalizations have fallen apart in the face of events . . . of reality . . . of what is now so clear about that time.

"What I want, then, is some sort of explanation, after all of that, after all we've been through, for what I assume means, since you said what you did about Michael, that you would have encouraged our own children to fight in this war—this war, which I'm convinced will end up being a disaster on the scale of Vietnam."

She was silent for a moment before she said, "I don't know about it being a disaster. I think it's too early to tell. But for me this is different. It's Israel I worry about. The U.S. can survive almost anything. Israel can't."

"I'd say that's an argument for risking Israeli children, not Americans."

She nodded understanding and looked down at her hands, which in the bright light were obviously sun-splotched.

That self-possession, he thought again. It always seemed to come back to that, always seemed the defining thing about her—the assurance, the discipline, so enviable, so maddening.

"I suppose this must seem very cold to you," she continued. "Would I risk my own children in a war like this? I can't really know, of course. Maybe not. Maybe I'm just a hypocrite, since I'm obviously accepting my American grandson's sacrifice. Then, again, Sandra is here. Ethan is here. Deborah and Yoni are both required to serve in the military. And Yoni . . . what happened to him shows the risk. Maybe you should ask

336

them these questions. All I can say is that you've never shared my . . . well, I was going to say my love of Israel, but that would be too . . . I suppose the word is trite. My English isn't so great these days." She smiled.

"I understand what you're saying."

She went on. "You know, right from the beginning, when we were in Feldafing, you remember how I wanted to come to Palestine. But then there was us . . . kids in love and so forth. Still, I never—and I think you know this . . . you knew it even then—I never lost the feeling for Israel . . . for my people—I'd say your people, too," she added with a smile, "but you never felt what I did. And then for whatever reason, maybe at first it was to please Ethan, Sandra felt it too." Annalise cocked her head, and asked in a voice of idle curiosity, "I wonder if Henry would have come.

"So you see," she continued, "I can't say for sure how I would feel about my children fighting in Iraq. Maybe I spoke too quickly about Michael. And I've been careful to stay away from the subject with Ben and Martha. I don't believe they would understand. But I meant what I said just now about America and Israel. The U.S. is a big, powerful country. If it's wrong about Iraq, it will still survive. I don't mean to suggest that I don't care about America or that it might suffer. It's the country that saved my life once, and it was my home for all those years. But when it comes to Israel, I'm . . . I don't know the word."

"Determined?" Stephen offered.

"More than that—maybe worse than that. Ruthless, I think. I don't want to hurt anyone, but I *will* hurt anyone.

"The Palestinians say they've been wronged. They say the Jews suffered but it's not the Palestinians' fault, and Israel shouldn't have been built on their bones. You know what? They could be right. And yet, I can't allow myself to care. The rights and injustices of the world are much too complicated for me to understand. I didn't ask for Dachau, and I don't want to hurt anyone here. But I will do anything—anything—to make sure we get to stay here."

~ ~ ~ ~ ~

337

Chapter 40

Thursday, May 5, 2005: Wonders sans Signs

S ITTING WITH HUNDREDS OF others under a gin-clear blue sky, the unfiltered sun already making him regret not wearing something cooler, Stephen was conscious of the sheer improbability of the image. He had a sudden vision of himself with his parents, brother, and sister, all long gone, at the farewell party held for him and Henry back in '44. In the frozen tableau he was standing next to the farewell banner his sister had made. Sixty-one years later, here he was in Jerusalem, in a square named for the Warsaw Ghetto, sitting on a folding chair next to—perhaps even more improbably, for any number of reasons—Annalise.

Around them were seated the living and the millions of ghosts who brought them together: Sandra, Ben, their spouses and their children. Deborah wore her IDF uniform. Michael, in his dress blues, was given admiring looks that were sometimes laced with sympathy when notice was taken of the bionic legs. And of course there was Jacob. And Henry. And in the crowd somewhere, one person Stephen thought—long hoped—he would never see again. Then, when he did see him, it didn't matter.

The ceremony began with the traditional two-minute siren heard throughout the country. During this time, everyone stopped whatever they were doing to remember. People in the street came to a halt. Cars stopped in place or pulled over to the side of the road. At Yad Vashem, always a solemn place, the atmosphere of solemnity deepened. In the plaza, wreaths were laid. The ceremonies would continue throughout the day. The names of the six million would be read in the Hall of Remembrance.

It was the second day in a row that Stephen found himself in the presence of a who's who of the State of Israel. Today he watched as the president, Moshe Katsav, placed a wreath to mark the sixtieth anniversary of the liberation.

The previous evening, the formal opening of the events, he sat not with his family, but together with other liberators as they listened to the prime minister, the famous or infamous, take your pick, Ariel Sharon.

And the shock of that evening: As he looked across the room, he caught sight of someone he thought he knew. No, he was sure he knew. And then he wasn't sure after all whether the bald man hunched over an aluminum-frame walker was who he thought it was. That's what the passage of sixty or so years will do. After the ceremony, he edged closer, trying to figure it out, wanting to say, "Don't I know you?" Both wanting and not wanting to hear, "You certainly should! I'm . . ."

Stephen approached and ventured, "You're Riggs."

And it was. John Riggs, as it turned out—they had never called one another by anything but last names. The same John Riggs who might have witnessed Murch's murder, who himself might have played a part in the Dachau retributions—the retributions Stephen had helped cover up but which became a weapon he could use against Riggs, but only if necessary. How long had it lasted—and was it even shared, this fear that each might turn the other in, with neither man willing to be the first to broach the subject and confirm what one or the other actually knew? It would seem they had spent forever in a state of purposeful ambiguity. Of reciprocity based on uncertainty.

And all of this seeming more surreal to Stephen for viewing it now, through a window distorted by time, as gravity will have its way with old glass, making it flow in waves from top to bottom. All the more surreal because the only thing Stephen was able to establish even now was that he was in the presence of someone named John Riggs, who served in the same unit during the war. These were the morsels that were confirmed by Riggs's daughter, who insisted on bringing him to the ceremony in what was likely a final tribute to a father who, as Stephen could see by looking into his confused eyes, possibly didn't even know where he was.

* * *

TODAY, SITTING IN the hot sun, Stephen recalled the central theme of this year's Remembrance Day—"The Anguish of Liberation and the Return to Life"—and the testimony he read of one of the survivors, someone named Bela Braver, which had special resonance. He looked down at the paper in his lap, read Braver's account.

> *The camp guard who came to open the gate said, 'You are free and you can leave.' . . . No one moved, no one went out. We did not laugh, we were not happy, we were apathetic –and the Russians came. A general came in; he was Jewish. He told us that he was delighted to find that there were still people alive in the camp. He started to cry, but we didn't. He wept, and we didn't.*

This, Stephen thought, in everything but name, described his memory of the day he first met Annalise—everyone overwrought, some of them to the point of murder, while she seemed composed.

These images left Stephen in a state of wonder. He marveled over the speed of the transitions, the innocence of his youth demolished so quickly by his war, the army, Henry's death, and all that followed. Each front.

As the ceremony on the square drew to a close, out of the corner of his eye he saw Annalise discretely wipe away a tear. He reached over, tentatively covered her hand, and when he met no resistance, held it in his.

From her seat behind, Sandra leaned in, came up with the flippant, uncharacteristically insensitive, remark: "My, my, look at you two. Divorced lovebirds."

"Don't say such stupid things," Annalise said sharply, without turning around. "Don't make a big deal of something that's not a big deal," she amended, less fervidly, yet the tone still one of more than mild annoyance at Sandra's trivialization of something both Annalise and Stephen might have viewed, or wanted to be viewed, as casual, but not trivial.

However they regarded it, as they continued to look straight ahead, they didn't let go.

He pictured himself floating over the event. It was a feeling akin to the one he'd had mere weeks before as he stared at the black-and-white photo with the scalloped edges, his comrades staring back. He was not having a mystical out-of-body experience as people sometimes described it. But still, seeing himself—seeing his family—in this unlikeliest of poses, in this unlikeliest of places, was startling and filled him with awe.

He wondered at the memory of falling in love with Annalise, of bringing her home—to his home, where she would be grateful but never completely feel it was hers. If ever there were a time when gratitude might have turned into belonging, that time was killed by Vietnam, the loss of Jacob, and the temporary loss of Ben, all of which had convinced her otherwise.

He should not have been surprised. After all, grateful or no, America was not her first choice, as she herself only recently reminded him. Although the circumstances under which she acted could not have been foreseen, she remedied this problem of belonging by making the move to Israel. It occurred to him now that the bar to his truly understanding her loyalties might have been his inability to fully comprehend her experience of being abandoned and set upon by Germany, her own country, in a way he could never imagine happening to him in his.

He thought about all the people he had left behind, or who had left him. His parents, Henry, Jacob, Ben, Annalise—their lives, as all lives, a complicated mix of cause, intention, and chance, of one temporarily outweighing the other: Sometimes, as with Annalise or Henry, the most malign of causes; at other times, as with his parents, the good fortune of a normal (not to say problem-free) life—a simple exhaustion of life's permit.

* * *

IN TWO DAYS he would return to the place that was home to him in every respect. Annalise had found a home here. He wondered about Sandra, Ethan, Deborah, and Yoni. Would they ever feel rootless, stateless? Yoni probably not—the family sabra (there were other, more worrying things about his feelings), nor Deborah, born in the U.S. but having left too young to have formed an attachment.

And Sandra and Ethan? In Israel they had found something—a place, a cause, an existence they could believe in. He wondered if their feelings might change over time, or whether their loyalties were divided. Would something happen to shake their faith, and if so, could that faith find another home, in a sense be restored? Stephen's parents had found the kind of refuge in the States that Annalise found and then lost there, and found again here.

It had taken Stephen literally a lifetime to reach the conclusion that people take lessons from life—hold on to them, act on the most urgent of them—mostly without having any way of knowing if they're the right lessons. In the face of uncertainty, they seek the comfort—the anchor—of belief, whether in nation, philosophy, or religion.

What he knew from his own experience was that the world was rarely kind to people who held rigid, impervious loyalties. The world was simply too fluid—too slippery—to sustain verities, let alone to have faith in them. Such unthinking loyalties, such true believing, all too often resulted in potentially useful lessons being learned too late, if at all—and in failure and disillusionment of one kind or another, often with a high cost.

Wasn't he a prime example? How much pain resulted from his unquestioned assumptions about his country, its motivations, and its leaders? He could console himself with the thought that he, like many of his generation, had a good excuse. His was the rare war, the righteous war, unambiguously won and leaving the country in an unquestionable position of global influence. His conclusions thereafter were based on that experience. His error was in using these conclusions, however justifiable at the time, without due consideration for their possible inapplicability to subsequent events.

He was hardly alone in this. What was the turmoil of the Vietnam era all about if not the pitting of Stephen's generation and its expectations of patriotism and duty against his children's generation and its skepticism, cynicism, and rebellion?

His rigidity came into play when he thought about his cavalier dismissal of Henry's certainty over the Nazis' atrocities. Gradually, he arrived at an understanding that this failing was bound up in a larger one—a general reluctance to alter course in the face of solid evidence that such change was warranted. Over the years he had become increasingly willing—sometimes eager in a self-flagellating way—to accept that he was easily trapped in the things and situations that were extant, rather than embrace change. He resisted even when in his gut he knew that change had occurred around him. It was a personal failing—a basic lack of courage and reluctance to leave the comfort of the known for the uncertainties and ambiguities of the unknown—and a character flaw, as he saw it.

Of course, it didn't help that Henry possessed these attributes Stephen lacked, probably to a fault. Henry swam happily in roiled waters, often as the source of the turbulence.

Still, while Stephen's failings were the source of regret, and sometimes, as with Jacob, deep remorse, he never gave up hope that they were failings that possibly, with diligence, could be overcome.

Possibly.

Sisyphus was condemned to spend eternity pushing a rock up a hill only to have it roll back as it neared the top. But Stephen's preferred metaphor was to see the world as an enormous mountain made of cloth and filled with sand. It could be moved, but only with concentrated force applied sharply, or assiduously over eons. Even then the sand would likely push back in the same place or elsewhere.

A friend once said such a view was devoid of hope and could only be held by a supreme pessimist. "If everyone believed it, nobody would try to change anything." Perhaps. But what did that have to do with reality or truth?

Santayana was wrong. The problem with failing to learn from the past wasn't that you were condemned to repeat it. It was that barring some miraculous improvement in the human genome, you couldn't really learn from it in the first place, or not in a way that mattered. The few who succeeded in learning from the past were still likely to repeat it—or some unforeseen or unforeseeable variation of it—or at any rate to be caught up in the repetition.

If he had to boil it down, he'd say that everything should be informed—but, even if it were possible, not determined—by the past. Yet it was a conclusion that made him sad, because even this more pliable guide would be without real, practical meaning. If the lesson was that one should be constantly open to new ideas and changed conceptions . . . well, it was both banal and useless. It still demanded too much of humans, who had evolved to a point where scientific and technological progress was advancing light-years ahead of fundamental biological change. Forces of destruction were being devised at a much faster rate than the means to control them. Meanwhile it was the primitive brain—the reptilian brain it was sometimes called—that was likely the real driver in human affairs. As the gap has widened between skill and emotion it has become ever more a case of the child being given the keys to the machine writ large.

In short, human activity was advancing rapidly in all fields except those of the most essential aspects of human activity. Perhaps the most that could be expected of a person was honest effort—determination to strive for the right decision, the better decision. To hope that the child can mature before the machine eats him alive.

And yet, for all the world's grim prospects, one should be always open to the possibility of surprise . . . of serendipity. Certainly, there had been many unpredictable events in his life. One of them was occurring at this very moment, in this most unexpected place. He'd always thought the bromide "never say never" was just the kind of flippant thing one said to fill a void. But maybe it was the only reason to hope. Never say never. Small comfort. Possibly all there was.

The ceremony ended. The participants stood and stretched, milled about, and began to make their way inside. Annalise looked toward Ben and Sandra, who had come around from behind. "The kids," she murmured to Stephen. "The kids who have kids," she added with a wistful smile.

"I liked the image of you holding hands," Ben said as he approached. "I'd never have expected to see it."

"Nor would we have," Stephen said.

"You can add it to the list of life's surprises and wonders," Annalise said. "At least when we return to our normal lives—the little that remains of them for your father and me—it can be with kinder, more tranquil thoughts."

Sandra said, "Well, if ever there were to be a place for reconciliation and kinder thoughts, this would be a good one."

"I think it's a sad place," Ben said.

"It is," Sandra agreed. "But uplifting, too. A reminder that good things can come from bad."

Stephen nodded. He thought, but did not say, *though not necessarily in equal measure.*

Just then he caught sight of Michael impelling his new legs across the plaza and called out to him. Michael turned and waved.

Stephen cupped a hand over his mouth, making a megaphone. "Hey, Mike! It has to have been worth it, right?"

After a moment in which incomprehension registered on his face, Michael smiled. "Probably," he called back.

Stephen laughed. "Probably," he said to himself.

THE END

Acknowledgments

Many people and organizations helped in the research, writing, and general encouragement of this book. The manuscript was read at various stages, each time resulting in valuable comments, corrections, insights, and outside perspectives. Thanks to Jessie Thorpe, Donna Salem, Laura Flaherty, Angie Gray, Adrian Wolff, Barry Stauffer, Lynda Bradley-Slesinger, and Andrea Robins. Thanks to Kario Salem for use of "Morning Coffee, Creamed with Dread." Thanks as always to my family for their constant encouragement. Above all, love and thanks to my most tireless reader and sanity checker, my wife Jo.

The United States Memorial Holocaust Museum in Washington, DC was, as always, an invaluable source on the Holocaust and its aftermath. Unique insights on the Feldafing displaced persons camp were drawn from Simon Schochet's *Feldafing* (November House, 1983).

Source material on America's wars is, of course, voluminous. Two books were uniquely helpful for this project: *War Letters: Extraordinary Correspondence from American Wars*, edited by Andrew Carroll (Scribner, 2001); and John Hagan's *Northern Passage: American Vietnam War Resisters in Canada* (Harvard University Press, 2001).

This is a work of fiction. Except for well-known historical figures, all of the actors are my own invention. While taking the usual novelistic liberties with people, events, and places, I have endeavored to create an accurate portrait of the tumultuous historical periods depicted in the story. I apologize in advance for any errors or misrepresentations; they are inadvertent but in any case my responsibility alone.

Richard Samuel Sheres
Alexandria, Virginia, 2019

ABOUT THE AUTHOR

Richard Samuel Sheres is a writer and former U.S. Government foreign affairs and intelligence senior executive. He is the author of the acclaimed novels *Keeping Gideon* (a San Diego Book Awards finalist) and *Ingersoll*. Born and raised in New York City, he has visited or resided in over sixty countries. He and his wife live in Alexandria, Virginia.

Made in the USA
Middletown, DE
13 January 2021